UNWINDING THE SPIRAL

UNION: BOOK 1

PETA HAWKER

First printing, 2022

Print paperback ISBN: 978-0-6453832-0-1

Ebook ISBN: 978-0-6453832-1-8

Cover design by Jordan Lewerissa at Good Food Design Studio.

For Mandi

GODS AND KIN

HIGHKIN
JESMA - sunkin
WEDERLLY - moonkin
EVERLUOF - starkin

MIDDLEKIN
SETUNIL - skykin
LERINIAL - waterkin

LOWKIN
NEFFREN - animalkin
FERENGÜN - plantkin
ERITOGONE - earthkin

PROLOGUE

TWO LITTLE GIRLS sat around a small campfire on the edge of the desert. A low tent nestled against a red dune, their mother lowering the flaps to keep out the oncoming chill. Shifting sand stretched in all directions. Above them, the night sky was dark, vast, full of glittering stars.

'Mumma, tell me the story of Setora again,' the older girl said.

'You never tire of her, do you, Siska?'

'It's Wave's favourite story too.'

The mother chuckled, glancing out over the sand dunes. Her husband—the father of her two girls—was out there somewhere, making sure they were safe for the night.

'Please, Mumma?' Siska whined.

Taking a seat by the fire, the mother pulled her youngest daughter onto her lap.

'All right, then,' she said, clearing her throat.

In a time so long ago that the truth has been clouded, the people of Heredour lived in harmony with one another and their gods. The youth felt the call of their god early, committing their young lives to study, to devotion, to service. There was strength in the power of the gods; it was a time when humans could match the magic of the wizards. Different kin lived side by side, celebrating the varied gifts that each god's power could offer their society.

In the grand towers of the South Claw, the starkin were captivated by the heavens as they studied the movements of the stars and planets. Philosophers and soothsayers of Heredour, the starkin held high honour among even the middle- and lowkin. It was their advice that kings acted upon, their words of wisdom that a housewife recited to her children before bed.

A prodigy of her generation, Setora rose quickly through the ranks of starkin scholars. Her devotion to Everluof was great, as was her power. When she didn't have one eye attached to a star-watcher, she would sit in meditation and prayer for hours.

So fervent was her devotion that she sometimes forgot to eat or sleep. Her greatest desire was to visit the stars—the only way she could truly deepen her connection to Everluof, or so she thought. One night, as she sat on one of the high mountain ledges, a shooting star crossed the sky and crashed into the ground below her seat.

Entranced, Setora climbed down and dug the rock from its grave. Cool to the touch and no bigger than her head, the star hummed beneath her hands. Setora knew the star was a gift from Everluof—if she couldn't visit the stars, he would send them to her instead. Despite the star's weight, Setora trekked down the mountain to show her kin what she'd received.

The starkin elders were amazed at what she'd found, but they were wary of the star. They warned her that it could be dangerous, and that she shouldn't have touched it. Laughing off their warnings, Setora took the star back to her quarters and spent the next day with it, looking, touching, hoping. The star revealed no new insights into Everluof or his power, but Setora was confident that she would discover something.

Each night she went back to her mountain ledge, praying to Everluof to send her more gifts. For several days, stars of all shapes and sizes buried themselves in the earth somewhere on the mountain. Setora would dig each of them out and carry them back to the starkin quarters.

Within days, one of Setora's mentors became ill. Setora was worried, but her obsession with the stars was so all-consuming that she didn't visit him. Other people the elder had encountered began to fall ill, and the lowkin medics announced there was a contagious disease making its way through the starkin community.

Obsessed to the point of insanity, Setora ignored everything around her, devoting every hour to prayer, begging Everluof to send her more stars. The sickness spread through the city, moving through each kin with increasing speed. The cause of the disease remained unknown until the starkin elders revealed Setora's gifts from Everluof.

The medics didn't know whether a star could cause such a wasting, contagious illness. They consulted with the wizards, whose knowledge and magic were unique and undisputed. After a careful inspection of the original star, the wizards decreed that the stars were the cause of the sickness spreading through the city.

Setora argued vehemently against the wizards. She had never been sick even though she handled the stars every day. The wizards realised that the stars themselves weren't the problem. They hypothesised that there was some sort of curse on the stars that passed from Setora to those she touched. Skin-to-skin contact was all it took for the curse to spread like wildfire.

Nobody died, but nobody recovered. Setora tried to convince the starkin elders and the wizards that the stars must hold some sort of cure, but they'd run out of time. Within weeks, everybody in the city was so ill they couldn't move—everybody except Setora and the wizards.

Although the people of the city didn't seem likely to die from the curse itself, they were too sick to care for themselves or anyone else. Setora's attention was finally drawn away from the stars as she watched her kin, her friends, her entire city succumb to the illness she had unknowingly inflicted on them.

Distraught, Setora went to the wizards and begged for their help. They knew there was only one way to fix the problem. The entire city and its people needed to be destroyed to stop the curse from spreading into the rest of Heredour. Setora agreed to stay, committing herself to own death as the price for her misguided actions. At the end, she wept beside her old mentor as he crossed over to the land beyond the stars.

Little did Setora know that the wizards were still learning the breadth of their destructive power. When they came together to destroy the city, their combined force was so great that they obliterated the entire South Claw. Everything was gone—Setora, her stars, her city, an entire swathe of the landscape.

Standing safe on the outskirts of Kochee, the wizards contemplated their actions. Though they hadn't meant to remove an entire part of the continent, they knew that at least nobody else would suffer from the terrible curse of Setora's stars.

Now, the white cliffs south of Kochee stand guard over the endless ocean, the place where the South Claw once existed. Thanks to Setora the Star-Caller, all Heredourians remember the danger of a fallen star and the terrible power of the wizards.

———

'Do you think a star would ever visit us?' Siska asked.

4

The three of them looked up at the vast blanket of the night sky.

'No, darling,' the mother answered. 'We're safe from Setora's curse.'

In the distance, they heard a low whistle.

'Daddy!' Siska squealed.

'Time for bed,' the mother said, lifting Wave up onto her hip.

Siska ran ahead, disappearing behind the tent flaps. Nestled against her mother's shoulder, Wave stared up at the sky, the stars glittering in her wide eyes.

1

BINDOCK

A GROUP of waterkin students lounged in the outdoor classroom, shading their eyes against the morning sun. Their ages were varied, some as young as twelve; the oldest, seventeen. Barefoot, the students dug their toes into the warm sand that made up the floor of the classroom.

Twisting her fingers together in front of her skirt, Wave stood before them, their tutor, Ealen, beside her. Wave chewed on her lip as the others looked up at her, some with bored expectation, others with outright hostility. Though she was dressed as they were, in a light cotton skirt and blouse, and though she looked just like them, with her bright blue eyes and sandy brown hair, she'd never felt like she belonged.

'As promised,' Ealen said with a wide grin, 'Wave will be taking us through the abridged history of our gods.'

One of the students, a boy only a year younger than Wave, groaned. Wave's stomach churned.

'Yes, Iberon, I know you've heard this more than once.' Ealen glared at the boy. 'But we have two new students who've only just arrived in Bindock, and we need to ensure everyone understands where we came from.' He gestured at the two youngest members of the group, who looked almost as nervous as Wave.

In a few weeks, those two would be settled in and feeling at home in the waterkin community. Wave often wondered what her world would have been like if she hadn't been ostracised the moment she'd arrived. What would it have been like to have friends her own age, to have people to go swimming with, to giggle with? Wave pursed her lips. She had one friend, thankfully, and although he was an elderly starkin, at least she had someone to keep her company. Her time in Bindock could have been much worse.

'Wave,' Ealen said. 'Will you take the class through the histories?'

'Yes.' Her voice came out in a rough whisper, so she cleared her throat and glanced at her tutor.

Ealen wasn't much older than Wave, in his midtwenties, she guessed. The older girls in the class simpered over him. His eyes were the bright turquoise of a skilled waterkin, framed by a strong jaw and close-cut dark hair. On the inside of his right wrist, the waterkin tattoo was almost invisible against skin as black and glossy as a night-cast river. Wave supposed he was handsome, and his smile was easy and genuine, but she wasn't sure what they saw in him other than a teacher.

'Wave?'

'Yes,' she said with a start, forcing her gaze back to the students. 'Heredour was created by all the gods; they birthed one another during the process of creation. First came Eritogone, mother of the earth. She created the dirt and stones and the layers of the world. Then came Ferengün, father of all the plants. From Ferengün came Neffren, father of beasts.'

'Lowkin gods are so boring,' Iberon whined, rolling his eyes. One of the older girls, Yllia, giggled and touched his arm.

'Hush Iberon,' Ealen said. 'If not for the lowkin gods, none of us would be here. Carry on, Wave.'

Wave took a deep breath.

'Well, once the lowkin gods had made the earth, they realised they were missing one crucial element. Together, they created Lerinial, who filled the oceans and built the rivers.'

'Yeah!' Iberon called out, his face a menacing snarl. He had all of Lerinial's fire, but none of her grace.

'Then they came together again and created Setunil, sky mother.'

Some of the girls looked up at the sky with wistful smiles.

'But the sky was empty and dark, so they created Everluof, and he filled the sky with stars.'

The class was strangely quiet about Everluof. Wave wondered if it was because of her friend, X'olea, the only starkin in a town full of waterkin.

'Then they created Wederlly, moon mother, so that the stars wouldn't be alone.'

The unsettling image of Wederlly's shimmering, iridescent eyes rose to Wave's mind, distracting her for a moment. Unlike middle and lowkin—with irises ranging from deep brown to emerald green to ice blue—all the highkin had unusual eye colours.

'The seven gods thought their world was complete, until they realised that the moon and stars were only visible for a short amount of time,' Wave continued. 'So together they birthed Jesma, and he created the sun so that all could appreciate the incredible world the gods had built.'

The class sat in hushed silence as Ealen opened a book to an image of Jesma. The god of the sunkin shone in gold silk robes, with golden-bronze skin and hair. Prominent amber eyes were highlighted by sharp cheekbones and a well-defined jaw. He was beautiful, but there was terror in that beauty. All the stories spoke of his arrogance and self-righteousness, but it was obvious in the set of his lips, in the slight lift of one eyebrow.

'As the bestower of light,' Wave continued, 'Jesma became the leader of all the gods. He encouraged them to divide into smaller groups, and he ordered the first high king to establish the same order among humans. And since then, we've been divided into our three classes—lowkin, middlekin, and highkin.'

One of the new students put her hand in the air and Ealen nodded at her.

'Can we hear about the other creatures?'

'If Wave is happy to continue,' Ealen answered.

Wave glared at him. This wasn't what they'd agreed on, but Ealen was still hopeful Wave would become a teacher like him.

'Come on, Wave,' Iberon said, frowning at her. 'Don't be lame.'

Wave clenched her fists as a sharp spike of frustration rose inside her.

'Fine,' she said, taking a few deep breaths to calm herself. 'In the beginning, Heredour was full of all kinds of majestic creatures that Neffren had created. There were human-like beings—'

'Elves!' Iberon said, his eyes wide.

'Gnomes,' someone from the back called.

'Pixies!' another student cried. 'Trolls!'

'Yes, all of those,' Wave said once they'd calmed down. 'But there were also other creatures. There were giant eagles.'

'They still exist,' the new student said with an eager nod.

'That's right,' Wave said. Her older sister had befriended a great sea eagle, not that she'd tell anyone in her class about her family. The people of Bindock already thought of her as an anomaly. And anyway, a skykin sister would undermine the lie that kept Wave and her family safe.

'There are a few giant eagles still in existence. But there were also ...' She paused, waiting for the hubbub to die down. 'Dragons.'

The girls squealed in delight and Iberon threw his fist in the air.

'Dragons! Dragons! Dragons!' The class erupted in excited chatter.

Wave smiled. The idea of dragons existing was endearing. Vicious, wiser than any man, and ageless, they'd always protected Heredour in times of need. Too bad they'd all been lost when the South Claw had been destroyed.

'And what about the Black Cloaks?' the other new student asked, his voice soft among the bubbling conversation.

The class fell silent. One by one, each student turned to look at Wave and Ealen.

'Okay,' Ealen said, his easy expression gone. 'Let's talk about the Black Cloaks another time. Why don't you all head over to Elder Zenebe's house for morning tea?'

Iberon shot Wave an unreadable look before scrambling after the rest of the class. Once they'd all disappeared into the main street of the town, Wave let out a big sigh.

'You did well,' Ealen said. 'What do you think?'

Wave shrugged and looked down at the ground. 'They don't like me.' The sand was warm on the soles of her feet, the sensation soothing her anxiety.

Ealen moved in front of her. 'That's not true, Wave.'

When she didn't respond, he took her chin in his hand and tilted her face up. They were uncomfortably close to one another, but Wave got the sense that Ealen enjoyed their proximity.

'You're the most powerful waterkin this town has seen in generations, Wave, perhaps even a thousand years,' he murmured. 'You don't need to worry about what they think.'

Wave jerked her chin out of his grip. 'If I'm to be a teacher, they need to respect me. That's not going to happen here.'

'You're still set on leaving, then?'

Wave nodded. 'There's nothing for me here, Ealen. Nobody wants me to stay.'

'I do.' He peered into her eyes, as if holding her gaze would keep her in Bindock.

'Thanks for letting me take the class,' Wave said. She turned away from him and stuffed her books into her satchel. 'I think I should probably find a different profession, though.'

Without looking back, Wave turned on her heel and left the classroom. She jogged between wattle and daub houses, the compacted sand of the street warming her soles and soothing her anxiety. When she reached the main street of Bindock, she turned away from Elder Zenebe's house. Many years had passed since she'd shared any meals with her classmates. Heading east, Wave passed the baker and tailor—both of whom watched her from their open shopfronts with wary eyes—before making it to the two-storey timber house near the end of the road.

Wave took the the steps two at a time and leapt onto the long verandah. Before she raised her fist to knock, the door eased open and a cool breeze rushed out to greet her.

'Teatime already?' a silvery voice said from the darkened hall.

Wave grinned at the hint of a smirk she heard in her friend's voice.

'My class was a raging success, X'olea,' she said as she stepped into the hallway and waited for her eyes to adjust.

The elderly starkin kept the house as dark as possible during the day. Though the summers in Bindock weren't as hot as the towns along the Swishdine Coast, and certainly not as humid, X'olea was from the mountains of Condor, a place where summer was more of a mild spring.

When she could see better, she let herself be pulled into a brief but friendly hug. Wave led the way through the hall and up the stairs. At the landing, she pushed the sitting room doors open. Shafts of sunlight pushed against the drawn curtain edges, and the room was filled with muted lamps. Long bookshelves lined two walls, filled to overflowing. A chaise lounge and two wide armchairs sat around a low table, also covered in books.

Wave dropped her bag on the floor, stacked the books in uneven piles on the table, and threw herself into one of the armchairs. This was her safe space, the only place in Bindock she felt at home. She'd tried to convince the council to let her move into X'olea's spare room so she could leave the shared dormitory and the sullen stares of her classmates. In their wisdom, the council had denied her requests each time, reminding her that it wasn't proper for a young girl to spend so much time with an old man, let alone live with him unaccompanied.

As if summoned by her thoughts, X'olea strode into the room, an ornate platter in his hands. He leaned the tray on the edge of the table and shifted a steaming teapot, two mugs, and a plate of biscuits onto a placemat. The empty platter he propped against one of the table legs.

The council didn't understand the nature of Wave and X'olea's friendship, and nothing Wave said would change their minds. There was nothing sinister about the hours Wave spent tucked away in X'olea's library, her head buried in one of his many ancient texts, a cooling mug of tea on the table.

'So your class was a success?' X'olea asked as he perched on the edge of the other armchair and offered Wave a biscuit. His violet eyes were no longer unnerving, but they always seemed to pierce her soul.

Wave snorted and took one of the proffered treats. 'I was joking.'

'What happened?' X'olea leaned back into his chair, a biscuit in hand.

'They don't listen to me because they don't respect me. It was a bit of a riot, honestly. And then,' Wave said, lowering her voice, 'one of the new kids asked about the Black Cloaks.'

X'olea chuckled. 'That must have gone down well.'

'That's why I'm here earlier than usual.'

There were many frustrations in Wave's life, but the inability of every single adult to speak openly about the Black Cloaks was often at the top of her list. X'olea had spent a lot of time educating her on their history—what little was known of it. For a well-respected scholar, even X'olea knew very little about the race of beings that held so much sway in Heredour.

Wave's thirst for knowledge was unquenchable, and any information about the Black Cloaks was so fragmented, so lacking in detail that her unmet desire often drove Wave to silent fits of rage. What she couldn't fathom was how these beings, with their unique and fearsome magic that humans couldn't access, had somehow been allowed to gain control over the lives of regular Heredourians.

'Your face is a picture of frustration.' X'olea's voice was gentle, soothing.

'Isn't it always when the Black Cloaks come up?'

'Best not to worry about them, then,' X'olea said. 'Just stay far away from them and you'll be fine.'

Wave grimaced. The phrase was almost identical to her mother's parting words when Wave left her tiny village as a twelve-year-old to trek to Bindock.

'But what about the Law of Kaiāho, X'olea?' Wave's voice was tight. 'What about Buduwai? I know it's High King Reuben's law, but it was their idea. And it's their job to ensure compliance!'

X'olea sighed. 'You know how I feel about the law. It's wrong, unjust, and inhumane. But I'm not going to run around town trying to convince others of that truth. You'll end up with a Black Cloak after you if you're not more careful.'

It wasn't the first time he'd lectured her, and it wouldn't be the last. Wave was trying to be good, though, keeping her mouth shut around the rest of the townspeople when it came to the Kaiāho. Bindock hadn't lost too many youth, though there were still a few houses that hung the black curtains of mourning. No matter what the Black Cloaks or the high king said, those young ones named Kaiāho might as well be dead.

The Law of Kaiāho was ancient, abandoned long ago for good reason. Under the Black Cloaks' guidance, the high king had reinstated the devastating law that saw children called by a god higher or lower than that of their parents taken away to be re-educated. None of the children had ever returned from Buduwai, the camp run by the Black Cloaks, even though the law had resurfaced eleven years ago. For most kin, training shouldn't take more than five or six years.

The plight of the families who'd lost a child was close to Wave's heart. Both she and her older sister, Siska, should have been named Kaiāho, but instead of being taken by Black Cloaks, they'd been able to assume new pasts and get the training they deserved. Their mother was earthkin, the lowest of the lowkin, but Siska had been called by Setunil, and Wave by Lerinial. Both middlekin. The only reason they'd escaped Buduwai was because of their family's remote location. Nobody bothered the farming villages of the Barancha Plains. Not yet anyway.

'You're thinking of your mother again, aren't you?' X'olea reached forward to pour them each a cup of tea.

'It's been so long since I've seen her, or my sisters,' Wave said as she accepted a mug. 'My studies are almost complete, but I wish I could see them now.'

'Because you're not sure what you should do?'

Wave shrugged. 'A second opinion would be nice.'

'I think your mother would tell you to follow what's true in your heart.' X'olea grinned through a swirl of steam. 'Or she'd tell you to stop getting so worked up over this decision.'

'That's easy for you to say,' Wave said. 'You had friends, peers, people who respected you by the time you finished studying. Staying and furthering your career as a scholar was an easy decision.'

'It was easy. But yours could be too.'

Wave cursed under her breath.

'How can it be easy?' Anger bubbled beneath the surface of her skin, instant and ready for action. 'Ealen would have me stay here and teach beside him. But the town doesn't want me here, and if I'm honest, I don't want to stay, but I'm scared to leave. Gah!' Wave balled her free hand into a fist. 'Where would I go? What would I do? I don't know anyone out there in the world!'

What she really wanted was to become a scholar like X'olea. There was so much to learn, and everything that was taught in their classroom was lacking in depth, and sometimes, honesty. In the five years of their friendship, X'olea had taught her more about history, religion, and politics than she would have learned alone in twice the time. He'd taught her some of the secret knowledge as well, and that drove her thirst for more.

'Whether you stay or go, Wave, someday you'll have to learn how to let people in. You won't find people who respect you or who want to be your friend unless you open up to them.'

Wave looked down into her mug. The steam had gone, and she stared through the pale green tea to the intricate flower design at the bottom of the cup. Just when she thought X'olea understood her better than anyone in the world, he came out with supposed wisdom that made no sense. Why in all the gods would she open up to people who didn't like her or respect her?

'You don't have to do everything alone, Wave,' X'olea said softly.

'I'm not trying to,' Wave hissed. 'I thought you understood.'

'I do, Wave, but—'

Wave set her half-empty mug on the table and stood, the china banging against the wood.

'Thank you for the tea, but I need to get to class.' Wave shouldered her satchel.

'Don't go like this.' X'olea stood and reached a hand out towards her, but she was already by the door.

'See you tomorrow.'

Wave clattered down the stairs, angry at herself. She knew she was being childish; X'olea was the last person who deserved her anger. There was no one else she could talk to, though, nobody who cared about her like he did, and sometimes her frustration boiled over when they were together. At least she could be honest with him.

There was still an hour before her next lesson started, and Wave paused on X'olea's verandah, uncertain where she should go. Bindock stretched away from her on one side, but there was no solace in the town. She could hear waves crashing in the distance, felt her namesake call to her. Giving in to the pull, Wave wandered away from the town and headed for the ocean.

2

MILLEN

In a tall, ornately framed mirror, Jessandra studied her reflection with a small frown. There were no wrinkles in her dress, and she'd already smoothed the few flyaway hairs that had tried to escape her reddish-gold braid. She'd touched her lips with the new lipstick from her mother and applied a little kohl to the edges of her eyes, but she didn't want to bring too much attention to that area of her face. Her eyes remained a slate grey, the colour of uncalled children.

'Ready, Princess?' a voice called from outside her dressing room.

She was never ready to face her father, but there was nothing she could do to avoid their weekly dinners. With a sigh, Jessandra patted her skirts one last time and left the mirror. Her handmaidens, two skykin named Siska and Inska, waited beside her curtained bed. They wore simple dresses in the grey of the city's servants, though a bright silver star was emblazoned on their chests, marking them as King Mascerab's. Both shared the ice-blue eyes of the skykin, but their hair and skin tone spoke of the different regions they'd been born to.

'Let's go,' Jessandra said, unable to hide the resignation in her voice.

Siska pushed the bedroom door wide, and Jessandra made her way through the hall, her handmaidens following close behind. Other servants dressed in grey offered small bows as she passed, though they watched her with greedy eyes. They all wondered if she'd be the next to fall, just like her sister, and they couldn't wait to watch the spectacle. At least, that's what Jessandra read in their eyes.

Dusk was descending outside, and the bright lanterns lining the castle's walls created a muted glow. Rich carpets softened Jessandra's footfalls and tapestries of ancient battles, long dead kings, and Marbin's varied landscapes marked her passage.

The trio reached the doors to the family's dining room. Jessandra took a deep breath and checked her skirts again.

'You'll be fine,' Siska whispered as she grasped the handles.

Jessandra wished she was right, but as days turned into weeks and then months, she was less sure that everything would be okay.

The doors swung inwards and Jessandra entered with as much formality as she could muster. She'd never understood her father's obsession with ceremony. It was just a family dinner after all, but Mascerab never let anyone relax in his presence.

The cavernous room was taken up by a long, wooden table, big enough to seat several families. At the far end, Queen Elisayn sat to the right of her father. Jessandra offered a deep curtsy before walking the length of the table to sit opposite her mother. Siska and Inska stood by the door with the other servants, hands folded in their skirts, eyes downcast.

'Hello, Jessandra,' Elisayn said with a small smile.

Her lilac eyes swept over Jessandra's appearance and she gave a small nod.

'Mother, Father,' Jessandra replied, nodding at each of them.

Mascerab grunted at her. She'd always been his greatest

disappointment. When he'd exiled Lenta, he'd realised that Jessandra was all he had left. Since then, she'd only continued to prove the validity of his disappointment.

'How was your week, dear?' Elisayn asked.

Jessandra shrugged. Her father often forced her to sit in on the daily court sessions, but he never spoke to her. At least Elisayn made an effort to see her daughter every day.

'How have your lessons been going?'

'Terrible.'

Mascerab grunted again. Servants appeared at the table, their arms loaded with rich food. Velvety butter beans in gravy, a rainbow trout resting on a bed of delicate vegetables, and bowls of dried fruits and small cakes were laid between the family. The scents were overpowering and Jessandra's stomach somersaulted. Mascerab waved the servants away with a hand.

In silence, the royal family of Marbin served their own food. Jessandra took only small portions of everything; she knew she wouldn't eat much. It had been the same the last few weeks, her anxiety causing her to push her food around her plate as she wondered what was wrong with her.

'Have you felt anything yet?' Mascerab asked as he shovelled pieces of white flesh into his mouth.

Jessandra looked down at her plate, but the food only made her nausea worse.

'No,' she whispered.

'Nothing?' he asked. 'Still? Not even the faintest breath of Everluof?'

Jessandra shook her head.

'I took her to the priests this week,' Elisayn said, her voice low.

The bones from Mascerab's meal clattered to the plate. 'She's already seen the starkin priest.'

'Not the starkin priest.' Elisayn's voice was little more than a whisper. 'Like we agreed, husband. I took her to the moon and sun priests.'

A muscle in Mascerab's jaw worked hard even though he'd stopped chewing. 'And?'

Nobody answered, the silence stretching uncomfortably, like a too-thin dough trying to hold together a stuffed pie.

'Jessandra?' Elisayn said.

'Nothing, Father.' Jessandra lifted her gaze. 'I felt nothing.'

Mascerab slammed his hands down on the table. The crockery jumped and fell, clinking against one another and jarring Jessandra's fraught nerves.

'How can you feel nothing? You're almost sixteen, girl. Sixteen! It's not normal.'

'I know.'

'Nobody else has this problem.'

Mascerab's voice began to rise, and Jessandra felt herself shrinking.

'Nobody, Jessandra! Are you listening to me?'

'Yes, Father. Something is wrong with me, it must be.' She hated how shrill her tone had become, hated how she couldn't hide the tremble in her voice. 'If we could just find a way to fix me, then everything will be okay.'

'Fix you?' Mascerab banged his fists on the table again. 'Fix you? This isn't a thing for fixing, girl. This is the natural order of things! You'd be worse than a Kaiāho if you aren't called.'

'Worse?' Jessandra's lip trembled. 'You can't send me to Buduwai, Pa, you can't! I haven't done anything wrong!'

'You're not to call me that. Anyway, I've no power to send you to Buduwai, fool child. The Black Cloaks handle that. I wonder ...' Mascerab paused, a thoughtful look taking over his hard features.

He turned to Elisayn, his violet eyes narrowing.

'Perhaps we should bring the Black Cloaks to her, see if they can ... encourage her to feel the call of Everluof.'

Elisayn's eyes widened.

'No, Pa!' Jessandra screeched as she pushed her chair back from the table. 'You can't bring them here. You can't subject me to their ... their magic. The people wouldn't stand for it.'

'Pssh.' Mascerab glared at her, somehow managing to combine all the spite he'd ever shown her into a single look. 'The people? They wouldn't know.'

'You have no idea what they'll do to her, Mascerab,' Elisayn said.

'They'll torture me, or hurt me, or get in my mind. And then they'll take me to Buduwai.' Jessandra jumped to her feet. 'You'll never see me again!'

Mascerab's face told her exactly how he felt about that prospect.

'I'm your heir, Father. I know you'd have preferred Lenta, but you exiled her. You're stuck with me now. If you let them take me away, you'll have nothing.' She slammed her palm on the table, mimicking her father without meaning to. 'Then what will Uncle Reuben say? You'll be powerless, they'll have to find a new ruler.'

In truth, Mascerab and Reuben were cousins. There were no other siblings on her father's side, so he'd become her uncle, at least in name.

Mascerab stood, his huge body towering over her. 'How dare you threaten me, little sprite? You are powerless—weak-willed and harebrained. I'd be better off taking one of these servants as my heir.' He waved a careless hand at the far end of the room, his eyes never leaving hers. 'You are spiteful, just like your sister, and you don't deserve the crown of Marbin, even if you did feel the call of Everluof.' He took a deep breath. 'Get out of my sight.'

Jessandra scrunched her face up at him, trying to look as menacing as she could. Inside, she felt like a piece of jelly, ready to fall apart at the slightest hint of heat. When she couldn't take her father's ferocity any longer, she turned and hurried from the dining room, her handmaidens close behind.

Once the doors had closed behind them, Jessandra set off at a run, tears streaming down her face. That jelly part of her had melted, and she ran to ignore the trembling of her body. She wanted to be angry at her father, wanted to rage at him and curse at him, but in the end, she knew he was right. There was something wrong with her, something no priest could fix. Maybe she belonged with the Black Cloaks, or in Buduwai, just as he said.

Ignoring the surprised servants who stumbled out of her way, Jessandra burst into her bedroom and threw herself down on the bed. She grabbed one of her pillows and squeezed it as hard as she could. Sobs wracked her body. She wanted to scream, but she sensed Siska and Inska were nearby, hovering uncertainly by her bed.

The youth of Heredour were always called by their god at a young age, sometimes as early as eleven. Almost all felt the presence of their god by the time they were fourteen. If they were Kaiãho, they were snatched up by the Black Cloaks and taken to some unknown place to participate in Buduwai, the re-education program. If they were called by the same god as their parents, or at least no higher than the highest-kin parent, the youth went to study under their god, often in a different place to where they were born.

But Jessandra? She was about to turn sixteen, and she'd felt nothing. Elisayn had dragged her to the starkin priests multiple times. They'd explained in great detail what it was like to feel the blessings of Everluof, but it made no difference. The more stressed she became about the whole situation, the more fights she got into with her parents, and the less likely it seemed that she would ever hear her god.

'Jessandra?' Siska's voice was soft, floating somewhere in the background of Jessandra's awareness. 'Princess?'

Her tears had subsided, as had the urge to scream or throw things. Once again, she felt hollow inside, like one of those unusual trees that grew out in the desert beyond the Barancha Plains, their trunks all bulbous and empty.

'I'm okay,' she said, her voice muffled by the bedspread. 'I'm okay.'

'Inska's gone to warm some honey milk for you.'

Jessandra sat up, pushing loose hair out of her face. The room was blurry. She scrubbed at her eyes, but the sensation worsened.

'It's the kohl,' Siska said. 'Here, let me clean you up.'

With a damp cloth, Siska wiped around Jessandra's eyes, cleaning off her makeup and her tears.

'There we go.'

'Thank you,' Jessandra said.

Siska sat down beside her on the bed and began to undo her braid.

'If you sleep with this in, we'll have a rough morning with the brush,' Siska said.

Jessandra let herself be soothed by her handmaiden's voice.

'What can I do?' she murmured, as much to herself as to Siska.

'Hold on to hope,' the older girl replied. 'Pray to Everluof, even though you can't feel him yet. Ask for guidance.'

'I don't think Everluof is coming for me,' Jessandra said.

'What makes you say that?' Siska's tone was soft, and there was no accusation in it.

Jessandra turned to face her. For a long moment, the princess studied her servant's face. Could she trust this woman? They'd been together since Jessandra's twelfth birthday; she'd all but grown up under Siska's care.

'I don't want to say,' Jessandra whispered. How could she trust anyone in this castle?

'You don't have to if you don't want to,' Siska said. 'But I have secrets of my own. I swear, as I swore when I took this job, that I will keep your secrets as my own.'

It was the oath all the servants took, but too many didn't keep it. Siska had always been true to her, though. She'd never revealed any of the tantrums or breakdowns that had happened in this room to her parents.

'When we were outside the orchard the other day, Skoa came to see you.'

Siska nodded, her hands clasped in her lap.

'I thought I felt ... something.' Jessandra thought her throat might close over at the admission.

'You thought you felt Setunil?' Siska whispered, eyes wide.

'Maybe?' If Jessandra thought she'd felt sick at dinner, it was nothing compared to the roiling of her gut now.

Siska was quiet for a time; Jessandra could almost see the thoughts taking her shape in her mind. If Setunil was calling Jessandra, she would be named Kaiāho and sent to Buduwai, never to return.

'You have to run away.'

'Run away?' Jessandra stood and turned her back to Siska. 'I can't run! I'm the heir, the last one left to take this throne.'

'And if you are being called by Setunil, you'll be named Kaiāho! What good is an heir stuck in Buduwai?'

'But after I'm re-educated ...' Jessandra trailed off. She already knew that there was no return from Buduwai. The city was full of houses with black curtains; a tribute to those young ones lost to the law.

'Don't be foolish, Jessandra,' Siska said.

Jessandra laughed, the sound ragged and nervous. The audacity of a handmaiden calling her master foolish was the least strange part of their conversation.

'Maybe they won't be so harsh on me?' Jessandra asked, looking to the ceiling as if it would help her. 'I'm the only heir now. Maybe Reuben won't let the Black Cloaks take me.'

'They exiled your sister because she got pregnant out of wedlock. What do you think they'll do to a Kaiāho? Kingdom be damned. You know what your the high king is like.'

Crazed. Delusional. Terrifying. Jessandra shuddered. Reuben's visits to Millen were few and far between, but she'd be happy if she never had to see him again.

'Where would I run to, Siska?'

Jessandra walked over to her balcony and pushed the curtains wide. Night had set in, and a waning moon rose over the mountain ranges of the North Claw to the west. Lake Armansis shimmered beneath the moonlight, small waves crashing on the false shore far below the castle.

'I'm useless at hunting and wildcraft, so I can't disappear into the forest. And no sensible citizen would harbour me, not when my father, Uncle Reuben, and the Black Cloaks would be after me. I wouldn't last a day out there!'

'Let me think about it, maybe there's something we can do.'

The stars were only just starting to show to the west. Jessandra glared at them. Those winking, glinting lights seemed to mock her, laughing at her inability to feel their presence, to know the call of Everluof.

'Curse you,' Jessandra whispered to the stars. 'Curse you all.'

3

BINDOCK

THE RIVERBANK of the Armansis was shaded from the afternoon sun by the dense tea tree forest—known as the Nagahere—that surrounded Bindock. Wave sat a little apart from Iberon and Yllia, her eyes steady on Ealen.

'You see, it takes a lot of focus for me just to stay in control of these droplets.'

A handful of water droplets hovered above the river, moving in a sinuous line around one another. Sweat beaded on Ealen's forehead.

'It would be foolish for me to try to carry any more than this.' He let the water splash back into the surface of the river.

Wave admired how instantly the droplets were absorbed back into the main body of water. That was the beauty of Lerinial's power—nothing would stand between water separated from itself.

'The three of you are about to graduate from your studies. What you really need to understand now is how to stay within the boundaries of your own energy. You've all done it when you were first learning—tried to push past your inbuilt limits and exhausted yourself.'

'I haven't seen Wave do that,' Iberon said with a smirk.

All three of them turned to her and she shrugged. She'd pushed as hard as the rest of them throughout their years of training, but she'd never burned herself out.

'I believe that's because there's nobody in Bindock who can match her strength.' Ealen watched her with a wistful smile.

'How does that make a difference?' Wave asked.

'You can't push past your boundaries if you've never learned the skills that would allow it. Our prowess is limited here. We all know the powers have been waning for several generations.'

'So what's wrong with her, then?' Yllia asked, pointing at Wave.

Wave clenched her teeth. It wasn't the first time Yllia had asked the question, and she wasn't the only one who thought such things, but it still sent Wave into a spiral of rage.

'There's nothing wrong with Wave,' Ealen said with a sigh. 'And you should know better than to speak unkindly, Yllia.'

Yllia blushed. Though his words were light, they were still the only form of reprimand anyone would get from Ealen.

'Unlike the rest of us,' he continued, 'Wave doesn't seem to be affected by whatever it is that's causing our power to fade. I anticipate Wave will be very important in relearning some of our lost waterkin skills.'

'I don't want to be important,' Wave muttered.

Behind Ealen, the water began to churn.

'You certainly won't get a husband,' Yllia whispered, Iberon laughing beside her.

'Shut up!'

A jet of water shot into the air. The stream jumped over Ealen and collapsed onto her classmates, drenching them. Yllia squealed, but Iberon kept laughing. Not a single drop landed on Wave or Ealen.

'Wave.' The frustration in Ealen's voice only just masked his laughter.

'Sorry,' Wave said.

She felt better now. Channelling water always helped calm her anger. Iberon and Yllia were often at the receiving end of a stream of water, though seawater was always more fun, especially if they forgot to close their eyes.

'You two, head back to town and get some dry clothes on,' Ealen said.

Wave stayed where she was, her eyes downcast.

'You're a freak,' Yllia hissed as she stomped past.

When the forest was quiet, Wave lifted her gaze. Ealen was watching her, his expression unreadable.

'Sorry,' she said again.

'You really need to learn how to control your anger.'

Wave nodded.

'You could do great things in this world, Wave, really important things.' He reached a hand towards her. 'But if you let your emotions get the better of you, nobody will want to be around you.'

His words were similar to X'olea's, but she had no anger left to argue with her tutor. She took Ealen's hand and he pulled her up. Suddenly, he was too close, his breath warm against her forehead. Wave tried to take a step back, but Ealen grasped her by the upper arms and peered down at her face.

'I know why you want to leave Bindock,' he said, voice hoarse. 'Let me go with you.'

'What?'

'It's obvious, Wave. You don't feel like you belong here. Nobody has made an effort to include you since the day you arrived and showed us all how powerful you were.'

Ealen leaned down until their eyes were level. They were the same ocean blue as hers, though his were several shades lighter. Flecks of grey marred the pristine colour of his irises.

'But if you want to leave, you'll need someone to guide you through the world. You're from a village in the Barancha Plains, the middle of nowhere! All you've seen of the world, and its people, is when you made the journey here. It's not safe for you to be out there all alone.'

Wave wrenched herself free from his grip. The anger was there, waiting for her, always hungry.

'Why do you always assume I don't know what I'm doing? You think I'm some idiot from the Plains, that I don't know how the world works? Well, let me tell you.' She stabbed a finger into his chest. 'The world won't want me, just like Bindock didn't want me. That's how it works, that's how people work. They pull you in close, and then they leave you. I'm no fool, Ealen.'

Despite her outward aggression, Wave trembled inside. No matter what she said, she was terrified of what she might find out there—not just the people, but the truths she might stumble upon. Though his words stung, he was right. She knew nothing of the world.

'You're too young to be so fatalistic,' Ealen whispered.

He didn't look upset. There was a fire in his eyes now, a hunger that Wave had never seen before.

'Yet I'm old enough to know better,' she said, pushing away from him and storming into the Nagahere.

The tea trees passed by her quickly, their white and pink blossoms dancing in a light breeze. Tiny grey-green leaves dotted the pathway, whisked from their branches during some heavy wind. Wave knew Ealen wouldn't follow her, but she couldn't stop herself from marching all the way to the inlet. She headed north, putting as much space as she could between herself and the town.

Down at the water's edge, Wave let her feet drag on the damp sand, her steps slowing. The crash and pull of the waves calmed her anger. She walked until she felt in control of herself again.

She should have seen it coming. Ealen had been acting strange towards her for weeks now, maybe even months.

Touching her arm after class, smiling at her when he thought others weren't watching, standing up for her against the rest of the town. She supposed it was normal to him—the age gap between them wasn't too big—but she saw him only as a teacher, one who couldn't give her the level of training she needed.

His offer to leave with her had come as a surprise. Ealen seemed happy in Bindock, his experience of the town the complete opposite to Wave's. She'd expected him to beg her to stay, to follow in his footsteps and become a teacher. What did it mean that he was willing to leave his home, his beloved profession, to follow her into ... gods knew what?

Wave shook her head and tried to clear her thoughts. Dwelling on whatever it was Ealen thought was going on between them wouldn't get her anywhere. It only firmed her resolve to leave, perhaps as soon as she graduated. There was nothing stopping her from travelling back to the Plains to see her mother and younger sister. Maybe she'd have a better chance of working out where to go from there, when she was with people who loved her.

Up ahead, a series of boulders reared out of the ocean. When the tide was high, small pools formed among the rocks, filling with tiny fish and scuttling crabs. The tide was drawing out, so Wave climbed onto one of the boulders and sat looking out over the ocean.

The horizon was dotted with little black marks—the indistinguishable shapes of the town's fishing skiffs. A group of young children were playing in the shallows close by, splashing each other and falling into fits of squealing laughter. Wave smiled. Her sister Winter was still that innocent, playing freely among the fields and waterways of the Plains. Wave couldn't remember feeling like that. She'd always been angry, but maybe she'd had a childhood just like Winter's, a childhood of freedom.

Thinking about Winter made her decision to go home easier

to accept. She wasn't going backwards; she was going home. To a place of calm, a place where she belonged. She wouldn't get stuck in the Barancha Plains like her mother; it would just be a temporary visit, a chance to see her family before she made her next move.

The group of children were leaving the water. One little girl was still in the shallows, her arms crossed over her chest. The others called to her, taunted her, but she didn't move. One by one, the other children walked away from the water, heading back towards town.

Seemingly happy to be left alone, the little girl began to play her own game, prancing around in the shallows and chatting to the water. Wave giggled. She was too far away to tell who the girl was, but Wave was reminded of herself. Wilful, alone. Always going her own way, her mind already made up. Perhaps she could take this little creature under her wing, give her the support that Wave never got.

With a sigh, Wave closed her eyes. The sun warmed her eyelids, the tip of her nose, the backs of her hands. Not long to go now, and then she could be free of the town that despised her. She wondered if she could convince X'olea to travel home with her. He'd get on well with her mother, and he'd been in Bindock for nearly as long as she had. Maybe he could do with a holiday. If she was clever, she might even convince him to continue travelling with her. Together, they'd have a better chance of finding someone who could teach her more about her power. She didn't really want to make that journey alone.

A strangled scream pierced the air. Wave's eyes shot open, and she looked up and down the beach. Nobody was in sight. Down in the water, Wave could see the little girl's arms flailing in the air. She was out too deep. In a heartbeat, Wave realised the girl was caught in a rip. She was drowning.

Wave threw herself off the boulder and ran to the shore, her bare feet pounding over hot sand and into the coolness of the ocean. The waves surged at her as she struggled against the tide. The girl was out too far; she'd drown before Wave could reach her.

Thigh-deep in the water, Wave closed her eyes and sent a stream of her power coursing through the ocean. Dipping, diving, darting; Wave was one with her power as she searched for something recognisable, something human.

There. The sound of a heartbeat. Not so much a sound as the feel of another heart beating within Wave's own body. The stream of power shot towards the fatigued girl as she began to sink. Wave wrapped her up and pulled her towards the surface.

She was caught in a rip, though, a snare set by Lerinial to trap unwitting humans. The rip fought against Wave's power, resisting her attempts to rescue the girl. They battled over her, Wave and the rip, and the girl's heartbeat continued to slow.

'No!' Wave cried in a panic.

Every ounce of energy she could find went into the stream of power. Wave pulled the girl towards the surface, her breath ragged with effort. Each time she gained some ground, the rip fought back harder, pulling the girl deeper.

'No,' Wave whispered.

There was nothing left. She'd reached the point of burnout, just as Ealen had warned. The rip was winning; Lerinial was set to claim her prize. Another life lost to the cruelty of an uncaring god. Wave tried to channel more and more power into the stream, but she faltered, her legs wobbling in the waves.

'No!' she shouted at the sky.

The heartbeat stopped. Anger filled Wave; a blinding, searing rage like nothing she'd ever felt before. An image appeared in her mind's eye—the girl sinking silently to the ocean floor, her hair spread out like tendrils, her dress ballooning with water, her lips parted in surprise. Only it wasn't the girl from Bindock, it was her sister Winter. And then it wasn't Winter, it was Wave's own reflection staring back at her as her lifeless body sank to the bottom of the ocean.

'She is not yours!' Wave screamed.

Rage spiralled through her. A blinding light—so brilliant it became dark—consumed her mind, her body, her soul. All she could feel was the light, all she knew was the light. She became the light of her rage.

Something slammed into her body and she was pushed back into the shallows. The light shattered into a million shards, fracturing the strange place Wave had disappeared to. She opened her eyes. The world re-formed around her; the crystalline blue of the wild ocean swirling around her ankles, the cloud-studded sky above her, the tremble in her body.

Wave looked down. In her arms lay the little girl, unconscious. The exhaustion returned and Wave's legs collapsed beneath her.

'Henny?' she whispered.

The firstborn child of Bindock's maire.

'Henny?'

Wave touched the girl's face, recoiling from the feel of her cold, clammy skin. Fingers trembling, Wave pressed against Henny's neck, feeling for a pulse. Nothing responded to her touch, not even the faintest glimmer of life.

'No,' Wave whispered. 'No. No, no, no, no.'

She grasped Henny's hands, shaking them. Nothing. Slapped her cheeks and pushed her eyelids open. Nothing. Called her name a hundred times. Pressed her ear against her tiny chest. Nothing.

The ocean slammed into Wave. She could have sworn she heard Lerinial laughing, the sound for her ears alone. The salt water stung her eyes, mixing with her tears, and she knew it was vengeance.

4

WATERFALL CITY

THERE WAS a wind in the northern quarter of the castle, strong enough to make Mortius pull his cloak from his shoulders. The stairs to the parapet were long and narrow, and the cloak was spending more time wrapped around his legs or tangled in his hair than keeping him warm.

Dawn was about to break, and Mortius anticipated he'd see the first rays of the sun once he reached the top. Most days, dawn was a time of peace and quiet for the senior adviser to the high king, but not today. He'd woken while it was still dark to a note from Reuben requesting his company. Little did he know that the king wouldn't be in his quarters, though he shouldn't have been surprised. More often than not, Reuben could be found in strange places in the castle, in an equally strange mood.

A dawn meeting on the northern wall didn't bode well. Twenty-five years he'd been at the king's side, but each year it grew harder to stay, and Mortius no longer knew what to expect when he went to see Reuben.

With the top of the wall in sight, Mortius paused to take a few breaths. He wasn't as young as he'd once been, but he was still fit, his body lithe. His close-cropped sandy hair was more silver than anything now, and he wore heavy lines around his violet eyes. Both hair colour and lines had been earned from the stress of his role, from the constant anxiety of managing a country with a delusional king at its helm.

The deep breaths were more of a mental preparation than a physical rest. Who knew what message Reuben had received and what fit of madness he'd spiralled into since? Had he slept at all during the night? Releasing his breath in a final, slow exhale, Mortius climbed the last few steps.

Absurdly wide and edged with crenellations, the parapet was empty except for four guards, two at either end where the wall ended in watchtowers. Mortius swept his gaze back and forth, his gut sinking. Reuben was nowhere to be seen.

Just as he was about to ask the guards if they'd seen the high king, he heard a high-pitched, manic voice calling his name. With a sigh, Mortius expanded his line of vision to see if he could find the imposter, this clown who'd taken over the mind and body of his king.

A hand waved from one of the eastern watchtower's unsealed windows, followed by Reuben's head, his hair blowing around his face. At least Mortius could pretend it was just the wind mussing his hair and not the night he'd no doubt spent sleepless.

Mortius closed his eyes for a moment, asking for strength from a god he had no faith in.

'Mortius!'

Reuben's voice was insistent, almost whining, and when Mortius opened his eyes, he saw Reuben waving him over like a small child with a new toy. Steeling himself, Mortius jogged along the parapet. The guards moved aside for him with a respectful nod, and he climbed the spiral staircase to the tower's platform.

'Hurry,' Reuben said.

'What is it, Majesty?'

Reuben grasped his arm and pulled him to the window.

'Look!'

The sun was just peeking over the Kirsky Forest in the east. It was beautiful, but the tangled mess of the city below them marred the view.

'You didn't come here to watch the sunrise, did you?' Mortius asked.

'No,' Reuben said, shaking his head. 'But it's nice to know that Jesma still has faith in me, that the sun rises another day to watch us attempt to keep our necks off the chopping block.'

Mortius blinked. It was an unsettling analogy—not that something strange coming from Reuben's mouth was a surprise —but the mention of the chopping block was a little disturbing. Only traitors were sent to the headsmen.

'I came here to look north.' Reuben turned to face Mortius. 'Obviously. Why would I come to the northern wall to watch the sunrise? That's absurd.'

Mortius shrugged. 'It was just a question.'

Reuben stepped back from the window. His hair had settled somewhat, though it was still a tangled, chaotic mess. It was gold and soft as spun silk, and he loved to keep it shoulder-length, as had been the style in his youth. The other highkin laughed behind his back, but he either didn't know, or didn't care. His eyes were the honey amber of the sunkin, but unlike his brethren, a dark ring ran around the outsides of his irises. When they were young, the ring had been imperceptible. Every year it grew infinitesimally, darkening his once seductive golden eyes. And with each year the ring grew, Reuben descended deeper into a spiral of madness and delusion.

'I came to the northern wall to look north.' Reuben strode to one of the north-facing windows. 'I would have expected you to understand such logic.'

Mortius rolled his eyes and followed his liege. The mountains directly before them were much smaller than those the city nestled against. From their high vantage point, they could see the grazing fields of Lashameg, the large town of Meisha Rony, and in the distance, the ring of mountains that encased Condor Province. The view was breathtaking.

Waterfall City sat high in the Paravat Ranges. Descending down the mountains in a series of terraces, the city was protected from the monstrous waterfalls on the north and south side by enchanted walls thicker than a house. The entire city had a bird's-eye view of any enemy who might approach the capital, though none had done so for hundreds of years. Just like his forefathers', Reuben's rule was iron-fisted and merciless.

'Why are we looking north, High King?'

Reuben extended one hand and pointed to the ring of mountains directly north.

'Condor.'

He didn't elaborate.

'What's happened in Condor?'

'Happened?' Reuben snorted. 'Nothing's happened. That's the problem.'

Mortius' pale eyebrows drew together. He had no idea what Reuben was talking about, and the king wasn't exactly forthcoming.

'What hasn't happened, then?'

'Ah!' Reuben spun to face Mortius again. 'It's the same lowkin dust we've been getting from Lashameg.' Reuben affected a whining, child-like voice. '"Oh, High King, our crops are failing. Our animals are dying. There's no fish in the sea. The wood rots as soon as its cut. We don't know what's wrong!"'

Mortius' gut clenched. Reuben could afford to make a mockery of Condor's concerns, but the regional issues had Mortius worried. They'd had almost identical reports from Lashameg. Condor wasn't a large producer compared to the other regions—the nation was tiny and mountainous—but they supplied much of the timber for the capital. If the wood was rotting before they had a chance to prepare it …

'Did you hear me, Mortius?'

'Yes, Majesty, I heard you.' Mortius pulled himself from his reverie. 'It is somewhat concerning, given that Lashameg has said much the same.'

Worse, if he was honest. The last report from Hinchka had spoken of entire herds of stillbirths. Not a single lamb born alive. Mortius shuddered.

'How bad can it be, Mortius?' Reuben turned back to the window. 'They've grown soft, thinking they can get away without paying the king's bounty. They must think I'm a pushover, and that perhaps they could rule Heredour.'

'We haven't heard from Triné Empire yet,' Mortius said, hoping to divert Reuben's attention from ideas of treason. 'Perhaps they're fine, just like Marbin.'

'Why haven't we heard from Triné? Too much time goes between reports from Kadesh. What is he thinking? Maybe he's like the others and thinks he should secede, or make a claim for my throne. Would he be a better ruler than me?'

Mortius ground his teeth. Treasonous rulers was the latest idea in a string of fancies Reuben seemed to enjoy entertaining.

'The regions have been united as one country under one high king for thousands of years, Majesty. I see no reason for them all to decide they'd like to secede.'

'What if they're working together, and that's why Marbin stands alone as loyal? Mascerab would never betray us.'

Mascerab was the most likely to betray Reuben. The assumption that his loyalty was ensured because they were cousins was laughable. Mascerab was as greedy and power-hungry as Reuben had been when he took the throne.

Lost in his thoughts, Mortius jumped in surprise when Reuben turned back to him. His hands gripped his hair, pulling it up towards the sky. The wild look in his eyes was back, the one that meant he hadn't slept all night.

'Why are they doing this to me, Mortius?' Reuben hissed, baring his teeth in a rictus snarl. 'Why couldn't they just be happy with what they have? Why me? Why me? Why me?' Reuben closed his eyes, rocking on his heels.

'Why me?' he cried over and over again, falling into a crouch. 'Why me?'

5

MILLEN

A BEAD of sweat dotted Jessandra's forehead, but the hot wind that had blown in from the Plains did nothing to cool her skin. She stood beside her parents in the courtyard, a small retinue of her father's army surrounding them. Other highkin gathered nearby—not only the many starkin families of Millen, but also the two moonkin families had come to witness this meeting.

Silver banners flew from the castle's battlements and the city walls. In the distance, Jessandra could see a carriage making its winding way towards them, mounted infantry in the lead. Much of the city was out to watch the procession—women and children hung from second- and third-storey balconies, and shop owners wiped their hands or smoked pipes from their doorways.

The corset beneath Jessandra's dress was stifling. She had no love for the garment, unlike her sister, and Elisayn always had trouble getting her into one. Today was different, though. Today, everything changed.

Jessandra lowered her eyes to her new dress, noticing the thin film of sweat that coated her chest. Her father had ordered the creation of a new wardrobe now that she was becoming a woman. The skirt was modest—dark silver silk rent with lilac slashes, hitched a little above her right foot to show matching silver slippers. The bodice was the same colour, with elegant starbursts stitched in mauve and long, spangled sleeves. She would have enjoyed the dress if it weren't for the absurdly low neckline that showed too much of her bosom, or the reason that she had to wear it in the first place.

With a sigh, Jessandra lifted her chin and squared her shoulders. She could ignore the shallowness of her breath for a little while longer. A rumble in the distance pulled her attention away from the city. Dark clouds were gathering to the east, somewhere over Condor's mountains. Summer storms were uncommon in Marbin Province, but when 'they did happen, they were vicious. Jessandra chewed on her lip.

'Your hair is everywhere,' Elisayn murmured.

Jessandra glared at her.

'It's a tad humid, Mother,' Jessandra said, nodding to the growing storm.

'Well,' Elisayn said, pursing her lips. 'Do something about it.'

Jessandra patted at her thick braid, knowing it would do no good. What she wouldn't give to turn and run to the lake right now. She'd spent every summer down there with her sister, imagining they were mermaids, waiting for some prince of the water to whisk them away. Mascerab had banned her from swimming with the locals this year, telling her it wasn't proper for a princess to debase herself with the lower kin.

'Don't forget what happened to your sister,' he'd said, as if she hadn't spent every day wishing Lenta was still with her.

Maybe the lordling in the carriage would have an adventurous spirit and he'd sneak off with her to swim, or walk through the orchard at midnight. A soft smile lit Jessandra's features. Maybe, just maybe, the lordling would be everything her family wasn't, and maybe, she'd have a chance to enjoy her life.

'Good girl,' Mascerab said. 'That's the kind of smile you want to put on. Show them nothing is wrong.'

Jessandra's face fell. No matter what this starkin boy was like, she still had a much bigger problem to solve before they could get married.

The procession reached the castle gates. Where the starkin of Marbin all sported a dark grey with shades of purple undertones as their kin colours, the banners of the newcomers favoured a silver so pale it was almost white and a deep, rich violet as a contrast.

Retainers appeared from the back of the carriage and opened the doors. Jessandra took a shaky breath as thunder boomed in the distance.

A herald—still seated on the back of his horse—blew a shrill horn and began to speak.

'Announcing Lord Azanya starkin, of X'xix, and his wife, the Lady Xan of X'xix.'

The couple stepped forward from the carriage, Lady Xan's hand resting on her husband's extended arm. Both were as pale as the silver robes they wore, with long, almost-white hair and violet eyes. They seemed to have descended from the home of the gods themselves.

The pair stopped before Mascerab and Elisayn and bowed deeply.

'Presenting the Lord Jai'til.'

A young man with the same bearings as his parents stepped forward from the carriage. His hair was as straight and white as a ghost-tree and fell to his shoulders. A cloak the colour of deepest night—embroidered with sparkling silver stars—sat on his shoulders, covering the simple off-white shirt and fawn breeches beneath. Tall purple boots with elegant inscriptions were laced around his calves. Unlike any of the starkin Jessandra knew, his eyes were such a deep violet that they were almost indigo.

Jessandra's breath caught in her throat. It had nothing to do with the stifling humidity, or her corset. Jai'til was beautiful, more handsome than any prince she could have imagined, more breathtaking than any person she'd seen in real life.

Following his parents' lead, Jai'til bowed deeply. Mascerab's herald took a step forward.

'May I present our righteous ruler of the Marbin Province, King Mascerab, cousin to the High King Reuben. His wife, Queen Elisayn, and their daughter and heir, Princess Jessandra.'

Mascerab dipped his head, and Elisayn and Jessandra dropped small curtsies. They were the ones with more power in the situation, though as Jessandra glanced at her family, she somehow felt that they were inferior with their bronzed skin and red-gold hair. Jai'til's family looked just like Everluof did in the history books.

Placing his right hand over his heart, Mascerab offered his left hand upright to the X'xix family.

'Welcome to our city,' Mascerab intoned. 'May our home feel like your own, and our family, your family.'

Azanya mimicked his hand movements. 'Your blessing is welcome and well met. Let our families unite in shared goals and shared dreams until we shall depart.'

They were far more formal than Jessandra was used to; it was clear they spent a lot of time in the capital. Jessandra tried to recall all of her lessons in etiquette, but her brain felt like it was full of clouds. A company of highkin had come with Reuben on his last visit, and she tried to remember how they'd acted. That was over two years ago now, and she'd been too sad about Lenta's exile to have paid much attention. She cursed herself inwardly.

'Let us take some refreshment,' Mascerab said with his most winning smile.

Jessandra always thought he looked like a wolf when he smiled like that; his teeth too pointy, his gaze too hungry.

'Refreshment is greatly appreciated,' Azanya replied as he removed his wife's hand from his arm. 'The road to Millen is long, and the weather has been frightfully hot.'

A bright spark of lightning forked across the sky to the east. Several members of Jessandra's party jumped, but the X'xix family didn't react at all. Summer storms weren't unusual along the Swishdine Coast.

Mascerab and Azanya bent their heads together as they followed the herald into the castle. Lady Xan offered her own arm for Elisayn to take as they followed their husbands out of the heat. Suddenly, Jai'til was in front of Jessandra, his eyes locked on hers.

'My princess,' he said, 'shall we cool down inside?'

Jessandra's heart fluttered in a panicked beat.

'Of course,' she murmured, hoping her voice sounded normal. She certainly didn't feel capable of holding a conversation with the ethereal creature before her.

Jai'til took her hand and hooked it into the crook of his arm. His hand was cool and soft, almost like the feel of her special suede blanket, or the skin of the kitchen dog's newborn pups.

Being so close to him only made her breath sharper in her throat, her body temperature rising as they entered the relative cool of the castle's lower levels. Jessandra was acutely aware of the sweat on her face and chest, of the flyaways sticking out of her braid, of the grey slate of her eyes.

'May I call you Jessandra?' Jai'til asked as they followed the party through the cool halls.

'Of course,' she said, not knowing what the right answer was.

If they were to be married, she didn't know what else he should call her except her name. She'd never heard her mother call her father 'King' in private before.

'Jessandra is fine,' she said.

'You can call me Jai.'

Jessandra risked a glance at her betrothed and saw he was wearing a cheeky grin.

'Not in front of my parents, of course,' he added, his grin widening.

'You can call me Jess,' she said, surprising herself as she smiled back at him. 'But not in front of my parents either.'

Jai threw his head back and laughed. Jessandra found herself giggling too, though she wasn't sure why. She felt as if she were in a fever dream. Those thoughts she'd had moments before he arrived—what if they were true? Jai'til certainly seemed to have a fun-loving nature beneath the stiff, formal front his family presented.

'You're quite a delight, my sweet Jess,' he said. 'Tell me, what sort of mischief do you get up to here in Millen?'

Jessandra opened her mouth to answer when she was interrupted by servants offering bowls of water and a tray of warmed flannels. The door to the sitting room stood open before them; Jessandra hadn't even realised they'd arrived.

With a grateful sigh, Jai'til wiped his face, neck, and hands clean with the water and cloth. Jessandra did the same, careful to avoid her kohl-lined eyes and bright lipstick. With her back slightly turned to her betrothed, she made sure to wipe the swell of her chest as well. The servant nodded in approval at the motion, and Jessandra frowned at the girl.

'Ready?' Jai asked.

Patting herself with a dry towel, Jessandra turned towards the doors.

'Yes.'

Jai'til took her arm again.

'I still want to hear what you get up to for fun here,' he whispered as they entered the dining room.

A long serving table was set with beakers of iced wine and tea, small cakes, and trays of fruit. Both sets of parents were already seated in deep, plush chairs around a table crowded with thick candles. The low hum of their murmured conversation didn't drown out the single harpist in the corner.

'What would you like, Princess?' one of the servants asked. 'My lord?'

'Just an iced tea for me,' Jessandra answered.

'Too early for wine?' Jai said in her ear, the smirk in his voice unmistakable.

'Too early in our new friendship for wine,' she shot back as she accepted a glass of tea.

He laughed again, the sound like chimes dancing in the wind. Jessandra caught their mothers watching them with appraising looks.

Jai'til took a plate of fruit and an apple cake along with a glass of iced tea. Feeling bold, Jessandra led him to where their parents sat, but she lowered herself into a chair that was a little removed, and less reclined.

Although she could feel their eyes on her more often than not, Jessandra ignored her parents and turned her full attention to Jai'til.

'What do you think of the fruit?'

His eyes widened as he chewed on the cake.

'I've never tasted a cake like this,' he said after he finished his mouthful. 'What's in it?'

'Haven't you heard we grow the sweetest apples in all of Marbin?' Jessandra asked, feigning innocence.

Jai'til's eyes tightened ever so slightly. He looked at her as if seeing her in a new light.

'I had heard the rumour,' he said, leaning in close to her, a small bunch of grapes in one hand. 'But I can only believe it now that the sweetest thing in all of Marbin is before my eyes.'

Jessandra blushed and looked away.

'Grape?' Jai asked.

His voice drew her gaze back to him. The look he wore sent butterflies spiralling through her stomach. She wondered if the boy who got Lenta pregnant had made her sister feel the same way.

'Please,' she murmured.

He rested one of the dark, oval fruits on her lips. His dark eyes held her, paralysing her. With his tongue pressing against his top teeth, he pushed the grape into her mouth.

In that moment, Jessandra knew she'd never be able to say no to him. Anything he asked of her would fall freely from her lips, regardless of whether it condemned her or not. He'd ensnared her—body, mind, soul—and she didn't care.

6

BINDOCK

THE ENTIRE TOWN of Bindock stood on the shoreline where Wave had tried to save Henny just days before. Muffled sobs and low chatter weren't enough to drown the crash and pull of the waves as they churned against the rocks.

A small boat with a rounded hull lay propped on a makeshift platform. The boat was filled with a bed of soft material, and bright streamers hung from the tall pole at the back. Wave couldn't look at the boat, or the crowd gathered around the platform. Her thoughts swirled like a storm-driven ocean and her heart ached. X'olea stood beside her, solemn and quiet, but she found little comfort in his presence.

The crowd fell silent, and Wave lifted her eyes. The maire moved towards the boat carrying a tiny, muslin-wrapped figure, his wife a half step behind. Tears traced the lines of her face. Seeing them, Wave thought her heart might shatter. The figure in his arms was so small, so impossibly tiny. Wave squeezed her eyes shut as her anger at Lerinial's cruelty clashed with her crushing sadness.

Side by side, the maire and his wife laid their only daughter into the belly of the boat. Henny's tiny body disappeared beneath the soft material, her final resting place. Her parents joined the crowd, holding hands and facing the ocean.

Elder Felin stepped onto the platform. He was wrapped in a white sarong, and his weathered face was consumed by the large wire-framed looking glasses he always wore.

'We have been brought together today through a shared grief,' he said, addressing the crowd. 'Our goddess has chosen to take one of her children home, and though it fills all of us with a great sadness, now is the time to let Henny go, to let her walk beside Lerinial in eternity.'

Wave could hear soft sobs and whimpers throughout the crowd, but she had no tears left. Her tears had burned hot the day she rocked Henny's body on the shoreline. Those tears had flowed freely as she delivered Henny to her parents, and later, they'd turned to gut-wrenching sobs as X'olea held her in his sitting room. Now, she felt like a sea sponge left in the sun too long. Withered and parched, unable to make sense of her own mind or the world around her.

'Henny was a shining light in our community. All of the children adored her company, and every adult she came into contact with was delighted by her presence. Today, we lose one of the sweetest creatures to bless this town. But we also know that Lerinial will take Henny into her loving arms and be blessed as we have been.'

How could Wave ever forgive Lerinial? Her goddess had betrayed her; betrayed Henny and the sanctity of life. Like a piece of flotsam swirling across the surface of the ocean, Wave felt lost and alone in the world, untethered from her goddess and her sense of self.

Something very strange had occurred when she'd tried to rescue Henny, something she had no way of comprehending. Using her god-given power against her goddess should have been impossible, but somehow, she'd bested Lerinial and plucked Henny's body from the ocean.

Henny's lifeless body, she reminded herself. Whatever strange power she'd tapped into didn't matter. In the end, Henny had still died. What good was this new thing she'd discovered if she couldn't save anyone?

Worrying about it was pointless, but Wave couldn't stop herself trying to understand what had happened when the blinding rage had turned into all-consuming light. It was as if she'd accessed the power of some other god. The thought was blasphemous, though, and illogical.

'It is time to release Henny back to the water. As she was born into this earth, from Lerinial's hand to her mother's womb, so we return her body to the greatest connection we have with our goddess.'

A group of men—their chests bare and lower halves wrapped in embroidered white sarongs—hefted the boat onto their shoulders and moved down into the shallows. The crowd surged forward, following them until the water lapped at their ankles. Wave hovered at the back of the group, X'olea by her side.

The men lifted the boat above their heads and pushed past the low waves. Once they'd made their way into calmer water, they lowered the boat and gave it a strong shove. At first, the boat seemed to push back at them, as if Henny wanted to come home. Eventually, the undercurrent took hold and pulled the boat further and further away. The town stood in silence, watching the girl's final journey.

As the afternoon wore on and Henny's funeral craft became little more than a speck on the horizon, the townspeople began to drift back towards Bindock. Unable to take her eyes off the near-invisible boat, Wave realised with a start that only the elders and Henny's parents stood on the shore. She felt awkward, as if she was imposing on something private, and she motioned to X'olea with her head. They strode in silence all the way back to his house.

A feeling of solemnity consumed Wave as she tucked herself into her favourite armchair. For a change, X'olea opened one set of curtains so they could look out over the Nagahere.

When X'olea came back to the sitting room with a tray of tea, Wave studied her friend. She hadn't had a chance to talk in detail with him about how she'd managed to retrieve Henny's body. The uncertainty was burning her up, a fire of questions seared onto her tongue.

With a big sigh, X'olea sat back into the other armchair.

'It's not your fault,' he said without any preamble.

Wave nodded. 'I know.'

'They're grateful you were able to bring her body back to them. That is a small gift usually stolen from us when a rip takes someone.'

'I know.'

They fell into silence as they waited for the tea to cool.

'Something else is on your mind,' X'olea said as he poured two cups.

Wave lifted the tea to her nose and inhaled. Peppermint and orange peel. Soothing for the stomach, uplifting for the heart. X'olea had been teaching her herb lore, a topic she was fascinated by. Too bad they had to keep the study a secret—the details of herb lore were only meant for plantkin.

'Did something happen that day?' X'olea asked. 'You were a mess by the time you got here. Of course you were,' he added with a small shake of his head. 'What I mean to say is that you looked like you'd burned yourself out.'

Wave wanted to tell him, but she didn't even know where to begin.

'Ealen always said I'd need a stronger teacher to show me how to push my waterkin power further,' she said, her words coming out slowly at first. 'But I fought so hard that day, I fought Lerinial with everything I had. And I went too far. I've never felt myself run out like that, but it happened.'

'Was that after you'd reached Henny?'

Wave swallowed and set her tea back down on the table.

'No.'

X'olea raised an eyebrow.

'She was already gone when I ran out of energy. I felt my power failing, felt my body losing control. Henny was sinking. Lerinial had her.' She paused. How could she describe what had occurred next with human words? 'And then I was angry. So angry. At myself, for not being able to help Henny. But mostly I was angry at Lerinial. Angry that she could just snuff out a life like that. Angry that she was so cruel. I could hear her laughing at me. It drove me mad. And then ...'

X'olea leaned forward, resting his elbows on his knees, his gaze intent on her.

'And then ... it's so hard to explain, X'olea. It's like I was consumed by this dazzling, brilliant light. I don't know how long I was lost in the light, but it felt like an age. And then something slammed into my body and I was back in the world. When I opened my eyes, we were in the shallows, and Henny was in my arms. But she ... she ...'

'It's okay,' X'olea murmured, resting a hand on her arm.

'Lerinial was angry, then,' Wave whispered, remembering the way the waves had splashed her face, how the water had stung much worse than salt water should. 'She's still angry at me. And I her. We've betrayed one another.'

'Tell me more about the light.'

'I don't know how else to describe it.' Wave shrugged. 'It was this blinding light that consumed me from inside out.' An idea struck her. 'You know how if you're looking at a stormy sky and there's a big shaft of lightning, your eyes are blinded for a moment?'

X'olea nodded.

'It was like that, I suppose, but it came from inside me.' Wave gestured at her chest and threw her hand out wide. 'I can't understand it, no matter how much I think about it. What do you think it means?'

X'olea leaned back into his chair and sipped at his tea. His gaze wandered out over the tea tree forest.

'X'olea?'

'I'm not sure, Wave. It's certainly nothing like Lerinial's power, nor anything like Everluof's. I've never heard anyone describe any of the other gods' powers in that way either.' He tapped one finger on his chin, his gaze disappearing into the distance. 'I wonder ...'

'What?' Despite her grief over Henny's death, Wave couldn't quench the insatiable desire to understand what she'd experienced.

'I'm not sure.'

Wave glared at him. X'olea threw his hands in the air.

'Truly! I have an idea, but I need more information first. Let me write to one of my old friends about it.'

'Will you tell me what you find out?'

'Of course.'

Wave picked up her cup and took a long swig of tea. 'I can't stay here, X'olea.'

'I agree.'

'Honestly, I want to leave right now. After what happened with Henny, though ... it's changed everything. I wanted to leave to get away from these people, but also to find a teacher who can help me push my power further.'

Wave nestled back into her chair again. 'Now it feels like there's some knowledge just waiting there for me, at the edge of my awareness.' She shrugged. 'But I have no idea what happened. Who would be able to help me understand? Where should I go? The world feels like this huge puzzle and I don't even know where to look for the pieces.'

'Be patient, Wave,' X'olea said. 'Once I hear back from my friend, we might have some more answers. And if not ... we'll go searching for answers anyway. Just wait till you've graduated.'

'We'll go searching?' Wave raised an eyebrow.

'Humph. Did you really think I'd let you run off to have exciting adventures by yourself?'

Wave laughed, the first time she'd been able to since Henny died.

'And I know you, Wave. No matter where we go, you'll find all sorts of strange knowledge. You seem to pull it towards you, like a lodestone. I wouldn't want to miss that.'

'So you'll come with me?' Wave asked. He'd already admitted it, but she wanted to be certain. 'Even to visit my family?'

X'olea grinned over his teacup. 'I think your mother and I will have some very interesting conversations.'

7

BARANCHA PLAINS

THE TAIL END of the storm had cleansed the atmosphere in the Barancha Plains. In a village several hours' ride from Essenné, Larka stood on her front step and breathed in the cool air. Summer's hot, dry winds would be back soon enough, so she relished the brief refreshment that came with the rain.

In her pocket was a letter, and she turned it over and over with one hand. Mail found its way to the village sporadically with the merchants from Essenné, though there was almost never mail for Larka. So few people knew where she and her family had been holed up these past fifteen years.

'Mumma, can I go and play?' Winter asked, her little face peering up from under Larka's elbow.

'Have you done your chores?'

'Yes!'

'Brushed your teeth and hair?'

Winter groaned.

'Go on, inside.' Larka pushed her daughter back into the house. 'You can play when you're ready for the day.'

Winter stomped inside and Larka followed her. Their house was small, just a simple kitchen with two bedrooms, but it had been home for a long time. This tiny space was the closest thing Larka had felt to safety since she'd left her hometown as a naive seventeen-year-old.

The water in the kettle was still warm, so Larka filled the small tub and washed their breakfast dishes while Winter brushed her hair.

'All done, Mumma.'

Larka tousled her daughter's hair and Winter wiggled away from her.

'All right, be safe out there. Remember, the creek can be unpredictable after a big storm.'

'I know,' Winter said. 'I'll stay with the others too.'

She smiled up at Larka, all wide-eyed innocence. Larka gathered Winter into a tight hug before she pulled on her boots and ran out the door. For a moment, Larka's throat closed over, as it did every time she watched Winter leave. She took a deep breath, and the moment of panic passed. They had years before she would feel her calling, years before Larka had to work out how to protect her youngest daughter from the fate her older two had escaped. No matter which god called to her, she would never let Winter be named Kaiāho.

Another day of working in the fields was before her, but the letter in her pocket burned a hole in her mind. She'd received it yesterday when the merchant had come through and she'd gone to buy new needles and thread.

The barley could wait a little while longer. Larka pulled out a chair and sat down, laying the crumpled letter on the table. The parchment was thin, cheaply made, and the wax bore no seal of kin or country.

Working carefully so as not to tear the fragile paper, Larka slid her finger beneath the wax and opened the note.

Dearest Larka, it began.

She perused the letter and let out a small sigh. Part relieved, part sad, Larka folded the parchment up and pushed it into the bottom kitchen drawer. It was from her old friend, Hasting, writing to let her know that he'd left his home in Harba Din and moved to the other side of Condor. He'd given her his address in Gardar Mae and invited her and Winter to visit whenever they liked. The journey from the village was still a long one, but he was closer now than he'd been in a long time.

Gods, the last time she'd seen Hasting was when she was pregnant with Winter. Since then, he'd lived in Lashameg Kingdom before moving to Condor Province six years ago. Letters had started arriving from him soon after his move with invitations for her to visit him. She'd never gone. At least he never tried to come to her; he had too much respect for her family and their safety to come looking for her out in the Plains.

Maybe it would be good to take a break from her work. Larka hadn't left the Plains since Samson had set them up here. He'd chosen this tiny, remote village to ensure her safety and the safety of their daughters, but it meant she was incredibly isolated. Fifteen long years in the Plains, but she hadn't seen anyone from her old life since before Winter was born.

This life was very different to what she'd imagined. When she'd met Samson, she knew she'd found her soulmate. What she hadn't known was that marrying him meant committing to a life as a fugitive, never certain of her safety or her place in the world. That was fine when it was just the two of them, exploring the world together with Hasting at their side. Once Siska had been born, and then Wave … once she had daughters of her own, safety became her biggest priority.

Larka dug around in the kitchen drawer, looking for a letter she'd read a thousand times. The parchment was worn thin, not because it was cheap, but because her fingers had caressed it so many times. The edges were starting to tear along the fold creases, so Larka avoided looking at it as much as she could.

My beloved,

Know that no matter what happens, I am yours. The safety of our girls is my priority now, and it means I cannot stay. I don't know how often I'll return, as I don't want to attract unwanted attention. I will fight for us. You are in my heart, forever and always.

The letter had been on the table the morning she conceived Winter, though she was unaware of the seed growing inside her at the time. Samson had disappeared before she woke, but she hadn't worried back then. It was part of the plan to keep them safe. They'd never committed to a schedule of his return, but she thought he'd continue to show up whenever he could, when it was safe for all of them.

She hadn't expected that she wouldn't see him for nine whole years, that he wouldn't even know he had another daughter. Disappearing off the face of Heredour had never been a part of their plan.

As each month and long year crept by, Larka felt more and more unsettled. His absence could only mean one thing—the Black Cloaks had found him. And if that was true, it was unlikely she'd ever see him again. Her heart fractured a little more every time the thought surfaced.

More importantly, his absence made her less and less certain of her security in the Plains. If he'd been captured, the last thing he would do is give up their whereabouts. But she knew as well as he did that the Black Cloaks had special ways of making humans speak things they'd sworn never to tell.

Hasting would know what to do. He'd been with them every step of the way. Her best friend since childhood, he and Samson had become fast friends when Samson showed up in their town. Hasting would be able to assuage her concerns, or help her make the decision to move, if that's what was needed.

Yes, maybe it was time for a holiday to Condor.

8

WATERFALL CITY

A FEW DAYS after their strange meeting on the northern battlements, Mortius received another early morning summons, though this one wasn't from Reuben. The script was familiar, but Mortius couldn't place whose hand had crafted it.

He was in his office, the sound of the waterfalls a distant rumble. One of the many benefits of living in the highkin quarter was the sound barrier that protected them from the monstrous falls. Dust motes floated around his head, but it wasn't yet light enough for Mortius to pay them any attention. He lit another candle and flipped the letter over, smiling as he recognised the seal.

The note was short, and Mortius tucked it under a pile of parchment before rising from his desk. He traipsed down the near-dark staircase and took a cloak from the peg. A light from the kitchen showed the cook already up, kneading bread by the growing fire in the hearth.

'I'll be back for breakfast,' Mortius said as he slipped through the doorway.

'You'll go hungry if not!' the cook shouted.

Cook had worked for him since he'd opted to move out of the castle early in his career, some twenty-odd years ago. He appreciated her audacity and quick wit, but he was more grateful for her ability to provide him with a steaming pot of tea before he realised he needed one.

A lowkin streetsweeper hurried along the paved walkway, trying to stay out of Mortius' gaze, but there was little activity in the highkin quarter otherwise. The city's highkin were a lazy bunch, soft and secure in their relative positions of power. Mortius had often thought about moving to the middlekin district just to get away from them, but he knew it would be a foolish move. There were too many people ready to supersede him who would see it as an act of weakness.

Mortius snorted. They wouldn't last more than a day trying to manage Reuben. Mortius and the High Council held a tenuous grip on the king these days. Despite the mess they were in, Mortius was considering leaving the city for a few weeks. The idea seemed like insanity, but so did staying. Maybe if he left, the council and the other highkin would get a taste of an unbridled Reuben.

The overpowering perfume of the highkin district faded as Mortius moved into the middlekin district. The houses here were smaller and less grand, though not by much. Instead of the ornate statues that guarded the highkin mansions like sentinels, the middlekin quarter housed manicured gardens and trickling water fountains. The clink of dishes being plated and the low murmur of voices gave the district a homely feel. In the belly of the darkened shopfronts, Mortius could see people moving around, preparing to set up for the day.

Mortius strode into the huge market square that straddled the middle- and lowkin districts. The area was a hive of activity —fruiterers unpacking produce from mule-drawn carts, bakers laying out fresh bread in wicker baskets, tailors shouting at one another as they pulled protective oiled cloth from their tables. The square was lined with smaller shops, taverns, and large warehouses. Ignoring them, Mortius strode around the market, angling for a warehouse on the northern edge.

The Master of Trade, Unner skykin, made his home behind the wide windows of the top floor so he could watch the movement of the market from his sitting room. Beneath his apartment was the warehouse that contained a treasure trove of luxury items for those with the funds to buy them.

The oversized wooden doors of the warehouse were still closed, so Mortius made his way to the smaller door at the centre of the building. He knocked and was greeted almost instantly by Unner's butler.

'Lord Mortius,' the man said with a deep bow.

'I'm no lord, Emmit, and you know better.'

Emmit bowed his head in supplication. 'Of course. Will you follow me? The master is expecting you.'

He was dressed in a fitted cotton suit of pale blue with glossy low-cut boots. The outfit looked almost proper enough to wear to a formal event. Nobody else in the city dressed their servants as flamboyantly as Unner. Mortius shook his head.

Up a flight of stairs, Emmit left Mortius in a semidark hallway as he went to check on his master.

'The Lord Mortius,' Emmit said as he ushered Mortius into the room.

From his daybed, Unner rose to offer his greetings. He was a large man, but not overweight. He stood a full head taller than Mortius, and Mortius wasn't short. Although Unner hailed from southern Lashameg, his shining ebony skin was often cloaked in the rich, brightly coloured fabrics favoured by the Trinian, his neck and fingers draped in heavy chains and jewels.

'Lord Mortius,' Unner declared in a voice that boomed across the room like a storm rolling over the ocean. 'Please sit.'

One giant, gem-encrusted hand gestured towards a reclining couch opposite his own.

The room was embellished in a similar fashion to its owner. Mismatched but luxuriously upholstered chairs and lounges filled the room. Paintings depicting sweeping Lashamegian landscapes hung on every wall, nestled between ornately framed mirrors. The carpet was a violent shade of purple, and the heavy drapes hanging on either side of the floor-to-ceiling windows were burgundy velvet, tied back with thick golden rope. Garish and outspoken, just like Unner.

Inclining his head, Mortius sat in the proffered chair, though he chose not to recline. He was a man of purpose, of intention, and spending the morning lounging around was not in his nature. The butler returned with a tray of exotic fruit and a steaming pot of black tea. Unner and Mortius sat in silence as the tea was poured for them.

'That will be all, Emmit,' Unner said.

'Actually,' Mortius said. 'Would you mind summoning Aymn to take tea with us?'

Emmit looked at his master for reassurance.

'Bring the boy,' Unner said.

With a final nod, Emmit left the room.

'I trust I find you in good health?' Mortius asked as he lifted his cup.

The master loaded a plate with sliced melon, peaches, and grapes. 'As ever, my good friend.' He smiled, big lips parting to reveal slabs of gleaming white teeth. 'I trust that you will be happy with my purchase.'

'You have never failed me before.'

Unner nodded and turned his pale blue eyes out over the market still setting up in the square. 'It is below, in the warehouse.'

Mortius nodded. 'How is your apprentice?'

The master turned back to Mortius. Determined not to give

away even the slightest hint of his purpose, Mortius didn't flinch from the other man's calculating gaze.

'He is diligent. Precise.' The master paused. 'Some days, one could be forgiven for thinking just how similar he is to his guardian.' Unner raised an eyebrow.

Mortius knew he was probing, baiting, testing him. Nothing shifted on Mortius' face, though he smiled inwardly. Unner was stuck on the notion that young Aymn was Mortius' son, despite the story they peddled that Aymn was his nephew. Either tale was safer than the truth. Nobody could know whose son he really was.

'I raised Aymn, it is only natural that he should have some of my traits.' Not entirely untrue.

Unner sniffed. 'He will make an excellent Master of Trade when the time comes. Far better than I have been.'

'That certainly says a lot.'

A knock at the door paused their conversation.

'Aymn,' Emmit said with no preamble.

'Good morning,' Mortius said.

Aymn grinned at his guardian from beneath a blond, shaggy fringe. Not for the first time, Mortius was glad they'd agreed to let the boy be raised in his care. There was enough of a similarity to their fine features that they could pass as uncle and nephew. As if in homage to his true identity though, Aymn's eyes hadn't taken on the violet shade that came with the use of Everluof's power, though he'd been schooled as a starkin. The boy's eyes remained an obstinate, nondescript grey, which nobody had dared to question. At least, not in front of Mortius.

As Aymn settled into manhood, though, his face began to take on the features of his mother. A delicate equine nose, a smattering of freckles over his cheeks, and even more surprising, the grace he carried with him in every movement. The resemblance between them was uncanny. Thankfully, his mother was a recluse who hadn't been seen for decades, even though she lived in the capital.

'Will you sit with us for a time, and share in tea and conversation with two old men?' Mortius asked.

Unner snorted in indignation.

'The pleasure would be mine,' Aymn answered, perching himself on the edge of a chair.

Emmit's lips thinned, but he poured Aymn's tea without a word. No doubt the man would have trouble accepting Aymn as his master if and when Unner retired. Mortius wondered if that day would ever come for Aymn, though.

'How are you finding the trade, nephew?'

'I feel as though I was called to do this,' Aymn said, his eyes lighting up. 'It's funny, I could almost say I feel the calling of the trade stronger than I do the call of Everluof.'

Unner and Mortius laughed, but there was a forced, uncomfortable nature to their mirth. Nobody of their generation was comfortable acknowledging the severely waning powers of humans, but the youth seemed apathetic about it. Those who had managed to avoid being named Kaiāho, at least. It had taken years of coaching and a mite of indoctrination to convince Aymn he would be called by Everluof. With the same intensity that Mortius defended the boy's fake heritage, he also needed to make sure he wouldn't be lost to Buduwai and the Black Cloaks. Aymn was the contingency plan he'd hoped not to need.

'You must be near the end of your apprenticeship by now?'

Aymn glanced at Unner before answering.

'The learning will never cease, not while the master is my master.'

'But in terms of his skills?' Mortius turned his attention to Unner. 'Would you say he is capable, fit to take over if you wanted to, say, have a holiday?'

The skin around Unner's ice-blue eyes tightened. There wasn't meant to be a threat in Mortius' words, but with

Reuben's current volatility, no high- or middlekin felt secure beneath his rule.

'He would be more than capable.' Unner's voice was light, bereft of emotion.

'Excellent,' Mortius said. He placed his teacup back on the table. 'I hope you're not planning any holidays, Unner?'

The large man opposite him shook his head. As the Master of Trade, he was used to being in charge of the direction of a conversation. Mortius had watched him in action countless times. Now, Unner was unnerved, his breath shallower than it had been, his half smile a mask of civility.

'Aymn, I'm considering making a trip away from the city for several weeks. I would like you to accompany me.'

Both men blinked in surprise before sharing a long look.

'I ...' Aymn started. He cleared his throat. 'I don't wish to leave the trade.'

'Oh, my nephew, I have no intention of tearing you from the thing you love.' Mortius sat forward on his chair, clasping his hands before him. 'Think of it as a learning holiday, a chance to have a break from the world you know, an opportunity to learn a wealth of other skills you could never pick up in the city.'

Aymn frowned, his eyes darting back to Unner. It was clear to Mortius that whatever loyalty he once held over the boy was almost gone; his heart and mind belonged to the Master of Trade. Exactly the time to separate them, to remind Aymn of his place in the world. Perhaps it was even the time to reveal the truth of his heritage. Mortius swallowed the thought.

Too soon. None of us are ready.

'If that wouldn't impact your work, of course,' Mortius added, turning back to Unner.

'Of course not,' Unner said, the corners of his mouth lifting in surprise. 'How long would Aymn be out of the city?'

'Five, maybe six weeks. I'm not certain yet, but we'll need to visit most of the regions. There will be a lot of time on horseback.'

Aymn's eyes lit up. There was little opportunity for the traders to ride out of the city, but Aymn had loved the hours he'd spent riding through the Kirsky Forest as a youth.

'And when are you leaving?' Unner asked. 'I'll need to be prepared for his extended departure.'

'I'm not certain yet.' In truth, he wasn't even certain if he should go. But he wouldn't leave the city without Aymn, wouldn't risk the Black Cloaks getting to him. 'But I will make sure I give you ample notice.'

'You have my permission, not that it's needed.' Unner grimaced a little, but lifted his cup to hide his discomfort.

'And you, Aymn?' Mortius asked. 'Are you willing to spend a few weeks out in the country with your uncle?'

Indecision played out on the boy's face. Mortius wondered how he could be good at striking trade deals if he couldn't keep his emotions off his face.

'I will miss the trade,' Aymn said after a few moments of silence. 'But I would like to see more of Heredour. I'm sure I will be able to establish new partnerships for our trade?'

'You will have plenty of time to do so,' Mortius said.

'If the master is okay with my absence, I will join you.'

Unner nodded. Mortius took it as consent. He wasn't likely to get anything more from the man.

'Thank you both for your understanding. And of course, this conversation stays between us, just us, until it's time to go.'

They both nodded their assent. Mortius eased back into his chair, and they sipped at their tea in silence. The low murmur of the market bubbled up from below the windows.

'I brought your package up from the storeroom,' Aymn said, breaking the quiet.

'Excellent.'

Aymn stood and sat beside Mortius, placing a container on the low table before them.

'The work of a true craftsman,' Mortius said as he ran one finger along the length of pale wood.

'Wait till you see what's inside,' Aymn replied, his eyes never leaving the box.

Mortius lifted the lid, a tiny gasp escaping him. Nestled on a bed of dark silk lay three pieces of the most exquisite jewellery Mortius had ever seen. Fine threads of interwoven silver made up the structure of a thick choker, designed to hold in its centre an egg-shaped moonstone. The stone would rest perfectly in the hollow of a woman's collarbone. Matching earrings completed the set; long works of entwined silver held tiny stones at random intervals, as though the piece was a spider's web catching dew drops in the early morning sun.

The moonstone at the centre of the choker was milky white with flecks of blues and greys and the occasional hint of green. The sheer beauty of the stone alone dazzled him. Mortius ran a gentle finger around the large gem. He remained silent for a long while, studying the pieces he'd waited so long for.

Knowing this would go unworn and unappreciated was almost too much to bear. The thought of the box growing dusty on some forgotten shelf made a lump rise in Mortius' throat. Such a waste. He snapped the lid closed.

'Will your buyer like it?'

Mortius clenched his teeth to stop his tongue from betraying him. When he dragged his gaze away from the pale wood, he noticed that there were tiny golden flecks in Aymn's slate-grey eyes. A shiver passed over Mortius.

'Definitely,' he said, attempting a smile. 'This set is the most exquisite thing I've seen in my whole life.'

'Me too,' Aymn murmured.

In the background of Mortius' awareness, Unner nodded his agreement.

'Nobody knows of this?' Mortius asked.

'Only Unner and myself.' Aymn tucked a strand of fair hair behind his ear. 'The seller. You. That's it.'

'Excellent.'

'The master has taught me the value of silence.'

One corner of Mortius' mouth lifted. 'Silence pays far more than many care to understand.'

9

MILLEN

A FULL WEEK had passed since Jai'til's arrival, and Jessandra was still as besotted as she'd been on the day of his arrival. They spent hours together every day—traipsing through the orchards, riding out to hunt in the nearby forests, puttering around the lake in a little rowboat.

The sense of being in a dream was heightened each and every moment. Jai'til was never improper towards her, despite his inherent mischievous nature, and the delight he showed when they were together was never feigned. It felt too good to be real, but Jessandra tried to remind herself that she was allowed to have something good happen in her life, even if just once.

At the end of each day, though, Jessandra's nerves began to fray. Distracting herself with entertaining Jai'til was fine, but it didn't help with her calling. She'd successfully managed to avoid the topic or speak carefully when it came up, but she knew that until she felt Everluof call to her, their marriage would never go ahead. Her father made sure she didn't forget, visiting her room most nights to glare at her in silence.

'Are you sad Jai'til is leaving tomorrow?' Siska asked as she pulled a brush through Jessandra's thick hair.

Jessandra looked at her handmaiden in the mirror and shrugged. Behind them, Inska moved about the room tidying clothes and making the bed.

'We get on so well,' Jessandra said. 'And this week has been ... perfect. But I still haven't felt anything from any god. He won't marry me if I haven't been called.'

Siska paused in her brushing, a bundle of Jessandra's hair in her hand. They stared at one another, as if sharing a secret conversation that only they could hear.

'You're right,' Jessandra murmured. 'It's not just Jai. It's Father. It's Uncle Reuben. It's Marbin, it's Heredour. I won't be good enough for any of them if I have no god, no power.' She squeezed her eyes shut. 'What is wrong with me?'

Siska went back to brushing her hair. 'It's your birthday next month. Jai'til and his family will be back the week after that for your wedding.'

'And?' Jessandra was all too aware that her time was running out.

Siska leaned down close to Jessandra's head, their eyes still locked in the mirror, ice blue and slate grey.

'Four weeks,' Siska whispered. 'That's all you have left.'

'You don't need to remind me,' Jessandra hissed.

'You can't leave this to chance,' Siska said, her voice urgent. She pushed a note into Jessandra's lap, making sure it was covered by her hand. 'You don't want to end up like your sister.'

Jessandra ground her teeth. How did Lenta's exile have anything to do with her dilemma?

'Siska, Inska,' Jessandra said in a loud voice. 'I'm ready to retire for the night. You may leave me.'

'Yes, Princess,' Inska said, laying a last pillow on the bed.

Siska continued to stare at Jessandra.

'Siska?' Inska asked from the door.

71

With a curt nod of her head, Siska turned on her heel and followed Inska through the door. When the door clicked shut, Jessandra let out a low growl. Who did Siska think she was, talking to a princess, an heir no less, in such a manner? For a moment, she forgot the note Siska had given her. When she went to stand, anger bubbling beneath her skin, she felt the parchment crumple beneath her hand.

Curious, Jessandra looked at the weathered parchment. There was no name on the outside, but when she opened it, she was shocked to see the familiar handwriting.

'Lenta?' she whispered, then shot a furtive glance around the room. It was empty, of course, but her heart raced anyway.

Jess.

> *I'm not pregnant. It's Lerinial who summons me.*
> *They'll take me away. I wanted you to know.*
> *I love you.*

A shiver ran over Jessandra's entire body, and her skin broke out in goosebumps. Mouth open, she stared at the last words her sister had ever written.

Not pregnant.
Lerinial.
I love you.

Tears sprang to Jessandra's eyes. Lenta. Lenta was Kaiāho. She hadn't been exiled. She'd been sent to Buduwai. The implications of her father's actions dawned on Jessandra. She forgot to breathe. Her heart raced in her chest, her whole body vibrating.

A knock at the door broke her terrible reverie.

Jessandra dashed the tears away from her cheeks.

Another knock.

She stuffed the note into her jewellery box.

'Come,' she said. Her voice shook a little, but less than she expected.

'My darling,' Jai said from the door.

Jessandra spun around. He stood in the doorway, all soft, pale skin and elegant fabrics. The corner of his mouth lifted as he regarded her.

'May I come in?'

It wasn't proper, but Jessandra nodded anyway. He perched on the edge of her bed and patted the covers next to him. Like a mindless puppet, Jessandra sat beside him. The delicate perfume he always wore, lilac and sandalwood, softened her uncertainty.

'In the morning we'll be surrounded by courtiers, our parents, horses, knights, all of it. I wanted a moment alone with you before we're separated.'

Jessandra smiled, her lips trembling.

'Oh, my dear.' Jai'til rested a hand on her cheek. 'I'm also sad that we must spend the next four weeks apart. But we've spent a lifetime separated before now. We can do it.'

The letter from her sister burned in Jessandra's mind. Lenta had been betrothed to Jai'til since they were toddlers. Only in her exile had the betrothal shifted to Jessandra. Not exile—Kaiaho.

'I don't know if I can,' she murmured.

Jai'til frowned, his face a mask of concern. 'What do you mean, sweet one?'

Jessandra shook her head. 'I can't.'

'Can't what?'

Squeezing her hands into fists to relieve the pressure she felt in her heart, she opened and shut her mouth. The words wanted to come out, but she couldn't let them. Jai had been so honest with her, sharing secrets from his childhood and time in training. He seemed to accept her exactly as she was, but she couldn't tell him the truth of her calling.

'My darling Jess,' he crooned. 'You can tell me anything.

Although we're not yet married, my heart is yours. I will hold your secrets as close to my chest as I hold my own.'

'I can't,' she whispered, but she felt her resolve crumbling at his caring tone. 'I can't.'

'If it tears at you this badly, you must tell me. A trouble shared is a trouble halved, so the priests say.'

'You won't want to marry me,' she whispered, hating herself as she spoke. Why couldn't she just keep her mouth shut?

Jai's eyes widened. 'Nothing you could say to me would turn me away, Jess. I stand beside you, now and forever.'

He spoke in earnest, Jessandra was sure. Unlike everyone else in her life, Jai'til said what he meant. If they were to be married, he deserved the truth. And if, as he said, he would stand beside her regardless, then it wouldn't hurt to tell him now.

'Your burdens are mine,' he murmured, taking her face in both of his hands.

Jessandra nodded. She could trust him. She could.

'It's just that ...' she started, but didn't know how to continue.

'Take your time,' Jai said. He released her face and took both her hands in his own. His smile was so warm, so genuine that Jessandra felt the last shred of her willpower waver and fade away.

'I haven't been called yet,' she whispered, so soft she barely heard herself.

'Pardon?'

Taking a deep breath, Jessandra lifted her face a little. 'I haven't been called yet.'

Jai frowned, but there was amusement on his face. 'What do you mean?'

'I haven't been called.' Jessandra wiggled her shoulders. 'Everluof hasn't yet called me to his side.'

Silence fell between them. Jai'til's face became the picture of neutrality, though Jessandra sensed his mind was whirling beneath his still exterior.

'So, you haven't done any training?' he asked.

Jessandra shook her head.

'And you haven't ... felt Everluof?' He lifted one hand, palm up, as if he could feel the god on his skin like rain.

'No.'

Jai blinked.

'How can that be, Jess? You're almost sixteen!'

'I don't know,' she whispered, looking up at him from beneath her eyelashes.

'Surely you must have felt something by now, some inkling of Everluof's grace?' A bemused frown marred his perfect face.

'Well, sometimes ...' Jessandra tried to stop the words spilling from her mouth, but her tongue wouldn't obey. 'Sometimes I think I might feel Setunil.'

Jai's frown was replaced in an instant by a stony, impenetrable mask.

'Setunil?' Even the timbre of his voice had changed, become harder, more brittle. He pulled his hands away from hers.

Jessandra's heart leapt to her throat. How could she have been so stupid?

'I mean,' she said, hesitating, wondering how to fix her mistake. 'I don't think it's Setunil, not really. My handmaidens are skykin, and I'm so desperate to feel something, anything.'

Jai'til stood, his eyes staring through her.

'It's just my imagination, I'm sure. Everluof will call to me, he will!'

'If you are skykin, then ...' He didn't finish his sentence.

'I'm not!' Jessandra's voice rose with each syllable. 'I'm not, I promise! Jai?'

He turned and walked away from her.

'Jai, please.' Her vision blurred with tears. 'I will be a good wife. I'll make you proud, I swear it!'

At the door, he stopped for the space of a heartbeat.

'I must speak to my parents,' he said.

The door clicked shut behind him. Jessandra clutched at her chest as a wave of absolute terror rolled over her. Everything was ruined. There were no chances left to fix her mistake.

Hiccupping sobs wracked her body. The room seemed to press in on her. Her clothes were too tight, her skin the same. She squeezed her eyes shut to block out the sensations, but they only became worse.

Everything was ruined because she couldn't keep her stupid mouth shut. Jessandra prayed to all the gods to come and take her away. She asked her bed to swallow her up. She begged Everluof, for the thousandth time, to come to her, or at least to make her disappear.

She didn't notice the door open again, or the quiet person who slipped inside her room until she felt warm arms around her body.

'Hush now, Princess, hush.'

It was Siska's voice, but Jessandra barely registered the sound. She pushed her handmaiden away and clawed at her own face.

'What is it, Jessandra?' Siska asked. 'What happened?'

'I told Jai,' she said in an uneven voice. Her sobs had subsided, but her chest still heaved. 'Told him I hadn't been called. I'm so stupid. I told him I might feel Setunil.' She smacked her forehead, over and over again, as if it might make the memory of her incompetence disappear. 'Everything is ruined.'

Siska was silent.

'I want to die, Siska. Anything would be better than this.'

'Don't say that,' Siska said. 'Don't ever say that. There is always another way.'

'Another way? What if it's Setunil calling me? I'll be just like Lenta.'

'You haven't gone through your calling ceremony yet.' Siska rose and began to pace the room. 'So the Black Cloaks can't take you. You've still got time.'

'You gave me Lenta's note. Did you read it?'

Siska nodded, though she looked uncomfortable admitting it. 'Your sister told me to give it to you when you were called. I know what it says.'

'Lenta never had her calling ceremony!' Jessandra said, ignoring the fact that Siska had held on to the note for years. 'They whisked her away in the middle of the night. Not into exile, but to Buduwai!'

Siska chewed on the insides of her cheeks. 'Then you have to run. Jai will tell his parents, and then the Black Cloaks will find out, they always do.'

'Where would I run to, Siska?' Jessandra threw her hands in the air. 'We already talked about this. I'm useless.' She started crying again, her disgust at herself growing with each second. Lenta would never have let herself get into such a precarious position.

'I'd never make it out of the castle, let alone the city.'

'Skoa,' Siska whispered.

'What?'

'Skoa will take you. Nobody would be able to follow you then.'

Jessandra's eyes widened. 'Are you insane? I can't fly!'

'Why not? If Setunil is calling to you, then Skoa might take you.'

Ignoring Jessandra's stuttering, Siska strode to the balcony. She gripped the railing and bent her head down. The sudden quiet made Jessandra nervous, so she stood, but didn't know what to do. Only powerful skykin could befriend a great eagle. What madness possessed Siska to think that Skoa would take Jessandra on his back?

'He's coming,' Siska said as she strode back into the room.

'Pack a bag, make it light. Only things you need. Warm clothes. And a dark cloak.'

Happy to be distracted by something to do, Jessandra stuffed a few items of clothing into a hunting bag, along with a few apples from her fruit bowl. The action felt surreal, as if she was watching herself from a great distance. She looked around the room, not knowing what she would need. Almost as an afterthought, she grabbed a small purse from her bureau, the gold and silver coins clinking inside.

'Put on your riding clothes,' Siska said as she rummaged through the closet. A divided skirt landed on the bed, followed by a long-sleeved shirt and jacket.

'What if it doesn't work?' Jessandra asked. She fingered the clothes, her mouth downturned. 'What if he won't take me?'

'Get dressed,' Siska said, glaring at her. 'He's almost here.'

Jessandra had no idea how Siska could know such a thing, but there was no time to ask. She shrugged herself into her riding outfit. Siska arranged her heaviest, darkest cloak over her shoulders and fastened the ornate clasp.

'You must keep your face hidden,' she said as she raised the hood over Jessandra's face.

From the open door of the balcony, she heard the sound of beating wings. Her heart pounded in her chest, but it wasn't the pulse of terror this time.

'Come on,' Siska said.

'Wait!' Jessandra rushed to her jewellery box and pulled out Lenta's note. She tucked it deep into her hunting bag and hurried over to the balcony. 'Okay. I'm ready.'

The eagle towered over both of them. Pale grey wings tucked into his snow-white body, Skoa watched them both with shiny, black eyes. His feathers gave the impression of the finest silk, and his long legs ended in powerful orange talons.

Siska had one hand resting on his curved beak.

'Come forward,' Siska whispered.

Skoa turned his great head towards Jessandra and stared at her with a single beady eye. Under his piercing stare, Jessandra felt her soul being washed clean. She took a shaky breath.

'Lean your head against his forehead,' Siska said. 'He needs to delve into your mind.'

Jessandra stared at her handmaiden with wide eyes. She knew Skoa wasn't dangerous, at least not with Siska around, but the knowledge didn't make getting closer any less scary.

'Come on,' Siska said, frustration pushing her voice to a low growl.

Skoa lowered his head towards Jessandra. Ignoring her better instincts, she closed her eyes and rested her forehead on the space above his beak.

She gasped. The sensation was like cool water sliding into her mind. A series of images played themselves out in her mind's eye, moving so fast that she couldn't make sense of them. Then he was probing her mind, summoning memories, feelings, and thoughts, and investigating them one by one. Together, they studied exactly what it was that made up the being called Jessandra. She couldn't have pulled away, even if she wanted to.

Without warning, Skoa jerked his head back. Jessandra blinked a few times as she tried to make sense of what she'd just been through.

Skoa unfurled one wing and extended it to the ground. Beside her, Siska smiled in relief.

'He will take you,' she whispered.

Jessandra looked at her. 'Take me where?'

'To safety.' Siska shrugged.

'What does safety mean to a giant eagle?' A tiny tremor shook Jessandra's voice.

'I'll be able to find you, I promise.'

Siska steered her towards the eagle and boosted her up. Jessandra slid into place above his wing joints, her skirt sliding over his silky feathers.

'Skoa will always be able to find you, now that he knows you. Great eagles never forget a soul.'

Jessandra looked down at Siska. 'Where is he taking me?'

Skoa hopped up on the balcony rail and unfurled his wings.

'Siska? Where is he taking me?'

Jessandra swallowed a scream as Skoa leapt from the balcony and they soared off over the lake.

1 0

BINDOCK

THE PRIEST'S rooms were bright and airy; long windows opened up to the north to let in the sea breeze. Wave pressed her thumb against each of the other fingers on her left hand. She wasn't supposed to move her legs, but she wiggled her toes. Anything to dispel the itching discomfort she felt in her right forearm. She stared at the top of the priest's head as he bent over her arm, a sharpened needle in one hand and a shallow ink dish in the other.

Across the room, Iberon and Yllia muttered in low voices, their forearms already wrapped in linen gauze. Iberon's foot tapped an uneven beat against the floorboards and Yllia twirled her hair in her fingers, a bored look in her eyes. They were eager to be out of the room, but Wave had sat through both of their tattoos, watching them squirm beneath the priest's needle. She wasn't about to give them the luxury of missing out on the boring part of the ceremony.

As the priest got closer to completing her tattoo, Wave felt herself get hotter, her skin growing clammy and sweat beading along her forehead. It was the middle of the day, but Wave knew it was just her reaction to the ink being forced under her skin.

The other two had been pale and sweaty by the time the priest was finished.

Using a soft cloth to give a final wipe over her arm, the priest lifted his head.

'All done,' he said. 'Remember to drink plenty of water, all of you.'

Once her forearm was neatly wrapped in gauze, the priest waved the three of them out. Iberon and Yllia rushed ahead of Wave, ignoring her as they so often did. They were both staying in Bindock to pursue uncertain careers. Bindock had a way of keeping the waterkin it trained; once again, Wave would be an outlier just because she wanted to leave.

The official graduation ceremony would happen in the evening, followed by feasting and celebrating. Wave wandered towards her dorm room, wondering if she should take a nap. The tattoo burned her skin, making her weary, but at least she had it. No matter where she went now, she was truly a part of the waterkin community.

A few hours later, Wave woke up groggy and parched. She tried to lick her lips, but her mouth was sandpaper. The jug she filled of an evening still held a bit of tepid water. She swirled the warm liquid around her mouth, not feeling in any way satisfied. There wasn't even enough left to splash her eyes.

The small window in her quarters was open. Dusk was setting in, and Wave realised with a panic that she didn't have long to get ready. Not bothering to pull on her boots, she ducked out of the trainee hall and ran through the sandy back streets towards the river. Not as far from the town as she'd usually like to be, Wave tossed her blouse and skirt on the river-bank and waded in. Washing in her slip wasn't ideal, but there was little privacy here, and not enough time to head inland to any of the private rock pools.

With one hand, Wave scrubbed at her face, underarms, and chest, working hard to keep her wrist wrappings dry. Good enough. She'd never been one to spend a lot of time focused on her appearance, unlike Yllia and the other girls. Just another thing that separated from her from them, another reason for them to look at her like she was a strange creature.

Grabbing her clothes, Wave jogged back to the house the students shared. The halls were silent, and Wave frowned. Surely Yllia would be in her room, dusting her face with powder and winding her hair into elegant curls. Water dripped from Wave's skin and pooled on the tiled floor as she paused, listening for any sound. Silence, except for the steady *drip, drip, drip* from her drenched slip.

Maybe she was late. Her heartbeat began to race as she trotted to her room and towelled herself dry. What if they started without her? Would that mean she wouldn't graduate?

The last pearlescent light of day filled Wave's vision as she tugged on her finest top, a pale green linen blouse embroidered along the collar with whorls. The neckline was a little lower than she liked, but at least it was cool and breezy. Rummaging through her few sets of clothes, Wave pulled out the silk skirt her mother had gifted her when she left home. A deep peacock green, it was gathered at the waist and fell in beautiful folds around Wave's calves.

Pulling her wavy hair back into a thick braid, Wave tried to study her reflection in the tiny, tarnished mirror. At least the skirt fitted her now, and she could make her mother proud. A few stray tea tree flowers were scattered along her desk, so she picked them up and tucked them haphazardly into her braid. Ornamentation wasn't a skill set she'd ever bothered to develop, but Wave thought she looked nicer than she had in the last five years. A fitting way to say goodbye to the town that had rejected her.

Back out in the hall, Wave grabbed her cloak from the cupboard, still listening for any sound in the aching silence. She slid her feet into boots she almost never wore, and headed into the street. The evening was warm, but Bindock often grew chilly overnight, even in summer. Graduation festivities were known to continue long into the night, though Wave didn't expect she'd stay up late with the rest of the town. It wasn't like they'd have anything to talk about.

Taking the back streets to avoid as many people as she could, Wave hurried to X'olea's house. Townspeople were starting to gather in the main street, and Wave breathed a sigh of relief. The graduates were always presented from the maire's verandah, and his house was conspicuously quiet.

Gathering her skirt into one hand, Wave climbed through the railings of X'olea's verandah and tiptoed to his front door. After a few unanswered knocks, Wave heard him moving around upstairs, so she let herself in.

'X'olea?' she called.

'Up here, Wave. Am I late?'

'Not yet.' She took the stairs two at a time, enjoying the feeling of the silk swirling around her legs.

X'olea's head was buried in a cabinet when she got into the sitting room.

'What are you looking for?'

'Oh!' X'olea banged his head on a shelf as he straightened. 'Just a book ... Wave!' He stared at her in surprise. 'You look beautiful.'

Wave laughed. 'I thought I should scrub up a little for graduation.'

With a grin, X'olea deposited a pile of books onto a nearby chair. He wore a pale grey shirt tucked into dark trousers and a silver circlet around his head.

'You know, I've never seen you wear it.' Wave gestured at his head.

X'olea's hand caressed the formal jewellery of the starkin. Where waterkin received a tattoo to mark their kin, starkin received a specially designed circlet. Nobody needed a tattoo or jewellery to show their kin—eye colour alone was enough—so the graduation gift was entirely ceremonial.

'I have little cause to wear it,' X'olea said, his voice soft. 'There would be some who'd wish to take it from me.'

Wave blinked. She knew X'olea was a rebellious scholar, a researcher who sought to uncover the lost, the hidden, the deliberately buried, but it had never occurred to her how many enemies he might have made along the way. Her own experience had taught her how easy it was to become an outcast, so she could see how X'olea had likely pushed his kin to disavow him.

'We should probably head down,' Wave said.

She was uncomfortable talking about his past. X'olea had lived a long life before they became friends, but he only ever shared stories that were useful, or necessary for Wave's learning. If she was honest, she didn't know much about X'olea's life before Bindock. Maybe she didn't know him at all. An alarming thought to have after five years of friendship, especially on the eve of their leaving.

'Before we do,' X'olea said. 'I received a reply from my friend in Condor.' He pressed a folded piece of parchment in her hand. 'I'd like you to read it, but not until later. You might be a little shocked, or confused by what he has to say. Let's get through graduation first.'

'That doesn't make me feel any better!' Wave said, her heartbeat speeding up again.

She turned the parchment over and over in her hand. The quality of the paper was thin, and there was no seal. Who was X'olea's friend in Condor?

'In your pocket now, Wave.'

With a sigh, she tucked the letter into one of the skirt's deep pockets. Resting his hands on her shoulders, X'olea turned her around and pushed her out of the room with a gentle shove.

'You should let yourself have a bit of fun tonight,' he said as he followed her down the stairs.

Wave snorted. 'Fun.'

'Let loose a little bit. You're about to leave Bindock, probably forever. Why not let go, just for a night?'

Wave didn't answer him. He was right, but she wasn't even sure she knew how to have fun. Since she'd arrived in the town, since she'd been relegated as the strange but powerful outcast, she'd dedicated herself to her study, to her goddess. Fun was for people with friends, with family. Fun was for people who belonged. Her heart ached as she realised just how alone she'd felt in Bindock.

For a few moments, Wave and X'olea stood on his verandah to admire the town. Night had set, but the street was full of long tables, towers of guttering candles at each end. Tall stands had been placed down the length of the street, and the light from the oil lamps was protected from the ocean winds by glass lanterns. Multihued streamers were tied between the houses, and the tables were covered in bright tablecloths.

Wave and X'olea descended into the throng. The compacted sand beneath their feet was strewn with pink and white tea tree flowers. Wave smiled. If there was one thing she'd miss from Bindock, it was the beauty of the tiny blossoms.

The rest of the townspeople were dressed in their best festival clothes. Bright skirts and long ribbons jostled with tailored coats and jaunty hats. X'olea shooed Wave through the crowd, pushing her to the front of the people standing expectantly before the maire's house.

'You made it,' Iberon said, disappointment plain in his voice.

'Of course I did,' Wave said, not bothering to acknowledge him with a glance. 'I wouldn't miss it.'

From Iberon's other side came a derisive giggle. Wave peered around Iberon to see Yllia decked out in all her finery. There was so much powder on her face that she looked like one of the pale-skinned people from the Paravat Ranges. The rouge on her lips was too bright for her pasty face, and her hair was bundled in an elaborate tower of curls, little gems intertwined here and there. If they were in the court of Millen, she might have fit in well.

'You look … nice,' Yllia said, pouting at Wave.

Wave laughed, unable to help herself. 'You look … different.'

Yllia glared at her, but their conversation was stopped by the sudden silence of the crowd. The maire had taken his place above them, and the congenial smile he wore belied the fact that he'd lost his only daughter a little over a week ago.

'You're still wearing your bandage,' Iberon growled at Wave's side. 'Are you really that dumb?'

Wave's heart leapt to her throat. Trying to be as circumspect as she could manage, Wave unwound the gauze as the maire called for the town's attention. Her unprotected wrist throbbed, but Wave pushed the feeling aside as she pocketed the bandage.

'Welcome, everyone.' The crowd grew so silent that they could hear the waves crashing in the distance. 'Tonight we gather in celebration.' The maire motioned to Wave, Iberon, and Yllia with one hand.

The other two climbed the short staircase to the verandah, Wave not far behind them. Iberon and Yllia stood to one side of the Maire, Wave on the other. He looked down at all three of them fondly. Wave wondered if he'd locked his grief up in some box in his heart so that he could carry out his duties for the night. Even though she believed X'olea when he said it wasn't her fault, she was plagued by an unreasonable guilt whenever the maire looked at her, so she lowered her gaze to the crowd.

'Taking in waterkin youth from all over Marbin, and some-times further afield, is a responsibility and honour we have always carried proudly in Bindock. While some youth are trained in townships full of many kin, here in Bindock, our young waterkin can learn not only to hone their power, but also what it truly means to be a waterkin, a child of Lerinial.'

A smattering of cheers travelled through the gathered town. Above them, the stars twinkled, distracting Wave for a moment. The moon hadn't risen yet, and the only light in the sky came from the stars.

'These three have been with us for five years. Iberon was born in Bindock, but Yllia and Wave travelled here from Essenné. Over the years, they have become a part of the wider family of Bindock, and I know I speak for all of us when I congratulate them on completing their studies.'

Wave clenched her teeth together and forced a smile. The townspeople whooped and clapped, but Wave knew it wasn't for her. They hadn't allowed her to be a part of the supposed family of Bindock, unlike the other two standing beside the maire, their faces split wide with genuine smiles.

Near the front of the crowd, X'olea smiled back at Wave while everyone else had eyes only for Yllia and Iberon. Wave's face softened as she looked at her old friend. How would she have gotten through her training without him by her side? Standing deeper in the crowd, Wave noticed Ealen watching her. His face was sombre, his gaze intent on her. She looked away, wondering why he hadn't got the message that she wasn't interested.

'Today, our three graduates received their tattoos. Waterkin across Heredour all carry this mark, an ancient symbol repre-sentative of the unique way we are tied to our country by the waterways. This symbol is the original shape of Heredour, reminding us of Lerinial's importance in the making of our world.' The maire lowered his voice. 'Show them your arms.'

Wave and the others held their right arms aloft. The tattoo itself wasn't large, but Wave's was still swollen and stood out against her sun-tanned skin.

'With this tattoo, we welcome you to the ranks of waterkin. We welcome you to bear the responsibility of using Lerinial's power with grace and humility. We welcome you to the honour of being an adult child of Lerinial, to bask in the ferocity of her spirit forevermore.'

In silence, all of the adults in the crowd raised their right arms into the air. A shiver passed over Wave, and she adjusted her stance, feeling strangely off balance. There was no sound, no movement for several long moments. Wave felt as if they were the leaders of some bizarre army, her and the maire and the other two. The sky was too dark, the stars too bright in the sky. Wave blinked.

The crowd lowered their arms.

'I present to you now, my people of Bindock, Iberon waterkin, Yllia waterkin, and Wave waterkin.'

Cheering, clapping, and whistling started from the first few rows of people, rolling through the crowd like thunder. The noise was deafening, and for a moment Wave felt a part of something. In front of the joint adulation of the town, Wave forgot what it had been like to spend her entire life here as someone they looked at with wary eyes, someone they preferred to avoid.

'Now,' the maire called, trying to force his voice over the din. 'Let's celebrate.'

He turned to shake their hands, then Iberon pulled Yllia down the stairs and into the crowd. People hugged them, touched them, spoke to them. A little reluctantly, Wave followed them. The sound of a dulcimer and a hand pan drum started up —the local musicians were set up on a verandah a few houses down.

People clapped Wave on the back, their smiles wide and

genuine. She found herself feeling more comfortable than she had in years, smiling at people and accepting their congratulations. Without warning, she was pulled into a tight hug, her face muffled against a slender chest. When she was able to move back, she saw X'olea beaming down at her.

'You made it,' he said.

'We made it,' she agreed.

He pushed her into the crowd, as if his presence was no longer enough for her. Wave tried to turn back to him, but she was swept along in the movements of all the happy people. Eventually, she found herself seated at a table next to Iberon and Yllia. The rest of their table was occupied by the council elders and the maire.

The evening flew by Wave in a whirlwind. Plates piled high with all sorts of exciting food were delivered to the tables by various wives and children. The men tapped barrel upon barrel of ale, and even opened a barrel of the special apple cider from Millen. Alone among the merriment, Wave accepted a glass of the cider, though she promised herself she wouldn't have any more. Yllia already had pink spots high in her pale cheeks, and her hair had become unpinned, tumbling around her face. No matter how the night progressed, Wave refused to make a fool out of herself.

People came and went, stopping to speak to the other two, occasionally asking Wave about her plans. Each time, she said she was off to visit her family, but after that, she wasn't sure. She didn't want to ruin everyone's effervescent mood by telling them she never intended on returning to Bindock because of the way they'd treated her. A few of the young men—fishermen and carpenters and shiphands—stopped by to tell Wave how pretty she looked. She smiled and acknowledged them all but gave them nothing else. One by one, they drifted off.

The night wore on, and Wave grew tired, but somehow, she couldn't drag herself to bed. Being almost the centre of atten-

tion was a bit of fun. As the middle child, she'd never had attention exclusively lathered on her, so the fact that Iberon and Yllia
were the focus didn't bother her. They were both getting
progressively drunker with each hour that passed; Iberon's eyes
red and glassy, Yllia's lipstick smudged and her hair in shambles
around her shoulders.

By the time the quarter moon was high in the sky, most of
the townspeople had retired to their beds. The elders and the
maire were gone, along with all the families who had young
children. Wave watched the musicians packing up their instru-
ments, rubbing at their eyes as they moved. A yawn cracked
Wave's jaw, and she blinked her eyes a few times. Gods, but she
was tired. X'olea had gone home half an hour ago, and Wave no
longer felt any desire to stay.

A few tables away, a group of men had gathered to sing some
of the old sea ditties unique to the northern coastal towns. With
their ruddy faces and drinks sloshing in their hands, Wave
could see how drunk they were, even from her distance. Iberon
waved one hand in the air, his eyes closed as he bellowed whatever unintelligible song they were singing. Ealen was among
them. He'd only come to speak to Wave a couple of times.
Perhaps he'd finally accepted that she wasn't interested.

Forcing herself to her feet, Wave bundled her cloak around
her. The temperature hadn't dropped much, but in her aching
tiredness, she felt a chill that shouldn't have been there. A few
paces away, Yllia slumped over the table, her head resting on
her arms, little snores erupting with every exhale. Wave
chuckled to herself as she picked up the girl's cloak, rested it
over her shoulders, and tucked it in around her legs. Yllia would
be miserable if she woke up with a cold as well as a hangover.

Ignoring the singing group, Wave started down the street,
her feet dragging with every step.

'Wave!'

She stopped, surprised to hear her name.

'Wave!'

Against her better instincts, Wave turned towards the group of men. Ealen stood on top of one of the tables, beckoning to her with one hand.

'Wave, come down here!'

She chewed the inside of her lip. All she wanted was to lie down and sleep away the strange mix of shame and loneliness rolling through her body.

'Please?'

The earnestness in his voice changed her mind. Still dragging her feet, Wave made her way down to them. The men watched her with greedy eyes.

At the table, Ealen reached a hand down. Wishing she'd ignored the call, Wave placed her hand in his. He pulled her onto the table. Closer now than they'd ever been before, Wave noticed his bloodshot eyes and the shaky hand holding a tankard of ale. Snaking an arm around her waist, Ealen pulled her even closer, so they were standing hip to hip. The stench of stale drink was so overpowering that Wave leaned her torso away from him.

'I didn't realise you were leaving,' he said.

'I'm tired,' she replied. 'And I'm off to visit my mother in the morning, like I told you.'

'You can't go yet.' He turned his face towards the group.

'Friends, may I have your attention for a moment?' Ealen called, his voice too loud for the night.

Their attention was already on Ealen and Wave, drunk excitement rolling off them. Even the few women still scattered around the tables had turned towards them.

'I have tutored Wave for five years now. Five years I have taught her the ways of our people and the power of Lerinial!'

The men cheered, though Wave knew it was for Lerinial, and not for her.

'Wave is by far the best student I've ever had the pleasure of teaching.' Ealen cleared his throat. 'More importantly, I've had the honour to know her as a person.' He stressed the last word.

Wave resisted rolling her eyes. They barely knew each other.

'She is kind and big-hearted. Although she sometimes lets her anger get the better of her, she is gentle and so very clever.' Pulling his gaze away from the crowd, he turned to face her, his eyes clear now, his smile broad. 'And it is my honour, before men and goddess tonight, to ask a very important question.'

Wave's stomach lurched and she tried to pull away. His grip around her waist was surprisingly strong. Ealen passed his tankard to one of the onlookers and grasped both her hands in his.

'Wave waterkin of Bindock, would you do me the honour of becoming my wife with Lerinial as our witness?'

Eyes wide, Wave stared at Ealen as if seeing him for the first time. She knew he liked her a little more than a tutor should, but this? Marriage? They weren't even dating, hadn't shared any time alone together to check their compatibility.

Her throat went dry, drier than the desert wind that blows into the Plains in the middle of summer. As the realisation of what he was asking sank in, Wave felt anger rising within her. Why would he ask her such a thing? Why now, when he was drunk, and she was about to leave? He knew she had no intention of returning.

'No,' she whispered. Seething inside, she pulled her hands free.

Ealen's face fell. 'But—'

'No,' she said, making her voice a little firmer.

A look of complete and utter defeat consumed Ealen's face. His shoulders slumped and he curled in on himself.

'I'm sorry,' Wave said, even though she wasn't. She was angry.

The silence from the group was deafening. Wave jumped off

the table and ran down the street, away from Ealen, away from her rage.

A high-pitched hissing sound pierced the air above her. Wave stopped. The sound grew louder with every heartbeat until it consumed her ears, her entire body. She turned back to the men; they stared at her, their faces a mirror image of her confusion. Some covered their ears with their hands.

Wave spun around, trying to find the source of the overwhelming noise.

'There!' someone shouted.

An outstretched hand pointed at the sky and all eyes followed. A shooting star was arching its way across the sky above them. Wave had seen plenty of shooting stars, but she'd never heard one make a noise.

In a moment of terror, Wave realised that the star wasn't trailing across the heavens. It was heading straight towards them.

Every single person had their hands pressed over their ears. Everyone except Wave. She stood alone, immobile, mesmerised by the star.

Time stood still. For several long moments, nothing moved except the star and the eyes of every person watching.

With a sudden crash and a burst of steam, the star buried itself in the sand at Wave's feet. She stood on the precipice of a small, damp canyon. At its heart, the star seemed to throb with a life force all of its own. Wave kneeled at the edge of the depression and reached in.

The star was little more than a lump of rock, but it fitted between her two hands as if it had been moulded from their shape. The surface was lumpy, though smooth to touch, similar to a stone polished by the movements of a river.

Warmth seeped into Wave's cold fingers. Droplets of water rose from the ground and streams of water lifted from the jugs on the table, all coming to dance at her fingers, to encase the star in her palms. She lifted it from the canyon and held it to her chest. Elation filled her with an intensity she'd never experienced before. She was under a spell, and she didn't care.

With a wild grin, she stood and turned to the group of townspeople. The shocked faces began to turn sour as she held the star out towards them. Despite the great distance between them, the group took a collective step back. Some of the men began to growl, a low buzzing sound that shook Wave out of her spell.

'Blasphemer,' someone murmured.

Wave pulled the star back towards her, cradling it against her chest.

'Star-caller,' another said, a little louder.

'Cursed!'

'Setora's curse!'

'Star-caller! Star-caller! Star-caller!'

Their faces blended together in an awful mask of fear. The crowd's shouting became cries of anger, became screams of terror.

A sob tore itself free of Wave's chest. She turned and fled, her legs pumping beneath the swirling green silk, her heavy cloak trailing behind. Down the street and out into the Nagahere, she ran, never stopping to see if they followed her.

11

WATERFALL CITY

ANOTHER EARLY MORNING greeted Mortius with yet another summons from Reuben. No doubt he'd have something else to lament about the regions who were failing him. At least it would give Mortius more reason to leave, more justification to desert the capital.

Although he didn't have any desire to toy with Reuben's mental health further than necessary, Mortius had already decided to delay visiting the king. He wanted to deliver the jewellery Unner and Aymn had purchased, and he hoped that particular meeting would go long into the morning.

Taking a fresh piece of quality parchment from the pile in his drawer, Mortius began drafting a response to Reuben's summons. It looks several drafts to get it to sound exactly as he wanted, but Mortius was no stranger to wasting good paper. One didn't become the senior adviser to the High King of Heredour without churning through parchment, ink, quills, and wax.

I will arrive later than expected to discuss the news, and therefore, miss breakfast with you. An anticipated gift has arrived, and I expect to deliver it this morning. We can share tea after midmorn, if that is preferable.

Enough information for Reuben to understand why he wasn't coming, but sufficient lack of information that if any of the servants read the message, as he expected several would, none would understand exactly what Mortius was doing. Perfect.

He folded the note several ways so that the contents were protected, then sealed the edge with hot wax. Mortius slid the heavy ring of office from his left middle finger and pressed the sigil of senior adviser into the wax.

Cook was in the kitchen, stirring something over the hearth fire. One of the two serving girls who worked for Mortius, Eveleen, stood at the bench, transferring herbs from market bags into tall jars.

'Good morning, Cook, Eveleen,' Mortius said.

'Morning, sire,' Cook responded without turning.

Eveleen ducked her head in what Mortius had to assume was a deferential acknowledgement. The girl had only come into his service recently as payment for a debt someone owed the crown. Mortius had no need for two servants and a cook, but it was safer to take the girl into his service. She was just shy of twenty, quiet, and a lowkin. Perfect for Reuben's serving staff, but Mortius hoped to save as many young girls as he could from the king. Heredour's queen was barren and docile, but Reuben's appetite was voracious. He took what he wanted, when he wanted, and it was rarely Queen Terinnien.

'I'm heading out.'

'Again?' Cook asked, turning to face him.

Her ruddy face was weathered, and she had none of the plumpness that he associated with those animalkin who worked in the castle kitchens. Squinting up at him with bright hazel eyes, she regarded him with suspicion.

'Are my breakfasts no longer good enough for ye, sire?'

Mortius smiled, a rare sight in their household. 'Your break-fasts are the only thing keeping me tethered to this world, Cook. Our precious king has become fond of requesting my company early in the day.'

Cook shook her head.

'In saying that,' Mortius continued, 'I have a parcel to deliver this morning, so I'll come back for breakfast and then meet with the king. Eveleen, this note needs to reach Reuben's office before sunrise.'

She took the proffered parchment quickly, her gaze lowered.

'Eveleen,' Mortius said, but the girl wouldn't raise her eyes.

'Yes, sire?' she asked, voice as timid as her exterior.

He grasped her chin with two fingers and gently tilted her face towards him. He didn't want to scare her. Although her breathing was shallow, she lifted her eyes. They were a vivid emerald; looking into them was like gazing into a deep forest pool. Mortius felt his breath catch in his throat as she regarded him.

'I know not what troubles you've suffered in the past,' he said, forcing himself to speak. 'Know that I brought you into my service to keep you safe. You have nothing to fear from me or mine, and if any harm comes to you from those in the castle, I expect you to tell me as such.'

Eveleen swallowed. 'Yes, sire.'

'Good.' He released her chin and felt a sense of loss he couldn't comprehend. 'Make sure this gets to High King Reuben.'

'I will.' There was a newfound confidence in her voice. She met his gaze for a moment, then lowered her eyes. 'The high king's office before sunrise,' she repeated.

Mortius nodded. 'I look forward to whatever breakfast you have planned, Cook.'

He turned away from them, a strange feeling taking over his body. Was this the feeling of premonition the starkin sooth-sayers spoke of? As a starkin, he should have known, but his powers were as weak as the rest of the humans'.

At the door, he took a dark cloak and settled it over his shoulders. The streets were already warm at this time of year, but he needed to remain unseen for a time. Before he opened the door to the world, he threw the deep hood over his head, his mind full of the green pools of Eveleen's eyes.

Through the back alleys of the highkin district, Mortius strode between the slumbering manors. Rosewater and lavender perfume hovered in the air, so thick it made Mortius want to wretch. He pushed the sensations aside. There was nothing more he despised than the fact that the highkin paid to have their district perfumed. It was the culmination of every-thing he hated about them; their pomposity, their assumed superiority, their utter disdain for the basics of life.

As he slipped across one of the main streets, he caught a glimpse of the manor he sought. An elegant, two-storey building with curling balustrades reared before him. Ivy climbed the walls and the long windows were cloaked in heavy drapes. Mortius ducked around the back of the building to the servants' quarters.

He rapped his knuckles on the courtyard door. It had been years since he'd been in this house, but he remembered the layout as if it were his own.

A young boy opened the peephole and looked at him with wide eyes.

'I'm here to see the Lady Frieda,' Mortius said, keeping his voice gentle, unobtrusive.

After a moment of consideration, the boy slammed the peephole shut. Mortius heard the sound of his footsteps hurrying away from the door. Anxiety rippled through Mortius' body, and he fingered the wooden box in his pocket, as if it might provide some antidote.

The peephole opened and an ageing woman stared back at him.

'The Lady Frieda isn't expecting anyone at this hour, sire.'

'I wasn't able to send advance warning of my visit.' Mortius pushed his hood back a little, just enough for the woman to see his features.

She baulked.

'Senior Adviser,' she breathed. 'My apologies. Please, come in.'

The wooden door swung wide and Mortius stepped in. They were in a walled stable yard, the ground beneath his feet smooth cobblestones. Garden beds surrounded them, and the boy who'd answered the door stood near the stables, twirling a hay fork in his hand, uncertainty wrinkling his face.

'I'm Matron Paose,' the woman said, drawing Mortius' attention back to her. 'Please, wait here a moment while I summon the lady.'

Mortius nodded as the portly matron ducked through another door leading into the manor. No doubt Frieda was like the other highkin—slovenly, lazy, sleeping in until the late hours of morning. Paose would likely have to rouse her, dress her, ensure she was ready for company. That is, if she accepted his presence. It was just as likely that she'd send any guards she had at her disposal to kick him out.

He only hoped that his position was enough to get him an audience. Frieda wouldn't have forgiven him, and he didn't blame her. He couldn't forgive himself.

The stableboy watched him with a bemused expression on his face. In the sky above the manor's walls, the first rays of sun pierced through a veil of low clouds. Mortius hoped Eveleen had delivered his message on time. As soon as the thought entered his head, he was consumed by the memory of her eyes. There had been a certainty in her gaze when she looked at Mortius, despite her presentation as a shy, meek lowkin.

'Senior Adviser.' Paose's voice dragged him from the vision of Eveleen's eyes.

'Yes.'

'Lady Frieda is ready to receive you.'

Mortius started. Paose had only been gone a few minutes. There was no way a highkin could get ready that quickly, even one who spent her life as a recluse. The speed of Paose's return had to mean that Frieda was not only already awake, but ready to receive visitors. And she'd chosen to see him. Mortius was glad, but a little disconcerted.

He followed Paose through the lower levels of the house and up a steep staircase. The walls were strangely bare, though Mortius could see the places where paintings would have once hung—rectangles of bright wallpaper gleamed in contrast to the faded walls. Mortius hadn't realised her family had become destitute.

At the top of the stairs, Paose stopped him with a lifted hand and ducked through another door. Again, Mortius noticed that any obvious signs of wealth were absent. There were no paintings, no sculptures, no idols to Wederlly or any other god. Frieda's family had always been wealthy, powerful, prosperous. Her parents had retired to their country estate a good decade ago, but where had the tokens of their wealth gone?

'Lady Frieda will see you, Senior Adviser,' Paose said as she opened the door wide, bowing as Mortius entered the room.

The room was nearly as empty as the rest of the house. Two worn, high-backed armchairs stood before the cold hearth, the walls and mantle empty of any adornment. A low table featured an array of crystal bottles, each one holding a selection of dark liquids.

'Senior Adviser,' Frieda said as she turned from the empty fireplace.

She was as beautiful as he remembered, perhaps more so, now that she had matured. Once pale skin was now tanned, suggesting she spent a lot of time outdoors. Frieda had always loved riding, so perhaps she wasn't the true recluse he'd always assumed. Blonde hair was bound back into a thick braid with no flourishes. Freckles were spattered across her nose and the tops of her bare shoulders. A long, modest skirt was offset by a low-cut blouse that made Mortius avert his gaze.

'You are the last person I expected to arrive unannounced at my door,' she said.

Like all moonkin, her iridescent eyes were of no particular colour and all of them at once.

'And I am the last person to expect myself to arrive at your door,' he answered, hoping to maintain an edge by being somewhat cryptic. He'd always excelled at subterfuge, but now he was standing before her, he felt off balance.

'And yet, here you are.' She regarded him solemnly, perhaps as an equal, or an enemy.

She was nothing like the cowed recluse he'd expected. What had she been doing these past twenty years while the highkin spoke of her in hushed tones? Riding, no doubt, but to where? And why?

'Here I am.' He wasn't sure what else he should say. Gods, but he hated this feeling.

'I presume you have something to say,' Frieda said, and gestured to one of the armchairs. 'You may as well sit, before you fall.'

Mortius coughed, surprised by her boldness. There was no doubt he was rattled by her, but he'd always been able to hide his true feelings. He took the seat she offered. She sat opposite him, her gaze searing. It felt like a baptism, as if she were some priest of old. There was a damning judgement in her eyes, and he couldn't blame her. Sitting before her only heightened the guilt Mortius already felt.

'I have a gift.' He pulled the wooden box from his pocket and handed it to her.

One eyebrow raised, she took the gift.

'There's only one still foolish enough to send me gifts.' She eyed the box suspiciously. 'And only one foolish enough to deliver such a gift.'

'I take it you've ignored all the others.'

Frieda snorted. 'Sold them.'

She slid the lid open. A small gasp escaped her before she clamped her mouth shut.

'It's beautiful,' Mortius said.

'Achingly so.'

'You won't wear them, I imagine.'

'Where would I wear it, Senior Adviser?' The derision in her voice made his heart hurt. He'd made his bed twenty-five years ago when Reuben's father, High King Esra, was dying. Lying in it all this time was decidedly uncomfortable.

'I expected as much,' he said, holding his chin high. 'I hope you can sell it for some worth. To keep your household together.'

'Pssh, you think I sell my things to keep myself afloat?' Frieda barked out a laugh. 'You're more ignorant than I thought.'

Mortius wore the insult, refusing to react to her.

'I didn't come just to deliver this.'

'Obviously.' Frieda glared at him. 'You were more than content to deliver every other gift anonymously.'

How many years had he been depositing boxes at her door? The first five years, Reuben had pretended she didn't exist. And then at some point, he'd thought to win her back to his side. Mortius had tried to persuade him otherwise. There were few who knew that a nineteen-year-old Reuben had raped Frieda and blamed his younger brother for the crime.

'I know you don't like me, Frieda,' he began. 'And I understand. I don't like myself, most days. If I could take back everything that has happened these past two decades—'

'But you haven't.'

'No. I've dug myself further into this hole, buried myself alongside him.' Mortius shook his head. Trusting Frieda was a risk, perhaps the biggest he'd taken so far. 'Something is seriously wrong with him, and I need your help.'

'Ha!' she exclaimed, slapping herself on the knee. 'My help?' She laughed again, but there was an ancient bitterness in the sound.

'He's losing his mind. Every day is a different Reuben. Up, down, sideways. I never know what to expect.'

'Then you shouldn't have followed him.'

'If only I were as wise as you when I was young.'

Frieda grimaced at him.

'I mean that with every ounce of sincerity I own. I was too ambitious, too thirsty for power. But I had no idea what I was getting myself into.'

'Pity you,' Frieda said, her voice flat.

'That's not why I'm here. I don't want your pity, or your forgiveness. Gods know I don't deserve it. But I do need your help.'

'So you've said,' she replied, turning away from him to study the empty hearth. 'Yet you've given me nothing to do so far.'

Everything about this meeting was going sideways. Mortius had thought to find a miserable, wretched woman, but here she sat before him—self-assured, angry, full of Wederlly's fire. More perfect than he could have dreamed.

'I need you to speak to him.'

'Are you insane?' In an instant, she was up, pacing before the mantle, her face turned away from his. 'I vowed never to speak to him again.'

'I know.' Mortius often wondered if it was Frieda's vow that had broken Reuben. 'I know. But Heredour needs you now. I wouldn't ask unless it was dire.'

'Heredour needs me,' she spat. 'You have no idea what I do for this godsforsaken country.'

'I don't,' he admitted. 'All the same, you are my last hope. Reuben is losing his mind. I don't say that as a joke. He is paranoid, vicious, chaotic. Nothing he does or says makes sense anymore.'

'Did it ever?' Frieda murmured.

'He asks after you constantly. From my vantage point, you are the only thing in his life that provides stability, clarity.'

'Can you hear yourself, Mortius?' Frieda demanded. 'I'm not in his life! I haven't been since I gave birth. He's delusional.'

'He is delusional,' Mortius agreed. 'And he's losing his grip on reality, which makes it impossible to keep this kingdom and this country afloat. I've tried everything in my power to make him be reasonable. And I mean everything.' Mortius rose, unable to contain his angst. 'He won't see sense. He thinks all of his rulers are against him, he thinks the Kaiaho are out to undermine him. He keeps Black Cloaks as his close counsel, even closer than I am.'

Frieda shook her head.

'It's true, Frieda. My position is advisory, but nothing I say to him makes a difference anymore. General Juro has tried talking to him, and he had the same luck as me.' Juro had been there the night Esra died. The general knew all of the sunkin family secrets, the same as Mortius. There were so few of them left. 'Nobody can get through to him. Not his wife, not his council, not his general, not his senior adviser.'

'And what makes you think he'll listen to me?'

'Nothing.' Brutal honestly was all he had left now, but he

sensed it was all Frieda would respond to. 'But I am a desperate man, trying to keep this kingdom together. Left as he is, he will tear Heredour apart, undo all of the good work Esra and his forefathers did. And if you're half of the woman you were before he destroyed you, I know you'd want to save this country.'

His words had a visible effect; her face paled, her hands clenched into fists at her sides.

'I love this country,' Frieda growled. 'More than you could ever understand. But I will not degrade myself to speak to him.' She turned to face him. 'And he did not destroy me. I was reborn the day he cast me aside, the day he sent Samson into exile.'

12

THE NORTH CLAW

THE FIRST HALF hour on Skoa's back was the worst time of Jessandra's short life. As they flew over the lake, she cried and trembled and clutched at Skoa's silky neck feathers. When she realised that her life did indeed depend on her ability to stay on his back, she'd cried harder. Every part of her body shook. Nothing that had happened in her life so far had ever made her this afraid.

And then, once her tears had run dry, she felt okay. Skoa's flight was smooth, his wings barely moving as they soared through the darkness. Jessandra realised she was tucked in securely behind his wing joints, and she soon felt comfortable enough to release a little bit of the pressure from around his neck. She couldn't let go completely, but she was able to stop squeezing him so hard.

For a while, Jessandra allowed herself to feel excited. They'd done it, her and Siska. She was free of the city, free of her father, free from the pressure of something she had no control over. The darkness stretched out before her, a blank slate, with only the winking stars and a quarter moon to offer any light.

Perhaps all she needed was a little time away from the pressures of royal life. Even if Skoa took her out into the wilderness, at least she could spend some time in contemplation of the gods, just as the priests had told her to do. Maybe she would finally feel Everluof's gentle fingers on her skin. She tried not to think about what she would do if she discovered Setunil calling to her instead.

After what might have been an hour or two, Jessandra grew restless and bored. Where the endless night had been exciting and full of possibilities, it now served as a source of anxiety. She had no idea where they were, or where they were going. Skoa was silent, of course, and Jessandra was left alone with her thoughts. She'd never been particularly comfortable spending time in her own mind, which was why she was so fond of daydreaming. The note from Lenta kept returning to the front of her mind, as if there was some direct link between the parchment in her bag and her brain.

The temperature dropped suddenly, and a cold wind swirled around them, messing up Jessandra's hair. She tried to shrug her cloak tighter around her body, but she still wasn't ready to take her arms away from Skoa's neck. A shiver ran down her spine.

As if in response to the change in temperature, Skoa opened his beak and let out a low, strange call. Ahead of them lay the shadowy shapes of a huge mountain range, the peaks lost among the misty darkness. Jessandra's breath hitched in her throat, her mind racing to the geography lessons she'd never paid attention to.

They'd flown over the lake, so this must be the North Claw. There were only a few small towns scattered around the Claw's coast. The rest was an impenetrable mass of wilderness cut down the centre by the Kanrid River.

Skoa navigated between the mountains, still heading what Jessandra guessed was west. The air became even colder and she huddled closer to Skoa's neck.

The mountains around them were enormous, the snowy peaks lost to the fog above. In the pale darkness, they looked perfect. There were no hints of blemishes, no tumbled rocks or rents in the surface, no jagged edges or caves carving eerie mouths in the mountain faces. Jessandra gave up studying them when she realised that they all looked the same under the supernatural light of the fog-shrouded stars.

Tilting slightly, enough to make Jessandra squeeze her legs against his body, Skoa angled right. North, perhaps. It was hard to tell without the sun. Most of the light of the stars and moon had disappeared now they were beneath the peaks of the mountains.

In the distance, Jessandra could see lights. Not the compressed lights of a town, but certainly the light of fires. Several spirals of smoke rose from the same spot. Even with her minimal knowledge, Jessandra knew enough about wildcraft to know that smoke only spiralled out of a chimney—there was no way to make an open fire burn in the same way.

She frowned. They were in the middle of nowhere. At first she thought that perhaps it was a small group of people camping out in the mountains, hunters or the like. But the smoke said otherwise. There were chimneys, lots of them, which meant there were houses. Perhaps even a town.

A glint of pale white caught her eye as they flew over the lights. She peered around Skoa's neck. It looked like a building nestled down among the trees, a building made of white marble. Impossible. Marble was a rare, highly prized substance in Heredour. This was the North Claw—barren, desolate, isolated. There weren't even any marble buildings in Millen.

Within minutes, they'd flown on, and the smoke, the light, and the strange marble building were all lost to the darkness. Jessandra tried to bring to mind an image of a map of Heredour. She'd never paid much attention to her lessons when her imagination was far more interesting.

She was sure there were no towns within the impregnable centre of the North Claw—they were all on the coastlines, accessible only by ships. Nobody travelled through the mountains. So how could there be a marble building and chimney fire out here? Maybe she was mistaken. Maybe from this height, the world looked different and they were somewhere else entirely. Condor? The Paravat Ranges?

The sky was starting to lighten in the east by the time Skoa began to descend. Up ahead, Jessandra could see the glow of a township, and beyond, the shimmering surface of the ocean. If Jessandra hadn't completely lost her sense of direction while they were flying, she guessed the town in front of them was Jindar. They'd flown for too long for it to be Chok.

The mountains turned into forested foothills. Skoa circled a cleared patch of land near a creek and with a running hop, skip, and jump, he landed. Jessandra blinked. They'd been flying so long that she'd grown comfortable on his back. She hadn't thought about what would happen once they landed.

Skoa extended one wing to the ground. Easing herself from his body, Jessandra landed on the grass with an awkward stumble. Her legs were stiff and cold, and she thought she'd have to walk very carefully for a while to avoid an injury.

Gnarled, evergreen trees stood like ancient sentinels around them, and the burble of the creek was a soothing balm to the sudden anxiety Jessandra felt.

'Where are we?' she asked, glancing at Skoa.

One beady eye regarded her. Looking at him now, it was hard to fathom the level of intelligence she'd felt when he delved her mind. He was just a bird, and she, just a girl, all alone in the forest. Jessandra swallowed, her heart beating faster than was comfortable.

With an awkward waddle, Skoa made his way towards the creek. A packed dirt trail ran beside the boulder-strewn water, wide enough for a person and a goat. Jessandra followed him, but her anxiety didn't decrease.

'Where does this go?' she asked, then shook her head. Why was she talking to an eagle?

To her surprise, Skoa leaned his head down and nudged her back.

'North?'

Skoa nudged her again.

'Is Jindar that way?'

Jessandra stared down the track. All she could see were trees upon trees, even as the sky grew lighter in the east. Skoa let out a low call and unfurled his wings.

'You can't go!' A lump rose in Jessandra's throat. 'Please.'

He leaned down, resting the top of his beak against her forehead. Then he turned and took several strides down the path. In the space of a heartbeat he was in the air, long wings carving his path through the sky.

'Skoa!' Jessandra called. 'Skoa!'

The shape of his body was soon lost to the still-dark mountains. Jessandra squeezed her hands into fists by her sides, her heart beating a wild rhythm in her chest. She'd spent her entire life surrounded by people; servants, teachers, priests, and highkin of the court had always been with her wherever she went. Half the reason she preferred to stare into the distance and imagine different lives was because she was never alone.

Well, she had her wish now. Not only was she alone, she'd been thrust into a life completely unlike her own. Jessandra took a step down the track. This wasn't anything like her imagination, but if she was honest with herself, nothing in her life had gone how she'd imagined. Lenta being exiled, Jessandra becoming heir, the betrothal to Jai'til, her lack of calling.

She had no chance of surviving long out here in the wilderness. Cold, lack of food or water, or some terrifying beast looking for a meal would soon see her demise. At least if she got to Jindar, she could pretend to be someone else and maybe find a way to stay safe.

She took another step forward, and then another. Before Jessandra knew it, she was making steady progress towards the township. The stiffness in her legs eased quickly, and she settled into a comfortable stride.

13

BARANCHA PLAINS

THICK, crusting mud coated Larka's hands as she trudged her way out of a field of potatoes. The heavy, drenching rain from a week earlier was still feeding the Plains, so Larka was spending a lot of time picking fine weeds and adding mulch around the plants.

The summer sun pushed everything to grow quickly, and it was a constant battle to keep the plants stronger than the weeds. The plantkin of her village did a good job of imbuing resilience into their crops, but there wasn't much any of them could do with their power to combat the weeds that flourished after such a good downpour.

At the village stream, Larka washed her hands free of the muck and splashed water on her face. There were a series of intricate lines tattooed below the nail bed of each finger on her left hand—the sign of the commitment she'd made to Samson when they married. She scrubbed the muck from her finger-nails, studying the lines as she did every time, wondering where her husband was.

Larka waved goodbye to her fellow workers before heading home. Though she'd been living and working in the Plains for more than a decade, she hadn't let any of her neighbours get close to her or her family. Winter had made fast friends with the other village children, which Larka expected, but she kept herself removed from the adults.

Dusk was setting as Larka wandered past the last few houses on her street. She and Sam had chosen this house because it was the last house at the edge of town. The road went nowhere, disappearing into scrubby bush and then desert beyond that. Fields of tall barley grass grew opposite her home, so there was plenty of cover should she ever need to flee.

A warm glow came from the open front window. It was unlike Winter to light the lantern before Larka got home. Like most children, Winter hardly noticed the change from day to night.

Larka pushed open the door, her eyes widening in surprise. Looking very proper in her one good dress, Winter sat at the table wearing a huge smile. More surprising still was the person who moved around the kitchen as if she lived there.

'Siska!'

Her eldest daughter turned from the hearth and pulled Larka into a tight hug.

'I made stew,' Siska said as she released Larka. 'And I brought a fresh loaf of soft bread from the castle.'

'And she's got apples, Mumma!' Winter bounced around in her chair. 'Apples!'

Though Marbin was known for having the best apples in the country, they all grew up near Millen where the winters were colder.

'What a treat,' Larka said, looking at the bowl overflowing with fruit. 'I'll have to make a tart.'

'Sit, Mother,' Siska said. 'Let's eat.'

She ladled the stew out into earthenware bowls and laid them on the table. A vase of fresh-picked paper daisies sat in the centre of the table. Winter's favourite.

'This is such a surprise,' Larka said after they'd eaten a few mouthfuls. 'I thought you might come back with Wave after her graduation, but not before.'

Siska pursed her lips. 'That was my plan, but I guess I'll wait here until she arrives.'

'Has something happened in the castle?' Perhaps she'd lost her job over some petty misdemeanour; King Mascerab was fickle and punitive at best.

'The princess has disappeared.'

Larka almost choked on her soup. 'What?'

'Why would a princess disappear?' Winter asked, scrunching up her nose.

'She hadn't been called yet,' Siska said. 'Her sixteenth birthday is right around the corner, as is her impending marriage. I guess she panicked.'

A strange turn of events, Larka thought. The Law of Kaiäho didn't make any pronouncements on what to do if a youth wasn't called at all. King Mascerab must have been furious.

There was a place someone like Jessandra could go, a place she would be safe. A town where people were trained in the powers of all the gods, not just one. But not many people knew about its blasphemous existence.

'You always said she didn't have a lot of real-world skills,' Larka said, curious about the plight of Siska's charge. 'I imagine they'll find her quickly.'

Siska made a noncommittal noise.

'Even if she stole a horse, where is she going to go? Mascerab's army is well disciplined, and he would be swift to take action. Especially after what happened to Jessandra's sister.'

Everyone in Marbin Province knew the story of Lenta, once heir to the throne. Siska choked on her stew.

'Can we talk about this later?' she asked, sliding a glance at Winter.

Larka frowned. 'Of course.'

'But why did she run away?' Winter asked.

'I guess she was unhappy with the way her life was going,' Siska said gently.

Winter took a slice of the soft, white bread that was so rare in their home. 'You can't just run away because you're not happy. Mumma always says we have to face our problems with our chin held high.'

Larka laughed, but the sound left a sour taste on her tongue. Winter's words were true enough; anytime she came home with a drama from the village children Larka would remind her not to run from her problems. The irony wasn't lost on Larka. Here she was, isolated and alone in the middle of nowhere. Her husband, the love of her life, had been gone for nine years, and she'd raised their daughters in hiding. It certainly felt like she'd run away from her problems.

After dinner, Siska and Winter washed their dishes and tidied the kitchen. Larka made up the spare bed for Siska. The bed was supposed to be Winter's, but she still slept with Larka. It was one of the small comforts Larka held on to in the humble life she led.

They shared a pot of herbal tea before Larka sent a complaining Winter to bed. Siska tucked her in, kissing her on the forehead and whispering secrets meant for sisters. The side of the bed that should have been Sam's was now filled with the tousled brown hair of Larka's youngest daughter.

Larka drained the dregs of the teapot into two cups. Taking a worn silver spoon from the table, she stirred in some of the creamy honey from Millen. Another of those sparing purchases she made from Essenné's travelling merchants, the honey was a special treat rarely used.

'Something else is afoot, I take it,' Larka said as Siska joined her on the back patio.

'I forgot how dark it is out here,' Siska said as she stared up at the sky. 'Millen is so full of light, even in the middle of the night.'

'How did you get here so fast?' Larka asked. 'Did you come on Skoa?'

Siska nodded, though she wouldn't meet Larka's eyes.

'Where is he?' Larka asked, trying to push Siska into talking. She had a sneaking suspicion that her daughter had something to do with Jessandra's disappearance.

'Hunting in the fields, I'd say. He hasn't eaten in a while, and your fields make for good picking.'

Larka ignored the barb that her village's well-tended crops would be full of rodents.

'And Jessandra?' she asked.

'It's as I said,' Siska said with a shrug. 'She hasn't been called. She thought perhaps she felt Setunil, but even that was likely out of desperation. The marriage was all organised for the week after her birthday. The boy she was betrothed to had been staying in Millen.'

'The same one her sister was betrothed to?'

'That's right. They shifted the commitment to Jessandra once Lenta ... left.'

Larka frowned. The girl had been exiled.

'Jessandra got close to Jai'til and she let slip that she hadn't been called.'

'Foolish girl.'

'She is. But she has a good heart. She panicked.'

Larka was silent for a moment, but Siska said nothing further.

'You helped her.'

'I had to!' Siska's voice rose. 'Lenta left me a note, one I was supposed to give to Jessandra when she was called. I read it, of course, even though I shouldn't have.'

'What did the note say?'

'Lenta wasn't pregnant.' Siska turned to face Larka. 'She was called by Lerinial. She was Kaiăho, and they took her away, shipped her off to Buduwai in the middle of the night and fabricated a pregnancy to avoid the shame. So I gave Jessandra the note, and helped her escape. They'd do the same to her, or something worse if she wasn't called at all.'

Larka pinched the bridge of her nose. Siska's actions were done out of the goodness of her heart, but the last thing Larka wanted was any attention brought to their family. Especially not from the highkin in Millen.

'You need to be more careful, daughter.'

'How could I let them do ... whatever it is they would do? Take her to Buduwai, or worse? I couldn't, not knowing what happened to Lenta.'

'And what if they find out you helped her?' Larka clenched one hand into a fist. 'What if they start asking questions about you, your heritage?'

'I've lived my entire adult life pretending my parents are skykin. It's nothing new.'

'You'd be hard-pressed to keep up the facade if the Black Cloaks started questioning you.'

'There's no way they could connect me to her escape,' Siska said. 'I was careful, I promise.'

Larka shook her head. Even as a little girl, Siska had been headstrong and rash, so different to her younger sisters. Apparently the trait hadn't softened even though she was twenty-two.

'And how did you get her out of the city without anyone knowing?' Larka already knew the answer, and it made her furious.

'Skoa took her.'

Larka took a deep breath and tried to release the tension in her jaw.

'Skoa took her,' she repeated. 'What if someone saw them?'

'I put her in a hooded cloak. It was dark. Nobody would know it was her.' Siska looked down at her hands. 'I did everything I could to protect her, and us. Anyway, he flew away from the city, over the lake.'

'Over the lake?' Larka's face softened a little. 'Towards the North Claw?'

Siska nodded.

'Where was he taking her?'

'I'm not sure,' Siska said. 'But the feeling I got was one of safety. That's why I'm here. In the morning, I'm going to go and find her, make sure she's okay. Visiting you is a cover story.'

Larka's breath quickened. The great eagles were from the North Claw, the only home they had since the South Claw had been blasted from the face of Heredour. There was one place Jessandra could be safe in the wilderness of the North Claw, and perhaps Skoa knew it. He must have taken her to Larka's home-town. Sharvel.

14

OUTSKIRTS OF CHOK

ON A LOW HILL overlooking the ocean, Wave sat with her back against a tree trunk, her knees pulled in tight to her chest. The crash and pull of the waves didn't soothe her as they once had, but she watched them anyway.

Dawn had come and gone hours ago, but Wave couldn't move. She'd spent all night running blindly through the Naga-here, sobbing as she held the star close to her chest. When her legs stopped obeying her, she crawled into a hollow at the base of an aged tree, tucking herself in as deeply as she could.

The forest had changed by then, though she hadn't realised until she stopped. Tea trees still dotted the landscape, their papery bark soft beneath the starlight, but she was also surrounded by tall poplars and beeches, their canopy spreading wide above her.

They would come for her, the Black Cloaks. She'd touched a star, and now she was cursed. The understanding of what she'd done sank in as she ran, and she knew she couldn't stop. She couldn't go back to Bindock, and she couldn't go home.

Everyone knew the story of Setora and the South Claw. It was a story read to children at night, to remind them of the indomitable power of the Black Cloaks. Nobody expected a star to fall at a person's feet these days, but if they did, the legend of Setora was so ingrained that they all knew to stay far away until the Black Cloaks came to take the star with their special devices.

Wave knew the story, knew about the danger of a fallen star and the power of the Black Cloaks. Even so, she'd picked the star up. At the time, it had felt like compulsion, a spell of dreamy desire. She wouldn't have been able to stop herself even if she'd been aware of what she was doing. The spell had lasted only until she saw the faces of her kin. Then, she'd realised her mistake, but it was only deep in the forest that she began to understand the ramifications of her actions.

They would hunt her down. Nowhere would be safe for her. Besides, she could never touch another person again without making them sick. If Wave had thought her life in Bindock was hard, now she'd have to live the rest of her life in isolation, never being able to go near another living soul. She couldn't risk making people sick.

The weight of realisation was crushing. By the time she'd climbed her way through the low hills up to this spot to watch the sun rise, she felt utterly defeated.

The town of Chok lay somewhere to her west, according to her innate sense of direction, but that didn't help. There might be Black Cloaks there already, looking for her in the face of every waterkin. Even if they weren't, she wouldn't be able to go near crowds; she'd have to avoid letting anyone touch her accidentally. She would not let what happened to the South Claw happen to Chok, or Bindock, or any other place in Heredour.

She had no food, no money, and only the clothes on her back. Impractical clothes too. At least she had shoes and a warm cloak. Life was suddenly an impossible problem, a riddle Wave didn't even know how to begin solving.

Dragging her eyes away from the ocean, she looked down at

the star in her hands. It was little more than a lump of cold rock, though she could sense the tiniest vibration, a minute hum of life within it. She ran a thumb over the surface, feeling each crevice and groove as if it were a part of her own soul. How could one tiny little lump of rock cause so much damage?

Her arms ached from carrying the star through the night, and the skin around her new tattoo was red and throbbing. With a sigh, she pushed the star deep into one of her cloak pockets. There was no bulge, no way anyone would know it was there. But Wave knew. She'd never forget what she'd done.

And yet, a small part of her didn't regret it. She was tied to that star. It had fallen at her feet, and she knew it had come for her. But then she thought of her family, her little sister Winter, her friend X'olea, and the reality of her situation was a bitter balm on her tongue.

Immobile from fear and heartbreak and indecision, Wave cast her eyes back out over the ocean, pleading with Lerinial to help her. Moments later, she heard a strange sound. Wave frowned. The tone tickled something in the back of her mind, like she should remember the sound, but she was having trouble placing the memory.

Louder again, this time coming from the south-east. Wave shifted her position, studying the tops of the trees behind her. The day was cloudless, the sky a pristine blue.

A black spot hovering just above the tree line caught Wave's eye. Her heart leapt to her throat, her stomach twisting in fear. She didn't know if Black Cloaks could fly, but she didn't have any cause to doubt that they could. The hill she sat on was mostly bare—only a few mid-sized trees guarded the top, along with a few scrubby bushes. If she was going to run, she had to go now, before the thing in the sky got any closer.

Just as she was preparing herself to shimmy down the west side of the hill, the sound came again. Not a sound—a low, haunting call. She studied the mark against the sky, watching as it took the form of a bird, not a Black Cloak. Not just any bird, a giant bird.

'Skoa?' Wave whispered.

It couldn't be. There were other giant eagles, especially in the North Claw, and Chok was at the edge of the mountain ranges. Her heart sank a little. What she wouldn't give to see her sister just once before she descended into a life of hermetic exile.

Despite telling herself that the image before her was just another giant eagle flying home, Wave couldn't leave the hilltop, couldn't stop watching the creature that could be carrying Siska, even if only in her imagination. Crouching behind the tree trunk, she followed the path of the bird. Within moments, she could see a rider on its back. Her pulse quickened, and she tried to dampen her excitement.

There weren't many skykin left who'd befriended the great eagles. As the elemental powers of humans faded, many of the ancient skills were lost. Just like Wave, Siska was an anomaly for her generation. Even so, this bird could be carrying anyone.

As if on cue, the eagle dropped lower, the ends of its talons brushing the tops of the foliage. Eagle and rider slowed as they neared Wave's hill. Her heart thumped a hasty dance in her throat and her knuckles were white where she gripped the tree trunk. The eagle circled the hilltop twice, then came to a running landing at the other end of the clearing.

The hooded rider vaulted from its back and strode to face the eagle.

'Why have we stopped here, Skoa?' The voice was so familiar, so reminiscent of safety and home that Wave's vision blurred with tears.

'Is she here?' Siska asked, still addressing Skoa. 'Why did you bring me to this place?' The pitch of her voice rose as she spoke.

Wave stepped from behind the tree.

'Siska?'

The rider spun away from Skoa, throwing her hood back.

'Wave?' The shock in Siska's voice was lost on Wave as she burst into tears.

Siska ran to her, her arms open wide to encase her sister. For a moment, Wave forgot what was hidden in her pocket, forgot that she was now a danger to humanity.

'Stop!' she screamed through her tears. 'Stop, Siska!'

Siska stopped dead, her fingers within reaching distance. Wave took a few hurried steps back. Wiping her eyes, she took another step back, just to be sure.

'Wave?' Siska asked again, as if she couldn't believe what she was seeing.

Wave could hardly believe it herself.

'What are you doing up here?'

Unable to contain herself, Wave broke into tears again, crouching down against the ground. She heard Siska step towards her.

'No,' she said through her tears. 'Don't touch me, please don't touch me.'

'Why not, Wave?' Siska asked, squatting down nearby. 'What's happened? How ... why are you out here?'

Between sobs and hiccups, Wave told her sister about the star. Wave couldn't look up; she didn't want to see the terror that was no doubt plastered on Siska's face.

When she finished her story, Wave rocked back on her heels and sat in the grass, finally lifting her gaze to her sister. Siska was still hunched down, her eyes wide, her hands clasped together before her, knuckles white.

'I've done some foolish things in my life,' Wave said. 'But this is the worst. I can't touch anyone, ever again.'

Siska shook her head, licking her lips and opening her

mouth. No words came out, though, and she pressed her lips into a firm line.

'Maybe I should just let the Black Cloaks take me,' Wave murmured into her lap. 'It's them, or a lifetime of being an outcast, having to fend for myself in the wilderness.'

'You could go to Veija-Mens,' Siska said, her voice coming out in a croak.

A spark of hope burst into life in Wave's heart that she quickly tried to squash. She had no idea what Siska was talking about, but it didn't matter. Could there possibly be a way out of her predicament?

'Veija-Mens?' Wave repeated when Siska fell silent.

'Mother always said that the people who lived there are descendants of those from the South Claw. Maybe they've found a cure?'

Wave's heart sank. Veija-Mens was on the other side of Heredour.

'Be realistic with me, Siska. What are the chances they've spent the last thousand years trying to find a cure? Their home was blasted from existence. They're probably living peacefully, grateful they're alive.'

'No, Mother was very specific. Don't you remember her talking about the island?'

Wave shook her head. Her childhood memories were few and incomplete.

'She travelled there with Father, and their friend. She said it was a haven for those in trouble, that the people who live there are … unusual. They have different knowledge of the gods.'

'That doesn't mean they'll be able to help me.'

'I didn't realise you were such a fatalist, Wave.' Siska stood and walked away.

Wave opened her mouth to retort but found nothing worthwhile to say. Why shouldn't she be fatalistic in this situation?

'You never told me why you're here,' Wave called.

Halfway back to Skoa, Siska paused, her back still turned.

'I'm looking for Jessandra.'

'Jessandra?'

Though it explained why Siska had asked Skoa if *she* was here, the answer still didn't make any sense.

Siska leaned her head against Skoa's, ignoring Wave. After a few moments, they separated, and Siska made her way back to Wave, keeping an uncomfortable distance between them. Wave knew she had to, but it still hurt. Siska was family.

Taking a seat opposite Wave, Siska told her about Jessandra. Wave listened in surprised silence as Siska tossed her some apples from a satchel at her waist.

'You helped her?' Wave asked. She hadn't thought of Siska as someone bold or fearless, but they hadn't seen each other in years. A lot had changed for both of them.

'Wouldn't you, if you could?'

Wave bit into an apple gratefully, suddenly aware of her ravenous hunger.

'Of course,' she said, forming words around hurried mouthfuls. 'She's a bit like us.'

'If they find out about Mother's kin, you'll be in a lot more trouble.'

Wave laughed, bits of apple spraying onto the ground between them.

'I hardly think they'll care much about sending me to Buduwai when I'm star-cursed. That'll be a much bigger problem for the Black Cloaks.'

'And what if they go after Mother?' Siska pulled a loaf of soft, round bread from her bag. 'What about Winter?'

'How would they know where they live? Everyone in Bindock thinks I was born and raised in Essenné, remember?'

'You mean to tell me that you never told a single person in that town the truth?'

'Of course not!'

Siska laid portions of bread and cheese out on the cloth wrapping and placed them between her and Wave. Once she'd sat back down, Wave reached forward and pulled the food towards her.

As she pushed a wedge of cheese into the bread, X'olea's face sprung to mind.

'Oh no,' she mumbled around the bread already in her mouth. 'I told X'olea. But he would never betray me.'

'He wouldn't need to, Wave.' Siska sighed. 'The servants in the castle told me all about the methods of torture the Black Cloaks use. They can pluck a thought, a memory, even a feeling out of someone's mind, and we're basically powerless to stop them.'

The bread turned chalky and tasteless in Wave's mouth. X'olea would never betray her willingly, but if the Black Cloaks got to him ... Unable to think clearly, Wave wrapped the bread and cheese back up in the cloth.

'I'll visit her, once we've got you sorted,' Siska said.

Wave could see the pity in her sister's eyes, and a small pit of anger bubbled up from deep inside.

'Sort me?' Wave asked. 'This can't be sorted on a whim, Siska. You say I should go to Veija-Mens, but we're on the wrong side of Heredour for that.'

'Skoa can fly you there.'

Wave turned to look at the bird. One beady eye was trained on her, even as Skoa shifted from foot to foot.

'I'm not skykin,' Wave said. 'And what if I gave the curse to him?'

'You can't. The skykin in the South Claw were friends with all the great eagles, and none of those eagles got sick.'

'What if you're wrong?'

'I just asked him.' Siska stood. 'He doesn't communicate in words, like we do, but I got no sense of danger from him, even though he seems to understand the problem with the star.'

'But I'm not skykin,' Wave repeated.

'Stranger things have happened.' Siska shrugged. 'Skoa brought me here for a reason, though he can't express clearly to me why. I assumed it was because this was where he'd left Jessandra. But then you were here ...' Her voice trailed off as she frowned at the giant eagle. 'Come on, he'll have to delve your mind again. It's been years since he's been near you.'

Wave rose on unsteady feet. 'If you're sure.'

Keeping several feet between them, Siska and Wave moved over to the edge of the clearing. Skoa regarded Wave from his great height for a while, then lowered his head towards hers.

Wave tried to ignore the long, orange talons at the end of his feet, so close to her own. She swallowed. Their foreheads touched. Wave felt as though she would drown in the ebony pools of his unmoving eyes, but they disappeared before she had time to think.

Everything around her was gone: trees, hill, sky, Siska. She was flying, a million images whirling past her at an incomprehensible speed. Ages of men and beasts moved beneath her gaze; warring, loving, living, dying. She watched as civilisations rose and collapsed, dragons careened through the sky and then vanished, oceans shifted, masses of land were created and destroyed.

Beings shrouded in black cloaks watched the world from a high tower lost in the desert, pulling invisible strings with the deft hand movements of a fiddle player. Wave's vision zoomed in to the tower, her gaze landing directly in front of one of the puppetmasters. She stared at his colourless eyes, recognising his face from some life long lost, and he met her gaze.

For a heartbeat, the strings around his fingers were still as he studied her, his pock-marked face a mask of shock that mirrored Wave's surprise.

She blinked. Before her were two huge eyes, reptilian but all-knowing. They blurred into the unyielding depths of Skoa's black eyes. The trees swirled around her, and she fell to her knees.

The sound of footsteps running towards her almost brought her back. Siska. She tried to tell her not to come any closer. Blue sky and white clouds swirled into one monstrous vortex as Wave's head tilted back, and then all was darkness.

15

JINDAR

JINDAR WAS BIGGER than Jessandra had imagined. Tall-masted ships sat close to the town, and the dark shapes on the horizon suggested more vessels of all sizes. From where she stood on the sloping road leading into the town, she could see plenty of two- and three-storey buildings, their shingled roofs glinting under the newly risen sun.

The town had no walls and no guards strolled the perimeter, not that there was any obvious boundaries. Farms became warehouses became crowded streets, and before Jessandra realised, she'd strolled into Jindar proper. Thick beams supported whitewashed walls on most of the buildings, whether inn or shop or house. Black curtains hung in many of the windows; like other small towns, Jindar had been ravaged by the Law of Kaiāho.

The people were dressed similarly to Jessandra—many of the women wore divided skirts and loose blouses, the men in wide-legged trousers that ended halfway down their shins. They all donned wide-brimmed straw hats, though the women tended to decorate theirs with scarfs of different hues.

Jessandra saw all the eye colours of the low- and middlekin.

Deep brown, hazel, emerald green, and all shades of blue jostled among one another. Jessandra was suddenly glad her eyes remained the obstinate grey of an uncalled youth. She wondered if there were any highkin in the town, perhaps running the council, in the library, maybe even the prolific merchants. It didn't matter; she'd have to avoid them all.

There was enough coin in her purse for her to take a room in a decent inn. She took her time wandering through the streets, watching the people, reading the names of the shops and the taverns.

Near the heart of Jindar, Jessandra found a building with a foundation made of riverstone, its upper floors white-washed with dormer windows looking out over the street. The sign hanging above the door proclaimed it as the Merchant's Wife. The front windows looked clean, and the street around them was free of rubbish and questionable people.

Swallowing her pride and her anxiety, Jessandra pushed through the heavy wooden door. The common room was well lit, a warm glow coming from the coals of the hearth. There were few patrons in at dawn; those who sat at the tables were dipping hunks of warm, fresh bread into a yellow soup.

'Well met,' a voice called from Jessandra's left.

She turned. To her surprise, the woman calling out to her wasn't more than a few years older than Jessandra. With the pale blue eyes of a skykin, she could have been Inska or Siska. Unlike her handmaidens, though, this girl wore an alarmingly low-cut dress, cinched tight around her waist. Her ears were layered in heavy rings, as were her fingers. A snaking tattoo of curling lines rose from her shoulder and up her neck, disappearing into her hair.

'What can I do for you?' the woman asked with a pointed nod.

Jessandra blinked. She was staring.

'Oh, I … I need a room for a couple of days.'

The woman's eyes tightened slightly.

'You're young to be needing a room alone. Where are your parents?'

In a panic, Jessandra realised she was just as unprepared for this version of her imagined life as she was for the wilderness.

'I have none.'

'No parents?' The woman raised an eyebrow.

'They're dead.' Jessandra swallowed. 'You're not so old yourself.' She bit her tongue. It wasn't meant to sound like a retort, but she would have been offended if their positions were reversed.

The woman burst out laughing, the sound like a battered bell pealing in the distance.

'You've got a tongue on you!' she cried, slapping her palm on one of the wooden posts that supported the building. 'No doubt your parents are dead, with an attitude like that.' Wiping her hands on her apron, the woman smiled. 'I'm Kyan. I'm sure we can find you a room for the night. You have coin?'

Jessandra nodded.

'Come on, then.' Kyan motioned with one hand. 'All our rooms are upstairs.'

Eyes wide, Jessandra followed the other woman into a hallway and up two flights of steep, narrow stairs.

'We always put the young ones on the second storey,' Kyan said as they reached a landing. 'You're fit enough to climb both sets of stairs.' She laughed again, before unlocking a door in front of them. 'This should satisfy you.'

Jessandra moved into the room. It was plain, but she knew not to expect anything like home. A single bed stood in one corner, just large enough for two people to squeeze into. An open cedar wood chest stood at the end of the bed, the soft fragrance of lavender filling the room. Opposite the bed was an area hidden by folding screens.

'Change room,' Kyan said, nodding at the screens. 'There's a basin in there too, but there's a communal bathing room at the end of the hall.'

Jessandra coughed. 'Communal?'

'Used to bathing in private, are we?' Kyan smirked, not bothering to hide the up-and-down look she gave Jessandra's clothes.

'I can't bathe around men!' Jessandra knew how childish she sounded, but the words tumbled from her mouth anyway. 'It's improper.'

'*Female* communal bathing room.' Kyan rolled her eyes. 'Nobody expects you to bathe with men.'

Jessandra let out a breathy sigh. 'Okay.'

'You're not from around here, are you?'

Was it that obvious? Jessandra's pulse quickened in her throat. If she lied, like she had about her parents, how long till she was caught out?

'No.' Maybe if she didn't offer any more information Kyan would leave her alone.

'Tight-lipped, hey?' Kyan shrugged. 'Keep your secrets then, girly. Breakfast is at seven bells, dinner after sundown. If you need anything, I'll be downstairs.'

'Thank you,' Jessandra said.

With a curt nod, Kyan left, closing the door behind her. Jessandra waited until the sounds of her footsteps going down the stairs disappeared before she let out another big breath. This fugitive life was more nerve-wracking than she'd imagined.

Jessandra tossed her bag on the bed, undid the clasp of her cloak, and hung the heavy thing on the back of the door. Behind the screens she found a washstand and a small stool, but there was no water in the jug. If she wanted to freshen up, she'd have to brave the communal bath area.

One wall held a dormer window with a cushioned seat at its base. Jessandra kneeled on the cushions and peered out through the speckled glass. From her vantage point, she could see the street below and the people moving about their tasks.

Fatigue washed over Jessandra. Her eyes became heavy, and she felt as if she couldn't lift her limbs. At least she was safe for a time, though she tried not to think about what she would need to do next. Her coin would only last so long, and then what? Could she work as a barmaid under Kyan's watchful gaze? She hoped to find some peace for a few days, enough to let Everluof call to her, but what if it took longer? What if, after everything, she still felt nothing?

Anxiety gnawed at her insides as she stared out over Jindar, trying to decide whether she should sleep, or bathe, or simply sit here and watch, waiting for something to guide her next move. Jessandra sighed. She'd never felt more alone in her life.

16

WATERFALL CITY

AT THE ENTRANCE to the dungeons, Mortius paused with his hand on the door. There were a thousand reasons Reuben might have asked to meet him here, but none of them were good. What if Reuben suspected Mortius? He was so paranoid these days that even if Mortius had stayed an obedient, loyal adviser, Reuben was just as likely think he was out to betray him.

Mortius took a deep breath. There was no avoiding this meeting any longer. He pushed the heavy double doors wide. The first-floor landing was crowded with people, and Mortius blinked in surprise. He thought this was a private meeting.

Two guards in the golden-bronze uniform of the high king stood either side of another set of doors. A table and two chairs were pushed against one wall. Reuben stood in the centre of the room, staring at the ceiling, surrounded by retainers, a single Black Cloak standing aloof to one side.

'Senior Adviser,' a voice said from Mortius' right.

'General Juro.' Mortius dipped his head.

The grizzled old man beside him was still as well muscled as he had been the last three decades. He wore his silver hair long to match the trailing white moustache that mostly hid his displeasure with everyone he came across. There was a reason nobody had ever replaced him, despite his age, and it wasn't just because he was the best military man in Heredour. He'd been there, the night Esra died.

'I'm glad to see you,' the general said, his violet eyes a mirror of Mortius'. 'I was certain I was going to be put in a cell when he summoned me here.'

'That may yet happen to us all,' Mortius murmured, but he breathed a sigh of relief.

There were other members of the High Council in the room —the white-haired maire of the city, Gurnagal moonkin; wiry Chlothar starkin; even elder Marni waterkin was there. If Reuben meant to lock all of them up, he'd need an army of Black Cloaks, and for once, only one wizard stood at his side.

One of the retainers murmured something to Reuben. The high king spun on his heel to glare at Mortius. At least his hair was combed today. He'd managed to look the part of High King in a bronze tunic embellished with golden suns, belted at the waist with a thick braid of gold silk.

'We're all here, then,' Reuben said. Turning back to the guards, he motioned at them to open the doors.

The other council members glanced between one another, looking as disconcerted as Mortius felt. He was glad he wasn't the only one with no idea of what they were doing in the dungeons, or why only half the council were present.

Two of Reuben's personal guards led the way down the stairs, Reuben clattering behind them with a disturbing eagerness. The councillors looked at Mortius uncertainly, and he saw an opportunity to regain a position of power over them.

'You heard him,' he said, shooing them into the stairwell with a quick motion. 'Don't keep the high king waiting!'

Beside him, Juro snorted. 'I take it you know nothing of why we're here,' he said as they followed the last of the council down the stairs.

Mortius shook his head.

'Would that I was still in his close confidence,' he murmured, more to himself than to Juro.

The general made a noncommittal sound.

In silence, they followed Reuben and his entourage down three flights of stairs, only stopping at each landing long enough for the guards to open the next set of doors. The dungeons had been built deep into the mountain so that each floor was below the castle's ground level. The third floor was where they kept the worst prisoners, or at least the ones the Black Cloaks deemed too dangerous for the higher levels.

There was no landing on the third floor, only a door made of thick iron rods. No prison guards were assigned to this level either. Reuben's personal guard lit torches Mortius hadn't noticed they were carrying, passing them out into the crowd at random. The dungeon guard who'd travelled with them from the top floor unlocked the door with a set of keys looped around his belt.

Unlike the first two levels, there were no lamps housed in the intermittent wall sconces. If not for the torches, they would have been plunged into a complete, stifling darkness. There were no windows for light or air, though the smell of musty water left a tang on Mortius' tongue. In the distance, he could hear a small trickle—no doubt another leak in the supposedly impervious walls of the city.

Reuben stopped them in front of a cell. In the small pool of light cast by the torches, the cell looked empty.

'I've brought you here to do two things,' Reuben said, his voice uncomfortably loud in the muted space. 'One is to give you some dire news.'

Mortius and the general glanced at each other. A muscle popped in Juro's jaw.

'The second is to demonstrate why I'm in favour of having the Black Cloaks work with us.'

Mortius ground his teeth. If not for the Black Cloaks ... There was rustling at the front of the group, and two of the guards held their torches high. With his eyes finally adjusting to the low light, Mortius realised the cell wasn't empty. A man, cloaked in shadow, leaned against the back wall. His violet eyes were vibrant in the darkness.

Gods, Mortius thought. *Are we here to see the punishment of some ill-begotten highkin? Some twisted lesson to us all?*

'Here we have a creature by the name of X'olea starkin,' Reuben said. 'He's been hiding out in the town of Bindock, on the north coast of Marbin Province. The Black Cloaks tell me they've had problems with him in the past, but nothing like this.'

Mortius peered at the man. As if on cue, he took a step forward. His hair and beard were silver white, and his skin had the feathery, papery look of long years spent travelling. Though dirty, he wore a fine-cut pale grey shirt and dark trousers, the ceremonial circlet of the starkin resting on his forehead. Nobody wore those anymore, unless they were getting married, or going to a coronation. It was strange, to see it on the starkin's head, knowing his own gathered dust in a drawer somewhere.

'We have a problem, my friends.'

Mortius pulled his attention back to Reuben. The high king had his back to the cell, his attention all on them.

'There is a star-caller loose in Heredour.'

A series of gasps and shocked cries travelled around the group. Even though they were highly disciplined, the guards around Reuben paled, a few blinking rapidly at his words.

'Yes, a star-caller. There have been a few who tried to take up this mantle since the South Claw was lost, and we have snuffed each of them out. As you know, they can bring only pain and suffering to anyone they touch.'

The curse. Anyone a star-caller touched became ill, wasting away until they died. And it was contagious—a person touched by a star-caller could pass on the curse through touch alone. No healer could help them, no herb save them. No prayers to the gods, no sacred rituals, nothing at all would cure it. That was why the Black Cloaks had blasted the South Claw from the face of Heredour.

'Dyafirah and his kin are out hunting this star-caller.'

Mortius shivered. Any Black Cloak was bad enough, but Dyafirah the Dread was the worst. And of course, Reuben had taken him as some sort of personal adviser. At least that meant the Dread was out of the castle.

'Unfortunately, the star she summoned seems to cloak her from their view, making it challenging to locate her.'

The council members began murmuring to one another, their panic-stricken faces pale in the lamp light.

'Hush!' Reuben called, a deep scowl setting his face into sharp lines and contrasts. 'Hush, you fools. She's only just graduated, so they've taken all her details from the town. They know what she looks like, how powerful she is as a waterkin, where her parents live, all of it. And they were able to detain her one and only friend in the town.'

Without looking, he gestured at the cell. Mortius frowned at the starkin trapped behind the bars. If this star-caller was a newly graduated waterkin, why was her only friend an old starkin? Even more troubling was why this man had been in Bindock in the first place—they were one of the few towns left in Heredour to maintain their kin. Nobody of another kin was denied a place to live, of course, but who would want to live in a town full of waterkin unless you were also a waterkin?

'The Black Cloaks who remained in the castle will be questioning this X'olea starkin while the others hunt for the star-caller. We all know how imperative it is to capture her before she touches a single person.'

Another shiver passed over Mortius, as though he'd stepped under one of the waterfalls outside the city. The questioning techniques of the Black Cloaks were almost as frightful as the idea of a new star-caller. They had no need for the sharp tools of a torturer when they could inflict all their pain directly within the mind of their subject.

'It's also imperative that this stays between those of us who stand in this hallway. Those council members who deemed their lives more important than meeting with us will be left in the dark, as will all the non-council highkin. At this early stage, the issue of the star-caller is a matter best kept close to our hearts so as not to invoke terror among the people.'

Mortius shook his head. Those here would never be able to keep this a secret, not if their lives depended on it.

'And if I hear even a rumour, or a hint of a rumour about a star-caller, I'll have your tongues out, and the tongues of your children.'

The silence in the dungeon was deafening. Maybe that would do it?

'All of them, no matter who spoke out of turn.'

There was a collective swallowing.

'Do you understand?' Reuben glanced at the guards.

They saluted, right fist over heart, left palm face up at waist height. The council members followed suit, though they were hesitant and unfamiliar with being made to salute the king. Like rote, Mortius and Juro saluted. They were the only army-trained men among the council.

'Everyone out!'

Mortius and Juro pressed back against the wall as the councillors raced up the stairs. Mortius stared at X'olea. The old man met his gaze evenly, regarding Mortius with what looked like curiosity.

'Mortius?'

Reuben stood at the foot of the stairs with Juro.

'Do you want to question him, too?' Reuben's smile was mocking.

'Perhaps, my king.' Mortius dragged his eyes away from the

prisoner. 'Perhaps.'

The three of them traipsed back up the three flights of stairs, guards tailing them. Mortius lost himself in the rhythm of the climb. Anything to ignore the sinking sensation in his gut. Maybe Reuben wasn't paranoid. Everything was actually starting to fall apart, just as he'd lamented.

'Come to my office, Mortius,' Reuben called back as they climbed the last flight. 'There's another problem we have to deal with.'

Mortius blinked and almost stumbled up the stairs.

'Another one?'

Juro trudged ahead of them, but Reuben stopped midflight and turned to Mortius.

'Mascerab's daughter has gone missing.'

The twist in Mortius stomach had nothing to do with Reuben's proximity, or the way his eyes rolled in his head, unable to focus on Mortius' face. At least, Mortius could pretend to himself that he was used to the high king's bizarre behaviour.

If the princess was missing, then there was nobody left to take Marbin's throne. The last thing they needed was a war of succession. All this, right when Marbin was the only region doing well, paying the high king's bounty on time, flourishing under Mascerab's rule.

A star-caller, a missing heir, the suffering of the regions. Reuben's descent into madness. Was he the cause of these problems? Or were they coincidental and something much bigger was at work?

Mortius pursed his lips to stop them from trembling. Reuben turned and continued up the stairs. Whether or not Reuben was the cause of all of Heredour's problems, he was certainly the cause of Mortius' inability to sleep at night.

He had to get out. And he was going to take Aymn with him. The boy had to be kept away from his father.

17

CHOK

Darkness filled the streets of Chok. No boisterous sounds of mirth tumbled from the brothels or the drinking houses, and the single lamp hanging from the door of each establishment was the only light that pierced the night. The hour was late, or early, depending on whether the timekeeper was a sailor or a housewife, but no matter the profession, the town of Chok was safely asleep.

Wave and Siska hurried down the middle of the road, cloaks wrapped tight around their bodies, hoods up to cover their faces. They maintained a good distance between them, and the muffled sound of their footsteps broke the stillness of the town.

Every now and then, a night bird cried out from the forest, the sound drifting over the bay. Stray cats with high backs and bright eyes watched Wave and Siska's journey, assessing them from the walls and roofs of the town but never making a sound.

From the cobbled streets, the sisters descended onto the sleek wooden decking of the old wharf. Waves lapped gently at the pilings beneath them as they hurried towards the last berth and the small ship moored there.

The boat was old and well used; letters inscribed in peeling red paint declared the boat's name as the *Hand of Numen*. Another cloaked person stood waiting for them on the deck, the features of his face lost in a deep hood. He was shorter than both Wave and Siska, and much stockier besides, something his cloak didn't hide well.

They stopped in front of him. Siska pushed her hood back and faced Wave.

'It's all organised,' Siska said, her voice low. 'He'll take you safely to Jindar.'

Wave stared up at her sister without removing her hood. Though she opened her mouth, no words came out. Her stomach was a twisted knot of anxiety, made worse by the fact that they were around another person. What if they brushed hands accidentally?

'What if it's not safe in Jindar?' Wave asked, swallowing the lump in her throat.

Siska turned her back to the captain.

'Nowhere is safe for you, Wave,' she whispered. 'No now. But from Jindar, you must make a decision. Either find another passage around the North Claw to Messenien, or make the journey through the mountains to Kochee. From there, you should be able to get a ship to Veija-Mens.'

Wave shook her head. There were too many steps, too many unknowns, too many opportunities for it all to go wrong. Too many chances for the Black Cloaks to find her.

'What else can you do?' Siska muttered. 'We agreed this was the best plan.'

'It doesn't mean it's a good plan,' Wave said, but she nodded her head beneath her cloak. This plan was as good as any, better than her vague thoughts about hiding away from the world in the forest for the remainder of her life.

Siska turned back to the captain and dropped a small purse into his upturned palm.

'See that she reaches Jindar safe and untouched,' she murmured, stressing the last word.

Let him think whatever he wanted about that one.

'Nobody must know of her journey.'

The captain's hood jerked an unspoken agreement.

'Discretion has paid my way for many a year,' he murmured. 'If the wind favours us, we'll arrive in Jindar tomorrow at nightfall.'

Wave cast her eyes over the boat, taking in the weathered state of the sails and the worn-looking hull. A small part of her wondered if it would be better if the boat sank out to sea. Lerinial would take her prizes and her revenge. Wave would be free.

'Stay safe,' Siska whispered.

The ache in Wave's heart intensified as she realised that although they'd reached the part where they would separate, she couldn't even hug Siska goodbye. They'd been together such a short time, and Wave couldn't bear to part with someone familiar and comforting.

'Thank you, Siska,' Wave said. 'Take care of Mother, and Winter. And Jessandra.' The princess was an afterthought, but she knew how much Siska cared for her charge.

'Go,' Siska said, her voice thick with unspoken emotion.

Wave took a few steps towards the captain. Despite the dark, she could make out the glint of a pair of steely blue eyes perched above a thick, dark beard speckled with grey.

'It be best if we don't exchange names,' he said, motioning towards the narrow gangplank that shifted with the gentle rock of the boat.

Wave turned to look at Siska, but her sister had already drawn her hood over her head, hiding her face. Swallowing a few times, Wave made her way up the gangplank, drawing a little on Lerinial's power to keep her steps steady above the ocean.

'We'll not leave 'til daybreak,' the captain said once they were on deck. 'Else we might draw unwanted attention.'

Wave looked over the railings, but all she could see of Siska was a dark shape moving towards the township. The ache in her heart sharpened, and she clutched her chest.

With a wide-legged, confident stride, the captain moved down the deck, motioning for her to follow. There were no sailors around. Wave guessed they were catching a last bit of sleep before setting sail.

At the top of the stairs leading into the belly of the ship, Wave stopped. Across from where she stood, Wave could see the shadowy figure of a man leaning against the railing, watching her.

Not knowing what to do, Wave lifted a hand and waved at him. She felt like a fool when he gave nothing in return, so she hurried down the stairs after the captain.

'These are the officers' quarters,' the captain said, showing her a small cabin.

She squeezed into the room, holding her breath as if that would stop her from touching the captain. The room held a single bed and a tiny desk and chair in the corner, but nothing else. A small lantern, almost burned out, sputtered above the bed.

'Officers are expensive these days,' the captain added with a grimace, pulling a small vial of oil from his pocket. In one expert movement, he filled the lamp and the room flooded with light.

'Might be best you stay down here most times.'

Wave pushed back her hood and nodded at him.

'Crews these days talk quick enough for a dollar,' he added, as if answering a question she hadn't asked. 'Though there is another passenger aboard for a change. He's not much older than you, I'd warrant.'

The man leaning against the railings. Wave pushed him from

her mind. She'd stay in her cabin where she couldn't accidentally touch anyone.

The captain made to shut the door. 'I'll see that you get some food.' The words whipped through the closing gap, and then she was alone.

With slow, deliberate movements, Wave slipped the bag Siska had given her onto the wooden floor and sat down on the hard bed with a sigh. She was tired, her legs ached, and she was heartsore. Pulling her cloak over her body, Wave curled up on top of the bed, facing the door. She closed her eyes and let the gentle motion of the boat rock her into a fitful sleep.

A hard knock at the door tore Wave from an almost dreamless sleep. She stared at the door for a moment before sitting up.

'Come in,' she said, clearing her throat.

A shaggy head of brown curls popped through the gap in the door.

'I brought you some food.'

Hazel eyes flecked with green, blue, and perhaps even violet peered at her above a wide, toothy smile.

'Who are you?' Wave asked, gripping the edge of the bed.

'My name's Strath,' the man said. 'I'm the other passenger.'

Much to Wave's relief, he didn't come any further into the room.

'I'm Wave,' she said, then cursed herself. She wasn't supposed to tell anyone who she was, but the response was automatic.

'Could I come in? It's boring up there with the sailors running around like someone chopped their hands off.'

Wave swallowed. This wouldn't be the last time she'd be in a similar situation, with someone who wanted to be near her. She had to figure out a way to deal with it if she was she going to get to the other side of Heredour.

'Just ... don't come too close to me.'

Strath raised an eyebrow at her.

'I'm sick,' she said. It wasn't exactly a lie.

'Oh!' Strath opened the door and moved awkwardly into the room. He held two bowls in one hand. 'I have some herbs on me, I might be able to help.'

Wave was silent. She took the bowl he offered her, avoiding his fingers like he was the one with the sickness.

'I, uh, I don't think herbs will help,' she said, to fill the silence.

Strath pulled the chair out and sat down facing her.

'Well, that does make me curious. Herbs can cure most things.' He motioned at the bowl in her hands. 'But so can a good meal.'

Wave's stomach rumbled and Strath laughed, the sound like the wild dance of wind through a forest canopy. Unable to help herself, Wave smiled and lifted the spoon to her mouth.

The bowl was full of bland porridge, but it tasted less like chalk than the bread she'd tried to eat yesterday. Her stomach growled again. All she'd eaten since the graduation feast was a couple of apples.

'So, Wave,' Strath said once he'd cleaned his bowl. 'What brings someone like you onto a boat like this in the middle of the night?' He glanced at her right forearm, at the lingering inflammation in the skin around her tattoo.

'I'm travelling to the Chaba-Canez Islands,' Wave said as she shovelled the porridge into her mouth.

Strath's eyebrows disappeared into his hair. 'Only the exuberantly wealthy or the highly unusual go to Chaba-Canez.'

'Well, I'm definitely not the first,' Wave said, cleaning her bowl with her fingers. 'And I hope I'm not the second.'

'It's a long journey. Are you planning to find another ship from Jindar?'

Wave shrugged. 'I'm not sure if I have enough money to

travel by sea all the way to Chaba-Canez.' There was a little purse in her bag now, filled with everything Siska had on her at the time, but it wasn't much. 'I guess I'll have to go through the North Claw?'

'That's not a journey to undertake lightly,' Strath said, his face a mask of concern. 'The mountains are dangerous, and there's no path between Jindar and Kochee. You'd also have to cross the Kanrid River at some point.'

Wave turned her eyes down to her bowl. Strath seemed nice enough, and more genuine than most of the people she'd known in Bindock, but she couldn't tell him that the mountains were probably safer for her than being near people.

'I don't have many other options.' She set her bowl on the desk, and Strath mimicked her. 'What about you? Why are you heading to Jindar?'

'I've been on a bit of a mission, and I've been gone for months. I miss my home.'

'Jindar is home?' Wave asked.

Strath shook his head, the hint of a smile on his lips.

'Messenien?'

Strath shook his head again. His eyes twinkled in the lamp light. There were definitely flecks of all different colours in his irises, now that Wave was looking properly.

'Are there other small villages in the Claw that aren't on a map?'

The Barancha Plains were full of tiny unmarked farming villages like the one her mother lived in, so it made sense that there could be some hidden mountain villages.

'You could say that,' Strath said.

'Are you being deliberately mysterious?' Wave asked, frowning at him.

Strath laughed again, the sound a refreshing balm to Wave's aching heart.

'I don't mean to be,' he said, 'but I'm not supposed to talk about where I come from to strangers.'

The floor lurched beneath them. Wave gripped the edge of the bed, her eyes wide.

'We must be leaving,' Strath said. 'Do you want to come up and say goodbye to Chok?'

'No.' Her tone was sharper than she wanted it to be, but going on deck was too risky. What if she bumped into one of the sailors?

'Okay!' Strath raised his hands in the air, a smile still playing on his lips.

The floor lurched again and the bowls shot from the desk, landing on Wave's bed.

'Why is it so rough?' she asked.

'They rowed us out of the bay a little while ago, so I guess they're pushing us through the big waves. Once we're past the breakwater, it should be smooth sailing.'

'Oh.' Wave was glad she'd spent the last five years around the ocean. Unlike other kin, she had Lerinial's support to stop her feeling seasick, even if the goddess was still angry at her. 'I've never been on a ship this big, and never out into the ocean proper.'

'Honestly, it's pretty boring unless there's a storm,' Strath said. 'But at least the journey won't be a long one.'

Wave wished the journey would go longer. At least she could delay the inevitable decision she needed to make while she was out to sea.

'Do you know if Black Cloaks can materialise on a ship?' Wave asked. It was a question that had plagued her since her shared vision with Skoa, when Siska had explained that the giant eagle refused to go near her and that she'd need to travel by boat.

'I don't think so,' Strath said. 'I've never seen it happen, and I've been on plenty of ships.'

Wave nodded as the floor lurched again. The bowls clattered

against one another on the bed.

'Nobody wants to be too close to a Black Cloak,' Strath said, 'but I get the feeling you've got a particular reason to stay away from them.'

'I haven't come across them yet,' Wave said, wondering what she could tell Strath without giving too much away. 'And I don't want to.'

'The last thing you want is to be on the wrong side of the wizards,' Strath said with a grimace. 'Maybe I should tell you about my home, then.'

Wave studied him. There was something endearing about his easy smile and bright eyes.

'I'm sure your hometown won't be as crazy as what I've just gone through.' Wave bit the inside of her cheek. She shouldn't have opened her mouth.

'Perhaps not.' He picked up the bowls and placed them back on the desk now that the violent shifting of the floor had calmed. 'But my home is a safe haven for those who are lost, reviled, or hunted. I think you might find some solace there.'

'Safe even from the Black Cloaks?'

'They've only visited twice in the last thirty years.' Strath shrugged. 'And they only come when they're desperate.'

Wave thought they might be pretty desperate when it came to looking for her. They had no reason to suspect she'd be in this secret town though, wherever it was, so perhaps she could be safe for a little while. Even if she had to stay away from all the people.

'Where is your home, then?'

Strath smiled. 'Deep in the mountains of the North Claw our ancestors built a town on a plateau. They called it Sharvel, and from then on, the people of Sharvel dedicated themselves to being purveyors of the truth.'

'The truth?'

'You might not be ready for the truth, Wave.'

18

BARANCHA PLAINS

ANOTHER DAY of digging around in fertile soil had passed, and only four since Siska had left. Not that Larka was counting. With the princess gone, Larka had wondered if Siska might come back home for a time. Wave would be on her way down to see them after graduation. They could be a family again. Well, as much of a family as they had been since Winter was born.

The last golden-pink streaks of the sunset were disappearing from the sky as Larka cleaned her face and hands in the stream. She was unable to shake the small feeling of excitement growing inside her. Her eldest daughters had been gone so long, and her husband even longer. She had no idea when she'd see Sam, but to have all three of her children together again ...

Larka sighed and trudged her way down the road, her legs weary but her heart full. Lamps glowed behind the solitary windowpanes of the village houses, heavy doors closed against the night. A chill crept across Larka's bare arms and she frowned. The summer heat was still holding strong, and there was no storm-driven wind. So why did she feel uneasy?

An orange glow radiated from the window of her house at the end of the road. Larka smiled, shaking off the strange sensation as a ghost of her imagination. Before she reached the door, though, she heard the sound of strong wings beating the air.

'Siska!' she cried, spinning around.

In the twilight, she watched a giant eagle land a few paces away from her. Snow-white feathers shone in the eerie twilight glow, and Larka knew it was Skoa.

A hooded rider jumped from Skoa's back, and Larka took a few steps forward, ready to embrace her daughter.

'It's me, Larka,' the rider whispered, pushing her hood back slightly.

'Inska?' Larka's heart skipped a beat in surprise. 'What are you doing here?'

Siska's friend grabbed Larka by the upper arm and steered her up the steps.

'What's going on, Inska?' Larka asked as she pushed the door open.

'Inside,' Inska muttered. 'It's not safe.'

Her words made Larka's pulse race. Winter looked up in surprise from the wood stove where she was heating up yesterday's soup.

Inska banged the door shut and pushed her hood all the way back. Her hair was dishevelled, her eyes bloodshot and puffy.

'What's happened, Inska?' A leaden ball of dread was growing in Larka's stomach. 'Is Siska okay?'

'No, she's not, and neither will you be. You need to leave, you need to leave now.' Inska's voice shook as she spoke.

'Tell me what's happened, and I promise you we'll be out of this house before you can blink.'

Inska swallowed. 'You know about Jessandra?'

'Yes.'

'Siska came to visit you a few days ago. When she returned to the castle, we heard news, terrible news from the north coast.' Inska took a shaky breath. 'There's a star-caller in Bindock. A star-caller! It can't be real, it just can't be.'

The ball of dread in Larka's stomach soured, festered into something rotten. She clamped her teeth shut.

'But then the Black Cloaks came, and they were asking after Siska. The other servants rushed to tell us and Siska knew she wouldn't be able to hide from them. So she told me.'

'Told you what, Inska?' Larka squeezed out from between her closed lips. 'What did she tell you?'

'That she saw Wave in the mountains around Chok. And that Wave is the star-caller.' Inska's eyes widened even as her lips trembled. 'She made me promise I'd come and warn you before they drag your location out of her mind.'

Inska burst into tears. She buried her face in her hands.

'I was so afraid,' she mumbled into her palms. 'I should have stayed and tried to help her, but I went straight to Skoa and fled with him.'

Larka's mind reeled. Wave, star-caller. It seemed impossible, like some old fairytale come to life. Gods, how could this have happened? Her baby, her sweet girl Wave.

'Pull yourself together, Larka,' she whispered, swiping away the few tears that had fallen onto her cheeks.

Winter stood nearby, watching them with wide eyes, her mouth open. Inska sobbed into her hands.

'Inska,' Larka said, grabbing her by the upper arms. 'Inska, you did the right thing. You've saved us, Winter and I both.'

When she didn't lift her head, Larka grabbed her chin and forced her gaze up.

'Hear me, child, you have saved us.' She pointed at Winter. 'You did what Siska asked, and that's all she expected from you. And now, I need your help.'

Tears still tracking down her face, Inska nodded. 'Anything.'

'We don't know how long it will take them to break into Siska's mind, so I need you to stand guard outside. Black Cloaks can materialise wherever they want, as long as they've been to the place at least once. They definitely haven't been in my house, but some of them may have been to this village. Stand at the front door with Skoa and look out for them.'

Without a word, Inska headed out the front door. Larka kneeled down in front of her youngest daughter.

'It's going to be okay, Winter, but we need to move fast.'

Winter nodded. 'But—'

'I know you'll have a lot of questions, and I hope to answer them once we're on the move. Is that okay?'

'Yes, that's okay.'

'I need you to go and pack some warm clothes and your underclothes into your satchel. We can't take any toys, but you can bring your blanket.'

With a small smile, Winter darted into the room they shared. Alone in the kitchen, Larka became aware of the sound of her own hurried heartbeat. The whirling of her thoughts made her feel like vomiting, so she pushed all thought aside. There was freedom in action, that much she knew to be true.

She moved around the room gathering supplies and stuffing them into her own satchel. Minutes later, Winter joined her.

'What about your clothes, Mumma?'

'Good idea.'

Larka stuffed some winter clothes, fresh stockings, and a few slips in her bag. Back in the kitchen, she unhooked their cloaks and settled Winter's over her shoulders.

'Time to visit our friend Hasting,' Larka said to Winter with a strained smile. 'It'll be an adventure.'

Winter's eyes lit up.

At the door, Larka paused. The note from Sam was still in the kitchen drawer. If the Black Cloaks found that ... Larka emptied all the letters from the drawer into her bag as a precaution.

'Let's go.'

Night had set in, and Inska still stood guard on the road, her body a shadowed figure nearby. A little further down, Larka could see the white glow of Skoa's feathers.

'You must go now, Inska,' Larka said as she reached the other woman. 'If the Black Cloaks find you here, they'll punish you too.'

'Where will you go?' Inska asked without removing her hood.

'I won't tell you. It's safer for all of us if nobody knows.'

Inska nodded and squeezed Larka's hand. 'Stay safe.' She ruffled Winter's hair and hurried over to Skoa.

'Time for us to be off,' Larka said as she watched Inska climb on the eagle's back. 'Are you ready for our adventure?'

Winter nodded, but her face was sombre.

'It's going to be okay, Winter.' Larka smiled down at her youngest daughter. 'We're together, and that's what counts.'

Larka took Winter's hand and pulled her into the field of barley opposite the house. They'd expect her to follow the road, either into the village or out into the scrub. What they didn't know was how many years Larka had spent on the run, standing beside her husband during his exile. At least, she hoped they hadn't worked out that particular family connection yet.

The journey to Essenné would take most of the night, depending on how tired Winter became. Crossing the Armansis could prove a challenge, but that was a problem for tomorrow. Whatever happened, she would see Winter safe to Gardar Mae. If Sam couldn't protect her and her daughter, she knew Hasting would.

19

JINDAR

Jessandra woke covered in sweat, bright slashes of sunlight streaming through the window. Large pools of light reflected off the polished wooden floor and dust motes swirled in disordered spirals. Jessandra squeezed her eyes shut against the light, trying to work some moisture into her mouth.

Feeling groggy and just as tired as when she'd lain down, Jessandra forced herself to rise. She wandered over to the window. The sun was high overhead and she rubbed at her eyes. Her vision blurred for a moment, and then cleared. Down in the street, people moved at a steady pace—shoppers, merchants, guards, and sailors all wore the loose clothing and straw hats she'd seen on her arrival. She took a deep breath. Everything was as it should be.

Further down, Jessandra noticed two people in dark cloaks moving from shop to shop. Her heart leapt to her throat. The other people in the street made a wide berth around the pair who moved through the town with their hoods up, despite summer's warmth. They were Black Cloaks without a doubt, even if she couldn't hear their gravelly voices or feel the cold disdain from this distance.

She panicked, looking around the room. Kyan owed her no loyalty, and if the Black Cloaks stopped in to ask after a young female with red-gold hair travelling alone, Jessandra's position would be forfeit. Glancing out of the window again, she watched their movements to determine how long she had before they reached the inn.

What she saw, though, only confused her. The Black Cloaks stopped at each shopfront, demanded the shopkeeper come to the door, then handed him or her a piece of thick parchment. Some of the shopkeepers looked frightened, others borderline hostile, but they all frowned over the paper for a moment before nodding. One by one, the vendors plastered the parchment to a window or door.

Jessandra was overcome with a vision of her face on the parchment with the word *WANTED* overhead. Would her father go to such lengths? There were no Black Cloaks in the castle, though some frequented the city. Unlike his cousin, Mascerab preferred to avoid the wizards where possible. His fear of the Black Cloaks was the only thing that made him seem human in Jessandra's eyes.

If he thought she was this far into the North Claw, then it could only mean one thing. They'd caught Siska, tortured her, dragged whatever information Skoa had shared out of her mind. Jessandra pressed a hand to her mouth. She'd been so desperate to save herself that she hadn't really considered the danger Siska was also in.

Guilt turned her stomach sour and she ran to the basin, dry-retching over the bowl. Once the fit passed, Jessandra wiped her mouth with the back of her hand and hurried back to the window. She didn't have time to be sick, to feel guilty about Siska's part in her escape.

The Black Cloaks were too close now for her to get away. She watched from above as Kyan poked her head through the doorway and received the parchment. From Jessandra's viewpoint, there was minimal interaction between the innkeeper and the wizards, but she trembled with fear. What would Kyan say when she saw the face of one of her patrons on the poster?

And then they were gone, moving off down the road, pausing in front of other shops, handing out more parchment. Jessandra hung her head and let out a relieved sigh. When she lifted her hands, her fingers trembled and she bunched them into fists.

She thought about braving the communal bathroom, but she was too curious about the contents of the parchment. Without bothering to check her clothes or her hair, she locked the door behind her and clattered down the stairs.

'Decided to join the land of the living?' Kyan asked as Jessandra traipsed into the common room. 'Are you hungry?'

Jessandra nodded, unsure how she should approach her question.

'Take a seat,' Kyan said, gesturing at the near-empty common room. 'I'll get you some stew.'

Only one other person occupied a seat, his head bent over a bowl. Jessandra didn't know if the common room was empty because it was too early for lunch or for dinner. She took a table on the other side of the room, flicking her thumbnails while she waited for Kyan to return. The room was all heavy wooden beams, whitewashed plaster, and sturdy furniture. The hearth was empty, and over the mantelpiece hung a thin sword, its hilt wrapped in gold thread. Jessandra pursed her lips at the feature. Perhaps the owner had been part of Reuben's army, or Esra's. Seeing the gold thread made her squirm. She should have been loyal to her family, but how could she be loyal to people who had kidnapped her sister, who were no doubt hunting her because of something she couldn't control?

'Here you go.' Kyan placed a bowl of thick stew in front of Jessandra, startling her. A plate of dark bread followed, a knob of butter resting on the edge of the plate.

'Thank you,' Jessandra said.

Kyan smiled and turned to go.

'Can I ask you something?' Jessandra asked.

'Can't guarantee I'll know the answer,' Kyan replied, 'but ask away.'

Jessandra cleared her throat. 'I saw the Black Cloaks in the street giving out some parchment. I was curious what it was about.'

Kyan studied her with narrowed eyes, and Jessandra's pulse raced. Without saying anything, the innkeeper turned and walked away. Jessandra's shoulders slumped. Maybe she could find another way of seeing the parchment. Some of the shop-keepers had plastered it to their windows, so perhaps she could sneak a look that way if she had to. She didn't feel ready to face the world just yet, especially knowing the Black Cloaks were out there, but she also knew she couldn't stay hidden in the inn forever.

Before Jessandra had a chance to do anything more than butter a slice of bread, Kyan was back at her table, parchment in hand.

'They're looking for someone,' she said, then turned on her heel and left again.

Jessandra lowered her bread back to the plate with a grimace. They were looking for her, of that much she was certain, but she picked up the parchment with her clean hand.

The word WANTED was spelled out in big letters across the top of the page, just as Jessandra had imagined. A talented illus-trator had drawn a greyscale likeness of the wanted person's face. Jessandra was surprised to see a young woman of a similar age to herself, yet the image looked nothing like her. There was a familiarity to the woman's features, but the dark hair, wide cheekbones, and freckles were too dissimilar to Jessandra's face for the poster to be about her.

Beneath the image was a short paragraph of text describing

the woman, a waterkin, and her dangerous criminal history. She'd committed another great crime, the details curiously vague, and the Black Cloaks were hunting her to seek justice. Jessandra snorted into her stew. Justice.

The woman's face before her was so young, Jessandra had a hard time imagining how she'd become such a dangerous criminal during her short life, while also managing to evade the Black Cloaks. Something was suspicious about it, but Jessandra found she didn't care. It wasn't her face on the poster, nor her crime of running away from her future described in the text. She pushed the parchment to one side and tucked into her meal.

Afterwards, Jessandra felt warm and sleepy again. She searched for Kyan, finding her gossiping with the kitchen staff.

'What are you doing back here?' Kyan asked when she noticed Jessandra standing in the doorway.

'I wondered if I could have some water heated for a bath?'

Kyan nodded, her lips closed tight, and directed one of the maids to the task.

'The stew was delicious,' Jessandra added, half to Kyan and half to the cook. 'Thank you.'

The cook gave her a toothy grin, but Kyan regarded her suspiciously.

'You don't know her, do you?' she asked just as Jessandra was about to head upstairs.

'Who?'

'The girl in the image,' Kyan said. 'On the poster.'

Jessandra shook her head. 'I've never seen her in my life.'

'Why did you want to look at it?'

Thinking on her feet had never been something Jessandra was good at, so she shrugged and aimed for a look of nonchalance as she tried to think of a clever answer.

'I just didn't expect to see Black Cloaks in Jindar, let alone Black Cloaks handing out posters. It seemed like odd behaviour and I …' She shrugged again. 'I was just curious.'

The skin around Kyan's eyes tightened for a moment, and then she laughed. 'You are a strange one. What did you say your name was?'

Jessandra's eyes darted around the room. She couldn't give her own name; anyone who knew anything about Heredour's royals would know who she was immediately.

'My name?' she squeaked, berating herself internally. Why hadn't she spent all that time on Skoa's back coming up with a new name? 'My name's Siska. Siska skykin.' The name rolled off her tongue naturally, but the sound of it made her feel ill.

'Well, Siska, you're a funny creature, but I like you.' Kyan smiled. 'Go on, Merilee will have your bath nearly ready.'

Jessandra tried to smile back, but it felt false and uncomfortable, so she nodded at Kyan and the cook. As she climbed each flight of stairs, she made a promise to spend her time in the bath coming up with an alter ego so that she wouldn't be caught out again. She had no idea how long she'd need to stay in Jindar, and eventually she'd have to leave the inn. Better to have a false identity ready to go.

'Siska,' she said to herself as she reached the landing. 'My name is Siska.'

2 0

WATERFALL CITY

A BURLY GUARD stood beside his skinnier, shrewd-eyed counterpart at the door to Reuben's personal quarters. Both men dipped their heads and stood aside as Mortius reached them.

Mortius paused before the door and glanced at the guards, hoping to read something in their eyes about the king's state of mind. The face of the wide-set guard gave nothing away as he focused on some point in the distance. The eyes of the skinny guard narrowed a little as he regarded Mortius.

With a sigh, Mortius leaned against the heavy doors. Inside was a small sitting room, the antechamber to Reuben's office. Small, luxurious couches lined the walls, all red velvet and gold linings. Portraits of long-dead high kings hung on the walls between paintings of sweeping landscapes from various regions.

Mortius averted his eyes from the painting of Esra, Reuben's father. The guilt that plagued him in the middle of the night was only made worse by seeing Esra's visage.

A painting showing the sharp spike of Marash Mountain caught Mortius' eye near the door to the study and he took a deep breath. The image of the mountain stirred something deep within him. He couldn't recall the last time he'd made his pilgrimage to the sacred peak. Perhaps he could work out a way to incorporate Marash into his itinerary.

Mortius turned the ornate handle of the door and pushed his way into the high king's office. Reuben sat hunched over the simple but elegant desk he'd inherited from his father.

One arm moved furiously back and forth over a piece of parchment. The desk was littered with scrolls and maps and scrunched-up notes. A luxurious breakfast lay untouched atop a stack of documents and several tall-backed armchairs were spread in a semicircle in front of the desk. The Black Cloaks had been here, whether earlier today or yesterday. Mortius hadn't been in the office for several days.

'Your Grace,' he said.

Reuben jolted upright and peered at Mortius as though he didn't recognise him. The bleary amber eyes that greeted him spoke of another night spent without sleep, though the colour of his irises was nearly obscured by the dark ring. Reuben gestured for Mortius to sit in one of the chairs and pushed a scrap of parchment towards him. The high king scrubbed at his eyes before hunching over his writing once more.

The greasy eggs and cold mutton on the desk made Mortius' stomach curl. He picked up the parchment and scanned the words before him, written in the delicate, curling hand of a Trinian wordsmith. With a sigh, he let the paper fall back to the desk.

Another despairing note from another desperate region. The letter explained that on top of the problems they were experiencing with the fish in the Satin River, the sea trawlers were finding half their catch dead before it landed in their boats.

'Dire.'

Mortius nodded, his mouth a thin line.

'Do they do this because they hate me?' Reuben's words were hard to make out through his clenched teeth.

'Of course not, Your Grace,' Mortius said, adopting his most supplicating tone. 'They do the best they can, but times are hard.'

'Times are hard,' Reuben said with a snort, his brows furrowing together. 'Not for Marbin, at least, not in terms of crop production.'

Mortius shrugged. 'Aside from his children, Mascerab has led his people from strength to strength.'

'And he shares my blood,' Reuben murmured. 'How could the two girls be such disappointments?'

'The other rulers don't mean to disappoint, Your Grace.'

Reuben stood suddenly, scattering the papers along the table. The skittering sound was an odd comfort to Mortius. Reuben's rage was familiar, safe, in its own way. The anger had always been with him, before the madness set in, before the paranoia, before everything fell apart.

'Yet they do so disappoint me.' The high king's voice was soft, little more than a hiss. 'Even Mascerab. First child a Kaiãho, the second a runaway.' Reuben shook his head.

'You saw my note from the other day?' he continued. 'I've sent a company up to Millen to aid in the search.'

'A wise decision.'

'I sent a Black Cloak with them. They'll be able to advise if Mascerab is being truthful about the state of Marbin's produce.'

'You doubt his character?' Mortius asked, his tone betraying his surprise. Not only were Reuben and Mascerab cousins, the region hadn't missed a single payment of the king's bounty since Reuben had taken the throne.

Reuben threw his arms in the air. 'Everything is in disarray, Mortius! How can I know who to trust anymore?'

Mortius stayed silent.

'The regions are all claiming something's wrong with the

land, or the water, or the animals. Our best ruler now has no heirs, because even if they find Jessandra, how could we allow her to rule? There's a star-caller still somehow evading Dyafirah and his lot. And all these misers in my court, and the court of all the other rulers, demanding to know what's happened to their children. They're being re-educated, the same as they have been the past eleven years! What do they expect from me? I'm no god!'

Mortius shrugged, keeping his dissenting thoughts to himself.

'How am I supposed to get the measure of these rulers, of the regions? What if it's worse out there in Triné, Lashameg, Condor?' Reuben gnashed his teeth together. 'What if it's not as bad as they say? How will I ever know?'

Mortius knew Reuben was spiralling again, that he'd soon descend into a manic state. Hopefully his proposal would slow the king's decline.

'I have a suggestion for that, Majesty,' Mortius said.

Reuben spun on his heel, his eyes wide, his hands buried deep in his hair.

'You say that you don't know who to trust anymore.' Mortius swallowed. 'Do you still trust me?'

It was a calculated risk. Reuben was just as likely to deny Mortius' loyalty off a whim. Instead, he glared at Mortius as if he were a fool.

'Trust you?' Reuben said. 'You're perhaps the only one I trust. You and Juro. Maybe Dyafirah, though he infuriates me.'

Mortius tried not to let his relief show on his face.

'Let me travel to the regions, High King. Let me hold the rulers to account, and let me see with my own eyes the problems they describe.'

Reuben's eyebrows disappeared beneath his hair. Leaving the city wasn't an idea that would have ever occurred to him as an option, and it certainly wasn't wise for him to leave. Mortius, on the other hand, was in the perfect position as a trusted adviser to Reuben while also being a shrewd observer. There was no one better for the job, and they both knew it.

'Where would you go?' Reuben eased himself back into his chair. Some of the wild light in his eyes had dimmed, though Mortius could still see his pulse dancing in his neck.

'I'd start in Triné first. We have an old friend in Haba Sha who might be able to shed some insight.'

Beren.

Reuben nodded with a small grimace.

'Then up to Shebedie to speak with the emperor, though I don't expect I'll get anything useful from him.'

'The grand prince, though?'

'Yes,' Mortius agreed. 'I can hold the grand prince to account.'

The emperor was old and frail, a leader more in name than anything else these days.

'From Shebedie, I plan to head through the back passes to Meisha Rony and up into Condor from there. Straight to Hybra, to see their king.'

'Yes, no point stopping at any of the little towns.'

'I might, just to see the wood mills.'

They had another old friend, Rainer, hiding up in the hills of Condor, not that Mortius wanted to remind Reuben of that particular dissenter.

'From there I thought it best to take the northern coast road to Maidie, then inland to Hincka to see King Vysidia. That way I could see how the fishing towns along the coast fare before I visit the plantations and livestock farmers.'

'You would certainly get the measure of these regions,' Reuben said, chewing his lip as he nodded his head. 'What about Marbin?'

'You've sent a Black Cloak to determine the truth, so there's no real need for me to go there. But if you need me to, I can travel to Millen once I return from Hincka.'

He'd never really planned to go to Marbin. There were only three people he needed to speak to.

Beren.

Rainer.

Kali.

There was a small chance Kali was somewhere in Marbin, but he'd had no leads on her whereabouts for a good two decades. She certainly didn't want to be found. The other two, though, would be easy to find. The question was whether they'd be easy to convince.

'What will I do without you?' Reuben asked. His voice was soft, his gaze lost on some point past the desk.

'You have Juro and the council for all the governing things. And the queen is still here.'

Reuben made a noncommittal noise. Terrinien was timid, boring, and barren. He couldn't have picked a worse woman to make the Queen of Heredour. She was a moonkin, though, and pliable, and they hadn't known she'd bear no children when the marriage was arranged.

'I wish Frieda was here,' Reuben murmured, more to himself than to Mortius. This was the worst of his changeable moods. The depth of his sadness was unbearable and made Mortius question whether he was doing the right thing by trying to undermine him.

Mortius sighed. 'So do I, Reuben, so do I.'

21

THE NORTH OCEAN

TUCKED AWAY in the officer's cabin, Wave and Strath sat in a deep discussion. The bowls they'd reused to eat the midday meal—soft jerky and hard cheese from Strath's full backpack and hunks of dark bread from Siska's stash—were stacked on the desk. Wave sat cross-legged on the single bed, her elbows resting on her knees as she leaned forward. Opposite her, Strath leaned back into the lone chair, nodding.

'So you think waterkin and sunkin are inherently connected to the wizards because of this?' Wave asked, her brows furrowed so deeply that she felt an ache growing above the bridge of her nose.

'We've hypothesised that either the wizards are able to access Lerinial's and Jesma's powers in addition to their magic, which would explain their incredible strength.' Strath tucked one leg under the other and shifted his weight around. 'Or their magic is actually a fusion of water and sun power.'

Wave shook her head, her mind reeling. They'd been discussing philosophy and religion all afternoon, Strath revealing things about Heredour's history that made Wave feel as if she was normal for thinking things weren't quite right in their world.

If Wave had known all the things Strath had shared in just the last few hours, it would have made her feel more sane while she was stuck in Bindock. She couldn't assume X'olea knew all of it, but surely he'd known more than he ever let on, and it made her angry. Strath had shared that the library in Sharvel, a building made of white marble at the heart of their hidden town, held the biggest collection of ancient texts that were otherwise banned, burned, or lost.

'I've only seen Black Cloaks from a distance,' Wave said, trying to pull her jumbled thoughts into something that resembled order. 'But my mother has filled me with stories of the things that they can do, the ways their magic functions differently from our power.'

'She was afraid of them?'

Wave shrugged. 'Isn't everyone?'

'Most mothers tell their children scary stories of the Black Cloaks to make them do their chores or go to bed on time.' Strath tilted his head to one side. 'But from what you've told me, it seems like your mother knows intimately the power and danger of the wizards.'

'She's always been very closed about our father. I know we travelled a lot when we were younger, before Winter was born. He was around then, I think.'

A half-forgotten memory surfaced in her mind's eye as she spoke. Wave, in a smaller body, sitting on a big, strong knee, a book open in front of her. Siska, no more than seven, nestled on the ground below Wave. Siska, adoration in her eyes as she looked past Wave. A resonant voice, warm like honey, reading from the book. The feeling of safety and support so strong that Wave was sure she'd never need to be afraid. She turned to look up, following Siska's gaze. A body came into view, strong arms covered in soft, golden hair holding her tight. Her eyes lifted, the face of her father just out of sight. Her vision blurred, and she blinked.

'Wave?'

Strath's voice brought her back to the present. The bed, the cabin, the ship travelling over the sea.

'Sorry.'

'It's okay.' Strath smiled at her, his grin already as comforting to Wave as X'olea's face had been. 'Were you thinking about him?'

Wave nodded. 'I could almost see his face, but my memory always blurs before I can recall it. It seems so important, but I can never visualise him. Shouldn't we remember the faces of our parents?'

Strath's gaze dropped to the end of the bed, his smile slipping. It was the first time he'd looked away from her throughout their hours-long discussion.

'Strath?'

'Are you angry at him?' Strath asked, his fingers fiddling with the lace of his boot. 'For leaving you?'

'Sometimes I get angry that he left our mother to raise us alone in such an isolated place.' She hadn't told him exactly where she came from. Five years of lying to the people of Bindock about her home and her family hadn't worn off. 'I'm sure he had a good reason. Mother always maintained that he left to keep us safe, and I have to believe her in that.'

'I think it's often hard to understand our parents' motivations.'

Wave thought about all the strict ways Larka had raised her. When Wave had been called by Lerinial, she'd known that the lies and secrecy her mother forced her to repeat were to keep her safe. Travelling through Esseñe on her way to Bindock, Wave had seen the black curtains in some of the houses. That was when she really understood her mother's motivations. Her father's, though? Everything about him was unknown to her.

Larka had never shared his kin, where he was from, who his family was, or where they'd met. Their story was lost to Wave.

'I guess so,' Wave said. 'What about your parents?'

Strath finally lifted his gaze to her. His expression was sombre, the first time she'd seen a darkness linger over his features. Even his bright hazel eyes were muted, the skin around them tightening.

'I like to believe that they were trying their best to protect us.' He pursed his lips. 'But I also think they were misguided.'

'What happened?'

Throughout their many conversations over the course of the day, Strath had managed to avoid talking about his family and his kin in numerous clever ways. The more he'd shared about his hometown, Sharvel, the more comfortable Wave felt about sharing some of her life with him, though she hadn't told him about Henny, or that she should be Kaiãho. She definitely couldn't tell him about the star. Some secrets were better left unspoken.

Taking a deep breath, Strath clasped his hands together. Wave thought he was going to bypass the question again, change the topic to something so interesting that she got side-tracked.

'My brother, Ernad, was one of the first Kaiãho.'

Wave's eyes widened.

'We had wealth and standing in the community, but my parents changed after Ernad was taken by the Black Cloaks. It broke them. My father, a waterkin, was the Maire of Haba Sha, but they left the Triné and began travelling, looking for Buduwai. I guess they thought they could just take Ernad back.'

Strath sighed. 'Everyone now knows the youth don't come back from Buduwai, but the law was in its infancy then, and nobody really knew what was going to happen.' He untucked his foot and leaned forward on his knees. 'In their travels, they learned about Sharvel and thought that the people there might know where Buduwai is. It was perfect for my disenfranchised parents, so we settled in Sharvel for a few years. I went to school there, made friends there. But my parents were never satisfied.'

'They were still looking for Ernad?'

'Sometimes they left Sharvel for months at a time,' Strath said.

'What about you?'

Strath shrugged. 'Sharvel had become my home by then. Its people were my family. They left me in the care of one of the elders when they went out searching. Much of what I know about Heredour is because of her.'

'But they always came back for you?' Wave asked.

'They did, but they were never the same. The longer that Ernad was gone, the hollower they seemed to become. They were obsessed with finding him, and they pushed everything else and everyone else away. Including me.'

'Where are they now?'

Strath had told her how he often spent time away from Sharvel every year to see what was going on in the rest of Heredour. Wave guessed that his parents were still travelling too, still seeking their lost son, forgetting the one they had left.

'They were fanatical, opposing the Black Cloaks and the high ling at every possible turn, inciting riots and upheaval wherever they set foot. They were angry, but then they became maniacal, thinking they could get the people of Heredour to rise up and stand against the crown.' Strath hung his head, looking at the floor. 'One time, when they'd come back to Sharvel to share news of the country and what they'd learned, the Black Cloaks came. They were looking for someone else, the high king's exiled brother, but they found my parents instead.'

Silence fell over the pair of them. Wave didn't know what to say. The Black Cloaks must have taken Strath's parents. If they'd been out in the nation trying to turn Heredourians against the high king, the Law of Kaiāho, and the Black Cloaks, there was no way the wizards wouldn't hold them to account.

'How old were you?' Wave asked, unable to bear the crushing silence any longer.

'A teenager, maybe thirteen?'

'Have you seen them since?'

Strath lifted his gaze, looking up at Wave from beneath thick, curling lashes. He shook his head.

'I've lost everyone to the Black Cloaks, and although I can fairly place some of the blame on my parents' shoulders, if it wasn't for the law, I'd still have my family.'

The pain in Strath's voice was an echo of what Wave's life could have been.

'I don't understand the pain of your loss,' she murmured, 'but it feels like my family has avoided what yours has gone through.'

'What do you mean?' Strath pushed his weight off his knees and sat upright. The grief that had overtaken his visage while he spoke of his family passed, though his face was still sombre.

'I've never told anyone.' Wave took a deep breath. 'From all we've spoken about, I can see that you won't vilify me.'

The floor lurched beneath them. Strath raised his eyebrows at her as he adjusted himself on the chair.

'I should have been Kaiāho,' she whispered, as if saying it quietly might stop the truth of it being known to the world. 'My sister and I both.'

'How?' Strath's eyes were wide. 'How did you escape it?'

Wave shrugged. 'My sister is twenty-two. The law was still in its infancy. We were already in the Plains by then, in a tiny village, and the law wasn't concerned with the lowkin then.'

'Ernad would have been twenty-two by now,' Strath said with a nod. 'They took him because my father was maire, even though they were middlekin. Had to make a statement to those in power.'

'When it was my turn,' Wave continued, 'we didn't participate in the formal ceremony. Because we were so remote, our village so small, nobody noticed. Mother had been indoctrinating me with how to lie to people for years. I think she knew I would be called higher than her.'

'She was lowkin?' Strath asked.

Wave nodded. 'Earthkin. My sister is skykin, and a powerful one at that.' She didn't need to remind him. He'd nearly fallen out of his chair when she'd told him about Siska's friendship with Skoa. 'We were raised in the Plains. I left in the middle of the night, made my way to Essenné and then up to Bindock, where I felt Lerinial calling me. I've been pretending that I'm from a waterkin family in Essenné for the last five years. Mother told the villagers that I'd been called in the middle of the night by Ferengün and that I'd gone to Condor to study their trees.'

The law had no problems with lowkin being called higher than their parents, so long as they remained lowkin. A child of an earthkin could be called by Ferengün or Neffren and nobody would even notice. But if the child of a lowkin was called by Lerinial, Setunil, or gods forbid, one of the highkin gods, then they would be snatched away by the Black Cloaks.

'I know it probably makes you feel worse, that we escaped when your brother was taken, your parents too.' Wave gripped the edges of the bed as the ship heaved again.

'Quite the opposite, actually,' Strath said, attempting a small smile. 'Your story gives me hope. Nothing is random in this world, Wave, and the fact that you and your sister were never named Kaiäho says something.'

'What does it say?'

'I don't know yet,' Strath said. The bowls slid from the desk with another lurch and Strath caught them. 'But if you're both as powerful as you say, then there's a reason Heredour didn't lose you to Buduwai.'

'You make it sound like we've got something important to do,' Wave said. 'My ... sickness won't let me do anything.'

'That's why you have to come to Sharvel with me,' he said, his grin widening again. The happy, familiar Strath was returning. 'We can take a room in an inn for the night, then head south in the morning. Separate rooms!' he added with a laugh at Wave's scandalised face.

'Will I have a better chance of getting to Veija-Mens from Sharvel?'

'Absolutely. You'll be halfway to Kochee.'

'You have to swear on everything you hold dear that you won't touch me,' Wave said in a small voice.

'I would never,' Strath breathed, his mouth open in shock. 'I'm not like that.'

'No!' Wave said with a sad laugh. 'No, I mean you can't touch me at all. Don't grab my hand, don't touch my shoulder to show me something, don't pass me food if we might brush fingers.'

'I wish you'd tell me what plagues you,' Strath said, but raised his hands in supplication at her glare. 'I swear, on all the gods from Eritogone to Jesma, and on the truth that rests in my heart, that I will not touch you in any way.'

Wave nodded with a grim smile. 'Okay. I'll come to Sharvel with you.'

Someone knocked on the door, startling both of them.

'Come in,' Wave said.

The captain peeked his head through the gap, giving a surprised look at Strath.

'Well, at least I only have to tell you once,' he said. 'We're pulling into the port of Jindar, and right on dusk, as I promised your friend.' He inclined his head at Wave. 'Most of the crew will leave before you, if you want to wait down here.'

'Thank you,' Wave said.

The door closed with a click.

'I better go and organise my stuff,' Strath said. 'I'll meet you up on deck?'

'To Sharvel,' Wave said with a nod, looking around the room at her meagre belongings.

Strath grinned. 'To Sharvel.'

22

JINDAR

Dusk came quickly to Jindar, nestled as deeply as it was in the North Claw mountains. Jessandra moved through the streets, sticking to the shadowed sides of the buildings, her hood drawn up over her hair.

She'd spent most of the day in the inn, enjoying a long bath in the surprisingly empty bathing room as she came up with a backstory for her new persona. The risk of confronting a Black Cloak in the daylight kept her confined, but as the light faded, Jessandra found her curiosity to explore was in itch she could no longer ignore.

From her vantage point on the third floor, she'd noticed that most of Jindar's people had dark hair and dark features, so she kept her hood up as she wandered through the town. Her hair would stand out here and that was the last thing she wanted. The shopkeepers were closing up and the taverns were full of the clattering sounds of a busy evening. Her eyes fell to the poster and the strangely familiar face over and over again.

There was nothing in particular that she was looking for. She'd been stuck in Millen her whole life, and an adventure for her had been hunting in the forests, or the once-a-year trip her family made to Essenné. In contrast, Jindar was a strange town, full of new faces, different shops, and the feeling of excitement. Even the fear of the Black Cloaks couldn't quell her curiosity.

As the last rays of light shot out over the western mountain range, Jessandra found herself down near the docks. The water was calm in the bay, but she could see waves crashing in the distance. There was a strange taste to the air—a tang of salty water, of seaweed, and perhaps the ocean scent of the day's catch.

'Need some dinner, miss?' a voice called out to her.

Down along the wooden slats of the dock was a collection of tiny huts. Jessandra made her way over to them and found a selection of food merchants. One sold fresh fish, another cooked, and yet another sold a selection of herbal liquors Jessandra had never heard of.

'The freshest fish you'll ever taste, miss!' the hawker selling cooked fish cried. 'The best meal you'll have all day.'

Jessandra strode up to the shack. 'How much for a piece?' she asked.

The man smiled wide, the gaps between his few teeth startling Jessandra. He looked clean enough, though, with dark curly hair, mended clothes, and a few golden hoops in each ear. There was no tattoo on his right wrist, and his eyes were the soft brown of an animalkin. He was the butcher, then, not the fisherman.

'For you, my lady, only a silver a piece.'

She heard the guffaw of the other hawkers and glared at the man. 'A silver? I could buy half of this stall with a silver.' She gestured at the man beside them selling fresh fish.

'Oh, my lady,' he crooned. 'You're right, but you look like a lady of such wealth that you could spare a silver for the likes of me.'

'I have little enough for myself, man,' she retorted. 'I'll give you a copper.'

'A copper!' he spluttered. 'A copper won't cover the oil alone!'

'Then I guess I'll go hungry,' Jessandra said, squaring her shoulders. If there was anything she'd learned from her father, it was how to strike a good bargain. The thought of him caused a bubble of anger to develop in her chest.

'Perhaps I can give you a grilled piece for the price of a copper,' the man conceded. 'Rubbed in some fresh herbs, no oil, ya see?'

'That sounds excellent,' Jessandra said through clenched teeth.

The hawker set to frying her fish and she wandered away, trying to let her anger subside. It wasn't the seller's fault that her father was a monster. She focused on the calming waters, watching as a ship pulled into port. This boat was older than most of the vessels in Jindar's bay, its hull a little more weathered than the ships it angled between. Jessandra wondered where it had come from, why it was so battered, but her attention soon meandered back over the dark, glistening sea.

'Your meal's ready, miss!' the hawker cried.

If he begrudged her haggling, it didn't show in his voice, or his face when she returned to the stand. A piece of white-fleshed fish, coated in a variety of nondescript herbs, lay on a few layers of butcher's paper.

'Thank you,' she said, laying a copper on the bench. 'I'm sure it'll be delicious.'

The man snatched the coin and shrank back into his shack, watching her from beneath half-lidded eyes. Fear was a common enemy, she realised as she wandered off the pier and up the street leading from the dock. She passed several closed shops, ignoring the posters in each of their windows. A few wooden seats had been placed along the street, and she sat down, still enjoying the view of the ocean. The moon was rising, casting a milky-orange glow over the water as Jessandra pulled the flesh apart with her fingers.

The hawker hadn't lied. There was nothing wrong with the food Kyan served, but this was without a doubt the best meal she'd had all day. The fish still had the taste of the ocean in it. None of the river fish they ate in Millen could compare. Jessandra leaned against the backrest and savoured each bite as she watched the moon rise. There were few people around to notice her or disturb her peace, so she pushed her hood back, enjoying the feeling of the cool sea breeze on her face.

She'd just licked her fingers clean when a group of sailors came up from the docks, shouting and laughing to one another. They called to her as they passed, inviting her to drink with them, crying loudly over her beauty, and making lewd jokes among themselves. Jessandra ignored them, keeping her gaze focused on the ocean until they were gone. She released her breath, hoping they hadn't noticed the colour rising in her cheeks.

More people were moving up the street from the docks, this time a young man and woman. As they neared, Jessandra thought they probably weren't much older than herself. Perhaps they were passengers from the ship that had arrived earlier.

The pair stopped nearby, staring at the baker's shopfront. They broke into an argument, the woman's voice high-pitched and panicked, the man's lower, softer. Jessandra squinted her eyes in the near-dark. There was something familiar about the girl's face.

The argument continued in hushed tones, and Jessandra could tell that the woman was in a state of distress. The man tried to comfort her, though he never touched her. When the woman turned to look up the street, her eyes wild, Jessandra realised why she recognised her face.

She glanced up and down the street. The inns and taverns were gathered in the centre of town, so the streets surrounding the dock were quiet. Without thinking, Jessandra rose and trotted over to the couple.

'Excuse me?' she said as she neared them.

The woman took several steps back, her chin trembling. The man stood in front of her, protecting her even though it was obvious there was something strained about their relationship.

'Can I help you?' the man asked, his voice neutral as he regarded Jessandra.

'I just wanted you to know that you should get out of town.' She spoke around the man, trying to speak directly to the woman. 'The Black Cloaks have been here today, handing out posters with your face on them.'

The woman nodded and gestured to the shop beside them. Jessandra didn't need to turn to know there was a poster in the window.

'You should be able to get through the town,' she added. 'I've been out this evening and I haven't seen them anywhere.'

The man's eyes narrowed.

'Why are you helping me?' the woman asked, frowning at Jessandra.

The question hadn't even occurred to her. Why was she helping this woman, warning her of the Black Cloaks' presence in Jindar?

'I … uh,' Jessandra began, but found her cleverly devised backstory had disappeared from her mind. 'I just—I wouldn't want to be caught by them.'

The man nodded as if he understood. 'What's your name, kind soul?'

'Siska,' she answered, full of confidence. While she was in the bath, she'd decided it was safer to stick as close to the truth as possible. There'd be less risk of a mistake that way.

The woman's eyes widened. 'Siska?' she repeated.

Jessandra nodded, suddenly unsure of herself.

'No,' the woman said. 'You're not. I know who you are.' She pointed at Jessandra's hair.

'I'm Siska,' Jessandra repeated a little louder, as if more volume would make it true.

'No, you're not. You're Jessandra.'

Jessandra's heart skipped a beat. She opened her mouth to deny it, but her mind was blank. Not even one whole day had passed in Jindar and she'd already been discovered. What idiocy had made her come and talk to these people?

'I know you are, because Siska is my sister.'

'Wave?' Jessandra said, her breath coming out in short, sharp bursts.

'You know her?' the man asked the woman.

Wave shook her head. 'Siska is her handmaiden.'

'Stop!' Jessandra cried.

'I know what happened,' Wave said, her eyes pleading with Jessandra. 'I know you ran. I saw Siska. She was looking for you, but she found me instead.'

The man looked between them with one eyebrow raised.

'I'm glad you two know each other, but we really need to go,' he said. 'Wave can't stay in Jindar.'

'You're right,' Jessandra agreed. 'But where are you going to go?'

'Strath is taking me to his home,' Wave said, earning a glare from the man, Strath. 'The Black Cloaks never go there.'

Jessandra's eyes widened. A place free from Black Cloaks? It couldn't be true.

'You should come with us,' Wave said, glancing up and down the street as if she expected a Black Cloak to appear out of nowhere.

'What?' Jessandra and Strath said at the same time.

'She's in a similar position to me,' Wave said to Strath. 'She needs to stay free of them.'

Strath studied Jessandra, his head tilted to one side.

'Come with us,' Wave said. 'Siska wanted to help you, but she can't help you if the Black Cloaks are already in Jindar. What happens when they start looking for you instead of me?'

Jessandra nodded. She'd been hoping that some opportunity would present itself so she knew what steps to take next. And here was Wave, the supposed hardened criminal, her handmaiden's sister, asking her to follow her to a place of safety.

'Yes,' Jessandra said. 'I want to. But my things are back at the inn.'

Strath shook his head. 'We can't risk it.'

'I haven't paid for my room either,' Jessandra added. Her clothes were one thing, but she didn't think she could deal with the guilt of not paying her dues, of Kyan thinking poorly of her. 'I have to go back.'

'You know Jindar, Strath,' Wave said, her eyes wide, pleading. 'Is there somewhere we can meet?'

Strath took a deep breath. A muscle in his jaw popped as he ground his teeth.

'Fine,' he said. 'There's an old warehouse at the south end of town, on the road out to the farmsteads.'

Jessandra pushed her lips from side to side.

'Do you know the road that heads west from the council building?'

'Yes,' Jessandra said. She'd spent some time studying the council building from the shadows, watching for any sign of other highkin.

'Follow that until the end. At the junction, take the road heading south. You'll see the warehouse; it's been abandoned for so long it looks like it's melting.'

Jessandra nodded. 'I won't be long.'

'Go,' Wave said. 'We'll see you soon.'

There was a promise in her voice, the kind of hope only a friend offered. Jessandra's heart expanded. Since Lenta had been exiled, or sent to Buduwai, as she now knew, she'd felt alone in her trials. Even though Jessandra had no idea why the Black Cloaks were after Wave, her immediate acceptance of Jessandra's plight and her offer of help was the closest thing she'd felt to friendship since she'd lost her sister.

As she climbed the streets of Jindar, her eyes stung with unshed tears. She brushed them aside roughly. This was no time for tears. Even though Strath was reluctant to include her, Wave had offered to take her to safety. She wasn't going to miss this opportunity the gods had aligned for her.

Back at the inn, she hurried past the common room. Kyan was too busy serving patrons to notice Jessandra. She stuffed her belongings back in the bag, including the coin purse and Lenta's letter. After looking around the room and peering under the bed, Jessandra decided she had everything and she ran down the stairs.

Kyan was still serving when Jessandra arrived back at the bar, and she tapped her foot impatiently. Another serving girl came up to her, but when Jessandra explained she needed to pay for her room, the girl shrugged and told her to wait.

'Leaving so soon?' Kyan said from behind Jessandra.

'Yes,' she replied without turning. 'And in a bit of a hurry.'

'All right, milady,' Kyan said with mock respect. She pushed a slip of parchment across the bar to Jessandra. 'Your room for the night.'

Jessandra portioned out the correct coins from her purse and pushed them towards Kyan. 'Thank you for your hospitality.'

'Any time, Siska,' Kyan said with a lopsided smile. 'You're mighty strange, but you're welcome any time you need a place to rest your head.'

Jessandra dipped her head and slid an extra copper over the bar. Kyan's smile widened, and Jessandra hurried out the door and into the street. No matter Kyan's unusual manners, Jessandra had appreciated the fact that a young woman had been running the Merchant's Wife. The last thing she'd needed was a suspicious man asking too many questions or looking at her the wrong way.

Sliding through the darkness, Jessandra followed the streets she remembered until she arrived at the council building. She breathed a sigh of relief and took the street running west. The street ended, just as Strath had explained, and she turned south.

The buildings here were run-down compared to the rest of Jindar. A corner sagged here, a roof was missing shingles there. Jessandra ignored them all, looking for the collapsing warehouse that hid Wave and Strath.

'Siska?' a gravelly voice called from behind her.

Jessandra's heart leapt to her throat and she kept walking, glad her hood was up. No human man had a voice like sandpaper on metal.

Up ahead she could see a large building, each corner appearing to sink into the street around it. The warehouse.

'Siska skykin?' the voice called again.

Jessandra glanced behind her and nearly cried out. A whole day in Jindar without running into the Black Cloaks, and here they were at the moment she was about to meet up with Wave, someone they wanted even more than her. Jessandra turned her face forward, her lips trembling.

Two figures appeared from the shadows of the warehouse in front of her. In the darkness, Jessandra could just make out Strath's brown curls.

'Go!' Jessandra hissed at them, but they were too far away to hear her.

Hurried footsteps gathered speed behind her.

'Go!' she shouted.

This time, they reacted. Whether they'd heard her, or they'd seen the Black Cloaks following her, both figures turned and ran up the street.

'Stop!' a Black Cloak cried.

Not stopping to think, Jessandra lifted her cloak and ran. Her feet pounded on the cobblestones; her heart pounded in her chest.

Indistinct, guttural words rose from behind her, and she knew they were casting their magic.

'Watch out!' she called to the figures in front of her.

The corner of a building beside her exploded, chunks of stone and mortar falling around her. Jessandra dodged as best she could. A large chunk hit her shoulder and she stumbled, crying out wordlessly.

23

JINDAR

A BUILDING EXPLODED around Wave and Strath. Behind them, Jessandra cried out. Wave stopped, turning back to the other woman.

'No!' Strath cried.

Wave strode back to where Jessandra was finding her feet, nursing her shoulder with one hand. Two Black Cloaks streamed up the street behind them. Without even closing her eyes, Wave could sense all of the water sources around them. Bores, wells, and the ocean further away all suited her purpose, so she summoned them towards her. The water swirled above her head. She shot it at the Black Cloaks in a powerful stream until they were forced backwards.

'Come on!' Wave shouted at Jessandra.

They ran, the cries of the Black Cloaks following them.

'Stop, star-caller!'

'Star-caller! Star-caller!'

The Black Cloaks recovered quickly from her attack. Buildings exploded around them as they ran. Ahead of her, Strath spread his hands wide and pushed them down. The ground behind them shifted and erupted in small waves, the cobble-stones shattering. There were no cries after that.

They didn't stop running though, even after they were out of town. The road turned to dirt, the shops gone. Fields surrounded them and the soft glow of farmsteads were visible in the distance, like little stars in the night sky.

'Can we stop?' Jessandra shouted from behind. She sounded like she was in pain.

'Not yet,' Strath called back.

Wave's heart beat painfully in her chest. Within moments, they heard shouts from the town, and Strath led them into a field of potatoes. The plants offered no cover, but the field provided an easy path to the foothills nearby.

If they could make it into the hills, Strath could hide them among the mountains. That's what they'd argued about when they first arrived in Jindar. He'd said that he was strongest in Ferengün's power, and although she wanted to question what exactly he'd meant by *strongest*, she trusted him to protect them in the forest.

'Stop, star-caller!' a voice called from the main road, all sandpaper and knives dragged across crockery. 'Star-caller!'

'Strath!' Wave cried as the potatoes exploded around them.

He stopped, spinning on his heel to face the Black Cloaks. A wall of earth lifted behind them, blocking them temporarily.

'Run!' he screamed.

The wall crumbled against the Black Cloaks' attacks. Then they were in the hills, calves straining against the climb.

Strath caught up to them. 'I can't do much more,' he said, his breath coming in sharp bursts.

Earth exploded around them. They stumbled as the whole hill shook.

'Get us to the forest, Wave,' Strath said, his voice rasping from his throat. 'I can hide us there.'

Wave didn't want to stop running, didn't want to face her

enemies again, but she could see Strath's energy was spent. She stopped before they reached the top of the hill.

The Black Cloaks were still some distance away, making their way surprisingly slowly through the torn-up potato fields. Wave realised it was because they didn't care. They were so confident in their ability to capture her that they strode through the fields as if they had all the time in the world.

Wave drew a deep, forceful breath through her nostrils. There was a lot more water for her to access out here. All the farms had large dams fed by inlets coming down from the mountains.

She gathered them up, combining all the water sources together above her. The jet she'd used last time hadn't done enough damage, so she used the anger in her heart to heat the water.

'Star-caller,' one of the Black Cloaks called, somehow injecting nonchalance into his raspy voice.

Above her head, the water boiled and bubbled, enough to fill a small lake. When she couldn't bear the temperature any longer, feeling her own skin searing from the heat hovering above her, Wave cast the water out.

Dirt exploded around her, but she ground her feet into the earth. The water was high enough that the wizards hadn't noticed it. Once it was hovering above them, she dropped it.

Screams rose from the potato fields. Wave grimaced, her own skin burning from the close contact, her raw tattoo throbbing. Steam rose from the ground, a blanket of mist as tall as a house standing between her and the Black Cloaks. Wave sent a weave of power through the air, just above the ground, enough to stop the mist from dissipating quickly.

She turned and fled, following Strath and Jessandra through the foothills and into the forested mountains. They'd been heading west through the fields, but once Strath saw Wave's veil of mist, he cut south again through the evergreens.

'Shh,' he whispered as he moved his hands around them.

Ahead and behind, leaves swirled and settled. Wave couldn't see or feel his plantkin power, one of the many frustrations she felt at the powers of humans, but she guessed he was veiling their path. Jessandra stood a little way away, clutching her shoulder, her red-gold braid in disarray around her face.

'I've hidden us,' Strath whispered, 'but if they're nearby, they can still hear us. So we keep going south at a fast pace, but we don't talk, okay?'

Wave and Jessandra nodded in unison. Strath led the way through the forest, taking a path visible only to his eyes. Curious, Wave watched as the leaves on the ground swirled and settled as they moved past, noticed the way the grass flattened and sprang back once they'd moved over it.

Hours passed in silence, and they didn't hear the Black Cloaks again. Wave started to worry that she'd hurt them badly with her boiling water. Even as the thought entered her head, Strath turned back to her with a glare. It wasn't the first time she'd wondered if he could read her thoughts.

By the time the moon had set behind the southern mountains, Strath stopped them.

'We can rest for a time,' he said. 'I think we've lost them.'

There was still a tightness around Wave's chest. Maybe it was just the last vestiges of fear. They'd come so close to being caught, and Wave wondered if it was her fault. If not for the delay while they waited for Jessandra, they wouldn't have come across the Black Cloaks at all. But where would that have left Jessandra?

Leaves swirled around them, and the trees sighed as Strath moved his hands in a smooth dance.

'We're protected,' he said. 'They'd have to be standing right next to us to even know we're here.'

'The forest is protecting us?' Jessandra asked, a hint of incredulity in her voice.

Strath nodded. His face was pale, and his skin seemed to sag from his bones.

'You should rest,' Wave said. 'You used a lot of Ferengün's power.' But hadn't he shifted earth as well? There was no way a human could use the power of two gods, so there must have been a trick.

Strath sat down with a sigh, leaning against the trunk of an old beech.

'You used a lot of power too,' he said, looking at her with his head tilted to one side.

Wave felt a little tired, mostly in her calves from the climb, but Strath looked entirely depleted. She shrugged. 'I feel okay.'

'I'm glad I've been able to see how powerful you are now,' he said, closing his eyes and resting his head back against the tree. 'You didn't tell me half of what you're capable of.'

Wave sat down beside him, leaving a decent space between them. 'I've never really known what I'm capable of,' she said. 'I haven't been pushed to my limits.' She pushed the image of Henny's lifeless body from her mind.

Jessandra sat down opposite her. 'You're more powerful than your sister.'

Wave shook her head. 'How can you compare someone who can change the weather with someone who shoots jets of water?'

'I've yet to see her change the weather,' Jessandra said with a small smile. 'But I've seen what you're capable of.'

'I'm going to sleep for a while,' Strath said, his voice hoarse. 'I'll know if they're coming close.'

He curled up at the base of the tree, his cloak tucked tight around him. One leg was bare, though, his pants bunching up and his cloak not covering him. Even though he'd just lain down, he was already snoring, the sound light and unobtrusive.

Wave wanted to pull his pant leg down, to lay his cloak over him properly and keep him warm. She was filled with a longing to protect him. The feeling was a new one for Wave, and it was more unsettling than anything else she'd experienced.

'Jessandra,' she murmured, battling her internal desire to stay isolated. 'Strath's leg is bare. Can you cover him?'

Jessandra looked at her askance. 'Okay?' She did as Wave asked, then sat back down, studying Wave with a strange expression.

'I know I invited you on this journey,' Wave said with a sigh. 'But I need you to promise me something.'

'Okay.'

'No matter what, you can't touch me.'

Jessandra frowned. Wave wondered if she'd heard what the Black Cloaks had shouted as they chased them.

'I'm sick,' Wave added, as if that was more than a poor explanation. 'You have to swear that no matter what happens, you won't touch me.'

'I promise, Wave,' Jessandra said, without any hesitation. 'I won't touch you. I'll probably forget, so I won't be upset if you have to remind me.'

'You can't forget,' Wave said. 'It's really important.'

'Okay, you've got a deal.'

'Thank you,' Wave said. They smiled at each other with a shared understanding that made Wave's heart swell.

'Get some rest,' she said.

Jessandra curled up in the hollow Strath had led them to, wrapping herself up in her cloak far better than Strath had.

Wave sat up for a long time. She pretended to herself that she'd volunteered for first watch, but in reality, she wouldn't have been able to sleep if she'd tried.

Her mind spun with the events of the last few hours. Finding Jessandra in the streets of Jindar had been bizarre enough, let alone Jessandra taking the time to warn Wave of the Black Cloaks. And then, the power she'd been able to weave together to defend them against the wizards.

Unlike the strange power she'd accessed when she'd tried to save Henny, her work tonight was all Lerinial's power. Just as Ealen had told her, she'd needed something to push her to test the limits of her waterkin power. Where Strath was exhausted from his incredible feats, Wave felt invigorated, more alive than she'd felt since she'd battled the ocean and lost Henny.

Again, she pushed thoughts of the drowned girl aside. Her heart still ached too much to think of her. The cruelty of Lerinial wasn't lost on Wave, especially as she thought of the boiling water she'd dumped on the Black Cloaks, heard their screams echoing in her mind.

There were too many things to think about, too many occurrences to digest. The star was still hidden in her cloak pocket, a secret from the two who lay before her. Wave shoved her hands in her pockets so she could touch the star. One hand brushed against something she'd forgotten was there. Frowning, Wave drew a piece of cheap, thin parchment out. The sharp block letters were unfamiliar to her, but reading who the note was addressed to was like a stab to her heart.

X'olea.

Your line of thinking is correct. What your friend experienced is identical to my first time. The anger, the blinding light, all of it. The inability to use the power in a useful way. It takes a lot of practice to hone this skill. Water and sun, Lerinial and Jesma. Lightning. You should bring her to me in Condor. I can teach her how to use it.

—Hasting.

Wave folded the note carefully and returned it to her pocket. Had she read it earlier, remembered it was there when she was in the Nagahere, or on the outskirts of Chok, she wouldn't have understood its cryptic meaning. But since then, Strath had revealed that the people of Sharvel believed the magic of the Black Cloaks to be a combination of Lerinial's and Jesma's powers. Water and sun. Lightning. What were the odds that this Hasting was referring to anything else?

Magic.

Wave's mind was so crowded with thoughts that she couldn't focus on any of them. What X'olea's friend was suggesting was impossible. Magic? It couldn't be.

Exhaustion soon overtook her, and, upright as she was, she slipped into a fitful sleep. Her dreams shifted between the gravelly voices of the Black Cloaks, to a land where all the colours were wrong, to a serpentine face full of overwhelming intelligence, to the faces of Jessandra, her sisters, her mother.

GARDAR MAE

IN THE DEEP mountain shadows that covered the small town of Gardar Mae, Larka mused over a steaming cup of tea while she watched the sky turning from peach, to lavender, to gold. She wanted to wait until after sunrise to wake Winter, knowing their long journey through the Plains had tired her.

Something shifted in the darkened doorway behind Larka.

'How long has it been?' a voice that felt like home murmured into the predawn silence.

Larka turned her head with a small smile. 'Too long, old friend.'

Hasting moved onto the patio and Larka stood to receive the tight hug he offered. They stayed like that for a while, happy to breathe in the scent of one another, to pause in remembrance of times long past.

'When I invited you and Winter to visit, I never expected you'd turn up in the middle of the night.' His face was all smiles, despite the admonition in his words.

'When I decided we would come, the circumstances were a little … different,' Larka said as she looked up at him.

Time had changed his face. Wrinkles etched from smiles and

tears lined his features and his hair had greyed around the temples, peppering through the rest of his dark brown locks. The colour-shifting irises that were his signature hadn't changed, though.

Larka dropped her eyes and took a deep breath. 'Tea?'

'Will you tell me what circumstances delivered you to my door at such an ungodly hour?'

Smiling, Larka pushed her way into the small wooden house. Behind her, Hasting chuckled, the sound little more than the wind rustling through leaves on a breezy day. Larka busied herself with the kettle while Hasting settled himself at the table.

'You've been behaving yourself for a long time.' Hasting took a loaf of dark bread from the counter and began to cut thick slices. 'It must be, what, nine years since I last saw you?'

'Before Winter was born,' Larka agreed.

'You were pregnant.'

Larka stayed silent. To think of Winter's birth was to think of Sam. Her daughter's conception marked the loss of her husband.

'And now she's all grown up,' Hasting said, his voice level as he shifted the conversation to the present.

Ever since they were children, he'd been able to anticipate Larka's moods and known how to give her space. She'd always been grateful for his steady presence in her life, his unwavering care for her. She needed it now more than ever.

'Did you run the whole way here? She looked exhausted.'

Larka turned away from the fire, pouring fresh tea into two mugs.

'We ran most of the way from Essenné,' she admitted.

'So what trouble brings you to my doorstep?'

Trouble always brought them together, Larka thought as she lowered the kettle onto a wooden board. She joined Hasting at the table with a sigh. A heavy ring threaded on leather hung around his neck, something she'd never seen him

wear before. He wasn't someone who appreciated ornamentation.

'You've let me into your home. I wouldn't want to burden
you with my troubles.'

'My home is yours, Larka, as it always has been.' Hasting laid
his hand over hers.

A bolt of energy ran up Larka's arm. It wasn't plantkin
power, nor any of the other gods' powers. Perhaps it was just
the familiarity of him, or maybe it was nothing more than the
simple presence of another human's touch.

'The girls are in trouble,' she said, removing her hand from
his and taking her mug.

The sun was high in the sky by the time she'd finished telling
him of Siska, Jessandra, and Wave. Hasting listened in silence,
never interrupting her except to make more tea or butter a slice
of bread.

'That is quite a lot of trouble for two young ladies to be in,'
Hasting murmured, a half-forgotten piece of bread in his hand.
'Quite a lot.'

'Three,' Larka said. 'And though only two are my responsibility, I can't help but feel connected to Jessandra's plight.'

Hasting nodded, his gaze lost on some spot over Larka's
shoulder. Larka added some blackberry jam to her bread, giving
Hasting time to think. There was quite a lot to digest, and the
news that her middle daughter had been named a star-caller
wasn't something to be taken lightly. If she was honest, she
hadn't really come to terms with it herself. How could she?
Wave was destined for a lifetime as a recluse if she managed to
evade the Black Cloaks.

Winter shuffled into the kitchen. Her ash-blonde hair was
tousled from the bed, her eyes bright and round with half sleep
as she folded herself into her mother's arms. Larka sat her at the
table and offered her bread and jam. Winter devoured the food,
scoffing half the loaf without taking her eyes off Hasting.

They'd met for the first time last night, but Hasting had been half-asleep, and Winter bone-tired.

'I bet you're tired from your long run?' Hasting asked.

Winter stared at him with wide eyes as she chewed on a mouthful of bread.

'Did you have a good sleep?' Hasting asked.

Winter nodded, but her mouth remained shut.

Larka could see the uncertainty in Hasting's eyes. He'd never had children of his own, though he was fond of them. As far as Larka knew, he'd never been married, or even in love with someone.

'Where do the town's children play?' Larka asked, combing her fingers through Winter's hair.

Hasting looked up at her with a relieved smile. 'They often play at the other end of town. Where Gardar Mae ends and becomes forest again.'

Larka took Winter into the small bedroom they'd shared for the night. She helped change her clothes and brush her hair, adding murmured words of comfort as she went. Winter was still tired, but her eyes were bright and she told Larka she was ready to explore.

Hand in hand, they wandered down the main road and through the town. Gardar Mae was much bigger than their village but it had the same comforting, homey feel that can only be found in small, isolated communities. Instead of large-scale farming, the people of Gardar Mae were mostly lumber-jacks and carpenters. The houses were all stained timber, as though they could merge back into the forest in a heartbeat. The mountain air was fresh and crisp, so different to the often arid air of the Plains. Larka breathed in deeply, her nostrils tingling with the mixed smells of pine needles and fresh-sawn wood.

At the end of the road, they found several of the local children kicking a ball to one another. The rules of the game looked surprisingly complex, the children shouting numbers at each other at random.

Larka gave Winter a gentle push towards them, but she wouldn't move.

'What's wrong, Winter?'

She looked up at her mother, her brows furrowed. 'I don't know how to play that game.'

'I'm sure they'll enjoy teaching you,' Larka replied. 'Just as you love teaching the younger children how to climb trees.'

Winter stared at the group and scrunched up her nose.

'Will you still be in the house when I want to stop playing?'

Larka pulled her daughter into a tight hug, clenching her jaw to stop the tears that sprang to her eyes.

'Of course. You know how to find the house?'

Winter nodded.

'I promise I will be there.'

Winter grinned, then ran towards the children. They screamed in delight when they saw her, and within moments she was part of a huddle, no doubt learning the rules of their strange game. Larka turned and walked away, ignoring the anxious tug in her heart.

The house was empty by the time Larka meandered her way back down the road. The air had warmed now the sun had peaked over the eastern mountains, but the house retained some of the coolness of the night. Larka paused in the dark hallway, breathing in the woody, earthy scent of the building, the familiar smell of Hasting.

Calling his name, she wandered through the house and into the garden. Hasting sat on a chequered blanket, reading in the shade of an old broad-leafed tree. He looked up as she crossed the sloping garden to join him. Lavender bushes crowded against peppermint, blackberry vines scrambled across a number of trellises, and raised vegetable beds abounded. Tucked to one side was a small, well-tended patch of rosemary and patchouli—an odd mix, but Hasting knew more about combination planting than she did.

Larka sat down beside him and leaned against the trunk, closing her eyes. They were safe, at least for a short while. The soft rustle of pages made her open her eyes. Hasting was watching her, his fingers running across the edges of the book.

'Have you seen him?' Larka asked, her voice soft as she tried to conceal the weight of her question.

'Not since I last saw you together.' Hasting's voice cracked when he spoke. Sam was his best friend.

'I haven't seen him since I conceived Winter,' Larka whispered.

'He doesn't know he has another child?'

Larka shook her head, biting her lower lip to stop it trembling.

'Near on nine years, then.'

'I could really use his support right now.' She hated how hoarse her voice was, but Hasting had seen her in every emotional state she possessed. He could handle it; she just wasn't sure if she could.

'Your daughters face a lot of danger.' Hasting laid his book down in the grass beside them, shifting his body so that he could look at her directly. 'You need somebody to help you. You and the girls.'

Larka nodded. 'I do.'

'Let me help you,' he said.

His voice had turned husky, and Larka's stomach twisted uncomfortably. There was something in his tone that she'd never heard before, an emotion she didn't understand.

'I can't burden you with our problems, Hasting.'

'Your burdens are mine, Larka, they always have been.'

'Hasting—'

'Please, Larka,' he said, 'let me explain.'

Larka closed her mouth and Hasting took a deep breath.

'There was a girl,' he said. 'Bella.' He fiddled with the ring around his neck.

With a frown, Larka admitted to herself that she was surprised. Hasting had never seemed to need anyone else in his life, anyone other than her and Sam. What truly surprised her was the small tinge of jealousy she felt.

'Six years ago, in Hincka,' he continued, his gaze drifting out over the garden to the patch of rosemary and patchouli. 'I fell in love with her, but I couldn't be with her.' He paused, his hand becoming a fist around the ring. 'I couldn't be with her because I hadn't let go of the past.'

A lump formed in Larka's throat as a memory of their shared childhood surfaced. The two of them, no more than fifteen years old, lying sprawled under one of the great oaks. Larka's head resting on Hasting's shoulder. Hasting stroking her hair. She'd thought then that she would never be happier in her life.

That was before Sam had shown up and stolen her heart. Before, when it had always been just the two of them. Larka and Hasting. She loved Sam, but could she honestly say that her life had been happier than that peaceful moment under the oak?

'Bella died before I understood how I felt about her.'

Larka covered her mouth with her hand, her eyes smarting.

'Her death broke my heart, Larka, and I realised then that my heart has been breaking every single day since Sam came into our lives.'

His words tore through Larka's body like a beam of ice.

'Larka—'

'Hasting?' a deep male voice called from the house. 'Hasting, where are you?'

'We're out here,' Hasting called, clearing his throat of emotion.

He looked at Larka, the longing in his eyes clearer than any words he could speak. She turned away from him, her insides roiling like a clod of disturbed earthworms.

A man, perhaps a decade or so older than them, wandered through the back door and into the garden. Iridescent eyes set against rich black skin made the man the spitting image of his goddess, Wederlly.

'Rainer!' Hasting exclaimed, all signs of his earlier emotion gone. He stood to greet his friend with a brotherly hug.

'Rainer and I became friends when I moved here,' Hasting said after he'd introduced them. The trio claimed new spots on the blanket. 'He's a skilled moonkin, and he's very, uh, knowledgeable.'

'Knowledgeable?' Larka asked, one corner of her mouth lifting.

'He's …' Hasting looked at Rainer for encouragement.

'A dissenter,' Rainer said with a broad smile for Larka.

Flecks of silver marked his thick curls at the temples, highlighting the silver shards in his irises.

'I was in the high king's army, a long time ago. I've seen too many atrocities to abide by the rule of our nobility.'

Larka shot an uneasy glance at Hasting. This man probably knew Sam, though it was unlikely he knew the truth about what had happened the night Esra died. Rainer probably believed all of the lies about Sam, probably thought his exile was a lenient punishment.

'Larka has come a long way to visit,' Hasting said. 'Her daughters are in trouble.'

'I have daughters,' Rainer said with a sad sigh. 'What cheekiness have they got themselves into?'

'Nothing that was in their control,' Larka said, working to keep her face neutral. Hasting might have befriended Rainer, but Larka was always primed to be suspicious of new people.

'Oh dear,' Rainer said. His smile slipped and a deep frown arched across his face. 'They're Kaiaho on the run? Rebels fighting against one of the rulers?'

Larka laughed, the sound forced and high-pitched, as if what he'd said wasn't so close to the truth.

'I failed my daughters,' Rainer continued, sadness etching lines on either side of his mouth. 'When I could no longer sit by and watch the circus show of this nation, I began to spread the seeds of dissent. I know things I shouldn't. They could have punished me, alone. Should have taken me to the dungeons, to the Black Cloaks, or taken my life. Those are the price of the secrets I keep.'

Larka and Rainer stared at each other for a long time.

He knows, she thought. *He knows about Sam, about Reuben, about Esra.*

'What did they do instead?' Larka asked.

'They murdered my wife in front of me.' Rainer's voice remained level, though his face paled. 'They took my daughters and spread them out across the country as servants in the highkin houses. But not until they'd watched their mother bleed out on our kitchen floor.'

'Rainer,' Larka said as she laid a hand on his arm. 'I'm sorry for your loss.'

In some ways, Larka understood what he'd been through better than she could explain. She hadn't watched Sam die, but every moment without him brought the possibility of his death. Nine years with no contact suggested that someone had finally achieved what Reuben had been trying to do all along. She couldn't think like that, though, couldn't give up all hope.

'Not as sorry as I am,' Rainer said. 'They thought they could cow me, silence me by taking everyone I loved.'

'Did it work?'

This time, Rainer was unable to contain his heartbreak. He lowered his eyes. Larka understood the feeling. Shame. Worse than sadness, loneliness, guilt.

'For a long time, I was broken by what they did. I was useless, a wasted man.'

They were silent for a time as Rainer's words settled over them. Birds whistled in the forest behind them. Larka stole a glance at Hasting, lifting her eyebrows in an unspoken question. He nodded.

'But then I met Hasting,' Rainer said, lifting his face back to them. Some of his composure had returned, and Larka could see the proud, strong man he'd been before his family was destroyed. 'And I'm beginning to find my resolve to continue fighting. If not for this country, then for my daughters.'

'I understand that,' Larka said. 'I feel it in my bones. I've given up trying to save this godsforsaken place, but I can't give up on my daughters.'

Rainer nodded. If only he knew who her daughters were. Larka opened her mouth to ask a pointed question about Sam, but closed it again. She wasn't ready. All those years alone in the Plains had made her wary of people. Defending her daughters had made her more protective than she'd ever imagined she would need to be.

25

OUTSKIRTS OF ORLANI

CANTERING DOWN WATERFALL ROAD, the autumn wind whipping his hair into a frenzy, Mortius felt an unrivalled freedom thrum through his body. He couldn't remember the last time he'd felt so good. Liberated from the constraints of Reuben's madness and the pressures of the kingdom, surrounded by the open expanses of the southern pass, Mortius felt a heavy weight slough from his shoulders. He was almost giddy with relief.

Riding behind Mortius were four plain-clothed men—a retinue of those he held a developing trust for. This would be their first opportunity to prove their loyalty and their worth. Among those four was the keystone to Mortius' plans.

Aymn rode with the others as befitted the supposed nephew of the senior adviser. There would be no special treatment for him out on the road, no acknowledgement of his privileged role under the Master of Trade. Here, he was simply Aymn starkin, another member of Mortius' crew.

Of all those who rode with him, it was Aymn he watched closely, waiting for an opportunity that would force Mortius to tell the boy about his heritage. The thought made Mortius' stomach churn, so he pushed it aside. For now, he could enjoy the relative freedom that came with riding unhindered through the country.

As the party of five moved closer to the Swishdine Coast, a looming structure appeared on the horizon. As tall as a mountain and more impassable than the Paravat Ranges, the structure was black and glassy, as if it was made out of some material that had never been seen in Heredour. No windows or doors marred its smooth surface, not that they could tell from this distance.

Of all the terrible secrets Mortius held close to his heart, it turned out that this structure was the one causing him the most distress.

Buduwai.

Nobody knew where the program was located, and nobody would ever wonder if it was here. The obsidian obelisk had reared from the southern horizon since the beginning of time and even the truth of its construction was lost to the ages.

Avoided for most of Heredour's history, only a select few knew that the Black Cloaks had finally worked out how to breach the perfect surface a few hundred years ago. When they convinced Reuben to bring back the Law of Kaiaho, they'd suggested the obelisk as the perfect home of Buduwai. What they did with the youth inside the structure had always been a mystery to Mortius until very recently.

The memory of that conversation between Reuben and the Dread was seared into his mind, like a hot iron on a fresh slab of meat.

'I need the truth, Dyafirah,' Reuben said, his posture rigid in his chair.

'You don't want the truth, King,' Dyafirah growled, his voice travelling from deep within his hood.

Reuben shot up from his seat and slammed his fist on the table.

'Where are they?' His voice was soft, deadly.

Dyafirah laughed, the sound more grating than his speaking voice. The hairs on Mortius' arms stood on end.

'If they can't be re-educated,' Dyafirah said, cutting his laughter short. 'They are disposed of.'

Mortius clenched his jaw as he recalled the Dread's words. Even Reuben had been shocked. Eleven years of the law, and not a single child had returned. How naive had Mortius been to not wonder why?

He knew the law was archaic and nonsensical, that a person had no control over the god that summoned them to their power, but he'd been so distracted by the kingdom—in truth, by his secrets and the weight of his guilt—that he hadn't stopped to question what was actually happening.

No wonder there were new families in each ruler's court every single day, begging for their young ones to be returned to them.

There was no end to the cruelty of the wizards. Against their insatiable lust for power and their ingrained reticence, Mortius felt like a drowning man.

As the dark structure grew in size ahead of them, its surface not reflecting the sun's light but instead seeming to swallow it whole, Mortius wondered if Buduwai was just a burial ground. After Dyafirah's revelation, he'd begun to think that perhaps the wizard wasn't telling the whole truth. The Kaiāho posed no risk to the continuation of Heredour's rule, but they were a threat to the Black Cloaks' vision of a highly regimented, ordered society. Why even bother attempting to re-educate them? He wouldn't put such a terrible possibility past them.

Soon enough, the road would divide to give travellers a wide berth around the monstrosity. One road headed west to Toohlio, the other east to Monera.

His horse began to slow as they drew closer to the monolith. From the corner of his eye, Mortius saw somebody ride up beside him, but he was unable to tear his gaze from the black mass ahead.

'What is it, Senior Adviser?' Aymn asked, the practiced deference in his voice overshadowed by his awe at the structure.

Mortius shook himself out of his stupor and turned to Aymn. The horses were trotting at an easy pace, and the other men remained a respectful distance behind.

With a sigh that carried the weight of eleven years, Mortius answered.

'This is Buduwai.'

The boy had to know what he would be inheriting, if Mortius' plan ever eventuated. Aymn's eyes widened, but he didn't turn away from the obelisk.

'This is Buduwai?' he whispered, the words almost imperceptible over the clatter of the horses' hooves. 'And to think ...'

Mortius' eyes narrowed. 'To think ... what, Aymn?'

Aymn was silent for a long time before answering.

'Would the dilution of our power also lead to a dilution of traits, do you think?' Aymn asked as his head tilted back to take in the structure's height.

'Traits?'

Aymn shrugged. 'My eyes have never turned violet, or even some pathetic, pale lilac.' He paused. 'And I'm a hopeless starkin.'

Unner had taught him well, taught him to speak a truth or ask a question without revealing the true purpose of the words. Perhaps he had felt Jesma call to him as a youth, despite Mortius' heavy-handed insistence on his starkin nature. Perhaps Aymn already knew what he was, already understood how precarious of a position that put both of them in.

'It is true that our powers are waning,' Mortius said, wanting to fill the silence, but not wanting to give too much away. He searched for something to say, anything that would articulate the path he wanted Aymn to take, without using quite so many words. 'Perhaps your eyes aren't meant to be violet.'

Mortius held his breath, shocked by his own audacity. Neither of them were ready for this kind of conversation, but here they were, on the precipice, ready to tumble into oblivion. Mortius lifted his gaze to the obelisk, uncertain of himself for the first time in thirty years. It wasn't a feeling he was comfortable with.

26

THE NORTH CLAW

THE MOUNTAIN AIR began to grow frigid the higher Jessandra and her new friends climbed. The peaks in the distance were snow-capped, and Strath explained that they were never without snow, even in the height of summer.

Jessandra was grateful for her cloak at night, though the days were warm enough to keep it tucked over her satchel during their hikes. Whether they were climbing up or down, Jessandra's leg muscles worked as they never had before, and she was always covered in a fine sheen of sweat. By the end of the second day, both she and Wave were exhausted. Only Strath appeared unperturbed by their journey.

'Why don't you two rest,' he said as the sun slipped behind the western peaks. 'I'll see if I can forage anything.'

Jessandra eased her satchel from her shoulders and massaged her neck.

'There's a stream nearby,' Wave said as she laid her cloak out on the ground. 'We'll go and fill the canteens.'

With a nod, Strath moved his hands around their makeshift camp. Leaves and grass rustled as if a wind had taken to them, and then settled. Jessandra knew now that this was the sign they were protected by Ferengün's power.

Strath took his flask from his bag and handed it to Jessandra before he disappeared into the trees.

'Which way?' Jessandra asked.

'Over there,' Wave said, pointing in the opposite direction Strath had taken. She didn't move, though.

'Are you coming?' Jessandra asked. 'I thought it might be nice to splash our faces.'

Wave stared at her cloak longingly, as if she didn't want to leave it.

'It'll help us sleep better if we wash away some of this sweat,' Jessandra added. She didn't want to try to find the stream alone and then risk losing them. She wouldn't survive long alone out here.

'Yes,' Wave said, dragging her eyes away from the cloak to study Jessandra. 'You're right.'

She led the way through the trees, Jessandra keeping her distance. They hadn't spoken much during the day. Strath had said the Black Cloaks would give up on them in the forest, so they could talk if they wished. Apparently, wildcraft wasn't something the wizards ever bothered to learn. The hills were too strenuous for any kind of conversation, though, and Jessandra hadn't found an opportunity to ask Wave about her illness or why she was on the run from the Black Cloaks.

The sound of trickling water danced through the trees and Wave broke into a run. Jessandra followed her, bursting out onto the bank of a small stream. Little waterfalls tumbled over tiny boulder-strewn ledges, and the water was so clear she could see the rocky bottom. Wave was already on her knees, splashing water on her face, and Jessandra kneeled down beside her.

She gasped in shock. The water was icy, colder than any water she'd ever touched. Wave laughed from beside her, shaking her head to stop the water dripping down into her blouse.

'It's so cold!' Jessandra said.

'This water feels different to the ocean, or the rivers,' Wave said. 'I guess it's from a snowmelt. It has this sense of agelessness, like it knows far more than I could ever learn in my lifetime.'

'Wow,' Jessandra said. She splashed her face again, revelling in the way the cold washed away her fatigue. 'I don't think I've ever washed my face in a stream.' There was something freeing about the moment for Jessandra, something she couldn't quite articulate.

'I imagine your life has been a bit different to mine,' Wave said between gulped handfuls of water. 'I remember when Siska started working for you, she was so amazed at all the technologies you had in the castle.'

Jessandra remembered when Siska had first come to Millen, but she'd been too young to understand the older woman's poorly masked surprise.

'Siska said your family grew up in Essenné,' Jessandra said, thinking back to the questions she'd asked in that first year, curious about someone's life outside her family. 'Surely you had access to the similar luxuries I did.'

Wave laughed, the sound bringing a smile to Jessandra's face.

'Latrines? Hot baths?'

'Oh Jessandra, I wish I could tell you.' Wave's laughter died.

'Tell me what?'

'You're the heir to the Marbin throne,' Wave said with a sigh. 'I know you're on the run at the moment, but there will be a time you'll return to claim your crown.'

'Maybe,' Jessandra said. She'd never been certain of her position as heir, and was even less so since she'd fled the castle. 'But why should that matter?'

'Because once you take that position, or even if you go back as queen-in-waiting, you'll have to do the right thing.'

Jessandra frowned. 'I don't think the right thing is so clear-cut.' She was learning that particular lesson the hard way.

'Really?'

'I'm almost sixteen, Wave, and I've never felt the call of any of the gods. They can't even name me Kaiāho because I'm some sort of anomaly.' Even being around Wave and Strath using their middle and lowkin powers, she'd felt nothing. 'What's the right thing to do in that situation? What should I do? What should my parents do? How can I be Queen of Marbin? A godless ruler? Impossible.'

Wave sat back on her haunches as Jessandra tossed a flask to her. 'Do you think the law is fair and just, though?'

'No,' Jessandra said, lowering her eyes to the burbling stream. 'The law is terrible.'

'Why?'

Jessandra sighed and sank to the ground, crossing her legs beneath her. 'Two years ago my sister was exiled. They told me she'd fallen pregnant to a lowkin and that the shame was too much to bear. So they exiled her to Triné, thrusting me into the position of heir.'

Wave nodded and sat down opposite Jessandra. 'I've heard of Lenta.'

'It was all a lie, though,' Jessandra said. 'Lenta was Kaiāho, she felt the call of Lerinial just like you. But to avoid the shame of having a Kaiāho daughter, my parents had the Black Cloaks whisk her away in the middle of the night and then concocted a story so that nobody would know.'

'I had no idea,' Wave said. 'It makes more sense than exile because of an undesirable pregnancy.'

'My uncle is insane,' Jessandra added. 'I mean, something is seriously wrong with him. My father is mean, but Reuben ...' She trailed off. There weren't enough words to describe her father's cousin. 'He's not right in the head. The law should never have been reintroduced.'

'I bet you can't say stuff like that in the castle,' Wave said with a small smile.

Jessandra laughed, but it was a sad sound. 'Sometimes I say as much to Siska and Inska, because I have no one else to talk to. But they're both such good girls, they listen to my rants and they take care of me, but they never share their opinions or their thoughts or their hearts' desires. It's not exactly a friendship when it's all one-sided.' She'd never spoken these thoughts out loud. Hearing the truth in her own voice only made it more real.

'It sounds really lonely,' Wave said. 'I know what that's like.'

'You?' Jessandra said, attempting a smile. 'I can't imagine that's true.'

Wave pursed her lips. 'I've been in training for the last five years, and I only had one friend.'

'I don't believe you.' Everything Siska had told her of Wave suggested a caring, loving person. There was no way she had no friends in Bindock.

'It's true!' Wave said with a laugh. 'And he is old enough to be my grandfather.'

'What?' Jessandra couldn't believe what she was hearing. 'How is that possible?'

Wave shrugged. 'They didn't trust me from the moment I arrived.'

'Why?' She knew what it felt like to not be trusted—her father always had people watching her, waiting to catch her in the tiniest mistake.

'I spent my journey up the river playing with Lerinial's power. By the time I got to Bindock, I was already more proficient in basic waterkin skills than half of the town.'

'You're like Siska,' Jessandra said. 'More powerful than anyone our age could hope to be.'

'I guess so,' Wave said. 'But it made the townspeople wary of me.'

'Jealous, more like it.'

'Maybe, but it set me apart. X'olea was the only one who'd talk to me. He's an old starkin scholar, and he taught me more than anyone else in that whole town.' Wave sighed. 'Gods, I hope he's okay.'

'Why wouldn't he be?'

Wave chewed on her bottom lip, looking at Jessandra anxiously. 'I can't tell you.'

'You can trust me, Wave,' Jessandra said.

The words resonated deep in her core. She'd thought she could trust Jai'til, but when it came down to the hard things, he hadn't stood by her. The words he spoke were hollow, meaningless. She'd thought she could trust Siska, and Siska had saved her. Trusting people wasn't easy when anyone could betray you, but she knew how to hold Wave's secret in her heart.

'It's not about trust, Jessandra,' Wave said. 'It's about fear.'

'I'm afraid of a lot of things,' Jessandra admitted. 'But who am I going to tell?' She gestured at the trees and the creek. 'The birds? The rocks?'

Wave laughed a little, and then studied Jessandra intently, as if she was a specimen that could be broken down and understood.

'Did you hear what the Black Cloaks shouted?' Wave said, her face settling into a semblance of calm. 'When they were chasing us?'

Jessandra frowned, trying to think back to those moments of terror. They'd called her Siska, the name she'd given at the inn. Then there was a lot of incoherent shouting, a lot of explosions, a lot of running, a lot of panic. She shook her head.

'After you were injured and I came back for you?' Wave asked, lifting one hand to her shoulder.

The pain had subsided over the days, though her muscles

were still a little tight. Jessandra touched the shoulder that had been hit by the building's shrapnel, trying to recall everything that happened within the chaos. Something shifted in the trees behind them, and they both looked up, but there was nothing there. A bird, perhaps, or just the wind. A memory returned to her while she was distracted.

'Star-caller,' she whispered, the name coming to her like a bolt of lightning. 'That's what they were calling out. "Stop, star-caller!"' Jessandra tried to mimic the raspy voice of the Black Cloaks, but she just ended up in a coughing fit.

Wave nodded, her eyes never leaving Jessandra's.

'They had some story in their head about us?' Jessandra said with a shrug. 'Star-caller?' She laughed. The story of Setora was a myth, a legend to scare children who wouldn't do their chores. Sure, there were some who said there was truth in the part about the Black Cloaks blasting the South Claw off the land, but Jessandra was too old to believe in bedtime stories.

'That's why you made us promise not to touch you,' Strath said as he stepped from behind a tree.

Jessandra jumped in surprise and Wave scrambled back-wards towards the stream, her eyes narrowed.

'Why are you sneaking around?' Wave asked, her voice as tight as her face.

'Tell me true, Wave,' Strath said, ignoring her question. He squatted down in front of her, carefully maintaining a distance between them. 'You're a star-caller?'

'No!' Wave exclaimed. 'I'm not.'

Jessandra rolled her eyes. She liked looking at Strath, with his strong shoulders and earthy nature, but he was far too dramatic for her liking.

'Then what's in your cloak pocket?' he asked, leaning closer to Wave. 'The thing you're always fondling when you think nobody's watching?'

Wave shuffled backwards until her fingers found the bank. She swallowed.

'I didn't do it,' she whispered. 'It just happened.'

Strath's shoulders sagged and he rocked back onto his heels. 'Gods,' he murmured, wiping one hand over his face.

'What is going on?' Jessandra asked. They were talking in riddles, and she hated the sudden exclusion, especially when she felt like she and Wave were just getting close.

'She's a star-caller, Jessandra.' Strath shook his head. 'I can't believe it.'

'I don't believe it,' Jessandra said. 'I don't.'

Without a word, Wave stood and left them. After a few moments of silence, Jessandra rounded on Strath.

'Why did you do that?' she asked. 'You cornered her like an animal! That's not nice.'

Strath turned to face Jessandra, regarding her with solemn eyes. They were hazel, flecks of blue and violet and green peppered throughout. Jessandra blushed and looked away. He did have a very handsome face.

Only a heartbeat later, Wave appeared between the trees, her cloak bunched in one hand. She sat beside the bank and spread the cloak out over her lap.

'Promise me you won't freak out,' Wave said, locking eyes with both Jessandra and Strath.

'You ask a lot from people you hardly know,' Strath said. There was a hint of laughter in his voice, though, and Jessandra shook her head at him.

'I promise,' Jessandra said, and she meant it. She had no idea what was going on, but she ached for the friendship she'd already found with Wave. Whatever Wave wanted to show them, Jessandra refused to react with the fear Wave was clearly expecting.

'I promise,' Strath said.

Wave dug her hands into the cloak pocket and withdrew

something hidden by her interlocked fingers. Taking a deep breath, Wave opened her hands. In the centre of her palms lay a rock, silver grey, lumpy and smooth all at the same time. Jessandra frowned, but Strath took a sharp inhale.

'That's not a star,' Jessandra said. The rock looked so boring, so lifeless. There was nothing of the enlightened nature of Everluof in that thing. 'No way. It's just a rock.'

'It's a star,' Wave said.

The corners of her mouth were downturned as she told them the story of her graduation night. When she was finished, Jessandra couldn't think, couldn't move. She blinked a few times, trying to give her mind a moment to process what she'd just heard.

'Does that mean you're cursed?' Jessandra asked. 'That's the sickness you spoke about, when you made me promise not to touch you?'

Wave nodded, her head lowered, her eyes on the star.

'How do you know?' Strath asked.

'Know what?' Jessandra said.

'How do you know you're cursed?'

Wave and Jessandra stared at him.

'There's a reason Setora's story has survived the ages,' Wave said, one eyebrow raised as if she couldn't believe he was even asking the question. 'To teach us a lesson. So that nobody has to go through what the South Claw went through. The loss of every single person, an entire land mass!'

'And what if Setora's story has been twisted?' Strath asked, his chin hidden beneath his fist. 'Her story has been passed down orally for generations. Things always get changed and meanings get lost when we share stories in this way.'

'I know what you're trying to do, Strath,' Wave said, 'but it won't work. Even if parts of the story were lost or changed, the essence is still there. Humans shouldn't touch a fallen star. But I did, gods know why, and now I have to bear the consequences.'

'No,' Strath said, shifting his gaze between both of them. 'No, there is more to this, I'm sure. We have to get to Sharvel. The elders will help us understand what this means. I already told you, Wave, the library of Sharvel holds all of the ancient texts, the lost stories, the forbidden knowledge. Maybe you don't have to go to Veija-Mens. Maybe we have an answer for you.'

Wave tucked the star away in her cloak pocket. 'Maybe.' Her tone didn't convince Jessandra.

'Come on,' Strath said. He jumped up, full of a vigour Jessandra didn't understand. 'Let's make camp. We're close to Sharvel.'

They set up camp and had their meal in relative quiet. Wave's revelation was a lot to take in, and Jessandra didn't know how to feel. Although she wanted to believe Setora's story was just that, a story, a fable, a tale, she couldn't help feeling anxious around Wave, and it made her heart heavy.

27

SHARVEL

THE SUN WAS NEARING its zenith when Strath came to a halt. In front of them spread a wooded plateau, surrounded on all sides by a ring of snow-capped mountains. At first, all Wave could see was a mass of ancient trees from end to end. As her eyes adjusted, Wave could see smoke spiralling from the heart of the plateau. Birds wheeled overhead, their shapes clear against the bright, cloudless sky. Wave wondered if they were giant eagles, or regular birds.

'Welcome to my home,' Strath said, a hint of pride in his voice. 'Welcome to Sharvel.'

Despite everything, Wave felt a small flame of hope flicker to life in her heart. What if there were answers in Sharvel? What if they found a way to cure her and she didn't have to try to fight her way to Veija-Mens? The way Strath talked, it seemed like anything was possible in this place.

'Where is it?' Jessandra asked, looking at Strath with doubt in her eyes.

Wave covered her mouth to hide a giggle.

'We keep ourselves well hidden,' Strath answered without

lifting his gaze from the plateau. 'How do you think we stay free of all of Heredour's politics and the Black Cloaks?'

Jessandra glanced back at Wave with her nose scrunched up.

Suppressing an urge to laugh, Wave spoke. 'How long will it take to get to the town?'

'About an hour or so,' Strath answered. 'Shall we?'

He lowered himself onto ledge and then dropped out of sight.

'Come on!' he called.

When Wave peered over the edge, she realised the drop wasn't much taller than they were.

'You first,' Wave said.

Jessandra eased herself over the edge, looking every bit the awkward princess who never spent time outdoors. Once she was hanging by her fingertips, she started screaming, too afraid to let go. Wave laughed, unable to help herself. With a sigh, Strath reached up and grabbed Jessandra's waist.

'Let go!' he shouted.

With a little sob, she did, and he took her weight, lowering her softly to the ground. Wave's laughter died in her throat. There was nothing like that for her; she'd have to find her own way down, no matter how afraid she was. Neither of them would touch her, and although she didn't blame them, it made her heart ache. She finally felt like she had people she could trust, people who were becoming her friends, but she could never have the kind of friendship she dreamed of. No hugs, no casual pats on the shoulder, no accidental brushing of hands. At least she'd been able to touch X'olea, even though they kept their contact minimal for the sake of propriety.

Knowing she may never be able to have that kind of close connection with another human was a crushing weight in her body. Any time Wave allowed herself to really feel it, she wanted to run away, hide from the world until she withered into nothing and was swallowed up by the earth.

'Are you coming, Wave?'

She pushed aside her miserable thoughts and slid over the edge, dropping to a crouch as she landed on the soft grass below.

'It wasn't that far down, Jess,' Wave said, laughing a little to cover her sadness.

Jessandra glared at her. 'I've never been allowed to do adventurous things. I was scared.'

From behind her back, Strath shared a secret smile with Wave. Her heart fluttered in her chest under his regard until the moment was crushed by the weight of the star in her pocket. Despite how connected she felt to Strath or how much he seemed to want to be near her, they could never be anything more than distant friends. Acquaintances, really. Wave supposed she should just be grateful that neither of them had run screaming into the forest when she showed them the star.

The journey across the plateau was peaceful and delightfully uneventful. Broad-leafed beech trees, the ends of each leaf tinged in orange, butted against oak and birch and pine. Tiny swallows danced from branch to branch, foreshadowing their path with delicate song. Above the canopy, the sky was cloudless, the sun high overhead. Wave hadn't felt this peaceful since … well, ever. Contentment wasn't a feeling she was familiar with, but beneath these trees she felt tension melt from her calves, shoulders, neck. A sense of ease entered her mind.

By the time her belly grumbled—a reminder that she'd been subsisting off foraged fruit and Strath's jerky for the past day— they'd found themselves on a dirt track that widened the further they travelled.

'The town is built on two roads,' Strath explained as they walked. 'Two concentric spirals that converge at the heart of Sharvel, the library.'

'I don't know what *concentric* means,' Jessandra said.

Strath paused to pick up a stick, drawing two opposing spirals that met in the middle into the dirt.

'This is the library,' he said, stabbing at the centre of the two lines.

'Doesn't that get confusing?' Jessandra asked as they started walking again. 'Everything must be built along a curve.'

'You get used to it,' Strath said, smiling into the distance.

Wave dragged her eyes away from him, trying to squash the envy she felt at seeing the physical closeness between Strath and Jessandra. There was no concern if they got too close to each other. Once again, Wave felt like an outsider.

A house appeared on the right of the path, but Wave didn't realise until they were almost upon it. Surrounded by lush, wild gardens, the circular mud brick home blended into the forest. Small dormer windows reflected shafts of sunlight and tinkling wind chimes hung from the extended roof beams. Wave got the impression that this house was made for practicality, but also to enhance the natural beauty of the forest. The design appealed to Wave's understanding of the nature of the universe, instead of some convoluted idea of what humans perceived as beautiful.

More houses sprang up on each side of the gently curving road. Each one was made of the same materials, but the design was always different. Some were more angular with two floors, others were comprised of multiple little domes connected by covered walkways, and some seemed to be more forest than house. Wave studied all of them with wide eyes.

'The people of Sharvel took architecture in a different direction to the castle builders,' Strath murmured.

'You're not wrong about that,' Jessandra said, her face scrunched up in puzzlement.

'The idea is to be completely hidden from the view of anyone who comes over the mountain passes, not that anyone does.'

Wave nodded in appreciation. She was beginning to see why nobody knew about the town, why it didn't feature on any of the sanctioned maps.

'You said the Black Cloaks have been here before,' Wave said, jogging to catch up with Strath and Jessandra. She'd been lost for a moment staring at a house that was built high off the ground, its floor beams spanning between four tree trunks.

'Yes, but only twice in thirty years,' he answered. 'And before that, almost never.'

'So they know about Sharvel, even if the rest of Heredour doesn't.'

Strath nodded.

'Which means that the high king probably knows about Sharvel,' Wave said.

'He does. It was he who sent the Black Cloaks last time. They were looking for his brother.'

'And he and the Black Cloaks are content to just …' Wave paused. She wasn't sure how to explain her question.

'Leave us be?' Strath finished for her.

'Yes.'

Strath shrugged. 'We don't harm anyone, and aside from my parents, nobody really leaves Sharvel. There's no impact on wider Heredour from our unorthodox philosophies.'

Wave and Jessandra glanced at each other.

'Unorthodox philosophies?' Jessandra asked as she turned back to Strath.

'You'll see,' Strath said with a mysterious smile.

The curve of the road continued to tighten, and the houses became smaller and closer together. Sometimes, a person working in their garden would wave at the trio, or a person walking in the other direction would smile and nod at them. There was no guarded suspicion of Wave and Jessandra, no concern over two strangers appearing in their town. Wave didn't know how to feel about their open acceptance. Neither Essenné or Bindock had been anything like this, and Wave had assumed that the inhabitants of small towns were always wary of newcomers.

'Oh!' Jessandra gasped.

Wave lifted her eyes and stumbled over her own feet. Before them was a grand building, more impressive than the castle of Millen she'd seen from a distance five years ago. White marble flecked with gold and grey shone like a beacon of hope in the sun, the land around the building cleared of trees. Eight steps, each spanning the width of the building, rose from the road to a colonnaded platform complete with giant terracotta pots holding plants with long stalks and huge, fan-like leaves. Each step was painted a different colour, and with a start, Wave realised they represented the eye colours of different kin.

'The library,' Strath said, sweeping his arms out in front of him.

'I think I saw this,' Jessandra whispered.

Wave was too enthralled to ask what she meant.

Vibrant lawns surrounded the library. Several townspeople lounged on the grass, books in hand or stacked beside them, sometimes alone, sometimes in groups. Scattered laughter and murmured conversation floated around the grounds, and Wave smiled to herself. Without even entering the library, she knew that this was the kind of place she'd been hoping to find when she thought about leaving Bindock. Before her were people who wanted to learn, who loved deepening their knowledge, and perhaps weren't afraid of uncomfortable truths.

'I want you to meet elder Kali,' Strath said, beckoning them up the stairs.

Wave followed him without hesitation, Jessandra a few steps behind. When they reached the top step, Wave turned to look back at the town. Even from her vantage point, it was hard to tell that the forest below her was full of houses and people. She shook her head in admiration. Perhaps she could stay in Sharvel after all. Perhaps she could live an okay life. She would be lonely, unable to get too close to another person, but at least she wouldn't be alone.

Strath led them past the main door and into a room off to one side. Bifold doors stood open to the lawns, and the room was sparsely furnished.

'Sit for a moment,' Strath said. 'I'll find her.'

He disappeared through a door at the back of the room, and Wave perched on the edge of one of the chaise lounges. Just as uncertain, Jessandra sat on a hard, wooden chair, her hands clasped in her lap.

'Where do you think we'll stay?' Jessandra asked.

Wave blinked. 'Maybe with Strath?'

She hadn't given it a single thought. Before the town had been unveiled, she'd expected to stay only a short time before making her way alone to Kochee, and onwards to the Chaba-Canez Islands. They'd been in Sharvel less than an hour, and already Wave felt like she was home. If the Black Cloaks never came here to look for her, and it sounded unlikely they would, why couldn't she live out her life as a hermit? Surrounded by books, and maybe some distant friends? It wasn't her dream life, but the moment she'd reached into the crater and taken the star was the moment she'd given up being in control of her destiny.

Each night, she lay awake, wondering what she would have done if she'd been able to live that moment anew. No matter how many times she replayed that night—trying to reason with herself that a smarter version of her would never have picked up the star—the weight of the rock told her she was lying. The star tugged at her soul, and unless she was asleep, she could always feel its pull.

A door at the back of the room opened. Strath walked in, his wide grin leading the way.

'Elder Kali,' he said, 'I want you to meet my friends, Wave and Jessandra.'

A woman in a loose white dress followed Strath into the room, her face the image of serenity. Tight, dark coils bounced around her shoulders without a tinge of grey, and her skin was a rich brown. Iridescent eyes regarded them below thick lashes, and her half smile said she knew more about them than she should have.

Wave and Jessandra stood, each offering a half bow as was courtesy when greeting an elder.

'Ladies,' Kali said, 'nobody bows to another in Sharvel.'

Wave straightened quickly, Jessandra a second behind her. Her smile widening, Kali placed the fist of her right hand over her heart, her left palm face up towards them. They copied her; the traditional greeting of Heredour was second nature to both of them.

'Be welcome in our home, Wave, Jessandra,' Kali said as she lowered her arms. 'Please, sit.'

Wave moved away from the chaise lounge. The risk of Kali sharing it with her or sitting too close was a risk she couldn't take. Jessandra resumed her place on the wooden chair, so Wave took the only remaining solitary seat—an ancient armchair with a high back. Kali and Strath sat beside one another on the lounge, and Wave was grateful she'd decided to move.

'You must be tired from your long journey,' Kali said.

'A little,' Jessandra said.

Kali turned to Wave, regarding her with those disconcerting iridescent eyes. She seemed to look through Wave, to see things Wave wasn't even aware of. Perhaps Jessandra was used to the colouring of moonkin eyes, but Wave's experience of highkin was limited to the violet eyes of the starkin.

'Sharvel has given me some energy,' Wave murmured. 'Your town is amazing.'

Kali laughed, a full, deep sound that made Wave smile, despite her nervousness.

'Normally, I'd offer you tea and the chance to sit and talk for a time. However, I wouldn't want to keep you from your much-needed rest,' Kali said as her laughter subsided. 'Strath said I might be able to help you, though, and it must be important for him to bring you straight here.'

Strath cast his eyes down, avoiding Wave's gaze. When she looked back at Kali, the elder had eyes only for her.

'Me?' Wave asked.

Kali nodded, her face serene.

'I can't,' Wave said, glancing between Jessandra and Strath as her heart began to beat fast.

'I realise you feel you can't trust me, Wave,' Kali said. 'And I understand your fear. I know not what plagues you, but Strath was certain that I would have something to offer you.'

Wave shook her head. She didn't know if she was more upset with Strath or herself. Maybe she was wrong to be vulnerable, to open herself up to them.

'She won't cast you aside, Wave,' Strath said, talking to his feet. 'Everyone is safe in Sharvel, even you.'

'He's right,' Kali agreed, leaning her elbows on her knees. 'Sharvel accepts all people, no matter the trouble that brings them here.'

She was cornered. The look in Kali's strange eyes invited trust, but Wave couldn't push the memory of the night of her graduation from her mind. Those faces full of unmasked fear and ill-contained rage still haunted her dreams.

'The trouble that brings me here is the worst kind,' she whispered.

If she could just make Kali understand that she was better off not knowing, then perhaps she could go back to her original plan. Stock up on supplies and head south. It wasn't an enjoyable thought, but it was clear she couldn't stay in Sharvel. Not if they wanted to know why she was here.

'Wave,' Strath pleaded, finally lifting his gaze. 'You want to go to Veija-Mens on the slim chance that they know how to help you. What if the answer is here?' He gestured at the walls around them. 'What if you don't need to go that far to find a cure?'

Wave couldn't turn away from his multihued eyes. If there was anyone she trusted more than herself, more than her family or X'olea, it was him. She didn't understand how she already felt such a kinship with him when they'd only been together a few days, but she couldn't deny the plea in his regard. Strath wanted to help her, not for his own sake, but for hers. When was the last time someone outside of her family had wanted to support her, help make her life better?

Swallowing a few times to calm her nerves, Wave put her hand in her cloak pocket. Her fingers closed around the cold lump, and the connection between her and the star vibrated like a divining rod. She paused for a heartbeat, praying to Lerinial that she wouldn't regret her decision, then pulled the star from her pocket.

'What is it?' Kali asked as Wave uncurled her fingers.

They locked eyes, all-knowing iridescent met uncertain turquoise, and an understanding passed between them. At least, that's what Wave felt. She took a deep breath.

'A star,' she said.

Kali's eyes widened and she straightened, her fingers clutching the fabric of her dress. The silence stretched as Kali looked at the star, looked up at Wave, looked at the star again. Just as Wave's heart began to pound painfully in her chest and the inward curses started, Kali spoke.

'How?'

Closing her fingers over her prize, Wave retold her story in more detail than when she'd first told Strath and Jessandra.

Once she was finished, Kali regarded her sadly.

'I understand your fear,' she said after another long silence. 'But Setora's story is not exactly what it seems.'

'What do you mean?' Wave asked. That familiar, tiny flame of hope tried to flicker into existence, but Wave squashed it. There was no point, not now, not when she'd already seen the sadness in Kali's eyes. The elder knew she was doomed, she was just more honest than the others.

Kali rose from her seat. 'Wait here.' She left through the back door.

Wave tucked the star back into her pocket and hung her head. 'I shouldn't have told her,' she murmured, more to herself than anyone else.

'She must know something,' Strath said, his voice hopeful. 'You heard what she said: Setora's story isn't what it seems.'

Wave shook her head. She felt like a piece of flotsam being tossed in an angry sea. There was no hope for the likes of her. A star-caller was a star-caller, destined to doom anyone who came near her. She screamed internally, the sound reverberating through her mind. It had been easy to ride Strath's waves of hope, pretending that there was a way to save her.

For the first time in her life she'd found people her own age she liked, respected, wanted to spend time with, but now she needed to face the reality that she had to give them up. All they'd been through together was in vain. She buried her face in her hands and tried to squash the terrible disappointment.

'Here,' Kali said.

Too lost in her own misery, Wave hadn't even heard her come back in the room. The elder held a book in front of her face.

Wave took it from her, unable to speak. Aged, dark blue leather bound faded sheafs of parchment. No title or author was inscribed on the cover. Wave turned the book over in her hands. The first page held a title, but nothing else.

The Blood of the Ehta.

'What is it?' Wave asked.

'Take it, and read it after you've had some rest,' Kali said. 'You should find some solace in one of the stories.'

'Which one?' Wave asked. Books had always held the answers for her, but she couldn't see how they would help now.

'The true story of Setora,' Kali said. 'The one not twisted and warped by those who would hide the truth.'

28

SHARVEL

IN A SMALL, circular room, Jessandra sat at a table grinding herbs in a mortar. Strath stood a few paces away, leaning over a large pot on the wood-fired stove.

'I think they're ready,' Jessandra said, handing the bowl to Strath.

'Perfect,' he said, offering her a small smile that made a lump rise in her throat.

She'd never ground herbs before, never made food of any kind. As children, she'd often followed Lenta into the castle kitchens to see what the staff were doing. They would be fed cakes and sweet apple juice before being sent back to their rooms. None of the cooks would ever let them near the food preparations, worried that they'd be punished by Mascerab.

Strath tipped the herbs into the pot, stirring a few more times before joining Jessandra at the table. He sat beside her, and her senses tingled at their closeness.

'I don't have any bread for our soup,' he said. 'That's the problem with travelling.' He shook his head with a sad laugh. 'Also the problem with having no parents.'

'I'd have the same problem even with my parents,' Jessandra

muttered, wrapping her hands around the mug of tea she'd poured earlier.

After Kali had given Wave the book, Strath had led them to his domed house. Despite the fact he'd been gone from Sharvel for months, his home felt fresh and alive. Strath had sent them both to rest in a bedroom that held two single beds.

Jessandra hadn't been able to sleep, and neither had Wave. As soon as they lay down, Wave began to read, flicking through the pages of Kali's book at a lightning pace. Jessandra was envious of her speed, but pushed her thoughts aside. Wave was her friend, that was all that mattered.

As Wave read, Jessandra let herself relax, getting lost in thoughts about Strath and Sharvel. Now that the stress of escaping the Black Cloaks was gone, Strath was much calmer. She couldn't deny the flutter in her belly when she was around him. When he smiled at her, she felt seen in a way she'd never experienced with Jai'til.

It felt like mere moments had passed while Jessandra lay back, lost in her thoughts, when she heard Wave sob.

'I have to see Kali,' Wave had said through her tears, taking the book and running from the room.

'Do you think Wave's okay?' Strath asked, dragging Jessandra's attention back to the present.

'I hope so,' Jessandra said with a shrug. 'Do you have any idea what was in the book?'

Strath shook his head. 'The library is full of ancient texts. I've read a lot of them, but I haven't read *The Blood of the Ehta*.'

'I wonder what's different about Setora's story,' Jessandra said, looking into the swirling colours of her tea. 'Maybe there's some sort of cure that was lost in the retelling?'

'I hope so,' Strath said, staring out of the window.

There was always something about the way Strath looked at Wave, the way he spoke to her that made Jessandra jealous. She couldn't be sure, but she got the sense that he liked her a little more than a friend should. The feeling tore Jessandra in two. Wave was her friend, and the closeness she felt for Wave was that of a sister. It didn't even make sense—they'd only known each other a few days, but Jessandra felt as if she and Wave had been friends their whole lives.

'Do you think I can stay in Sharvel?' Jessandra asked, trying to pull her attention back to her own future. Worrying about Wave and Strath was one thing, but she couldn't forget her own dilemma.

'Everyone is welcome in Sharvel,' Strath said, turning away from the window. 'I can't promise that your father won't be able to find you here, but I know you're safer here than anywhere else in Heredour.'

'Maybe I'll find my calling here.' The absence of her god-given calling was the root of all her problems, and she tried to put it back in focus. Traversing the North Claw with Wave and Strath had been a welcome distraction, but now that they could settle down in Sharvel for a time, she had to think about her next steps. 'Do your elders know how to help someone find their god?'

Strath laughed, long and loud, though it wasn't unkind.

'Oh, Jess,' he said. 'You have no idea.'

She frowned at him. 'I know, that's why I'm in all this trouble. If I knew which god I was a child of ...'

'That's not what I mean,' he said, grinning at her.

Before she could reply, the door to Strath's house banged open.

Wave stood in the doorway, tears streaming down her face, just as they had been when she'd run from the room earlier. The *Ehta* was still in her hands and she walked over to them, flopping the soft book open on the table.

'Wave?' Strath asked, his voice soft as the leather that bound the text.

Their friend cried openly, unable to speak. She flicked

through the tome, then pointed at a page. Jessandra and Strath crowded around the book, their faces almost pressed together as they looked at the page. Doing her best to ignore their closeness, Jessandra skimmed through the story as fast as she could. Wave sat down on the chair opposite with a thump, hugging her knees to her chest.

When they were finished, Jessandra lifted her eyes to Wave, her hands over her mouth. Wave nodded.

'It was all a lie?' Jessandra said. 'There's no curse?'

Wave nodded again, her lips trembling. Jessandra jumped up and wrapped her arms around Wave. Tears pushed themselves from Jessandra's closed eyelids. Wave held her tight as they rocked back and forth.

'You're not cursed,' she muttered into Wave's hair. 'You're not cursed.'

The *Ehta* had revealed the truth of Setora's story, the truth that had been wilfully lost to the ages. Setora's stars had never been cursed, and she'd been a star-caller for many years without any problems among her people. The Black Cloaks had been curious about her stars and offered to work with her to understand their nature.

Then the Black Cloaks had begun to do things to the stars, unspeakable things, and Setora rejected their work. She'd tried to reclaim the stars she'd offered them for research, but they refused to return them. When they finally gave in, offering Setora a single star as payment for allowing them to do their research, she thought the terrors of their experiments would be over. Soon after they returned the star, though, her mentor became ill. The rest of Setora's story was the same as the one modern mothers told their children—slowly, everyone who came into contact with Setora or her star became sick, until the entire city was ill.

Setora had been distraught because she knew the truth. The stars hadn't made everyone sick. The Black Cloaks had done something to the star they'd returned—twisted it, corrupted it, cursed it in some way nobody understood. They were the cause of the illness that wiped out the city, they were the reason the South Claw was blasted off the face of Heredour.

'Those bastards,' Strath hissed. 'How could they?'

Jessandra took a deep breath and released Wave.

'I'm so sorry,' Strath said, standing at the same time Wave did.

They held each other, the image of a lovers' embrace. Jessandra pushed aside her jealousy. Now was the time for rejoicing that Wave could live a normal life, that she could be a human alongside them. There was no curse, only another story full of Black Cloak lies. Jessandra felt a bubbling anger, similar to what she'd felt when she'd read Lenta's note. They were responsible for so much pain in their world. Bastards, Strath had called them, and Jessandra agreed. How did they get away with all the deceit?

'Kali confirmed it,' Wave said later as they sat over steaming bowls of soup. 'The *Ehta* came from Veija-Mens, from the descendants of the South Claw. It's the original story, not the warped version we know in Heredour.'

Strath reached over and squeezed her hand. 'You're free now.'

'Not quite,' Wave said.

Despite their shared relief at the *Ehta*'s revelation, Jessandra had noticed Wave was still holding on to some sort of sadness.

'Just because we know the truth, doesn't mean the Black Cloaks will stop looking for you,' Jessandra said, her spoon halfway to her mouth.

'They have a narrative to uphold,' Wave agreed. 'The people

ing, because she felt the same. Staying in Sharvel would mean an idyllic life, something most people only ever dreamed of. And yet, it wasn't enough. Jessandra had a kingdom to rule, and even though she wasn't sure she wanted the responsibility, duty called to her like a beacon. The feeling was a surprise—she'd always been too lost in her head to understand what it meant to be heir.

'I can't,' Wave said.

'Why not?' Strath asked.

'What if the people of Sharvel were harmed because the Black Cloaks learned they were harbouring a star-caller?'

Strath frowned before opening his mouth to speak. Jessandra cut him off.

'That's not it, Wave. Tell him why you can't stay.'

Wave stared at her with a frown that softened into a smile. Their friendship had only grown in the hours since they'd learned the truth of Setora and Wave's curse. There was an understanding between them, a shared sense of being wronged by the world for simply existing as they were. Although Jessandra couldn't explain it, the feeling made her heart full to bursting. She'd only shared that kind of closeness with Lenta. Wave's presence, her understanding, was the most welcome relief.

'I can't stay,' Wave admitted. 'My family is out there, likely suffering because of the lies about the star. I have to try to help them.'

Strath studied her, his face impassive.

'I understand,' he said. 'I would do the same thing. But there of time since she'd left Millen?

'Is it really almost Long Night?' she asked.

Strath and Wave nodded in unison. The festival wasn't a huge celebration for starkin, though they normally celebrated in a small way in the castle. Long Night held the most importance for water- and moonkin—they equally celebrated and mourned the aching distance in the sisterhood between Wederlly and Lerinial. It was always held on the first moonless night of the year, but Jessandra hadn't been paying attention to the phases.

'What difference will a couple of days make, Wave?' Strath asked. That look was in his eyes again, the one that was reserved for Wave, the one that caused a spike of jealousy in Jessandra's gut. 'I promise you, both of you, that what you'll learn will change everything.'

'Like how you can use both earth- and plantkin powers?' Wave asked, as she sat back in her chair, folding her arms across her chest.

Jessandra frowned. Nobody could use the power of two gods —to suggest such a thing was blasphemous. Strath stared into his soup with his favourite mysterious smile.

'You noticed,' he said.

Wave rolled her eyes at Jessandra.

'Noticed what?' Jessandra asked.

'When we were fighting the wizards,' Wave said. 'Outside of Jindar. Strath protected us with walls of earth, though it cost him dearly. And he knocked the Black Cloaks over by shifting the ground beneath their feet.'

Jessandra nodded slowly, realisation creeping across her

awareness. 'But you also protected us in the forest.' She turned to Strath. 'Shifted plants and leaves and gods know what else to hide us.'

He grinned at them both.

'How?' Wave asked. 'It should be impossible. Another person would call you a blasphemer.'

Strath laughed. Gods, how Jessandra loved the sound of his mirth.

'You think Setora's story is the only lie we live in Heredour?' He pushed his bowl away. 'I wanted to let Kali explain this, as she's far more eloquent than I, but since you've asked the question ...' He shrugged.

'Eloquence be damned,' Wave said.

'Come on then,' Strath called as he headed out the door and into the garden. 'The truth awaits.'

Dusk had settled over Sharvel, and twilight cast the plateau in shades of indigo and violet. Jessandra led the way out of the house, Wave close behind. Strath stood beneath an ancient beech, waiting for them.

'Are you sure you're ready?' he asked, a sly smile lighting his features as he regarded them both.

'My life has been flipped inside out twice in the space of mere weeks,' Wave said. 'I've never been more ready.'

Strath closed his eyes. The leaves above him rustled, even though the air was still. At their feet, fallen brown leaves lifted into the air, spiralling around Strath's face. It was an impressive feat of plantkin power, Jessandra knew, but it was nothing compared to the power Wave controlled.

'Oh,' Wave said, her smug smile falling as she watched Strath's demonstration. 'Setunil.'

Jessandra looked between Strath and Wave, not understanding. Setunil was the god of the sky, the god of Siska and Inska. He commanded power over weather, the air ...

'Oh,' Jessandra said, accidentally mimicking her friend. 'Setunil.'

Droplets of water rose from the birdbath near the house, adding themselves to the spiral of leaves surrounding Strath.

'No,' Wave said.

Jessandra's mouth opened. It shouldn't be possible. It couldn't be, not without unravelling everything she knew about how the world worked.

With a shaky breath, Strath released the leaves and water, letting them fall to the earth. He'd grown pale. They rushed to his side, helping him down to the ground.

'Working with Lerinial takes a lot out of me,' he murmured, smiling up at both of them.

Above his head, Wave and Jessandra stared at each other. The shock in Wave's face was a mirror of how Jessandra felt.

'Do you see?' Strath asked once he'd regained some of his colour.

'You can use the power of more than one god,' Jessandra breathed.

'No,' Wave said, 'no, it's more than that.'

Strath nodded.

'We think we're only using one power at a time,' Wave continued. 'I move streams of water, so I'm using Lerinial's power, right? But that's not true. They're intimately connected. We thought Strath was using Ferengün's power to move the leaves, but how could he move them through the air without some support from Setunil? How could I have heated that water to boiling without some sort of support from Jesma?' She stood and walked away from them, pacing as she spoke. 'We're not even aware of it, but we're tapping into the powers of multiple gods, even while we think we're just using the power of our singular god. And that's what they drill into us. My teachers would say that I can move water through the air because I have so much strength in Lerinial's power. But that's not it at all, is it?

Somehow, as impossible as it seems, I'm connecting with Setunil to move Lerinial's water through his air.'

Wave turned back to where Jessandra and Strath sat by side by side. Jessandra had her arm around Strath's shoulders, his head resting against her shoulder, but she barely noticed. The more Wave spoke, the more her mind reeled.

'They made us together, all eight gods,' Wave said, her eyes wild. 'Being called by one god is the lie, isn't it, Strath?'

He nodded. 'We can access all the gods' powers, and we do it without even realising.'

NO MAN'S LAND

IN THE HOLLOW silence surrounding the obelisk, the horses whinnied and bucked as they drew closer. Aymn's horse fought against the reins, and Mortius watched the other men struggle with their mounts as they reared on their hind legs or danced in sidesteps.

Mortius' mount, Sabré, didn't shy from the flick of his reins or the pressure of his knees, though her ears were laid flat against her head. He didn't blame the horses. There was an eeriness to this place, an unnatural quiet that made his skin tingle, his breath shallow.

The area all around Buduwai was barren, open land. No grasses, trees, or shrubs of any kind grew here; it was as if the desert had swept into this little pocket of Triné. Not that the empire would claim the obelisk, though neither would Lashameg. Buduwai was in no man's land.

'Where's the entrance?' Aymn asked, pulling Mortius from his reverie.

'There are none.'

Mortius glanced at his charge. A thousand unspoken questions simmered in his eyes, but he asked none of them. A minute frown crossed his features.

'Did the Black Cloaks build this ... thing?'

'Nobody knows who built it,' Mortius said with a shrug. 'It's been here for as long as we've documented our history.'

'How does anyone get in?' Aymn asked.

Mortius bit the inside of his cheek, the familiar guilt bubbling under the surface of his skin. 'I don't know.'

Just because the Black Cloaks were using the obelisk as their home for the Kaiáho didn't mean they were going to let the High King of Heredour in on their secrets. Revealing his ignorance pained him, but he couldn't lie to Aymn about Buduwai.

'When they've finished being,'—Aymn paused as he searched for the right word—'re-educated, how do they get out?'

Mortius didn't fail to notice the sarcasm, or the pain, in Aymn's voice. While Mortius carried the guilt and shame of failing to talk Reuben out of introducing the law, Aymn had no doubt lost friends to Buduwai. Aymn belonged to the city and the people in a way Mortius never could.

'They don't,' Mortius said with a swift glance behind them. The others still rode at a respectful distance, struggling with their horses in silence.

'Ever?' Aymn asked, mimicking Mortius' soft tone.

'I don't believe so.'

Aymn looked over his shoulder, checking the others were far enough away.

'Uncle?' he murmured as he turned to face the obelisk.

Many years had passed since Aymn had called him anything other than Senior Adviser.

'Speak freely, Aymn.'

'There is talk among the common folk about Buduwai.'

Mortius nodded. He'd heard all the rumours from his spies, but it was another thing to hear it from someone whose loyalties lay elsewhere.

'There are many who say that the Black Cloaks are doing something ... untoward with these misguided youth.'

Aymn kept his eyes forward, as if avoiding Mortius' gaze could help him avoid the weight of the question. For a long time, Mortius said nothing, trying to figure out how to frame an answer.

'I don't know what they do in there,' he answered finally. 'The Black Cloaks are reticent and guarded about everything, even around the high king. They still operate under the guise of re-education.' Mortius swallowed. 'But, like the common folk, I also hold grave concerns for those named Kaiāho.'

'What can be done about it?' Aymn turned to Mortius. 'How can we help them?'

The skin around Aymn's eyes was tight with a pain Mortius didn't understand. Mortius had never let himself get close to anyone, saving himself from experiencing the suffering of loss. The only person he'd ever felt even a hint of closeness to was the child Aymn. Back then, with the boy in his household, when there had been equal laughter and tears at any hour of the day, Mortius had felt like he had a friend.

'The high king has no intention of revoking the Law,' Mortius said. 'I have an idea, something of a plan that might help the Kaiāho. It may well fail, and it will require a lot of time to implement.'

'Can I help?' Aymn asked, the eagerness in his voice almost overshadowing the hurt in his eyes.

'It will be extremely dangerous.' Especially for Aymn. 'But if you want to help, I think you're well suited.'

Aymn nodded. 'I imagine it's not something we can discuss in great detail yet?' He gestured over his shoulder with a raised eyebrow.

'That's right. Part of my intention out here in the regions is to set my plan in motion. I'll tell you what I can, when I can.'

'Thank you,' Aymn said.

Silence settled over them as they rode past the structure. The only sound was the nervous whinnying of the horses. There were no crickets, no birds, no signs of life anywhere. Deep cracks spiderwebbed the space between the road and the monolith, as if no rain had fallen in a thousand years.

Before they reached the western coast road, Mortius called a halt to their journey. He ordered the others to make camp on the open land west of the path, as far away from Buduwai as they could be without losing sight of the road.

'Is it wise to camp so close, Senior Adviser?' one of the men, Lien, asked as they dismounted.

The sun was near to setting, but they had enough time before full dark to get further away.

'Perhaps not,' Mortius answered, his eyes on the huge structure. 'Yet I wish to study this place for a time before we move on.'

Mortius could feel Aymn's eyes on him, could feel the unasked questions burning in his mind.

The five men set up camp in silence, too aware of the ominous presence in the background to try to rouse a conversation. The air was warmer than in the city, even though it was early autumn, and they didn't bother setting up any tents. Each man rolled out a fur-lined bed roll in a circle around the fire pit.

Lien and Vir'n disappeared towards the setting sun to try to forage some kindling to start a fire. Before leaving the capital, Mortius had instructed them to bring some decent wood, anticipating that they'd have to camp somewhere along this barren stretch, but he'd said not to bother with kindling. The original plan had been to stay closer to the coast, where there was plenty of scrubby sea brush. For now, they had to make do with whatever pathetic sticks they could find.

Once the fire was set, the others unloaded supplies from their packs. There would be no fresh meat tonight; the barrenness surrounding them made hunting a futile task.

With the sun gone, a fine mist blanketed the sky, blotting out the moon and stars. Huddled by the flickering fire, Mortius couldn't avoid the quietness of his team. The three older men knew each other well, and had shown a strong sense of camaraderie on other ventures. Tonight, though, nobody wanted to share campfire stories, or jest at another's expense.

Mortius sat alone on one side of the fire, facing the obelisk. That he could see the structure against the lightless sky made his dinner curdle in his stomach.

'What do you make of this place?' Aymn asked Lien. They sat side by side, the structure to their right.

'Make of it?' Lien raised his eyebrows as he stared into the fire. 'I don't know what to make of it.'

'It's been here as long as memory,' Yll chimed in from a few paces away.

'Aye,' Lien agreed, 'I've been past here a few times.'

'But what is it?' Aymn asked in earnest, as if Mortius hadn't already revealed the secrets of the obelisk.

'Nothing important, I'd say,' Yll said with a shrug. 'Nobody knows how to get in. There's no doors, no windows, no entrances of any kind.'

'What if there are people inside?' Aymn asked.

Mortius swiped a hand over his face to cover his surprise. He didn't know what Aymn was up to, and it unsettled him.

'What do you mean?' Lien asked. 'How could there be people inside?'

'What if there's an entire city in there?' Aymn asked, throwing his hands in the air, his eyes wide. 'Maybe people have been living inside, trapped for an entire age!'

'What nonsense have you got into your head, boy?' Yll said with a laugh. 'I thought you said he was a bright one?' Yll turned to Mortius with a cheeky grin.

Mortius forced a smile.

'There are rumours about this place,' Vir'n muttered from his place outside the pool of light.

All four of them turned to him, watching him in silence.

'There are tales of a time when the ground wasn't always like this. That in another age, there was lush plant life, animals, everything.' Vir'n stared into the fire as he spoke, his hands clasped before him. 'Some have spoken of lightning appearing here when no clouds darken the sky.'

The fire crackled, and the mist deepened.

'And there are some who think that ...' He paused. With a fearfulness reminiscent of an oft beaten animal, Vir'n raised his gaze to Mortius.

The look in his eyes was that of a frightened animal.

'Speak freely, Vir'n,' Mortius said, his voice hoarse. 'You will face no persecution for words spoken in this blighted land.'

Some of the fear in his eyes subsided, and he turned to face the others.

'There are some who wonder if this is the home of Buduwai.'

Mortius couldn't hide his shock this time. His mouth opened and he inhaled sharply. The secret he thought they'd kept so well was burning quietly among the common folk like the beginning of a wildfire.

Across the fire, Aymn locked eyes with Mortius, a look of grim satisfaction on his face. He'd known, then, before Mortius had told him. Suspected, at least, based on the challenge in his expression.

One by one, the others turned to look at Mortius, the same question on their faces. As Lien tore his eyes away from the fire, a whip-like crack resounded through the air. They leapt to their feet, hands ready on their sword hilts. A streak of lightning arched down from the sky, piercing the barren ground on the other side of the obelisk.

Then, there was silence. Each man studied the area around

him. Mortius looked up at the vast, mist-riddled sky. No storm clouds marred the expanse above him.

Another deafening crack boomed through the open space. Moments later, lightning crashed from the empty sky into some point north of the structure.

'Senior Adviser!' Lien cried. 'We should get out of here!'

Mortius shook his head, though nobody was looking at him. The other men voiced the same idea, in an array of panicked pitches.

'No,' Mortius said as he tried to watch the obelisk and the sky at the same time.

'It's not safe!' Lien shouted as another bolt arced towards the ground.

'Calm yourself, Lien,' Aymn said once the lightning had disappeared. 'Haven't you noticed?' Aymn gestured towards the building. 'The lightning only strikes on the land around the building. It doesn't cross the road.'

Mortius blinked. The junctions of the three separate roads created a triangular stretch of land around the structure. No lightning pierced the ground outside the triangle. Aymn was right. They were safe.

'And see, men,' Aymn added. 'The ground isn't cracked on this side of the road, which may mean the lightning is the cause. We're safe here.'

Mortius breathed a sigh of relief. He wasn't concerned about the lightning; he'd heard all the reports before. What gave him hope was Aymn's discerning eye for detail and the way he calmed a group of frightened men using logic and a few choice words.

Lightning crackled through the air around them. Chains of light wrapped around the obelisk before striking at the ground. The time between strikes grew shorter, but they were in no immediate danger. The group stood in awe, watching the incredible display of raw power. As abruptly as it began, it was over, a deafening silence filling the darkness. Mortius moved back to the fire.

One by one, the others followed, Aymn in the lead. They sat in silence for a long time. Mortius felt Vir'n's eyes on him, but he didn't acknowledge the man. Mortius knew what they were all thinking. If the stories of the lightning were true, then couldn't the rumours of Buduwai being housed in the structure also be true? A clawing sensation rose in his gut, and he pushed the thoughts aside.

'We should sleep now,' Mortius said. 'No harm will come to us here, so rest easy.'

In silence, they tended to the fire and each man made their way to a sleeping roll. Mortius knew that, despite his words, nobody would sleep well tonight.

30

GARDAR MAE

AUTUMN SETTLED over Condor with the gentle whisper of cold wind in the trees and growing ice caps on the high mountain tops. Larka and Winter fell into an easy rhythm in Gardar Mae, sliding into Hasting's life as though they belonged there.

The wooden house was filled with laughter and warmth and the smell of freshly cooked food. Rainer visited every day, usually after Hasting had returned home from his work in the plantations, so they could share a meal together.

After dinner each night, Larka presented different plans to Hasting and Rainer. She'd grown comfortable enough around the other man to share the troubles of her eldest daughters, and she was rewarded with his compassion and offers of support.

'If you took the letter with you,' Hasting said one night, several days after Larka had arrived, 'they've got no reason to consider coming here.'

'Not for a while, as I've said,' Larka answered. 'Siska doesn't know you're here, so she can't provide that information to the Black Cloaks no matter how much they torture her.' Her heart ached just saying the words, but she pushed ahead. She hadn't the slightest idea how she could help her eldest daughter. 'But if they don't catch Wave, they're going to be looking for us under every rock and leaf. By then, it won't matter where they think we are. They'll be everywhere.'

'That's why you want to act sooner?' Rainer asked from the counter, his hands buried in soap suds.

'If I can organise for Winter to be kept safe,' Larka said, 'then I can try to rescue Siska.' One step at a time.

'I want to go wherever you go, Mumma,' Winter chimed in. She held a warm scone in her hand, blackberry jam and cream dripping over her fingers.

'I would never leave you unless I knew you were safe, my darling,' Larka said. 'But somebody needs to help your sister.'

Winter grimaced and shoved more scone into her mouth.

'I agree we need to keep Winter safe,' Hasting said. 'But we also need to keep you safe. There's no way any one of us'—he gestured at himself, Larka, and Rainer—'could get into the castle unnoticed, let alone down into the dungeons.'

'Then we have to come up with a better plan. I can't sit back and do nothing!' There was no evidence that Siska was trapped in Waterfall City, but Larka didn't think the Black Cloaks would want her anywhere else.

'Let me take you to Davej-Arne, to my friend who lives there,' Hasting said. 'Nobody in the capital knows of my connection to him. And Davej-Arne is so far-flung, it'll be the last place they'll look.'

Larka could think of other far-flung places that would actually make the bottom of a Black Cloak's list, but she kept her thoughts to herself.

'It will take months to get to Davej-Arne!' she insisted. 'Siska can't wait that long.'

'I told you,' Hasting said. 'There's another way.'

'Then why won't you tell me about this other way?'

'Because you won't like it.' Hasting grabbed a towel and

began drying the dishes Rainer had stacked to one side. 'It'll be easier for me to explain once we're in Davej-Arne.'

Larka let out an exasperated sigh. 'How long?'

'Very quickly.'

'How long is that?'

'Faster than any other plan you've come up with.' Hasting turned away from her to place the dishes in the curtain-fronted cupboard.

She couldn't understand why he was being so evasive. There were no direct routes to get to Davej-Arne from Gardar Mae, and they'd either have to go through the Triné Empire or past Waterfall City. Even if they had access to horses, the journey would take weeks at best.

'And what about getting from Davej-Arne to the capital?' Larka said, determined to either get her way or unearth whatever Hasting was hiding. 'Another month or two on foot to get around the Kirsky Forest isn't going to help Siska.'

'We won't have to wait that long,' Hasting said, his back to her. 'I'll just need a couple of days to regain my strength.'

Larka laughed. 'Are you going to fly us there? Morph yourself into a great eagle or a dragon and whisk us over the continent?'

'Something like that,' Hasting said.

She could hear the smirk in his voice. Had he always been this frustrating?

'I want to go with you,' Rainer said, surprising Larka from whatever retort she was about to spit back at Hasting.

'Why?'

Rainer dried his hands on a towel and sat back down at the table. 'There's nothing left for me here in Gardar Mae. My wife is dead, my children scattered. They hate me, anyway. I can't protect them, but I could try to protect you.' He turned to Winter at the other end of the table. With a small smile, he picked up a cloth napkin and wiped the remaining jam and cream from her face. She smiled back at him with genuine warmth.

'And Winter. The most important.' He tapped her on the nose and she giggled.

'We should get you ready for bed, little lady,' Larka said, realising she'd lost most of the evening explaining her latest plan to the two men.

'But I want to stay up,' Winter said with a frown. 'I don't want to miss out on what you're talking about.'

'We're done talking for the night,' Larka said with a sidelong glance at Hasting. If he wasn't going to be upfront with her, there was little else they could discuss.

Winter argued for a while, but Larka eventually wrestled her into the washroom to brush her teeth. By the time she was asleep in bed, Rainer had left and Hasting was lost in a book.

The soft orange glow of an oil lamp cast his brown curls in reddish hues, and the whisper of pages turning was the only sound in the quiet house. Larka's heart beat unevenly as she stood in the doorway watching him. An unfamiliar sensation tingled in her lower abdomen. She frowned at herself, disbelieving.

Am I ... attracted to him?

The thought was a revelation, shocking in its audacity. Larka let out a tiny gasp. It couldn't be attraction. Not Hasting. Not her best friend, the one who'd been by her side since they were children.

At the sound of her breath, Hasting looked up. A slow, seductive smile spread across his face. Larka felt the tingling again and she swallowed.

He opened his mouth to speak.

'I'm going to bed,' Larka said, cutting him off before he could say something untoward.

'May the gods hold you in the cradle of their arms,' he murmured.

She turned on her heel, unable to look at him any longer. In a daze, Larka readied herself for bed. She loved Sam, her husband. Something else must be going on in her body, but it certainly couldn't be attraction to Hasting.

Tucked under the covers beside Winter, it took Larka a long time to drift into an uneasy sleep.

———

There was a new quietness to the house the next day. Larka kept to herself, and there was less laughter, less joy. Hasting could feel it, from the way he studied her from afar, but so could Winter. She escaped as early as she could, hunting down the children and their strange ball game.

'I have a day off today,' Hasting said after Winter had gone. 'Would you like to spend some time together, just the two of us?'

Larka's fingers dug into the loaf she was tucking into the breadbasket. Taking a steadying breath, she released the bread.

'Okay.'

He'd know something was wrong if she denied his request.

'I've got a bit of gardening to catch up on, and a book I want to finish,' he said when she finally turned around. 'Perhaps we can potter among the vegetables and read under the old oak in the garden.'

Just like when they were teenagers.

'I don't have any books,' Larka said.

Hasting smiled. 'I've got some of your old favourites.'

Gods, his smile made her feel so uncomfortable. Heat rose to Larka's cheeks.

'What needs doing in the garden?' she asked.

'I'll show you.'

Hasting led them through the house and into the garden. Nestled among the herbs and vines were several raised vegetable patches. One was thick with potato leaf, while the others held an assortment of chard, carrot tops, onion, and rhubarb.

Without any preamble, they set upon the garden. Larka could feel the layers of earth that needed attention, and she was drawn to support them. When she asked for manure, Hasting pointed to a hessian bag behind the trellis, and when she wanted straw, he showed her a covered stack by the wood pile.

Relief flooded through her body as she and Hasting worked the soil and plants, side by side, just as they always had. Growing up in Sharvel, they'd learned how to access the power of all the gods, but it was still evident that every human was stronger in one element. Larka had always been closest to Eritogone; Hasting to Ferengün.

Out in the world they had to assume one kin, which meant that Larka had spent fifteen years working with Eritogone's power almost exclusively. It was refreshing to dabble in Ferengün's power, learning new weaves from Hasting as he encouraged the growth of struggling plants.

This was how it should be. The two of them, shoulder to shoulder, their friendship wrought in familiarity, tears, and dirt-covered hands. Not attraction, or whatever this strange feeling was growing inside her.

The sombreness from earlier burned away under the bright autumn sun as they spent the morning in quiet conversation, laughter interspersed throughout.

'I thought I'd find you two here.'

Rainer's voice made them both turn in surprise.

'Have you eaten lunch yet?' Rainer asked.

Larka glanced up at the sun with a wry smile. 'Not yet.'

'I went fishing this morning,' Rainer said. 'I've prepared us a meal.'

Hasting and Larka washed their hands in the barrel by the back door. Inside, Rainer stood in front of a towel-covered tray, which he whipped off in a great flourish. The smell of herbs and freshly cooked fish greeted Larka's nostrils and she smiled in appreciation. Beside the whole fish—some sort of cod by the look of its fins—sat a bowl of mashed potato and another bowl of wilted greens.

'What a treat!' Larka exclaimed.

Food like this would have been common in Rainer's highkin household before he lost his family. These days he ate much the same diet as Hasting and Larka.

The three of them sat down to eat, Rainer portioning out sections of everything into four bowls. One bowl he covered with the towel.

'Winter can't miss out,' he said, the fondness in his voice not missed by Larka.

There was no point summoning her; she lived on her own schedule, eating whenever her body required sustenance. Larka appreciated his thoughtfulness, though.

The meal was reminiscent of everything she'd left behind in Sharvel. Dense without being heavy, rich in nutrients without being boring, flavoursome without being oversaturated. Gods, how had she spent so long living off barley and stew in the Plains?

When they were finished, they ignored the mess they'd made and collapsed onto a blanket beneath the old oak. They discussed inconsequential things—the challenges of raising daughters, their favourite books, stories from each of their journeys across Heredour.

Larka had almost forgotten what it was like to have friends. To be surrounded by the companionship of adults was a balm for the hole in her life she'd chosen to ignore. She'd never felt safe enough in the Plains to let anyone in. Despite her earlier hesitation, Rainer's friendship soothed her aching heart, and Hasting's mere presence was enough to ease her worries.

'All right!' Larka said, holding up her hands. 'Even though

you won't tell me how, let's do it. Let's go to this friend of yours in Davej-Arne.'

Hasting grinned at her. 'I know you don't believe me, but just you wait.'

'I've seen his trick,' Rainer added. 'It's worth it.'

Hasting had never kept secrets from her before, so she knew it was something big. Larka opened her mouth to try to needle something out of him. The words died in her throat as Winter sprinted into the garden, her eyes wild.

'Men in black cloaks,' Winter cried as she ran towards them. 'In the town.'

Larka froze. Black Cloaks. Not here, not now. They weren't ready.

Hasting and Rainer leapt to their feet, Rainer scooping Winter up onto his hip.

'What do we do?' Larka whispered, looking up at Hasting.

All the roads leading out of Gardar Mae started in the town, so there was no way to get out without being seen. The mountainous forest around Hasting's house was too dangerous to try to traverse—sharp crags covered in slippery pine needles would see them dead before the Black Cloaks found them.

'Now's as good a time as any,' Hasting said, reaching his hand out to Larka.

She took it, and he pulled her up.

'We're not ready,' she said.

'Too bad.'

With a grimace, Hasting led them out of the garden and into the forest at a trot. The large fruit trees gave way to towering pines within moments and they struggled against the needle-strewn ground. The house was still in sight when Hasting stopped them.

'I'll have to come back for you, Rainer,' Hasting said. 'I don't think I'm strong enough.'

Rainer's eyes narrowed.

'You can't leave him behind now,' Larka said. 'They'll know he was with us.'

'I don't know if I can.'

Larka punched Hasting in the upper arm. 'This was your idea! You said you could take us, and now we're stuck!'

'I meant I could take you one by one!' Hasting said. 'It wasn't meant to be like this.'

'It never is, Hasting!' Larka cried. 'Nothing in our life is ever like we meant it to be, but we just have to deal with what we've got.'

'Please,' Rainer whispered. 'Please don't leave me here with them.'

Hasting grimaced. 'Fine. Do you all trust me?'

In unison, Larka, Rainer, and Winter bobbed their heads.

'Come in close.'

Hasting opened his arms wide. Larka tucked herself in under one arm, Rainer under the other with Winter still on his hip. To complete their tight circle, Larka wrapped her other arm around Rainer's waist.

'Good,' Hasting said. 'Winter, bury your head into Rainer's shoulder. Hold on to each other, and whatever you do, don't let go.'

The places where Hasting's body touched Larka's sparked, tingled, vibrated.

Not now! she screamed at herself.

'It's easier if you close your eyes,' Hasting murmured as he closed his own.

Heart racing, Larka did as she was bid. Beside her, Hasting muttered words in a foreign language of guttural, scratching sounds that she knew from her nightmares. He spoke in the language of the Black Cloaks. Power emanated from him, a power different to the plantkin energy she associated him with, different to the earthkin power he could use almost as well as her. Terrified, Larka opened her eyes.

They were wrapped in a veil that darkened with each heart-beat, as though thick clouds were consuming them. Larka could see the forest around them, but it was fading into obscurity. She glanced at the others. Their eyes were all closed. Hasting was still murmuring, his words like sandpaper to her ears. There was no elemental nature to what he was tapping into.

A movement in the forest caught her attention. Two Black Cloaks raced up the slope towards them. They shouted in the same grating tongue.

Darkness consumed them.

The forest disappeared, the advancing Black Cloaks with it.

Larka's heart beat a painful rhythm in her chest, and her fingers ached from the grip she held on Hasting's and Rainer's clothes. Her vision showed nothing more than her friends, her daughter's head nestled into the crook of Rainer's shoulder.

They stayed in pure, complete darkness for what felt like an age. Before fear of the unknown could take over, though, scenery began to assemble into being before her eyes. The pine forest was gone; instead, they were surrounded by tall evergreens with long buttresses, thick vines entwined along the branches. Vibrant flowers covered the undergrowth of small shrubs, their long stamen dripping with pollen turned viscous. The scene before Larka's eyes grew more visible with every second, materialising around them, growing in depth as she watched.

Hasting stopped chanting, his face pale and drawn. Solid ground pushed up against Larka's feet. The sound of leaf litter crunched under her toes as the visage around them crystallised. In slow motion, she watched Hasting's body falling away from her. Despite the hold she and Rainer had on him, he collapsed to the ground, motionless.

Magic.

Hasting had used magic.

31

SHARVEL

LIFE IN SHARVEL was like a warm blanket on a cold night. Several days had passed since Wave had discovered she wasn't cursed, since she'd been held by her friends, since she'd felt human again. Most nights, she cried herself to sleep with relief, and sometimes, Jessandra rose to comfort her. The touch of her friend's hand on her shoulder only made her tears flow faster. Sometimes Jessandra cried with her.

Autumn was starting to set in, the nights growing chilly and the sun rising later. Wave and Jessandra fell into the simple rhythms of their new life, following Strath's lead in growing and making food, meeting the community, spending time with the elders in the library. For Wave, it felt like coming home.

The day of Long Night Festival arrived without any disturbance from the outside world. Although Wave felt relieved that she and the town had been left alone, she had a feeling that they were all running on borrowed time. There would be a point, whether in two days or two years, when the Black Cloaks would arrive in Sharvel looking for her. She had to be gone by then. There was no way she could let any harm come to these gentle people who'd accepted her with open arms.

In the small room where she'd first met Kali, Wave reclined on the chaise lounge, her head buried in a new book. If her new friends, her broken curse, or the generosity of this town weren't enough to make her want to stay, the wealth of knowledge in the library might have done it. Since Strath's demonstration in the garden, Wave had been devouring every text on the subject she could find.

A woman in a loose white dress strode across the lawns towards the room, and Wave peered over the top of her book. Two teacups clinked together in the woman's hand.

'What are you reading now?' Kali asked as she set the cups down on the table.

Wave pushed herself upright, marking her page in the book with a sprig of dried artemisia Strath had given her.

'*The Diaries of Emmeth the Sage.*'

'Ah,' Kali said. 'A classic.'

'Not where I'm from.'

Kali chuckled and slipped through the back door, returning moments later with a steaming pot. Once the tea was sitting on a slab of wood, Kali sat back in the armchair with a sigh.

They sat in silence for a few moments, waiting for the tea to brew. Wave had come to Kali's office every day since arriving in Sharvel, and the elder had never failed to meet with her. They'd discussed everything—philosophy, history, geography, and more importantly, the use of different gods' powers. Kali was a fountain of knowledge and Wave soaked up everything she could from the other woman.

'I'm curious about your family, Wave.' Kali poured them each a cup. Steam rose from the surface in lazy, winding spirals.

Despite their many conversations, neither Kali nor Wave had shared anything overly personal. Everything else had seemed too important to Wave to even spend much time thinking about her family. Those thoughts were too painful anyway.

'What do you want to know about them?' Wave asked. She was no longer afraid of being honest about her family—Strath had made sure she understood that the people of Sharvel despised the Law of Kaiāho.

'You've only spoken of your sister, a powerful skykin. Your parents must be powerful in their own right, to bring the likes of you both into the world.'

'I know so little about my father that I have nothing useful to share,' Wave said with a shrug. 'My mother ... well, I wouldn't say this anywhere else. My mother is an earthkin.'

'So you both escaped the law, then.' Sipping at her steaming tea, Kali leaned into the soft armchair, her legs resting over one arm. 'I'm sure that's an interesting tale, but perhaps we can save it for another time. Your mother is strong in her earthkin power?'

'Not particularly,' Wave said. 'She doesn't stand out in the community. I guess you would say she's an average earthkin.'

Kali pursed her lips. 'We don't believe in the Law of Kaiāho here, as you know. How could we, when we know that humans can access the power of all the gods?'

Wave shook her head. The concept still rattled her mind, but already she was experimenting, reaching for the other gods in a haphazard fashion, hoping to explore what other power was available to her. One of the reasons she met with Kali was a vain hope that the elder might teach her how to access the gods.

'What we do understand,' Kali continued, 'is that strength of power is passed down generationally. No matter what kin your parents are, if they are strong in their power, so too will their children be strong.'

'So you think my father is very powerful?'

'He must be,' Kali said with a decisive nod. 'What is his kin?'

Wave frowned. 'I don't know. Mother always said it was safer for us the less we knew about him.'

'She's very protective of you.'

'She is.'

Wave studied the other woman through a veil of steam. Kali was the youngest elder she'd ever met; she was of a similar age to her mother. Unlike her mother, though, the lines around Kali's eyes suggested many years spent with an honest smile on her face more than the years of hardship Wave's mother had endured.

'What's her name?' Kali asked.

'Larka.'

Kali choked on her tea. She sat forward, almost dropping her teacup on the floor.

'Are you okay?' Wave asked.

'Larka?' Kali croaked as she waved away Wave's offer of assistance. 'What's your father's name?'

'Sam.'

Kali blinked once, slowly. Then, she dropped her face into her hands, cradling her head. The silence dragged on, Wave growing more uncomfortable each moment. She set her teacup down.

'Kali?'

Taking a deep breath, the elder lifted her head. 'I'm sorry, Wave.' There was a new light in her iridescent eyes, some strange mix of anger, shame, and hope.

'What for?'

'I knew ...' She trailed off. 'You don't know where your mother is from?'

Wave shook her head.

'Your mother, Larka, she was raised here.'

'Here?' Wave's eyes widened. 'In Sharvel?'

'Yes. I believe her parents moved here when she was a toddler.'

Wave flopped back onto the lounge. Why had her mother never told her? They'd never left the Plains, never come back to visit family. They could have been safe here, without all the lies. Why hadn't they stayed?

'Wave, you were born in Sharvel,' Kali said. 'So was your sister.'

No words formulated in Wave's usually quick mind. She stared, not at Kali, but through her, through the wall behind her, into the past.

'I'm sure this must be more of a shock to you than it is to me,' Kali said, keeping her voice low.

Wave focused her eyes back to the room, back to the elder sitting opposite her.

'I ... I don't know what to say.'

'You don't have to say anything,' Kali said with a small smile. 'But I'm happy to answer any questions you have.'

There was only one question.

'Did you know my father?'

Kali swallowed. 'I did.'

'Who is he?' Wave asked. She leaned forward, perching herself on the edge of the lounge. 'Kali, please tell me.'

'If Larka didn't want you to know ...' Kali trailed off. One eyebrow hunkered down over her eye as she chewed on the inside of her cheek.

'Mother wouldn't tell us because she wanted to protect us,' Wave said. 'And that was fine when we were young, naive to the world. But look at us now. Siska, saving princesses from the cruelty of the world. And me, a star-caller!' Wave threw her hands in the air. The memory of her attempt to save Henny floated to the top of her mind, but she shoved it back down. 'I'm missing vital information about where I'm from, about who I am. Anything you can tell me about him might help me understand what I should do now.'

Kali took a deep breath, letting it all out in a big sigh. 'I don't know if you're ready for the truth, Wave,' she whispered.

Her words shivered in the air like prophecy, an echo of

Strath's words on the *Hand of Numen*. Kali glanced around the room, as if by avoiding Wave's gaze she could avoid the story.

'I've never been more ready,' Wave replied, inflicting all of the earnestness she could into her voice. 'Please, Kali. I need to know.'

'Sit back, then.' Kali filled their teacups again, settling back into her armchair, tucking her legs beneath her body. 'It's a long story.'

'For once, I have all the time in the world.' Wave took her full cup and leaned against the lounge. The position felt wrong, the reclining pose in full contradiction to the wild beat of her heart.

'I came to Sharvel not long after your father,' Kali said. 'That's how I know your mother. I was here not long after they were married.'

'So he wasn't from Sharvel?'

'No. Sam and I ... I guess you could say we grew up together, in a manner.' Kali paused.

Wave became more uncomfortable. How bad could talking about her father be if someone as eloquent as Kali hesitated and stumbled over her words?

'Wave, before I go on, I want you to know that there are a lot of stories about your father. A lot of lies. There are very few people who know the truth of his family, but I am one of them. I'll tell you the real story, but when you return to the world, you have to understand that nobody will believe you.'

'I already understand that.' Wave took the star from her dress pocket and lifted it between their faces. 'Tell me.'

'Your father is Sam, but his real name is Samson sunkin. The high king's younger brother.'

For the second time in the same conversation, Wave's mind was utterly blank. She couldn't formulate a thought, an opinion, even a question. The high king's brother?

'You've no doubt heard the story of his exile. That he tried to steal the throne from Reuben, that he had a hand in their father's death, that he raped one of the highkin women. It's all lies. Your father isn't the arrogant sunkin his brother is. He's kind and gentle. He didn't do anything to Reuben, and he certainly didn't rape the woman.'

Wave stared at Kali, blinking slowly. Thoughts, memories, and emotions began flooding her mind.

'The woman, Frieda, was a moonkin like me. We grew up together, two young girls of highkin birth in the big city. When Wederlly called us both, we were overjoyed. We trained together, did everything side by side. She fell in love with Samson, and though he was kind to her, he didn't love her.

'Reuben couldn't stand it. He wanted to take everything from his brother, and so he tried to win Frieda over. But she didn't like him. None of us did, really. He was spiteful, mean-spirited, always jealous of his younger brother. She rejected him over and over again, until one night, he snapped. It was he who raped her, not your father. Samson would never ...' Kali trailed off, lost in her own memories.

Wave was flooded with a cacophony of thoughts, questions, memories, all spiralling through her mind. Her father ... how could he be the exiled brother of the high king? It wasn't unlikely, it was impossible. The story didn't add up, didn't amount to him and Larka meeting in this hidden town. Even if Samson hadn't done what the world claimed, that didn't make him her father.

'How ...?' Wave asked, still struggling to find words to articulate the storming ocean of her mind.

'After he was exiled, he found his way here, to Sharvel. You've seen yourself that this is a place of safety, a haven for any who are lost or cast out. Samson found a place here, a home.'

'He met my mother here?'

Kali nodded. 'Apparently they fell in love the moment they met. By the time I left the capital and followed Samson here, they were already married and as tight as thieves. Them and

Hasting.' Kali chuckled, shaking her head with a small smile. 'Your sister was born not long after I arrived, and a few years later you followed. They travelled a lot when you were both young, exploring the parts of the world that were open to Samson.'

'Not Heredour, though.'

'No. Samson's exile made it too dangerous. They spent a lot of time here, though, maybe half of every year.'

'So how did we end up in the Barancha Plains?' Wave asked. 'Without him?'

'We're not sure how, but somehow the Black Cloaks learned that he might have been hiding out in Sharvel. The first time they came, we had warning. Sam took Larka and you girls into the desert. You were just a toddler. But the Black Cloaks were watching the town, so your parents decided it was time to find a new way to protect you and Siska.

'They moved out to the Plains, and your father only visited intermittently, at least, that was the plan. Given that you don't know anything about him, it sounds like something went awry.'

'I have a younger sister,' Wave said, trying to understand the timeline in her head. 'Winter. She's eight.'

'She's Samson's? Your mother didn't remarry, or …?' The question hung in the air between them.

'As far as I know,' Wave said with a shrug. Everything about her family was a lie. Everything in her life had been a farce, from the moment she was born. 'I remember him visiting us when I was little, though I can't recall his face. If Winter is his, it means nobody's seen him in eight, no, nine years. What happened to him?'

'I have no idea,' Kali said. 'We haven't seen him in as many years. The last time the Black Cloaks came, they brought the high king with them. They were looking for Samson, but he wasn't here. That was nearly eight years ago.'

Realisation bloomed like a poisoned flower in Wave's mind. 'When they found Strath's parents.'

'Yes,' Kali said, her eyes downcast.

'My father is responsible for Strath losing his parents,' Wave whispered. 'He deserted us in the Plains, left us to a life of lies and uncertainty.' The familiar anger bubbled beneath the surface of Wave's skin. She didn't care that he was highkin, the high king's brother no less. He was her father, and he'd been responsible for Strath's pain. Because of him, Winter had never known her father, and Wave and Siska barely had memories of him. Because of him, Larka had been left in an isolated village to raise three children alone.

'Strath's parents weren't Samson's fault,' Kali said. 'It was entirely circumstantial that they were here when the Black Cloaks came. I'm sure you know how rarely they actually stayed in Sharvel. Other than your father, Strath's parents were some of the most wanted people in Heredour.'

'Not anymore,' Wave said, grinding the words out through clenched teeth. 'They're gone now, and I'm the most wanted person in Heredour.'

'Wave.'

'No, Kali.' Wave stood. 'I appreciate you telling me my family's origin, but you can't stop me being angry.' *Angry* didn't quite cut it. *Rage*—a burning and frothing fury—was a better description. 'How much of my life, Siska's life, Winter's life would be different if he'd been around?'

'You understand why he couldn't—'

'Then he shouldn't have had children!' Wave balled her hands into fists. 'He should have realised he wouldn't have been able to manage the responsibility of being a parent because he's an exiled royal! How much danger have we been in this whole time, completely ignorant to our own heritage?' Wave began to pace the length of the room.

'He was so young when he was exiled, Wave.' Kali was trying to placate her, calm her down, but it only enraged Wave further.

'Not much older than me, if I remember the story correctly?' she said, saliva gathering on her lips as she spoke. 'When I thought I was cursed, I took every possible precaution to protect others, not let them touch me, even by accident. I suffered, thinking I'd have to live my life alone, never getting close to another human again. But I knew that was my duty!'

'Then you are a better person than he is.'

Wave spun around to face Kali. 'Why are you defending him?'

'I'm not defending him,' Kali said, holding her hands up. 'I know you're hurting because of what I've told you. But I also know the depths of suffering he's been through in his life, and so I have compassion for him. He adored you all so much. Leaving you would have broken his heart.'

'It's not good enough,' Wave said. 'Not at all.' She turned and strode from the room.

The lawns around the library passed quickly as her legs picked up speed. The houses along the curving road became a blur as she jogged towards the forest.

'Wave!' a voice called out, but she ignored it.

Trees whipped past the edges of her vision as she began to run. There was nothing particular to her direction, she just needed to move. The further she ran, the more her anger subsided. In its place, a gaping well of loneliness opened, her heart aching for the singular aspect of her family she'd never known.

Out of breath, she stopped at one of the ancient oaks, resting her hands on the trunk. She screamed as if the world was on fire. Head tilted to the sky, her voice threw a wordless wail up at the canopy, the tips of her fingers digging into the bark. She screamed and screamed until all that was left was the hole in her heart that should have been filled by her father.

The scream dissolved into tears and Wave sank to her knees in the dirt. She clutched her face with her hands. Her fingertips bled, but she didn't notice the blood tracking across her cheeks, mixing with her tears.

Someone placed an arm around her shoulder and pulled her away from the tree.

'Let it out, Wave,' Strath's voice crooned. 'You're safe here.'

In the circle of his arms, Wave cried as she'd never cried before, feeling for the first time the reality of her absent father and how it had impacted her life.

Strath was right, though. She was safe. She was safe with him.

32

SHARVEL

THE AFTERNOON SUN crept its way towards the western mountain peaks, the temperature dropping the further it sank. A thick, woollen blanket was spread over the ground in front of Strath's house, and several patterned cushions were scattered around.

Tucked deep in a heavy coat, Strath sat with his back against the old beech tree, hands busy weaving pieces of soft bark together. Jessandra perched on top of a cushion, frowning at a pair of knitting needles held close to her face. In front of her downturned mouth hung several rows of lopsided, hole-riddled weave.

'Wave's coming,' Strath said without looking up from his work.

Jessandra looked up and twisted around, dropping her needles in the process. She groaned, knowing that she'd have to start all over again. Then she saw Wave making her slow way down the road, her eyes glued to the ground. The knitting didn't matter anymore. Wave was more important.

Wave joined them on the blanket, seating herself cross-legged in silence. There was a solemnness to her, an air of sadness tinged with despair. Jessandra reached over and laid her hand on Wave's knee.

'How are you?'

'Okay,' Wave said. She lifted her gaze to Jessandra. 'Before I agreed to come to Sharvel, Strath warned me I may not be ready for the truth.'

Strath laid his project down and studied Wave. The pair locked eyes, and Jessandra felt the familiar pang of jealousy in her stomach.

'When I learned that I wasn't cursed, I thought that's what you were talking about. And when we learned about using the powers of all the gods, I thought that was what you meant,' Wave continued. 'And maybe you did.'

Strath shrugged.

'But today I learned the truth about my family, and I definitely wasn't ready for it.'

Since they'd seen her running past the house, Jessandra's worry had been gnawing at her. Strath had followed Wave into the forest, then returned an hour ago, telling Jessandra that Wave was going through some strong emotions and that she wanted to spend some time alone. The worry was almost too much for Jessandra to bear.

'Do you want to talk about it?' Jessandra asked. 'I know what it's like to have a messed-up family.'

Wave turned back to Jessandra. Her eyes widened and she covered her mouth with her hands.

'Gods!' she whispered.

'What is it?' Jessandra asked.

'Jess,' Wave said, shuffling closer. 'Jess, we're sort of like cousins. Second cousins, I guess.'

For a moment, Jessandra just stared at her. She burst out laughing. 'Second cousins?'

'I'm not joking,' Wave said. 'My father is Samson sunkin.'

Jessandra's laughter died. 'Samson?' she whispered.

Wave shuffled closer again, grasping Jessandra's hands in her own. 'Samson.'

It only took Wave ten minutes to explain the story Kali had shared with her earlier. She touched on how angry she'd felt, and how let down, but didn't go into a lot of detail. Jessandra guessed that now they'd passed, those emotions weren't as strong. Or perhaps Wave wasn't ready to explore them yet.

Jessandra's heart felt full again, as it had when Wave had first suggested she join them. She may have lost her sister, but she'd gained a cousin, someone who understood the mess of their families almost as well as Lenta had, someone who'd chosen to be her friend.

Tears tracked down her cheeks as Wave revealed the lies at the heart of Samson's story. There was no doubt in her mind that Reuben had done all of the things Kali had said, those awful things attributed to his brother.

'I can't believe him,' she hissed. 'He's a monster.'

Strath nodded his agreement.

'I was so angry at Samson,' Wave said. 'For abandoning us, for shirking his responsibility as a parent. But once I'd exhausted my anger, I began to understand. He knew what Reuben had done to Frieda, but he realised that nobody would believe him.'

'Reuben can be very charismatic,' Jessandra added. 'When he wants to be.' Which seemed to be never these days.

'So he did what he thought was his duty. He was trying to protect his people. And all he's done is try to protect us, his family, despite the danger we're all in. His absence is the best protection any of us have, as hard as that is to face.'

'The high king is responsible for so much pain,' Strath said with a shake of his head.

'How can one man be so terrible?' Wave asked. 'It doesn't make sense.'

'My father is pretty awful,' Jessandra said. 'They're cousins, so maybe it's a family trait.'

'But Kali said my father was nothing like that. That he was kind, and gentle. And there's no way my mother would have fallen for a monster like Reuben, so I'm more inclined to believe Kali.'

'Maybe there's something wrong with Reuben,' Strath said, his gaze wandering over the treetops to the distant mountains and the setting sun. 'Maybe he's the one who's cursed.'

Jessandra chuckled. 'If only it was that simple.'

Knowing they were related felt as though something had clicked into place in Jessandra's mind. Despite the pain and confusion Wave was going through, she glanced at Jessandra, sharing a small, secret smile. This bond, whatever it was, was almost better than having a sister.

'I don't want to interrupt your sharing,' Strath said, 'but we should get ready.' He pointed to the western mountains and the sun nearing the peaks.

'My mind is in turmoil anyway,' Wave said. 'I don't know what to think, or what to talk about. We might as well get ready. At least it'll keep me distracted.'

A corner of the blanket in each hand, they shook the material out before carting it inside with the pillows. While Jessandra and Wave changed into their new dresses borrowed from the neighbourhood, Strath heated yesterday's stew.

They ate in relative silence, each lost in their own thoughts. Jessandra's mind was full of Wave, their family, and wondering how Long Night Festival might be different in Sharvel. When they'd finished, Strath lifted Jessandra's cloak and settled it over her shoulders as Wave secured her own cloak.

'Are you ready?'

Anticipation wrestled with the sleepy food-induced warmth in Jessandra's body. She watched Strath don his own cloak, taking in the shape of his face and his tousled dark curls with greedy eyes. Even though they were going to a celebration, he still wore his utility belt. Knives, rope, and a flask crowded against dried meats, tiny packets of herbs, and a small bottle of alcohol. There were more items, she was sure, hidden in secret pockets she'd only see if they needed something. Gods, he was clever.

'Ready,' she answered, her voice husky.

Wave nodded her agreement, and they headed out to the road. Strath's house was around the middle of one curving spiral, so there were already people on the road, making their way towards the library. The townsfolk waved and smiled, but otherwise kept to themselves. They were dressed in thick cloaks of varying shades, and many of the women and children wore mittens to protect their hands. Jessandra didn't feel cold, but she knew how frigid the air grew of a night on the plateau.

The three of them strode in silence, Strath between the two girls. Jessandra shared the occasional secret smile with Wave behind Strath's back. Whenever Wave's eyes were forward, or looking at other people, Jessandra found herself staring at Strath.

The library rose before them as they rounded the last bend, white marble reflecting the last rays of the sun, turning the walls almost violet. The lawns surrounding the library were already filling with people who stood facing the front entrance in silence or quietly talking to one another.

'Let's get closer,' Strath said, leading them through the gathered crowd until they stood near the centre of the green. Small children ducked and weaved between the adults. Some of the older ones had climbed into the tall fruit trees at the edges of the lawns.

Four huge bonfires, enclosed by rings of boulders the size of Jessandra's head, burned warm and yellow. The sight of the bonfires made Jessandra's heart sing. It wouldn't feel like Long Night without them.

The light was fading fast, and the crisp air tingled Jessandra's nostrils. She huddled deeper into her cloak. Millen could be cold in winter, but the cold in Sharvel was different. There was an iciness that got into Jessandra's bones and made her nose red and sore. It wasn't even winter yet.

Jessandra screwed her nose up, forcing her mind back to the present. Kali had explained that she should come up with an intention, something to channel her mind's energy towards during the ceremony. This was a new part of the festival for her, and nothing had come to mind over the last few days.

Two elders dressed in white cloaks—Kali and an unfamiliar man—climbed the steps of the library. They turned to face the crowd, serene smiles wrinkling the corners of their eyes.

'That's Estapol,' Strath murmured, nodding at the man. 'Welcome to Long Night Festival.'

A fresh shiver ran all over Jessandra's body. On the top stair, the two elders stood side by side, beaming at the crowd. Everyone began to settle. Parents gathered children towards them; each face rose in anticipation to those leading the ceremony.

For a few moments, the silence was so complete that Jessandra could only hear the sound of the wind rustling through the treetops. Then Kali and Estapol began to sing, the melody beautiful and lilting. The sounds tugged at her heart, as if pulling her towards a memory she couldn't quite recall. The people of Heredour only spoke one tongue, but Jessandra didn't recognise any of the words the elders used.

The song seemed to vibrate through the air. Jessandra could feel every individual hair on her arms, her legs, her face. Unable to help herself, she began to sway in time to the tune.

Evening darkened around them, pulling its soft blanket over the plateau. The song didn't stop, and Jessandra felt as if the elders were singing directly into her heart. She raised her head and saw the first star of the night twinkling above them through a film of light cloud.

A stand had been placed on the library's platform. An assistant stepped forward and placed a clay pot before Kali and Estapol. Without pausing their song, the elders descended the steps of the library and kneeled on the grass. With gentle hands, they dug out clods of soft earth and carried them back to the pot. Estapol continued the melody as he sprinkled earth into the pot, but Kali transformed her song into a wordless wail. The sound crashed over the crowd like a storm-driven ocean and Jessandra felt as if her heart might burst.

Then the song began to soften, growing quiet. Jessandra strained her ears to catch the melody. Kali and Estapol held their palms open towards the crowd. A tiny seedling hovered above each of their palms. Together, they planted the seedlings in the pot.

A tingle ran over Jessandra's body, and she glanced at Wave. Her friend had eyes only for the elders. This was what Strath had demonstrated for them on their first day—the intertwined power of multiple gods.

Without pausing their soft song, Kali and Estapol wove intricate patterns above the pot with their hands. Droplets of water began to fall over the newly planted seeds, though the rain didn't come from the clouds.

As the elders stood back from the pot, Jessandra was overcome with a new sensation, like being plunged into cold water.

I run towards the truth of who I am.

The sentence appeared from nowhere, but as soon as it was in her mind, she knew that this was her intention.

I run towards the truth of who I am.

The words were the heart of all of her issues. Who was she, really? A princess? An heir? A daughter, sister, friend? Lover? Godless? Skykin? Hopeless?

I run towards the truth of who I am.

She didn't have an answer, not yet, but Kali had told her the intention would give her something to grow into, a purpose for which the gods would fill in the blanks.

In a heartbeat, the rain falling from the elders' hands was gone. The shape of the song changed and the elders raised their arms to the sky. The fine spray of clouds cleared.

Jessandra felt the change of their power as a different vibration against her skin. She wondered if this was what they'd been trying to teach her all along. Was this what it felt like to be called by the gods?

Eyes lifted to the heavens, Jessandra was engulfed by the magnitude of the space above them. The sky was dark now, inky blackness stretching from mountain top to mountain top. An impossible number of stars winked at her, glittering in their bed of darkness. A deep sadness pooled in Jessandra's heart.

The people all around the green were starting to sing along with the elders, but the strong emotion closed Jessandra's throat over. She squeezed her eyes shut, unable to bear the brightness of those cold stars, not wanting to bear the memory of a life she wasn't even sure she wanted. So much had changed since those panic-filled days when she'd been Jessandra, Princess of Marbin.

From outside the darkness of her closed eyelids, Jessandra felt a growing brightness, almost as if the sun were rising too early. Squinting her eyes open, she saw the stars and moon growing bright above them. The light expanded with the swell of the elders' song until it felt like full daylight had descended over Sharvel.

As the light grew, Jessandra felt a gentle caress on her skin, as if the light was raining down on her in a soft mist.

Everluof.

Her heart beat in a panicked flutter. This is what she should have felt years ago; this sense of the god who would allow her to live and rule and love as a starkin queen.

A moment later, the feeling vanished. The stars settled back into the sky, dim now despite their constant twinkle. The terrified elation of a moment ago drained out of Jessandra, leaving her deflated and confused.

The song subsided and a murmur of soft conversation travelled through the crowd as they dispersed and began to gather around the roaring bonfires.

Strath grabbed her hand and pulled her and Wave over to the closest fire. Another tingle ran over Jessandra's body, but this one had nothing to do with the gods. Strath chatted to one of his neighbours, and Wave squeezed around him to stand beside Jessandra. Barrels of cider were tapped and mugs passed around. Jessandra wrapped her hands around the cold drink, grateful for the warmth of the fire. Her body was alive with sensation, but the heat was familiar, comforting.

'That was a bit different,' Wave said.

Jessandra nodded. 'I felt them, I think.'

'The gods?' Wave's eyes widened, her mug halfway to her lips.

'I felt Everluof, definitely.' Jessandra shrugged. 'And I could tell there was a ... difference between the others. When they were working with Eritogone, or Ferengün, or Lerinial. I don't know if I connected with them, but I could sense the differences.'

'Me too,' Wave said as she shuffled closer. 'I can't understand the others enough to use their power, but I can feel the difference in energy.'

'That's because you're so powerful with Lerinial,' Strath said, turning aside from his neighbour. 'It's harder for you to understand what the other gods might feel like when your power drowns them out.'

Wave crinkled her nose.

'That should make it easier for me, then?' Jessandra asked with a small laugh. 'Being godless and all?'

'Perhaps.' Strath's grin was wide and encompassing, taking in both girls.

Jessandra felt a sudden queasiness, and she frowned into her cup. She'd been drinking wine and cider since she was a child, as was the norm for highkin, but something didn't feel right.

'Are you okay?' Wave asked.

The sensation roared to life, demanding to be noticed. It wasn't nausea from the cider, as she'd first thought, but something else altogether. Jessandra frowned.

'Jess?' Wave asked. 'Jess?'

Jessandra pushed her mug at the others so she could hold the space below her ribs. There were no words she could use to describe the feeling that was rising inside her, but it made her want to run as far away from the library as she could. She fought against the feeling. This should be a time of celebration, or relief. They were safe, her and Wave, and free, and it was Long Night Festival.

'What is it?' Strath asked. He moved closer towards them until the three of them formed a tight circle. 'Jess?'

She shook her head. The more she struggled, the more urgent the feeling became. Every fibre of her body demanded that she turn her back on her friends, on these people who had taken her in. The sensations willed her to run into the forest and never return.

Flee.

The words resonated through her mind with a terrifying ferocity.

'Something's wrong,' Strath said.

Flee.

It definitely had a voice now, the sensation. What couldn't be articulated previously was now a demanding presence.

'Flee,' she whispered.

There was no immediate danger. So why did she feel this way?

Flee!

Strath nodded once and grabbed both their hands. He pulled them through the crowded green, jostling against the people of Sharvel until they broke free. They were on the curving road, the one that eventually pointed south.

'Run,' Jessandra whispered. 'Run!'

She lifted her skirts and ran. There were footsteps behind her—Wave's and Strath's, she was sure—but her mind was too focused on getting out of Sharvel to care.

As they curved around the spiralling road and the library disappeared from view, Jessandra swore she heard the sound of hooves.

'Horses!' Strath cried.

The people of Sharvel didn't keep horses. Jessandra willed her legs to move faster, and they responded. Running had never been something she enjoyed, unlike Lenta, and she'd no doubt pay for it later. It didn't matter, though. Nothing did. She was with her friends, the two people she felt more bonded to than any others, and they were escaping whatever was headed for Sharvel. Slowly, the sound of hooves faded.

They passed Strath's house without stopping, the house she'd finally felt at home in for a few days. The road ended, became a creekside trail outside of the town that she leapt onto, the others close behind.

Her breath heaved in her chest, and she could hear Wave panting behind her. If there were any horses coming, they wouldn't have been able to hear them. The trail ended suddenly, and Jessandra stopped, Wave crashing into her back.

A valley stretched before them. Steep mountainsides rose on either side of the shale-ridden path, the tree covering sparse. Giant boulders dotted the spaces between the trees like big, ugly boils pushing their way to the surface of the land. In the darkness, everything was shades and shadows, a muted visage of grey on grey on grey.

'Follow me,' Strath whispered.

Taking careful, measured steps, Strath climbed the steep slope to their left. Hand in hand, Jessandra and Wave followed him. Strath lowered himself down behind an enormous boulder, pressing a finger to his lips as they squatted beside him. Jessandra's chest heaved as her breath pulsed in painful bursts.

Strath moved his hands around them in a graceful dance. Jessandra couldn't tell which power he was working with, but she guessed he was hiding them. Of all the things he excelled at, using the gods' powers to conceal them had proved the most useful.

The sound of galloping horses echoed through the valley. Jessandra swallowed, her pulse still racing. Taking care not to loose any of the shale, she peered around the boulder and into the valley. Moments later, several horses cantered down the creekside trail.

At the front of the group was a sleek, ebony horse ridden by a tall creature in a long black cloak and raised hood. Jessandra's heart leapt to her throat.

Twice in thirty years, Strath had said. Now, because of her, or Wave, or both of them, the Black Cloaks had come to Sharvel a third time. Each visit was getting closer together. Although it pained her to think of it, perhaps Sharvel's luck was running out.

A host of the high king's men rode behind the Black Cloak. The gaudy golden uniform of the High Army stood out against the bleak mountainside, but the showy silver uniform of her father's army was nowhere to be seen. Maybe they were looking for Wave after all.

She shot a furtive glance at her friends. Wave's eyes were wide, fearful, but Strath's eyebrows hunkered down over his eyes, his face a vicious snarl.

Jessandra held her breath as the troops paused at the mouth of the valley. The soldiers peered down the path, squinting into the darkened forest at the other end. The Black Cloak didn't move. If a breeze rose, Jessandra expected that the cloak wouldn't stir. Her stomach churned.

Time seemed to stand still as they peeked over the boulder, watching the Black Cloak, waiting for something to happen. Jessandra had no sense of how much time passed before the Black Cloak finally turned his horse and cantered back towards Sharvel, the soldiers hurrying to follow. When they disappeared from sight, Jessandra let out a big breath and slumped down behind the boulder. Wave and Strath were beside her moments later.

'What now?' Wave asked.

Jessandra didn't miss the note of resignation in her voice. They'd thought they were safe in Sharvel, but only a few days had passed before they were back on the road again.

'We go south,' Strath answered, his voice resolute.

'Where to?' Jessandra asked. If Sharvel wasn't safe for Wave, or her, then nowhere in Heredour was.

'To Veija-Mens,' he answered.

It was as good a plan as any other.

33

HABA SHA

OUTSIDE A STATELY SALMON-COLOURED BUILDING, Mortius waited in the shadow of a street vendor's umbrella, watching Haba Sha's constituents come and go. The council building stood at the heart of the business square, and the maire's house stood opposite. Mortius averted his eyes from the house, keeping his focus on his target.

Beside him, Aymn studied the square with bright eyes. They were both dressed well; Mortius in his usual tight-fitting black silk, Aymn in loose trousers and a fitted shirt embroidered with Unner's symbol. The others were back at a local inn, instructed to gather gossip and keep their heads down.

Mortius tugged at the collar of his tight shirt. He favoured silk because it was cool, but it made little difference here. Haba Sha was one of the most southern points of Heredour and the humidity was still present even though it was autumn. It was still early, but there were only a couple of hours left before he'd have to change into something that didn't hug his body quite so well.

'Let's go,' Mortius said.

They strode towards the council chambers, Aymn falling in

step behind Mortius. A guard stood at the door, watching the townspeople with a bored look. His eyes fell on Mortius, and after a perfunctory glance, they widened in recognition. Back straight, the guard stood to attention.

'Senior Adviser,' he said, his voice breathy. 'We weren't expecting you.'

Mortius nodded. 'Perfect. I'd like to watch the petitioners.'

'We should arrange a formal welcome,' the guard said, stumbling over his words. 'Where are you staying? Maire Beren would have you stay in his own home, I'm sure.' He shifted slightly, edging his way between Mortius and the door.

'What's your name, soldier?'

'Cyeen,' the guard answered, his brows knitting together.

'Lt Cyeen, I would not stay in that place if it was the last house standing.'

Although the black curtains had been taken down by the house's new owner, Mortius knew what had happened in the maire's house.

'Yes, sir.'

'And the less who know of my arrival, the better. There will be no formal welcome.'

'Yes, sir.' The guard moved aside.

Mortius strode through the open door. The hallway was cool, and he breathed a sigh of relief. An older man hurried by, clutching his hat in his hands, offering no more than a subdued glance at Mortius and Aymn.

They sidled through the open door of the chamber, easing their way behind the row of empty chairs at the back. The sun shone through tall, open windows that took up the whole eastern wall. There were no decorations; no banners or flags or even tablecloths. For a town like Haba Sha—where every building and vessel was covered in multicoloured ribbons, flags, and curtains—the sparseness was unsettling.

Several petitioners sat in a disordered row before a long,

plain table. Beren sat on the other side with two advisers on either side of him, facing the door Mortius had just entered through. Seeing the man who'd once been his friend came as a shock, and Mortius bumped into one of the chairs. The sound caused Beren to look up from the petitioner standing before him, his eyes locking on Mortius.

Time had changed him, in much the same way it had changed Juro. There were wrinkles around his forehead, silver hair threading through pale locks. His posture had drooped, shoulders rounding over the table, his neck jutting forward. His eyes were heavy-lidded, and his clothes hung from his frame. None of the proud, cunning man Mortius had once known was even visible.

There was no surprise in his face as he studied Mortius, just a weary resignation. Beren turned back to his constituent.

'I haven't caught any fish these past three days,' the older gentleman said. 'Neither has my son or his crew.'

He wore the wide-legged trousers typical of Triné's fishermeen, and his felt hat was crushed beneath one hand. The other hand was bunched in a fist in the material of his trousers.

'Are you still using traps?' Beren asked with a sigh.

The man shook his sun-wrinkled head. 'None of us have used traps in weeks. But now we're not pulling up anything with the rods. At least, nothing you'd want to put on your table.'

The others seated around him nodded their agreement. Mortius grimaced. There'd been reports from Varachanas and Toohlio of too many dead fish, but it was hard for Mortius to imagine the reality of the situation.

Beren sighed again. 'Are you spending enough time in prayer, Jonarl?'

The older man drew himself up to his full height. 'I spend all the time I can praying to my goddess. But Lerinial is angry. She won't help us. I don't know what else I can do.'

There was a desperation in his voice that struck Mortius like a discordant bell. He knew the feeling all too well, even if his desperation had nothing to do with fish.

'We pray all the time,' another of the men chimed in. 'Has Lerinial forsaken us?'

'That is not a question for the maire,' the adviser to Beren's left snapped. 'Speak with your priest of such matters.'

'But what do we do about the fish?' Jonarl asked in earnest. 'How are we to feed our families?'

'There is nothing I can do,' Beren said. He sounded bored. 'However, the senior adviser of High King Reuben has deigned to visit our humble town. Perhaps he can offer more insight than I.'

Beren looked up at Mortius with a virulent smile. The fishermen turned in their seats, staring at Mortius and Aymn in surprise. Mortius clenched his teeth. At least he knew how Beren felt about him now.

'The High King Reuben is aware of your great plight,' Mortius said. He cleared his throat, trying to find the tone of authority he'd once carried with pride. 'All of the regions suffer in their own way, and it is for this reason I am visiting. I seek to get to the heart of why your fish are dying.'

'They're not dying, Senior Adviser,' Jonarl said, his gaze on the floor. 'They're dead.'

'Where do you fish from, Jonarl?' Mortius asked.

The older man looked up, uncertainty paling his face.

'We're of the sea, Senior Adviser,' he murmured. 'My son and I man a vessel called *Nolany's Worth*.'

'I will come tomorrow to witness your woes.'

'Thank you, Senior Adviser,' Jonarl said, clutching his hat to his heart. 'All honour to the high king and the senior adviser.'

'All honour to the emperor and the grand prince,' Mortius said.

The other fishermen repeated the intonation and as a group,

they rose and shuffled out of the chambers, bowing their heads to Mortius as they passed.

'Well handled, Senior Adviser,' Beren said when the room was empty.

One of Beren's assistants gathered the parchment that covered the table towards him, ignoring everyone else. The adviser who spoke harshly to Jonarl watched Mortius through narrowed eyes.

'Will you dine with me?' Beren asked, pushing himself away from the table with a listless energy. 'We take our tea earlier than you might be used to.'

'Not now,' Mortius answered as Beren meandered across the floor.

He stood before Mortius, eying Aymn curiously.

'But I'll dine with you this evening, just you and me.' He placed a hand on Aymn's shoulder. 'I wanted to introduce you to Aymn, my nephew.'

'Aymn starkin,' Aymn said, placing his right hand over his heart.

'Aymn starkin,' Beren repeated, the skin around his eyes tightening. 'Maire Beren skykin. The honour is mine.' He mimicked Aymn's gesture, but his lips thinned. Was it panic or anger? Mortius couldn't be sure, but he'd brought Aymn here for this exact reason.

'Beren and I were stationed together near Ergin during the Raider War,' Mortius said without taking his eyes off Beren. 'We were in Esra's army, Jesma preserve his soul.'

Beren nodded. 'We were Reuben's men back then.'

'Still are,' Mortius said.

Beren turned his gaze to Mortius. It was panic, he realised, not anger. The surprise visit, the way he'd dealt with the fisher-men, and now Aymn standing before him—Beren didn't know what was happening, but he knew something was up, and he was worried.

'Of course,' he said, his throat quivering. 'All honour to the high king.'

'I'm sure there'll be time for you two to get to know each other,' Mortius said. 'When should I visit the wharf?'

'You want to see the fish?'

'I do.'

Beren nodded. 'It's not pleasant. Go tomorrow, about an hour after sunbreak. That's when they come back to shore. And when the smell is the most manageable.'

'I'll see you for supper, then?'

'Of course.' Beren fingered one of his rings, twirling it around and around. 'You're welcome any time after sunset.'

Mortius stared at Beren for a moment longer before turning and striding through the door, Aymn trailing in his wake. Sweat dampened his armpits, but he strode through the square, ignoring the sun.

He was angry. What a sloppy mess of a man Beren had become. Maybe it wasn't anger, just disappointment. Beren wouldn't be much help to him, lazy and guarded and bitter as he was.

34

TRINÉ EMPIRE

BURIED DEEP in a forest she didn't recognise, Larka cradled Hasting's motionless body to her chest. Winter and Rainer squatted beside her, their eyes wide and alert.

'We need more water,' Larka croaked.

Winter nodded and rose to her feet. Taking the large leaf she was using to transport water, she turned and disappeared into the humid forest, Rainer close behind.

Despite splashing water over his face several times, Hasting still hadn't stirred. Larka closed her eyes and called on the deep well of Eritogone's power within her. Taking several deep breaths, Larka inhaled the scents of the forest and opened herself to Ferengün's power. She wove a cocoon around Hasting, taking aspects of the life-giving soil and the nutrient-dense plant matter to create an energetic wrapping around her friend. Eyes still closed, she whispered heartfelt prayers to her god and his, and then to all of them.

Fast footfalls on damp leaf litter announced Winter's return. Larka opened her eyes as Winter knelt beside her. Some way off, Rainer struggled through the undergrowth.

The huge leaf, heavy with water, trembled in Winter's hands

as she offered it to her mother. Larka dipped her hand into the well of water and sprinkled some onto Hasting's face, maintaining the weaves of earth and plant power holding him.

With a skill she'd secretly used in the Plains, Larka wove a thread of Lerinial's power through the clear liquid. Water rose from the leaf and hovered over Hasting before raining softly down on his face. His skin brightened wherever the water fell. Larka repeated the movement, adding silent prayers to the three gods.

Hasting coughed. Larka sprinkled more water over his body as colour bloomed in his face. With a deep breath, Larka began to unwind the cocoon that held Hasting safe. His eyes fluttered open and he looked up at Larka.

'Winter, go help Rainer,' Larka said. 'I need that extra water.'

Without a word, Winter disappeared into the forest once more, helping to clear a path for Rainer.

Birds chattered and sang above them. Hasting's eyes moved, following the sounds. Larka stroked his cheek and frowned at him.

'That was some trick,' she murmured.

Hasting managed a small smile. 'Told you … wouldn't like it.'

'I'm grateful, nevertheless.' Larka looked at the forest around them. 'Though I'm not sure where we are now.'

She had a nagging feeling that this wasn't Davej-Arne's forest. Although they were certainly in a tropical rainforest, her memory of the Kirsky was that the southern aspect was full of ferns and moss and ancient, reaching figs. This forest was different.

When Winter and Rainer returned, a new leaf shivering in Rainer's large hands, Larka lifted Hasting's head so he could drink. Each sip of water brought a brightness to his skin, clearing his eyes. They sat on the forest floor for a long time as they waited for Hasting to gather some strength.

'Where are we?' Larka asked once Hasting had found the energy to make a joke at Rainer's expense.

'Kirsky Forest.'

Larka frowned. 'Are you sure?'

Her words sparked an uncertainty in both men. They studied the trees, the plants, the angle of the sun.

'I don't know where we are,' Rainer said eventually, 'but I don't think this is the Kirsky.' His eyebrows drew downwards, making his eyes appear smaller than they were.

'I made a mistake,' Hasting said, his own frown gathering his eyebrows at the top of his nose. 'I wasn't strong enough to get us all the way across the country. I could be wrong, but I think we're somewhere in Triné.'

Larka pinched the bridge of her nose and squeezed her eyes shut. Triné. They could be near Shebedie, the capital of the empire, which would make them alarmingly close to Gardar Mae. Or they could be all the way down on the coast somewhere—Beestreb, or Haba Sha, or Toohlio. None of it was helpful, though. They weren't any closer to Waterfall City, and Winter was still at risk.

'This plan is in shambles,' Larka muttered under her breath.

'We can make a new one,' Hasting said, squeezing her hand. 'If we're near the coast, we might be able to get a ship to the Chaba-Canez Islands.'

Larka released the grip on her nose and looked up. 'Why would you suggest the Islands?'

'Veija-Mens was the place Sam felt safest in the whole world. What if he's been hiding out there this whole time? You know he always went back to see the seers.'

The possibility had crossed her mind a few times, though she'd never raised it during their evening planning sessions. Veija-Mens had seemed too far away to even think about, especially when she needed to protect Siska.

Rainer was studying her with an odd expression on his face.

Larka realised their mistake. Up until now, neither she nor Hasting had actually said Sam's name. It had been intentional, given Rainer's past with the sunkin family. Realisation was dawning on his face now, so Larka changed the subject.

'I didn't think we could access their power,' Larka said. 'Their race is not ours.'

'Everything we've been taught is a lie.'

'I know that, Hasting,' Larka said, rolling her eyes. 'We were raised the same way.'

Hasting sighed and tried to stand, but he struggled to get to his feet. 'I guess we're not going anywhere soon?' he asked Larka.

'You're not strong enough yet.'

Leaning back against the trunk of one of the strange trees, Hasting gathered them around him with a wave of his hand. Seated on the ground, they were hidden from sight by the tall, arching buttresses of the tree.

'You both know the history of our gods,' Hasting said, 'but it might be a good lesson for Winter.'

Winter's eyes widened and she shuffled forward.

'Larka, would you tell us how the Black Cloaks came to be?'

'If I must,' she replied. 'After Jesma was created, he decided the gods and their children should be separated, divided into kin. His intentions were pure arrogance, and Lerinial stood up to him in place of the other gods. They fought, water against light, and the Black Cloaks were born. Not men, not any of the lost creatures, but something else altogether. A race unto themselves.' Larka rubbed her earlobe. 'Unholy, we called them, because they weren't born of a god's joy at creating life. They were created because of a rift between those who are most holy.'

'Water and light, you say?' Hasting glanced between Larka and Rainer expectantly. Larka stared back at him; Rainer merely shrugged his shoulders.

'It's simple, really,' Hasting said. 'We're just blinded, as usual.

Blinded by history, our own fears, our human ignorance. The truth was always there, right in front of our faces, since the beginning of time.'

'So enlighten us,' Larka said. Her curiosity was piqued by the direction of his thoughts, but she still couldn't see where he was going.

'Water and light. Somehow, we decided that a clash between two elemental gods resulted in a race of beings who had access to something special, something different. Something men couldn't touch.'

They all stared at him, even Winter, leaning forward with her elbows on her knees. Larka felt the first spark of understanding in her mind, like a budding flower waiting for the first ray of sunlight.

'Friends,' Hasting said. 'Magic isn't a separate, special power. Magic is lightning, the power of electricity.'

Larka blinked in surprise. The flower in her mind bloomed in the radiance of understanding.

'Magic is elemental.'

35

THE NORTH CLAW

By the time Wave and Jessandra had followed Strath all the way to the Kanrid River, the exhilaration of the chase had worn off, and they were both exhausted.

Strath pointed out the shafts of silver between the trees as they descended into the river's valley. The water reflected the midday sun, and the closer they got, the more Wave found herself shielding her eyes from the glare.

When they arrived at the edge, Strath paused to let them wash their faces and take a drink. Wave eased her way down the bank, squatting by the wide river. The current was strong, gurgling around rocks and fallen branches. There was a different feeling to this river, something unique in the way it moved. But then, Wave had only known the languid pace of the Armansis, and she was beginning to understand that water felt different depending on its source.

Jessandra flopped down beside her with a groan. 'My legs hurt.'

'Mine too,' Wave said. She thought running up and down the wet sand of Bindock's shore most days had kept her fit, but the surrounding area was mostly flat. The mountain climbs she'd undertaken in the past week proved how much more difficult inclines were on her untrained body.

Now that she was sitting down, the weariness of a night with no sleep washed over Wave. She splashed her face a few times, but even the cold water didn't pull the tiredness from her bones.

At least the exhaustion squashed her anger.

'How will we get across?' Wave asked, looking up at Strath, who was scanning the river with narrowed eyes.

'We head west,' Strath said. 'The river narrows further up, and hopefully, the way across is still there.'

Wave frowned at him. As far as she knew, there were no crossings within the North Claw—no bridges, no ferries, no way to span the width of the Kanrid.

'Come on,' Strath said, holding a hand out to both of them. 'I'll feel safer once we're on the other side.'

With a sigh, Wave took his hand and let herself be pulled to her feet. She ignored the tingle that ran up her arm at Strath's touch, reminding herself that only days ago, she'd thought they'd never be able to be near each other.

'How will we be safer?' she asked as Jessandra groaned her way to standing. 'The wizards can materialise wherever they want.'

'There are no bridges over the Kanrid, and the current is dangerous. They'll never expect us to cross.' Strath started making his way through the dense undergrowth.

Wave and Jessandra shared a furtive glance before trudging after Strath. The river narrowed as they headed west, though they moved slowly due to the fine-leaved ferns crowding their path. Up ahead, Wave spotted their destination. What had once been a thick, tall Krakoa tree spanned the width of the river. Tangled roots reared into the air on their side of the river, the barren branches digging into the bank on the other side.

Strath stopped when they reached the roots.

'I haven't crossed here in years,' he said, turning back to

them. 'Many years. We'll need to be careful. The wood may have decayed.'

Testing his footing with each step, Strath climbed up through the roots. Wave followed his lead, Jessandra close behind. The wood felt solid enough beneath Wave's feet.

By the time Wave had pulled herself up onto the trunk, Strath was already edging his way across the river. The trunk had worn almost flat where they would walk, suggesting that it had spanned the river for an age. Strath tested the strength of the wood with a few tentative steps before continuing.

The length of the trunk was covered in broken branches. Some were worn smooth with age, but others were jagged enough to catch a long skirt.

'Watch the snags,' Wave said to Jessandra as her friend's face appeared above the tangled roots.

Jessandra smiled at her, and Wave felt her anger at the wizards disappear completely. This was what it was like to have friends. They were surrounded by danger, hunted by the Black Cloaks, and yet, they had enough faith in one another to smile despite it all.

Wave picked up the edges of her dress and grasped them in one hand so she could use her other hand for balance. The trunk was sturdy beneath her feet as she edged out over the river. Below her, the strong current diverted around boulders and branches. Lerinial delighted in the way her water could separate and divide with ease, always finding a way back to itself. Wave blew out her cheeks and let herself relax.

Blinking away the compulsion to dive in, to let herself be swept away by Lerinial's flow, Wave dragged her eyes from the river and continued forward. The trunk narrowed near the middle. Snags were more frequent and harder to navigate around. Wave sent a small prayer to Lerinial, asking for courage. In her heart, Wave was certain Lerinial was still angry at her, but she was Wave's goddess. If she couldn't ask the gods for help, what good were they?

Wave looked up and saw Strath watching them from the opposite bank. Perhaps she didn't need Lerinial after all. The courage she needed could be found in the man waiting for her at the other end of the log, the man who made her heart beat fast and her insides squirm, the man who saved her even when she thought she was doomed.

He grinned as she took his hand and jumped down onto the bank beside him. From behind her, Wave heard a frustrated cry.

Jessandra was stuck in the middle of the trunk, her divided skirt caught on a long branch. She tugged at the material, but the dress was caught fast.

'Don't pull it, Jess,' Strath called.

She looked up at them, her face scrunched up in consternation.

'Try to figure out how it's caught, and reverse whatever has caused the bind.'

Jessandra nodded and turned back to the branch, studying her skirt, moving the material in different directions as she tried to find the problem.

'Should I go to her?' Wave asked.

'Let her figure it out,' Strath said with a shrug.

'But what if—'

Jessandra shouted in frustration and stomped her foot against the trunk.

'No,' Strath whispered as a loud crack whipped through the air around them.

In a heartbeat, he was scrambling back onto the trunk. The decaying wood crumbled beneath Jessandra's foot. Her dress tore away from the branch and she fell with a terrified scream, crashing into the swirling river.

Wave's heart lurched. The current pulled Jessandra down and under, dragging her away from them.

'No!' Wave screamed.

She sent darting arms of power into the river. The current moved fast, and Jessandra was already far away. Using every ounce of waterkin strength she had, Wave hunted through the Kanrid for her friend. When she found the gasping princess, Wave wrapped her up in weaves of power and began to pull.

The power of the river fought against Wave. She dragged Jessandra to the surface so she could breathe, but the river wouldn't let her go. Debris from the shattered tree barrelled towards Jessandra. Wave diverted her power, deflecting the branches so they swirled away from the princess.

Strath tore his way through the undergrowth to where Jessandra floated, immobile within the battle of Wave's and Lerinial's wills. In silent desperation, Wave fought the river, a line of sweat breaking out on her brow. Her power was slipping, failing against the might of the river. Lerinial wanted her prize, just as she'd wanted Henny.

'No!' Wave screamed. The memory of Henny's dead body in her arms sent anger spiralling through her. She couldn't lose someone else.

Jessandra slipped beneath the surface. Inch by inch, she drifted further away from them. She was already too far away from the bank for Strath to help.

'No,' Wave whispered. The anger shifted, morphing into the unfamiliar blinding rage.

'No.'

Her whole being was consumed by light. This time, she was ready. She took control of the unknown power. Holding an image of Jessandra's face in her mind, she forced an imprint of the princess onto the background of light. From the depths of Wave's mind, she heard Lerinial cry out in anger.

'You can't have her!' Wave screamed into the blinding light.

Jessandra slid from the river and flew into Strath's waiting arms. The pair crashed into the ground.

Wave fell to her knees. The aftermath of the strange power ricocheted through her body. Gasping for air, she vomited up last night's stew, her vision blurring.

The power had nothing to do with her goddess, or any other single deity, of that she was now certain. This was something else altogether. Wave couldn't see how it was a combination of water and sun energy, as X'olea's friend had said, but she didn't know what else it could be. Pulsating energy moved through Wave. Spots appeared before her eyes and she squeezed them shut.

She'd done it. Saved Jessandra when she couldn't save Henny. Bested Lerinial. But what kind of power could beat a god? If the people of Sharvel were right, if X'olea's friend was right, then there was only one possibility, but it was too terrifying to contemplate.

Wave opened her eyes, her heart beating a wild rhythm in her chest, her healed tattoo throbbing. The spots were gone, so she wiped her mouth and sat back on her heels. Strath was still downstream, carrying a sodden Jessandra towards her. The princess clung to Strath like the limpets the people of Bindock harvested from submerged rock pools. A small pang of jealousy spiked in Wave's gut and she shoved it down.

When they reached her, Strath placed Jessandra on the ground next to Wave, prying her fingers from his body.

Pale as the new moon and trembling like a small leaf in the wind, Jessandra looked at Wave with big eyes.

'Thank you,' she said, choking on her words.

Wave nodded.

'We need to get you dry, Jess,' Strath said, glancing up at the sun. 'Before the temperature drops any further.' He turned to Wave with a meaningful look.

'Yes,' she responded, her voice flat and emotionless. 'I'll help you.'

They pulled Jessandra to her feet and Strath disappeared into the woods.

'Come on Jess,' Wave said, beginning to untie the princess' bootlaces. 'Time to strip off.'

With shaking hands, Jessandra began removing her layers until she stood only in her slip. Wave used the outside of her own cloak to towel Jessandra dry, then draped it over her shoulders.

'It's too warm for a cloak,' Jessandra murmured.

'Not for you,' Wave answered. 'You're only wearing a slip.'

Jessandra glanced into the woods, at the place where Strath had disappeared. A rosy blush flooded her cheeks and she swallowed.

'Hold the edges around your body,' Wave said, attempting a small smile at her friend's discomfort. She would have felt the same, had their positions been reversed. Together, they wrapped Jessandra up in the cloak, keeping her warm and protecting her modesty. Moments later, Strath emerged from behind the tree line.

'I'd like to be deeper into the forest before we set up camp,' he said. 'We'll need a fire, so I want to shield us as much as possible.'

'Jessandra's shoes are soaked,' Wave said.

The princess cast her eyes down.

'I'll carry you, Jess,' Strath said.

'I can walk,' Jessandra said, her blush growing to turn her whole face beet-red. 'You don't need to carry me.'

Strath offered her a generous smile. 'Have you ever walked through a forest barefoot?'

Jessandra shook her head.

'There might be prickles, insects, snakes. It's too dangerous.'

With a miserable sigh, Jessandra agreed. Again, Wave noticed the spike of envy that rose within her as Strath swept

Jessandra off her feet. Pushing the feeling aside, she bundled up the wet clothes and followed Strath into the trees.

They walked in silence. Wave studied the pair in front of her, noticing how Jessandra didn't cling to Strath in the same way now she'd recovered from her ordeal. The muscles in his back were taut, visible beneath his damp shirt from the effort of carrying the princess, and Wave felt a strange sensation, low in her body. She frowned. Nobody had ever made her feel the strange array of emotions she experienced around Strath.

Deep in the forest, he called a stop to their journey in a small hollow. They were all exhausted. Wave and Strath set up camp, making sure Jessandra was comfortable after her fall.

Strath built a small fire and disappeared into the forest to hunt for their dinner. Winter apples and mushrooms wouldn't be enough to build their strength after the day's events. Wave draped Jessandra's wet clothes over branches as close to the fire as she dared.

When Strath returned, she helped him skin and cook the rabbit he'd caught. Strath offered a quiet prayer to Neffren as they worked. By the time they'd finished their makeshift dinner, Jessandra's eyes were drooping, so Wave helped her get comfortable. Her friend was asleep within moments, her soft snores bringing a smile to Wave's face.

She joined Strath close to the fire. He was squeezing water out of his coat, saturated from when he'd caught the drenched princess. Wave took it from him and hung it near Jessandra's wet clothes.

'We'll keep heading south tomorrow,' Strath said.

Wave averted her eyes from the strain of his muscles beneath the loose white shirt he wore. She nodded at the fire.

'Lerinial is angry,' Strath said.

Other than the crackling fire, the night was quiet around them. Wave couldn't ignore his words.

'She is.'

'You've done that before, haven't you?' Strath poked a stick at the fire, even though it didn't need stoking.

'Yes.' Wave felt her mood darken, but she couldn't help it. The image of Henny's cold face hovered before her.

'What happened?'

Wave glanced over at Jessandra, but she was still asleep. There was no way she was going to get out of talking about it. She trusted Strath. He knew about the star, knew about her heritage, had taught her about using the other gods' powers. But this was different, and the possibilities terrified her.

In short, halting sentences, Wave described what had happened that day on the beach when everything had changed.

'But she was dead,' Wave said, her lower lip trembling at the memory. 'Even after what I did, I couldn't save her.'

Strath reached out and grasped her hand. A jolt of energy ran up Wave's arm, but she was too lost in her own misery to pay it any mind.

'You saved Jessandra,' he said. 'Perhaps that was the reason Henny died, so that you knew what to do to save your friend.'

Wave said nothing, staring down at the ground. Was Henny's death worth it, then, to teach her how to save Jessandra? How could she stack one life up against the other, deciding who was worth keeping and who wasn't? That was what the gods did, though, and it didn't seem fair.

Strath grasped her chin in his finger and thumb and lifted her face. As they locked eyes, Wave's heart began to beat fast, but it had nothing to do with the conversation.

'You know what this is?'

Wave shook her head. She wasn't sure if he was talking about whatever she could feel between them, or how she'd saved Jessandra. In truth, she'd prefer not to talk about either of them.

'Remember what I told you when we first met, back on the *Hand of Numen*?'

'No.' Wave tried to smile, and Strath dropped his hand from her face. They'd spoken of so many things over that trip, so it was easy to pretend she was clueless.

'In Sharvel, our philosophers came to the conclusion that the wizards either access Lerinial's and Jesma's powers in addition to their magic, or their magic is actually a fusion of water and sun power.'

The letter from Hasting burned in her cloak pocket, the pocket opposite the one she kept the star in. For some reason, she hadn't been able to let go of the crumpled parchment, and now she knew why.

'Wave,' Strath said, his hazel eyes blazing in the reflection of the fire. 'You used magic.'

36

THE NORTH CLAW

THE SUN HAD ALREADY RISEN when Jessandra stirred from her sleep. She sat up, rubbing her eyes and pulling the cloak tight around her. Her mind was foggy, and she stared at the cold fire, trying to recall what had happened.

On the other side of the fire, Wave and Strath were still asleep. Wave was tucked into Strath's side, his cloak barely covering their bodies. Jessandra's stomach clenched and she looked away.

Clothes were strewn all around their little clearing, but as Jessandra blinked the sleep from her eyes, she realised the clothing was her own. She glanced down at the cloak wrapped around her. The dark blue wool covered in swirling embroidered lines was Wave's, not hers. She pulled the cloak open and found she was only in her slip. No wonder she was cold.

Memories began to surface, but they were sluggish in their arrival. The snag had caught her dress. Trying to be responsible and patient and unhook herself. Getting frustrated. The sound of splintering wood. Ice-cold water taking her breath away. The pressure on her chest as the water forced its way into her lungs. Spluttering. Then drifting, mind and body.

Jessandra shivered and pulled the cloak tight around her. She'd nearly died. The drifting of her consciousness, almost like going to sleep, was a memory all too real.

There had been power with her in the water, she wasn't sure from which god, but it hadn't helped. As she drifted, there was a blinding light and an unknown force on her body. And just like that, she was in Strath's arms on the ground, bone-cold and so tired her mind ached. The trip into the forest was a blur; she couldn't even remember falling asleep.

No wonder Wave and Strath were sleeping next to each other. They'd all gotten drenched. The rest of their clothes were drying and Jessandra was in Wave's cloak. She rose on shaky legs, pushing down the pang of jealousy that lingered. Wave was her friend, and Wave had saved her.

Touching each piece of clothing one by one, Jessandra realised everything was still damp. Although it was probably risky, she guessed they'd need to start the fire again. She cursed herself inwardly. Why had she never bothered to learn wild-craft? She couldn't start a fire alone, and they needed one because of her impatience, her inability to look after herself.

Hoping one of the others would wake soon to help with the fire, Jessandra slid her boots on without any stockings. They weren't as wet as she'd expected, but they were still uncomfortable. Clutching Wave's cloak around her, she trudged into the forest to collect small sticks.

She wandered for a while, picking up twigs and branches, her mind drifting back to those moments in the river. In the light of that experience, all of her other worries paled in comparison. She hadn't been called, but what did it matter? None of the gods had tried to save her. Wave had.

'Jessandra?' Strath's voice called from the clearing.

'Coming,' she said, trying not to be too loud. They didn't really know how safe they were from the Black Cloaks.

When she made it back to camp, Strath was hunkered down over the coals, moving them carefully with a long stick.

'There you are,' Wave said from behind the tree line. She was dragging a fallen branch behind her. The skin beneath her eyes was shadowed.

'I went to look for kindling,' Jessandra said as she lowered the pile to the ground beside Strath.

He looked up at her, his smile genuine. 'Thank you.'

Together, they built the fire up from the warm coals. Jessandra stayed by his side as Wave collected more wood. She wanted to learn, wanted to feel less useless, but she found it hard to keep her attention on the task. Her mind wandered, still sluggish from her time in the water.

Once the fire was going, Wave and Strath cobbled some branches together to create a drying rack for the clothes. They snacked on dried jerky from Strath's belt pockets and some tubers Wave had dug up. They ate them raw, and Jessandra had to drink a lot of water to get the chalky taste out of her mouth.

'We'll need to go into Kochee once we get there,' Strath said as he poked at the fire.

'It's not safe for either of us,' Wave said.

She was plucking the tuber's hairy skin off her tongue as she spoke. Jessandra giggled and Wave stuck her tongue out even further.

'How do you think we're going to get a ship to Veija-Mens if you won't go into the town?' Strath asked, his eyes still on the fire.

'We can sneak in to get on a ship,' Jessandra said. 'Just like Wave did when she left Chok.'

'And how are we going to pay for this ship?'

Jessandra and Wave glanced at each other. They'd fled Sharvel with nothing more than the borrowed clothes on their backs. True to his nature, Strath had worn his utility belt to the festival, so he had lots of useful items. Even if there were coins hiding in his belt, they wouldn't be enough to pay their way out of Heredour.

Across the fire from her, Wave chewed on her bottom lip, no doubt coming to the same realisation.

'We don't have any coins,' Jessandra said. 'We don't have anything more than the clothes we wore to the festival. Do you have coin?'

Strath looked up from the fire. Jessandra found it hard to meet his hazel eyes, but she forced herself to not look away.

'Not enough,' he said, sliding his gaze away to study Wave.

Jessandra sighed.

'We'll have to obtain more,' Strath said.

'How?' Wave asked, her deep frown a mirror of Jessandra's.

Strath glanced between the two of them and burst out laughing. 'You two have never had to work to support yourselves, have you?'

Jessandra shook her head, but Wave glared at him.

'She's a princess,' Wave said. 'And I'm seventeen. I've been in training for the past five years.'

'Sorry,' Strath said. 'I'm not laughing at you, I promise. Sometimes I just forget that you've both led very different lives to me.'

For some reason, his words stung like a sun rash and Jessandra flinched. Maybe that's why he didn't respond to her in the way she wanted him to. He was older than her, and his experience of life had been the complete opposite to Jessandra's. Perhaps he thought that made them incompatible.

For the first time since she'd noticed boys existed, Jessandra wondered what being compatible with someone would look like, how it would feel. Her life had always been orchestrated by others, and there had never been an opportunity to even explore the idea of what a good partnership could be. Especially not when her husband was always going to be chosen for her based on his kin and his family's status.

'We'll go into Kochee,' Strath said. 'Carefully!' He threw his hands in the air at Jessandra's glare. 'We'll spend a bit of time working out what's needed. Wave, you'll be able to get work in the mines or a fishing boat easily, and I can get something in the fields. Jessandra, seeing as you haven't been trained in anything, I guess you could be a maid. There's no kin requirements for that kind of work.'

'Mines—'

'Maid—'

'I can't work in—'

'I don't know how to be a maid!'

Jessandra and Wave looked at each other for a moment, then started laughing. The tension among them eased a little, and they discussed the different jobs they could do.

'How long will we have to work?' Jessandra asked once she'd come around to the idea of being a maid. At least she had some role models, though she'd never seen Siska or Inska scrub a latrine.

Strath shrugged. 'That'll be part of our first venture. We'll find work, but we'll also work out the price of a fare to Chaba-Canez. Then we can figure out how long it'll take to save.'

'I don't think we can afford to be in Kochee for very long,' Wave murmured.

'Neither do I,' Strath agreed. 'I don't want us to get separated, but we may end up in a situation where you need to go one at a time.'

'No!' Jessandra cried. The idea of being separated from Wave was unthinkable. They'd only just found each other. They were family, both through blood and in heart. And although Wave was smart and powerful, Jessandra wasn't sure they'd get very far without Strath. His wildcraft skills were the only thing that had kept them alive this long. And besides, she felt safer with him around.

'Like I said, Jess, it's not ideal.' Strath stood and stretched his arms towards the sky. 'But nothing about this situation is ideal. We'll avoid getting separated, but we also have to be smart about this.'

Jessandra locked eyes with Wave. Her friend gave a small shake of her head, her lips pursed. At least they thought the same. Separating would only be done in absolute desperation.

'Fine,' Jessandra said.

'I'm going to see if I can hunt some more food for us, Neffren willing,' Strath said. 'I've got salt with me, so we can cook and preserve it, at least for a few days.'

'Enough to get us to Kochee,' Wave said.

'Exactly. Once the clothes are dry enough, we'll make a move.'

The sun was already high in the sky, but Strath seemed to think they were safe enough. Jessandra vaguely remembered him saying the Black Cloaks would never think they'd crossed the river.

'Come on, Jess,' Wave said. 'Let's see what else we can forage. The more food we have, the easier our journey will be.'

Strath took off into the forest in one direction, Wave and Jessandra in another.

Once they were far enough away from Strath's earshot, Jessandra spoke.

'I won't leave you,' she whispered.

Wave looked over at her with a small smile.

'And I won't leave you.' Wave squeezed Jessandra's hand.

Nothing about her life was going to plan, but in that moment, Jessandra had never felt more at peace.

37

HABA SHA

DUSK SETTLED over Haba Sha with the standard southern fanfare of humming insects and a collective sigh of relief. Once again, Mortius stood in the business square, only this time he was watching the maire's house. If he could have, Mortius would have avoided setting foot in the villa, but Beren lived there now, and dining there would afford the sense of privacy he needed.

A servant showed him into the two-storey house and led him up a set of finely carved stairs. They strode through the dining room, set for two, and onto a long stretch of balcony that looked down over the square.

'Senior Adviser,' Beren said, turning from the railing with a half bow. 'Please be welcome in my home.'

'Thank you, Maire Beren,' Mortius said, imbuing his words with as much sarcasm as he could muster.

Ignoring the barb, Beren gestured for him to sit in one of the easy chairs. The servant poured out two tall glasses of iced tea.

'Unless you'd prefer something stronger?' Beren asked, one eyebrow twitching as he tried to keep his face impassive. He knew Mortius didn't drink.

'Iced tea is perfect in this climate.'

Beren waved the servant away and took one of the glasses.

'Did you enjoy your journey here?' he asked, not looking at Mortius as he sipped his drink, cold condensation dribbling over his fingers.

'It was good to be on the road again.'

Peering over his drink into the growing darkness of the square, Mortius watched the city coming alive below him. Street lanterns guttered into life, attracting a plethora of flying insects. People moved through the square, going about their business in the relative cool of the evening.

'You've been in the city too long,' Beren said.

'Agreed. One must do what he can to serve the high king, though.'

Beren raised his glass.

'All honour to High King Reuben,' he muttered.

'All honour to Emperor Kadesh,' Mortius intoned without thinking. How easily he slipped into the customs of the Trinian.

'It's been long since I've seen you, Beren, or heard from you,' Mortius said after a lengthy pause. 'Do you still enjoy your position in Haba Sha? Or does being maire wear on your existence?'

It wasn't meant to be an insult, but Mortius knew that was how it sounded. One corner of Beren's mouth quivered.

'As always, Senior Adviser. There are many challenges, but none that are unbearable.' Beren raised his eyes from the square. 'None that could compare to the daily challenge of running the country, or handling the high king.'

The words were a challenge, one Mortius had been waiting for since their first interaction in the council chambers. He wondered if there was a hint of resentment in Beren's tone, though. All those years ago when they'd become a part of Reuben's inner circle, they were each promised positions of high power for their unwavering allegiance and their unconditional silence. Yet it was Mortius who held the highest position, had maintained it for over two decades. The others had been sent to outlying regions to manage smaller towns and cities, those who hadn't been disposed of. It was possible that Beren envied Mortius' position at Reuben's side. Mortius could have laughed. The man had no idea.

'There must be a great challenge for the kingdom if the senior adviser has been sent out into the regions.' Beren was probing, hunting for information Mortius wasn't ready to give.

Mortius grimaced and turned the conversation back on Beren.

'A lack of communication from my informants is the greatest challenge I face.'

Beren sat a little taller in his chair. 'We send weekly reports to Shebedie, to be collated for you.'

'The regularity of each transcript is not what concerns me.'

Beren frowned.

'The failure has been in documenting the reality of your situation.'

'So you've come to check up on us? To make sure we're telling the truth?' Beren's eyes narrowed. 'I don't believe it. You can't think I believe you're here about some godsforsaken fish!'

Mortius said nothing. They were standing on the precipice of a dangerous conversation, and he wasn't sure how to continue. Instead, he watched the people of Haba Sha move through the square. There weren't many—those who weren't out on their fishing boats would be in one of the taverns, or at home with their families.

'We should retire inside,' Beren said.

'Yes,' Mortius agreed as he got to his feet. At least there would be no risk of their conversation being overheard.

He looked over the street one final time. A small group, no, a small family, moved from one side of the square to the other. They kept to the shadows as best they could, though it was hard when the streetlamps were bright and well placed. Mortius squinted at them, curious about their suspicious behaviour. Two men and a woman, all middle-aged, and a small girl holding the woman's hand. They paused, talking quietly, and the woman's face was lit by one of the lamps as she turned to face the men.

Mortius' heart skipped a beat. He would have recognised that face anywhere. This was the woman who'd stood between him and Samson, the woman who'd forced him to let Samson slip out of the kingdom's grip one lonesome night in Hybra.

Larka.

Samson's wife.

One by one, the others shifted at the edge of the light. The first man was nobody he knew, certainly not Samson. The girl was unknown to him, though there was no doubt she was Larka's child. She shared too many of Samson's features for her to be anyone else's. But the girl was perhaps nine or ten, and Samson hadn't been seen in Heredour for at least fifteen years. There had been reports, glimpses of someone who might have been him, here and there. Nothing substantial, though. Was he here, in the city with them?

The second man passed through the pool of light.

Rainer.

Mortius clutched at his heart, his chest constricting. In a heartbeat, the group was gone, disappeared into the shadows consuming the other side of the square. What in all the gods were Larka and Rainer doing together?

'Mortius?'

Beren's voice was distant, a sound summoning him from the edge of a fathomless ocean.

'Mortius, are you well?'

They were gone, but there was still a chance he could find them. Even if Samson wasn't with them, he could at least try to talk to Rainer. This moment of chance would save him a trip to Condor.

Letting go of his chest, Mortius turned to Beren with a forced smile.

'I am,' he said. 'I thought I saw someone I knew down there, but I was mistaken.'

Beren glanced over his shoulder, but the square was empty.

'Come on.'

Inside, they sat opposite one another, though the distance between them wasn't great. After they'd settled, servants brought platters of food and jugs of wine. In the centre of the table was a large, baked fish. Mortius shook his head.

'You've some nerve,' he muttered.

Beren shrugged. 'Not everyone is a failure at their job.'

Though he spoke of the fishermen, his tone suggested otherwise. Mortius gritted his teeth, and they ate in silence until Beren waved the servants away.

'We'll pour our own wine,' he insisted until they left.

Alone with only Mortius for company, Beren sighed and pushed his half-finished food away.

'You carry a great weight,' Mortius said.

Beren glanced at the fish. 'Triné is troubled.'

'There is more to your burden than dying fish.'

Sitting back into his chair, Beren held the glass of wine close to his chest.

'It's a huge burden when there are no obvious solutions, no easy answers.'

'Of course. I didn't mean to dismiss your plight.' Mortius copied Beren's relaxed pose, nursing his mulled cider. 'But I have known you a long time, Beren, and I can see that more weighs on your heart than the fate of a city you don't love.'

Beren pursed his lips. The panic from earlier was gone, replaced by a wariness Mortius well understood.

'I know how you feel,' he continued. 'For it's the same weight that burdens my shoulders and crushes my heart.'

'We should not speak of that which remains hidden.' Beren's voice was tight, the warning clear in his tone.

'We must,' Mortius said. 'I can longer abide that creature as my king and watch the country crumble!'

'I'll have no part of your treason.'

'He is not fit to rule!' Mortius slammed his fist on the table. Cutlery jangled, plates clattered, but Beren shook his head. 'You weren't so concerned about committing treason when Esra was on his deathbed.'

Beren scrubbed his face with his hands, but said nothing.

'You haven't seen him, Beren. Everything's changed. You've been gone too long.'

'Or maybe you've been close to him too long. Maybe you've got a taste of power and want more.'

'I'm no sunkin, you fool. I can't sit on the Sun Throne, even if I had the slightest desire to do so, which I don't.'

'And neither is that boy you paraded in front of me.' Beren set his wine back on the table and waved his hands in the air. 'Aymn starkin, my nephew,' he said, affecting a voice he no doubt imagined was a good impression of Mortius'.

'I had to keep him free of Buduwai. And anyway, he's the backup plan.'

'Backup plan?' Beren sneered. 'Backup plan? Samson hasn't been seen in fifteen years. Fifteen years, Mortius! We might know what really happened that night, but how do you expect to convince the population of his innocence? We forged his guilt in the fire of public opinion.'

Beren stood and paced the room, his back to Mortius. At least he was rattled. Anything was better than the apathetic maire he'd seen this morning.

'His eyes are no longer amber,' Mortius said softly, hoping to draw Beren's attention.

'The ring?' Beren asked, his back still turned, his palms resting on the mantelpiece.

'It's been growing. The past five years or so it's been obvious to everyone. I'm worried.'

'It doesn't mean anything,' Beren said, but his tone told Mortius he didn't believe his own words.

'Maybe not, but Heredour is falling apart.' Mortius took a deep breath. 'We have regions struggling to produce anything, herds of stillborn calves and sheep, dead fish, rotting wood. Then we have the Law of Kaiãho and Buduwai, and the problems the parents of those unreturned youth will no doubt cause. And to top it off, we've got a star-caller running loose, evading the Black Cloaks without even trying!'

Beren turned, his face pale. 'A star-caller?' he whispered.

'This country is a powder keg, Beren, and even if it's not because of Reuben, he's not fit to help Heredour through its next phase.'

'Star-caller?'

Mortius grimaced. Of course he'd focus on the one thing they couldn't control.

'Now do you see why I'm here?' Mortius laid his palms on the table. 'On top of all of that, the Black Cloaks are pushing harder for control, for a place of power next to Reuben.'

'Why did you come here first?' Beren said, the familiar panic surfacing in his voice again. 'If I knew there were others on board, I wouldn't hesitate to help.'

'When did you turn into such a pathetic rat?' Mortius spat, unable to hide his contempt any longer. 'What happened to brave, cunning Beren? Where is the man who made the plans to ensure Reuben's rule in the first place?'

Beren shook his head. 'I don't know.' With slow steps, he returned to the table. 'I don't know.' He drained his glass, and then hung his head in his hands.

'I don't ever remember being so afraid of everything.'

'Neither do I,' Mortius said with a half-hearted laugh. 'But here we are. Two old men who set the nation on fire twenty-five years ago. Now we have to find the courage within us to put the fire out.'

'Why us, Mortius?' Beren mumbled into his hands. 'Why can't we just sit back and let this madness play out?'

'Because it's just as much our fault as it is Reuben's. And if not us, then who? Who, Beren? Are you happy to sit back and watch the demise of our powers, of our nation?'

'Maybe.'

'You want to be maire of nothing? Maire of a town that produces nothing? Dealing with unhappy, starving, dying citizens? You want that on your conscience on top of everything else?'

'No.' Beren raised his head. 'But you don't know that getting Reuben off the throne will change any of those problems.'

'I can't make any guarantees,' Mortius agreed, studying Beren with narrowed eyes. He was close to giving in now, Mortius could feel it, sense it, smell it. So close. Mortius just needed to push a little more in the right way, and Beren would be his.

'But you and I both know that things started going wrong with the regions after Reuben took the throne. The Black Cloaks started meddling. The Law of Kaiāho. A star-caller ...' Mortius paused. No wonder he was exhausted. 'All of it. Everything was flourishing under Esra and his forefathers. And everything is failing under Reuben. His reign is built on a bed of lies, deceit, murder. We didn't think that mattered at the time. We didn't realise the gods would forsake him.'

Beren looked at him, his mouth downturned, his fingers intertwined with one another in his lap. There was such a great sadness to him, as if the true weight was the guilt of all they'd done, all the wrongs they'd let slip past them unspoken.

I've got him.

'Let's be honest with one another, Beren.' Mortius shifted his chair closer, so he could hold the other man's gaze. Violet and ice blue met one another, neither of them flinching. 'Everything we've done, everything we've let slide. It's hurting Heredour, and it's hurting us too.' He stabbed one finger at his chest.

Beren pinched the bridge of his nose, squeezing his eyes shut. All throughout their long past, Mortius had kept his emotions close to his chest. The time for being closed was gone, and he was certain the way to turn Beren was to reveal that they shared the same burden. The same shame, the same guilt.

'I can't live with myself anymore,' Mortius said. 'I want to fix this.'

After a long moment of aching silence, Beren raised his head.

'I cannot promise to be brave,' he whispered.

'I don't need you to be brave,' Mortius said, holding his gaze. 'Not yet.'

Beren nodded. 'I'll do what I must, then.'

'Swear it.'

Right hand over his heart, left hand over Mortius' heart, Beren intoned the words that had bound them together over Esra's deathbed so long ago.

'I am your man. Your will is my own. I move as you move, I trust as you trust. I am your man.'

3 8

THE NORTH CLAW

DAYS OF TREKKING through the mountain ranges made Wave feel more alive than she had in her life. The ache in her muscles subsided, and for once, the unceasing questions burning in her mind disappeared quickly each night as she fell asleep.

The only regret she had was that she'd slept alone since their clothes had dried. The day she'd saved Jessandra, Strath had invited her to curl up with him for warmth because they were a cloak short. She'd hardly slept that night, hyperaware of the feeling of his body pressing against hers, the sensation of his breath brushing her neck. Despite the exhaustion, she'd do it again, a thousand times over. But the opportunity was gone— their clothes were dry, and everyone slept beneath their own cloak.

Each time the thought arose, though, Wave berated herself. It was only a week ago that she thought she'd have to live the rest of her life as a hermit, never to touch another human. All that had changed when she'd read *The Blood of the Ehta*, and here she was, lamenting the loss of the touch of a boy.

He wasn't just any boy, though. This was Strath, the man

who'd befriended her when she was at her most vulnerable, the man who'd brought her to the cure she hadn't even known to look for. The man who was guiding them through the wild forests of the North Claw to try to find safety. The man who took in all of the wildness of her life—powerful waterkin, star-caller, daughter of Samson sunkin, magic-wielder—and accepted her regardless. How could her heart not beat fast when he looked at her with his colour-infused hazel eyes?

One morning, several days after Jessandra's fall, Wave woke alone in her cloak by the cold fire. Her limbs were stiff, so she rolled over, stretching her arms and legs for a time before sitting up. Jessandra was still asleep opposite her, but Strath was nowhere to be found.

The rosy blush of dawn stained the sky to the east. Wave stood and eased the sleep from her limbs. The patch of forest was sparse to the south, so she wandered towards the empty space.

Strath sat cross-legged on a rocky outcropping. In front of him was a view unlike any Wave had seen. The mountains descended sharply into a small bay below. Further south, the land sheared off into giant white cliffs, their edges jagged as if some ancient giant had torn a section of land away. Spreading inland of the cliffs was the desert—white clay quickly turned to red sand dunes stretching far beyond the horizon to the east.

This was the edge of Heredour. And there, in the vast silvery ocean, was the place the South Claw should have been. Seeing it from this vantage point made the absence of the Claw seem unnatural, disjointed. The land wanted to continue, take up space, push itself into the ocean as it once had. Instead, there was nothing except the unmoving, unyielding sea.

A large town was tucked into the bay below them.

'Kochee,' Wave said, joining Strath on the outcropping.

'Yes,' he murmured.

The people of Kochee mined colourful gems and precious stones deep beneath the ranges of the North Claw. From all Wave had read of the town, the people who lived in Kochee were more interested in their wares and their wealth than they were in the pursuit of their gods-given powers.

Wave wondered if her parents had travelled through Kochee, perhaps working under an alias. One of the few things Larka had told her was that they had travelled a lot, and one of their favourite places was Veija-Mens. If they'd met in Sharvel, it seemed likely they would have travelled through Kochee on their way to the Islands. Curious, Wave realised, that the one place that represented solace for her family was the isolated island she was also headed for.

'How do you feel?' Strath asked, disrupting Wave's quiet contemplation.

'Fine,' she said, but the answer was automatic.

'I mean, how do you really feel?' He turned from his study of the bay to face Wave. 'The last few days have been ... big for you.'

'Days?' Wave asked. She laughed, though she wasn't sure why. There was very little that had been funny since Henny's cold body landed in her arms. 'Weeks? Months? I've lost count.'

'Exactly,' he continued. 'You tried to save Henny. Then a star fell at your feet and you fled your home, thinking you were cursed. You met me by chance, or fate as I think, and then Jess joined us. We fought wizards, and then when we got to Sharvel, you learned that you weren't cursed, and that we can use the power of all the gods, and then you learned that your father is the exiled brother of the high king.' Strath took a deep breath. 'Jessandra saved us from the Black Cloaks and the army, I'm still not sure how, and then you saved her from the Kanrid using magic.'

His list was incomplete, but she'd never spoken about the disturbing vision she and Skoa had shared on the hilltop above

Chok. Then there were the dreams that plagued her each night, of X'olea locked in a dark room, of the puppeteer wizard in his desert tower, of a land where the colours of the landscape were all wrong and dragons flew in the sky. They were only dreams, though, and nothing in the face of everything else she'd experienced.

'When you list it in such an ordered fashion ...' she murmured, attempting a small smile.

'I just want you to know that I'm here,' Strath said, reaching across the space between them to hold her hand. 'You can talk to me about any of it, if and when you want to.'

Wave nodded. 'I know. There hasn't really been a pause since Henny died, and I haven't had much of a chance to process it all myself.'

'Somehow, I don't think we'll be getting a break from the chaos just yet.' Strath sighed. 'Hopefully we can rest and process when we get to Veija-Mens.'

For the first time since he'd barged into her quarters on the *Hand of Numen*, Wave considered the fact that he was still here, by her side.

'You know, Strath, I'd understand if you've had enough of this insane journey.'

Strath's eyebrows shot up. 'Why would you think that?'

'Because you don't owe us anything.' Wave gestured over to the sleeping princess. 'We got ourselves into the mess, and you've been helping us try to get out of it. I appreciate it, as does Jess.' Wave paused. She appreciated him, more than she could ever articulate. 'But you lost your brother, your parents to the Black Cloaks. You lost your parents because of my father.' Her voice squeaked a little at the mention of Samson.

'I lost my parents because of their actions. Your father is not to blame for their capture, and from what you've told me, he's not to blame for most of the trouble that is laid at his feet.'

Wave nodded; though she still retained some anger towards her father, she didn't doubt the story Kali had shared.

'I'm here because I want to be,' Strath said. 'Like I told you when we first met, your story gives me hope. I can't help Ernad or my parents, but I can help you, both of you. You're way too valuable to lose to the Black Cloaks.'

Wave laughed.

'I don't just mean because of what you know, or how powerful you are, or who you're related to.' Strath shuffled over to her and laid a hand over her heart. 'This heart of yours is too precious to lose to those monsters.'

A lump rose in Wave's throat. She hoped Strath wouldn't realise her heart was beating so fast because of how close they were. Time seemed to stand still. Strath didn't move away, and she was consumed by his eyes, lost among the flecks of turquoise, emerald, and violet. When he blinked, Wave was distracted by the brush of his long lashes against his cheek. The hand he'd laid on her heart slid up to her face, cupping her cheek.

Strath pulled her face closer to his, his breath as heavy as hers. An unfamiliar feeling stirred deep in her abdomen, pulsing in time with the rhythm of her heart. Their lips brushed. Wave fought a rising crescendo of panic.

A loud snort made them both jump, Strath's hand falling from her face. He looked crestfallen, and Wave swallowed a few times, trying to find her breath. Behind them, Jessandra stirred in her sleep, then sat up with a strangled cry.

Feeling grateful but strangely dissatisfied, Wave hurried over to the princess.

'What is it, Jess?' she asked, squatting down and resting a hand on her friend's shoulder.

'I had a dream,' Jessandra said. Her hair was in disarray around her face, her eyes bleary with sleep. 'There was a tower —deep in the desert. A huge tower.'

Wave's mouth went dry.

'A man stood on a balcony. Gods, Wave, he was ugly.'

The pockmarked skin, the hooked nose, the white irises. Wave shuddered. Strath joined them, watching Jessandra intently and avoiding Wave's gaze.

'There were strings all around his fingers, threading out into the world like spider silk. A string wrapped around me, and he smiled, and started pulling. I felt like a little bug, incapable of escaping the spider's web.' Jessandra shivered. 'But then there was a golden man, shining like the sun. He stood between me and the spider-man. I was blinded by him, then ...'

Jessandra frowned. 'I guess I woke up then.'

'I've seen him,' Wave muttered. Strath finally looked at her.

'The golden man?' Jessandra asked.

Wave shook her head. 'The puppeteer. In the desert tower.' She told them about her shared vision with Skoa.

'That's him,' Jessandra said, her face paling. 'Why are we having the same dream?'

'Maybe it's not a dream,' Strath said. 'Your intuition is highly attuned, Jess. I don't know what it means, but you knew something was wrong at Long Night well before I did.'

'But what does that have to do with anything?' Jess asked. 'What does intuition even mean? Is it something to do with the gods?'

'No,' Strath said. 'At least, I don't think so. It's just something that I developed over the years. I think we all have it to some degree, but yours is ... on fire?' He shrugged. 'Maybe it ties into your dreams somehow.'

'Have you dreamed of him?' Jessandra asked, studying Wave. Her eyes were clear now. 'The spider-man, or the man of gold?'

'No.' Wave wasn't ready to share the strange things she did see in her dreams. 'Perhaps the golden man is Jesma?' The iconography Jessandra had described worked for the sun god.

'Makes sense,' Strath said. 'Are you okay?'

Jessandra nodded. 'It gave me a fright, but I'm okay now I'm awake.'

'Let's get ready, then,' Strath said.

'Ready for what?'

'Kochee,' Wave said. 'It's time to find a job.'

39

HABA SHA

THE PORT of Haba Sha was a vast, chaotic whirlwind of colour and sound. Larka and Winter stood hand in hand on a low rise, looking out over the bay. Rows of tall-masted sailing ships and wide-bellied merchant vessels sat abreast of smaller commercial fishing boats. On the distant horizon, dozens of sea craft—some only mere specks—travelled to and from Triné's main port.

There were no cliffs on this side of Heredour, and the rows of wooden wharves gave way to pebbled beaches and rolling hills of swaying seagrass. Though it wasn't the first time she'd seen the port, the vastness of the ocean still took Larka's breath away. Everything in the Barancha Plains operated on a much smaller scale, and she'd been stuck there a long time.

'Let's sit, Winter, and we can watch the ships.'

Larka led her daughter to one of the many worn wooden benches placed along the cobbled street. The stench here was awful, brine and rotting fish mixed with sewer water and piles of trash, but she'd promised Hasting and Rainer they wouldn't move far. The two of them were deep in the shouting, scrambling mess of the port, hoping to buy them all a passage far away from Heredour. Having a woman and child with them would have ruined their bargaining power, so Larka and Winter were left in an open place they could easily flee from if need be.

Once Hasting had recovered enough to walk unaided, they'd marched through the forest, following the scent of seawater. When they'd stumbled into the outskirts of Haba Sha, nobody had been more surprised than Hasting. His intention had been to take them to Davej-Arne, all the way over on the eastern coast of Heredour, but here they were on the Swishdine Coast.

Over a few conversations, they'd surmised that the strain on Hasting's grasp of magic from moving so many of them at once had forced him to jump somewhere much closer. Larka didn't mind. It had been easier to agree on the plan of taking a ship to Chaba-Canez now they were here. The plan wouldn't help Siska, but if Larka was honest with herself, she didn't have the first clue on how to help either of her adult daughters. Keeping Winter safe was something tangible she could focus on.

They'd taken lodgings in the outskirts of the sprawling town, paying for a cheap room with a collection of coins Hasting and Rainer kept tucked into secret pockets. Larka had been impressed. They were both more prepared to run than she was.

'They're so big, Mumma.'

Winter's gaze was distant, her eyes lingering over the swaying lines of ships.

'They are,' Larka said. 'We'll probably be on one of those wide-bellied ones.'

'But the water, it's even bigger.' Winter shook her head as she took in the ocean. 'It goes on forever.'

'It seems like that. But we'll head over the horizon and in a few days, you'll see the Islands. The main island, LaBraqi, has a volcano at its heart.'

'Volcano?' Winter turned to her mother, eyes wide. 'What's that?'

Larka explained how sometimes the gods made the earth

move in strange ways, how they made volcanos as a funnel to the fiery heart of the whole world. Anywhere a volcano could be found was a very special place to the gods.

Nodding slowly, her expression turning concerned, Winter looked out over the bay.

'The volcano on LaBraqi is inactive, so it's nothing to be afraid of,' Larka said, misreading her daughter's expression.

'Mumma,' Winter whispered. 'Don't look, but someone is watching us.'

Larka's heart leapt to her throat. She glanced around the people in front of them, but nobody paid her any mind. Easing her head slowly to the left, her gaze landed on an all-too-familiar face, one she'd hoped to never see again. The sounds of the port disappeared until all she could hear was the rush of blood racing through her eardrums.

Mortius.

Only a few metres away, he stood alone on the pier. No, not alone. Another man, unfamiliar to Larka, stood beside him chatting with a bored expression on his face.

He'd aged since she'd last seen him. The once-blond hair was silver now, and his face was marked with fine lines and deep furrows. The stress of his role, the secrets buried in his heart were obvious in those lines. Even so, he carried himself like someone half his age, his posture upright and his gaze as shrewd as ever.

There was no hiding from him. They locked eyes and the world around them ceased to exist. The man beside Mortius realised his words were falling on deaf ears and he turned to follow Mortius' line of sight. Larka and Winter were two unremarkable people in a crowd, though, and the man's gaze passed straight over them.

Taking slow, deliberate steps, Mortius moved towards them. His sidekick stepped in behind him with a bemused smile. A bevy of men followed, four in total, wearing dark riding gear.

He wasn't alone after all. At least there were no Black Cloaks with them.

'Winter, whatever happens here, don't say anything.'

Larka stood and pulled Winter up, tucking her in behind her skirts. The more distance she kept between Mortius and Winter, the better.

The group arrived quickly, and Mortius and Larka stood in silence facing each other.

Her whole body trembling, Larka made a small curtsy.

'Senior Adviser.'

She felt Winter bob beside her. The poor girl had never had to curtsy before.

'Larka.' His voice was crisp as a spring morning. There was no obvious emotion in his tone or expression as he regarded her.

One of the men stood close behind Mortius. He was young, younger than all of them, perhaps a few years older than Siska. There was something familiar in his bearing, though his pale hair and flat, grey eyes gave nothing away of his heritage or kin. The boy had eyes only for Winter, and the longer he looked at her, the paler his face became.

'Who's this?' Mortius gestured at the half-hidden form of Winter.

Gritting her teeth, Larka drew her daughter out from behind her body.

'This is Winter.'

The smile Winter gave him was all teeth. She was afraid.

'Winter?' The name made him pause, as if considering its meaning. 'Your daughter?'

It took Larka a while to answer. 'Yes.'

'You remarried?' He glanced at her hands.

Larka folded them into her skirts, but she was too slow. There were no rings on her fingers. A marriage in Sharvel was unlike the rest of Heredour. Her commitment to Samson was tattooed on her left hand. The absence of a ring wouldn't have gone unnoticed by Mortius.

'No,' she admitted.

His eyes narrowed. 'Is he here?'

'Here?' Larka's eyebrows shot up in surprise and she shrugged. 'I don't even know if he's alive.'

Mortius took a step back as if she'd slapped him. He didn't know where Samson was, but it was clear he also hadn't orchestrated his death. A small hope flickered to life in her heart.

'Who's this, then?' She gestured to the young man. Moments of opportunity only presented themselves for a very short time, and she wasn't about to miss this one.

The boy's eyes flicked up to her face, regarding her with a small frown. Winter squeezed Larka's hand.

With a very slow movement of his head, Mortius turned to where she pointed. He motioned with his head and the boy moved forward to stand beside him.

'This is Aymn starkin,' Mortius said, his voice tight. 'My nephew.'

Larka raised a derisive eyebrow at Mortius but smiled at Aymn.

'A pleasure to meet you, Aymn,' she said. 'I thought you must have been related to our senior adviser. You do look so alike.'

She couldn't keep the smirk out of her voice. Up close, the resemblance to Reuben and Samson was unmistakable. Even though Aymn lacked the golden hair and amber eyes of his true kin, the sharp jaw and the shape of his eyes told no lies. The face of Larka's husband was reflected back at her, but this boy wasn't his son.

Mortius glared at Larka, daring her to cross the line of propriety again. She wasn't ready to be cowed, though.

'Do you find Everluof's grace to be sufficient, Lord Aymn?'

Aymn blinked in surprise.

'I am no lord, only a master's apprentice,' he said, his voice as smooth as silk. As he spoke, his chin lifted, and Larka saw Reuben's face as if the best artist had painted it over the top of Aymn's.

'And an excellent one at that,' Mortius said.

'But no,' Aymn continued, his eyes on Larka. 'I do not find Everluof's grace sufficient. We all know there is little power left to be touched by our generation.'

When he spoke, every eye was on him. He had the charisma of a sunkin, the magnetic energy that attracted people into his orbit. Though she didn't know how he managed it, Larka realised Mortius must have convinced the boy at some young age he was to be starkin. If he was Reuben's son, as she guessed, then Mortius had put in the work to save Aymn from Buduwai.

As she studied him, Aymn knelt down in front of Winter, bringing his face level to hers. The likeness in their faces jolted Larka from her thoughts.

'And what of you, little Winter?' Aymn asked, his voice gentle. 'Have you felt the grace of any of our gods or goddesses yet?'

This time, Winter's smile was genuine. She reached a hand out and laid it on Aymn's face, shaking her head and saying nothing. The two cousins, unconnected all their lives, stared at each other, open curiosity on both of their faces.

Above their heads, Larka and Mortius shared a long, knowing look. When Aymn rose, his face a little more ashen than it had been before, Mortius took a step closer to Larka.

'Larka,' he said, lowering his voice. 'It is imperative that you visit me at Maire Beren's residence.' He waved a hand behind him, gesturing at the bored-looking sidekick.

Beren.

The name hit her, jarring her equilibrium. Another of the inner circle, one who was no doubt still on the inside if he was Maire of Haba Sha. Swallowing her bile, Larka focused her attention back on Mortius.

'I don't think that's in my best interest, Senior Adviser.'

He grasped her wrist, and for the first time, Larka saw desperation in his eyes.

'I know who you travel with, and I need to speak with him.'

Larka's breath caught in her throat. He hadn't stumbled upon them by chance. They'd been careless, and he'd come looking for them.

'No harm will come to you or your child.'

'I have no reason to trust you, nor any reason to visit you at his residence.' She flung one arm at Beren. He frowned at her. He had no idea who she was, thank all the gods.

'I don't expect you to trust me,' he said. 'Gods know I've given you every reason to hate me.'

Larka laughed, but it was a hollow, empty sound.

'Larka, we may have a common goal.' His voice was a whisper, his words meant for her alone.

'A common goal?' she hissed. 'Are you mad?'

'Undoubtedly. But there is one who is worse.'

Reuben's face swam before her eyes.

'My position has changed, and I think we should discuss how we might … assist one another.'

For the longest time, Larka stared at him. An eerie silence cocooned them, every person nearby intent on listening to the words not meant for them. Everything about the situation screamed danger. This was the man who'd been instrumental in Samson's exile. This was the man who'd supported Reuben through all of his evil actions. Even if he truly had chosen to cast aside his loyalty to the high king, that only made him less trustworthy.

And yet, if he had turned from Reuben, maybe he could help her. What if he was looking for Sam too?

'I promise, you and Winter will be free to leave Haba Sha as you wish. No harm will come to either of you.'

'Surely you understand that I can't do that, Mortius.'

A muscle in his jaw twitched. 'Then we must meet some-where neutral.'

'Neutral?'

Mortius shrugged, an unusual gesture for such a taut, controlled man.

'Somewhere you'll feel safe. Somewhere we won't be disturbed.'

'There is a place,' she said, wondering why she was parlaying with him but unable to stop the words from spilling forth. 'An open field with a copse of coarse-wood trees at its heart. Head west along the coast road until you reach the third small road running inland.' It was a nothing place, a place with no special memories or reasons to go there.

'Past the road to X'xix?'

'No,' Larka said, her voice terse. 'The third road after you leave Haba Sha. Half a mile up the road, you'll see the trees.'

'When?'

'Tomorrow, at dawn.' Larka paused, thinking for a moment. 'Nobody else is to come. Just you, and Aymn.'

'Of course.'

'And all four of us are free to leave. Not just Winter and me.'

Mortius grimaced. 'I need Rainer.'

'Rainer is pledged to me. He goes where I go.' There was no pledge, but Larka had no reason to be transparent with Mortius.

'Fine.' Mortius' hands balled into his fists. 'Fine. But I will speak to him.'

Larka nodded. 'Dawn, tomorrow. No weapons, no men.'

'No weapons,' Mortius agreed. 'Just Aymn and myself.'

Without another word, Mortius spun on his heel and pushed through his men, stalking down the pier. The others stared at Larka for a long moment before hurrying after him. Aymn glanced at Winter one last time, offering Larka a small smile before he disappeared after them.

Taking a shaky breath, Larka eased herself back onto the

bench. Uncertainty crept through her body, mimicking the grey clouds rolling over the horizon. Winter sat beside her.

'He understands, Mumma.'

'What do you mean?' Larka looked down to see Winter's serene smile.

'Aymn. He understands me.'

Larka didn't know what to say. Before she had a chance to respond, Hasting and Rainer strode up to them.

'I've got us a passage,' Hasting said. 'But we have to bide our time. We'll leave in two days.'

Rainer smiled at Winter, tousling her hair.

'Good,' Larka said. 'We have something we need to do tomorrow.'

Both men looked at her with eyebrows raised.

'We ran into someone,' Larka said. 'An old ... acquaintance.'

'Who?' Hasting's eyes narrowed.

'You should sit,' Larka said. 'Both of you. You're not going to like what I have to say.'

They sat, Hasting on Larka's left, Rainer on Winter's right. Rainer wore a bemused look, but Hasting folded his arms across his chest.

'Who?' Hasting repeated.

Larka took a deep, steadying breath. 'Mortius.'

They were both silent, though Rainer's face paled and he chewed the inside of his cheek.

'Fine,' Hasting said as he stood. 'I'm finding someone who can take us now.'

'No, Hasting.'

Ignoring her, he started walking down the pier. Larka grabbed his hand and pulled him back to the bench.

'Sit down, Hasting,' she growled, 'and listen to me before you do anything stupid.'

He clenched his jaw but did as he was told.

'We can't stay in this town, Larka,' he said. 'If he knows you're here, Winter's here, neither of you are safe.'

'He knows Rainer is here too.'

Rainer pinched the bridge of his nose.

'See, even more reason to get out of here. I'll get us some horses, we'll head up to—'

'Stop, Hasting!' Larka said. 'Mortius and I, we made a deal.'

Hasting's anger forced him to his feet. 'You what?' he whispered. There was violence in his voice, a tightness around his eyes Larka had never seen before.

'We're all free to leave Haba Sha, so long as we meet him tomorrow morning.'

Hasting opened his mouth to retort, but Larka raised one hand.

'Hush. He wants to speak to Rainer and me. He has some sort of plan. He's casting Reuben aside.'

'So?' Hasting said, his voice rising. 'You can't trust him! Look at everything he's done, every misery he's caused.' Hasting's face contorted in rage. 'And not just to your family, but to all the people of Heredour.'

'He's right, Larka,' Rainer added. 'I know him, more than any of you. He can't be trusted.'

'I don't trust him!' Larka exclaimed. 'I'm no fool, and I'd expect you both to think better of me than that. I need to know what his plan is, and whether it involves Sam.'

'This is insane,' Hasting said.

'It is,' Larka said. 'But I need you to trust me on this. He had a boy with him, Aymn.'

Hasting shrugged. 'And?'

'He's Reuben's son, I'm certain of it.'

'Gods,' Rainer said. 'Frieda's boy?'

'Perhaps. He's been raised as Mortius' nephew.' Larka flopped down on the bench.

Winter giggled from between them. 'He's not related to the thin man!'

All three of them turned to her.

'What do you mean?' Hasting asked.

'It's like …' she started, and then grimaced. 'I don't know how to explain it. But it's in here.' She stabbed at her heart with one finger.

'Can you try, Miss Winter?' Rainer asked. 'Us adults aren't very smart.'

Sighing, Winter looked around them for something to demonstrate with.

'Like this,' she said, grasping a loose thread of Larka's sleeve. She pulled the thread towards her and lay it over her heart. 'You see?'

Larka and Hasting stared at one another.

'And the sleeve is … Aymn?' Rainer asked.

'Yes!' Winter giggled again, grinning up at Rainer. 'You understand. And I have a thread to Mumma, and Siska, and Wave. But this thread, it's a little bit different.' She shrugged.

'They're cousins,' Larka murmured. 'And if Mortius wants to install Aymn on the throne, he'll have to ensure Samson never returns.'

'Exactly why you can't meet with him,' Hasting said. 'He could take you hostage, use you as bargaining power.'

'He's desperate. Something's not right.'

'Mortius has never been a desperate man,' Rainer said, his eyes still on Winter.

'I know,' Larka agreed. 'I wouldn't believe it either if I hadn't seen it. He wants us on his side. Gods know why he thinks either of us would agree to help him, though.'

'He'll try to capture you,' Hasting said, his anger replaced with anxiety. 'You can't meet with him.'

'It'll be the four of us, and just him and Aymn. No other men, no weapons. We'll be in an open field, far away from the town.

'You can't do this, Larka,' Hasting whispered, grasping her hands as he perched on the edge of the bench. 'After everything we've been through.'

'If he wanted to take us, he could have done it just now. But he led his men away and didn't tell them who we are. I'm going to meet him, and I hope you'll come with me.' Larka turned to Rainer. 'And I hope you'll come too.'

'I don't like it,' Rainer said. 'I don't like it one bit. But if you say it's the right thing to do, I'll follow you.'

Larka rested one hand on Rainer's shoulder. 'Thank you.'

'This is madness,' Hasting said, but there was a resignation in his tone.

'Absolutely,' Larka agreed. She squeezed his hands. 'But there is an opportunity here, I can feel it.'

Hasting shook his head and slumped back into the bench.

'Fine,' he said. 'What do we have to do?'

40

KOCHEE

THE TRIO HALTED on the outskirts of Kochee. Beneath the bright midday sun, Jessandra squinted at the buildings and streets of the town. Every surface glittered and sparkled. The town looked like an illusion, a hazy mirage bordering desert and ocean.

They'd noticed the way Kochee shimmered as they descended the final rocky mountainside, but it wasn't until they arrived that Jessandra realised how bizarre the town truly was. Gold, silver, and copper covered every surface. Walls, roofs, and window frames were studded with precious gems and stones.

There was a vast amount of wealth in her family and in the city of Millen, but the display before her was obscene. The only part of the town not covered in precious metals or gems was the road. Thick slabs of smooth, white stone guided them into Kochee.

Strath kept them close to the buildings, staying in shadows where they could. In whispers, he revealed that in the heart of Kochee lay the merchants' guild, a square where even the roads were paved in gold. Jessandra was used to being surrounded by luxury, fine silks and delicate jewellery, any coin she needed at her disposal. But this? A road paved in gold? It was obnoxious, unnecessary. Who were these people trying to impress? Nobody crossed the desert to come to Kochee—only the people of Geb traded by road, and the rest came by boat, if they came at all.

Before long, they reached an area filled with people. Carts pulled by donkeys pushed for space against horse-drawn wagons, while all manner of people hurried past in every direction. A lot of the civilians were wearing a strange contraption on their faces, kind of like a looking glass but so dark the person's eyes were hidden. There would be no easy way of telling a person's kin here, and it meant that Jessandra and her friends stood out as foreigners.

'We need to get some of those looking glasses,' Wave murmured, mirroring Jessandra's thoughts once again.

'Agreed,' Strath said.

He led them through several wide, straight streets towards the docks. There was always a market near a wharf, and it would be easy to disappear into a bustling marketplace without drawing too much attention.

Though most of Kochee had been built on flat ground, the markets sloped down to meet the docks, creating a maze of angled streets that left behind the white paving in favour of more practical cobblestones. The bay remained in view and Jessandra could make out huge ships rocking gently against their moorings. Many of them were decked out in as luxurious a fashion as the rest of the town; some of the giant unfurled sails even had glittering jewels sewn into their hems.

Down on the docks, people scurried about in all directions; captains shouting orders, sailors hauling ropes, workers stacking crates between the jetties. Chaos seemed to be the inherent nature of Kochee.

At the furthest end of the docks, Jessandra spotted a host of dark, dingy ships. They looked nothing like their glamorous counterparts, and Jessandra felt a spike of unease in her belly when she looked at them. She dragged her eyes away, frowning at the sensation in her body as she followed her friends.

The market was busy; shipments of fresh produce had just arrived and people were hurrying about making purchases. Hawkers crowded against one another, shouting over the top of the hubbub to make their special prices or unique gifts known to all. The market was a chaos of light and sound and colour, but at least there were no bejewelled buildings, and most of the people here had foregone the strange looking glasses.

Jessandra was overwhelmed by the place. She visited Millen's main markets once every year, on her birthday. The citizens were always on their best behaviour, though, moving out of her way, curtsying at her family, offering their wares for free. That experience was nothing like the chaotic dance happening around her. Jessandra realised her birthday must have been and gone, and she hadn't even realised.

Sixteen. It didn't feel any different, not compared to the wild changes that had happened over the past few weeks. Still, she was a little sad that nobody knew, that there hadn't been even a small celebration.

'My lady! Over here, great lady!' a merchant called.

Wave giggled. 'He's talking to you, Jess.'

Jessandra turned towards the peddler, noticing the simpering smile he plastered over his face as soon as her attention was on him.

'Great lady,' he said, beckoning to her. 'See my jewellery, the finest in all the market.' He waved a hand over his small stall. The gems were expensive and well cut, but the metal was cheap, the design poorly thought out.

'No, thank you,' Jessandra said, lifting her chin a little higher as she turned away from him.

Although Wave had stayed with her, Strath was nowhere to be seen, lost in the throng of marketgoers.

'Where is he?' Jessandra asked.

'Gods,' Wave said. 'It's going to be impossible to find him in this.'

Jessandra clutched Wave's hand, neither of them moving. The crowd flowed around them, as if they were ageless boulders in a fast-moving river. What would they do if they couldn't find him?

'Wave! Jess!'

Further down the road, Strath's body seemed to float above the crowd as he called their names. Wave moved through the milling people, pulling Jessandra in her wake. When they reached him, Jessandra realised he'd climbed the side of a stall to find them. He jumped down and pulled them in close.

'You've got to stay with me,' he said, as if he were admonishing them. His smile said otherwise. 'I've got good news.'

'You got a ship?' Wave asked.

'You found us jobs?' Jessandra asked.

'I found you both some paid work,' Strath said. 'How do you feel about polishing jewellery?'

Jessandra glanced at Wave, but she just shrugged.

'It sounds better than being a maid,' Jessandra said.

Strath laughed. 'Good.' He took their hands, leading them to a nearby stall.

'Aminy,' Strath called. 'I've got your workers.'

A shrewd-eyed man, not dissimilar to the one who'd called out to her earlier, ducked through a curtain to face them. With the pale blue eyes of a skykin, he looked Jessandra and Wave up and down.

'They'll do,' he said. From his pocket he took a small pad of parchment and a chiselled stick of charcoal. He scribbled something on the paper before tearing it loose and handing it to Strath.

'Take them to the warehouse district,' Aminy said. 'Ask for directions if you're not sure. The warehouse has a sign like this on it.' He stabbed at the parchment in Strath's hands. Above the scratchy, scrawled words was a symbol—a chain with a flagpole stuck through the middle loop.

'Thank you,' Strath said.

Aminy's eyes were already scouring over the crowd, so Strath turned away, Jessandra and Wave following. They struggled through the crowded market, Jessandra gripping on to the back of Strath's coat in an effort not to lose him.

As the market stalls began to thin out, so did the throng. Strath pulled them into a tight circle, a little away from everyone.

'Let's get you to that warehouse, and then I'll go and secure us a passage,' Strath said. 'Once that's done, I'll see what I can find for myself.'

'I don't like this,' Jessandra said. She'd been pushing aside the unease she'd felt since they entered Kochee, but she couldn't ignore it any longer. 'I don't think we should separate.'

'We have to,' Strath said. 'No captain is going to give us passage for nothing. And you're lucky I was able to get you two work in the same warehouse.'

'Did you see those ships, though?' Jessandra asked, looking between her two friends. 'At the other end of the docks?'

Wave shook her head, but Strath's smile died, his lips forming a straight line.

'Slavers,' he said.

Jessandra's eyes widened. Slavery was reviled in Heredour; an easy thing to do when the hierarchy of kin determined those who could be employed in servitude.

'I didn't think there were slaves in Heredour?' Wave asked.

'There aren't,' Strath said. 'At least, not any obvious slaves. But the people from lands across the ocean have slaves, and the slave traders operate from Jamari.'

The island was so far west of Heredour that nobody considered it a part of the country. No wonder the highkin never bothered to integrate the tiny island. It was typical highkin thinking—Heredour was free of slaves, everyone else wasn't their problem. Jessandra shook her head.

'Why are they here, then?' she asked.

Strath shrugged. 'I guess the same reason other ships stop here. Top up on supplies, give the sailors a break, all of that.'

His answers did nothing to quell Jessandra's unease. If anything, she felt worse now, as if she'd swallowed a vat of hot oil.

'Unless either of you have a better idea,' Strath said, 'we'd best find this warehouse.'

Jessandra pursed her lips. Any chance of using her royal status as a way of getting what they needed was out of the question—she'd bring the Black Cloaks down on them in a heartbeat.

'Fine.'

'Let's ask these stallholders for directions,' Strath said.

The crowd was much more manageable here, and despite hanging back, Jessandra and Wave didn't lose him again while he spoke to different people.

'All right,' he said, returning with a grim smile. 'This way.'

'Something doesn't feel right,' Jessandra whispered to Wave. 'Something's wrong.'

Wave chewed on her lip. 'I know, but what else can we do?'

Clenching her hands into fists, Jessandra followed Strath through the streets. They entered the wild dance of the main market again, and Jessandra pushed down the feeling of wrongness as she focused on not losing Strath again.

41

KOCHEE

THE PEOPLE CRASHED around Wave like the frothy breakers of a storm-driven sea. She was having trouble following Strath—her attention wandering to the discomfort she felt in her gut, her eyes roving over the slave ships at the far end of the docks.

The sensation wasn't really in her gut when she thought about it. If someone had a knife pressed to the back of her neck, that would be a more accurate description of how she felt. She wanted to turn and look behind them, but resisted. Beside her, Jessandra kept glancing backwards, her fingers entwined in her skirts.

'Strath,' Jessandra said. 'Strath!'

He slowed until he was between them.

'What is it?'

'We're being followed,' Jessandra whispered.

Wave's gut clenched and she fought every urge to turn around. Instead, she looked up at Strath. He would know what to do. A muscle worked in his jaw, but he nodded once, then continued walking, his stride quickening.

None of the stalls grabbed his attention, despite the merchants' invitations, and the two girls hurried to keep up with him. They were heading uphill, back towards the town. The market crowd was beginning to thin.

Wave's heart thrummed in her chest. A lump rose in her throat. The crawling sensation in her gut intensified and she turned to glare at Jessandra, willing her to move faster. When she was close enough, Wave reached out and grabbed her hand. Before she had a chance to speak, Strath turned and began heading back into the throng of marketgoers.

Jessandra stumbled over a cobblestone as they were swallowed by the crowd. Wave dragged her forward so she didn't lose her balance.

It was all Wave could do not to break into a run, to sprint out of this mad town with its sparkling walls and eerily reflective windows. In the forest and the mountains, she'd felt safe. They'd only been in Kochee for half an hour, and they were already in danger.

Keeping her eyes locked on Strath's bouncing curls as he cut a path through the people, Wave sent a hurried prayer to Lerinial.

'Let the people wash over us like waves, let them bury us, let them hide us,' she intoned under her breath, wondering if Lerinial cared about her anymore.

A wordless cry pierced the air. Jessandra's hand slipped from Wave's.

'No!' Wave cried, pivoting on one foot.

Two men in rough-spun miner's garb held Jessandra between them. One had a hand clamped over her mouth. Above the thick, dirty fingers, Jessandra's grey eyes darted about in desperation. Strath hurled himself at one of the men, attacking with the slim dagger that lived on his belt.

Wave followed him without thinking, flailing her arms at the second man. The first man let go of Jessandra to defend himself against Strath's blade. The other held Jessandra tight, angling the princess in front of Wave.

Noise came from all sides. Marketgoers turned to watch the fight, encouraging them with cheers. Jessandra freed one of her arms and twisted in the man's grip so she could hit him. Neither of their blows hurt him, strong as he was, but he couldn't do anything to stop them without releasing Jessandra.

Desperation consumed Wave. They were attracting too much attention. Just because they hadn't seen any Black Cloaks in the town didn't mean they couldn't arrive at any moment. What a prize they would find—not one but two of the people they were hunting, embroiled in a scrappy street fight.

Strath's opponent had drawn a large dagger. Its wicked, glinting edge caught Wave's eye, and she paused, her heart in her throat. Strath parried every blow the man sent his way.

The second miner caught her arm and yanked it behind her body. Wave cried out in pain. Forcing her to the ground, her knees crashing into the cobblestones, the man spun Jessandra until she was beside Wave.

'You little whores,' he spat. 'I'll never have to work again once I claim my prize.'

The second man was covered in fine nicks, blood trickling down his arms and legs. A cut above Strath's eye clouded his vision with blood. He fought with unrivalled ferocity, his movements cunning and quick. The pair darted back and forth, trading blow after blow. Strath was nimble, but the other man was like bedrock. And against his might, Strath was tiring.

Wave and Jessandra looked at each other. There was a grim determination in her friend's eyes, so unlike the panic Wave felt inside. Wave struggled against her captor. Pain seared through her shoulder, and she squeezed her eyes shut.

'Ooph.'

Wave's eyes flew open. The other man held his side, eyes wide in surprise. Panting, Strath squatted in a half crouch, waiting for the next attack. Blood dripped onto the cobblestones from his dagger.

The miner roared and ran at Strath, an enraged bull with an easy target. Stumbling, he fell to his knees. Hot, red blood rushed over his fingers. He pulled his hand away from his body. Strath had made a gaping, jagged wound. There was blood everywhere. Strath turned his attention to the man holding Wave and Jessandra.

Before he could move, a power stirred around them. A blast of air shot from the sky. The bleeding miner flew back into the crowd. Wave's arm wrenched free as the second man was flung backwards. She screamed in pain, her arm hanging limp at her side.

With a startled look on her face, Jessandra grabbed Wave's other hand and pulled her towards Strath. The crowd parted for them, allowing them free passage before crowding around the injured men. Strath sprinted away, dragging Wave and Jessandra behind him.

As they headed back through the town and the crowd thinned to only a few people, Strath let go of their wrists and slowed a little. Both Wave and Jessandra were struggling for breath. Wave's shoulder was a bright spot in her awareness, the pain almost as surprising as Jessandra's use of Setunil's power. Wave clenched her teeth and pushed all thoughts from her mind.

'Come on,' Strath called over his shoulder.

They were close now; Wave could feel the fresh breath of the forest filling her nostrils even as she raised an aching arm to shield her eyes from the shiny walls. She knew they couldn't stop until they were well into the forest, but the scent gave her hope.

At the edge of her vision, Jessandra panted beside her, sweat dripping from her brow. Sometimes their hands crashed into each other as they ran. Wave could hear Strath's laboured breathing only a few paces ahead, and for a fleeting moment she was sure they would be okay. The forest called to them. They were going to make it.

Jessandra disappeared from beside Wave. A heartbeat passed before she realised. With one hand she pulled at Strath's shirt, too exhausted to cry out. They both turned.

For a long moment, she saw nothing out of the ordinary. In the shadowy depths of a nearby alleyway, Wave saw two Black Cloaks, almost indistinguishable from the darkness. Jessandra hung between them, limp and unmoving.

Wave opened her mouth to cry out. Strath threw his body around hers, smothering her face with a rough hand. She struggled against his grip as he dragged her into the shadows of a nearby building. They stood in silence, Wave struggling against Strath as she peered into the alleyway. The Black Cloaks were discussing something, their backs to the street. And then, they were gone. They wrapped their cloaks around Jessandra, and the alley was empty, filled only with shadows.

Strath took his hand away from Wave's mouth but held her body against his.

'No,' she whispered, hot tears tumbling down her cheeks. 'Jess!'

With gentle hands, Strath turned her around and hugged her as she cried into his chest. She beat her clenched fists against his body, and he held her tighter.

'Jess,' she whimpered.

'There's nothing we can do for her now,' he whispered into her hair.

'But—'

'She could be anywhere by now. Waterfall City, Buduwai, Hinchka, anywhere.' Strath looked down at her, his eyes soft with compassion. 'There's no way to know where they took her. We have to make sure the same doesn't happen to you.'

He took her hand and began leading her through the shadows of Kochee's outskirts.

'Or worse,' he murmured.

The words were lost on Wave, her heart already in mourning. They'd had such a short time together, her and Jessandra, and now she was gone. The princess represented the first connection to her father's family. Wave felt as though a piece of her heart was missing, as though a tie she'd only just discovered had been cut short.

'Come on,' Strath said gently.

Wave wiped her face with the edge of her sleeve. Her shoulder throbbed in time with her heart, just as her tattoo had when she'd fled through the Nagahere. Hand in hand, Wave and Strath slid between the shadows, leaving Kochee one person lighter than when they'd entered.

42

HABA SHA

THE PALE, indeterminate colours of first light graced the eastern sky as Mortius mounted his horse. Low clouds hung over the horizon, but they held no promise of rain. Beside him, Aymn sat tall in his saddle, his gaze fixed on the changing sky. Beren stumbled into the courtyard, his dressing gown in disarray, his pale hair sticking out at odd angles.

'Are you sure this is wise?' Beren mumbled, looking up at Mortius.

'No,' Mortius said. 'But I'm going to do it anyway.'

'Tell Rainer I ...' Beren stared at the cobblestones. 'Good luck.'

Mortius gave a curt nod and flicked his reins. The walled courtyard was large, but it only took Sabré a few long strides to cross. He rode through the town, Aymn close behind. The stench of rotting fish rose to meet them, worse than the usual city smells of refuse and sewerage. Aymn lifted a veil of material over his nose and mouth.

The boy was smart, much smarter than Mortius had ever given him credit for. It wasn't enough for Mortius to realise Aymn would be a far better leader than Reuben, though. He needed the people of Heredour to accept Aymn. There had to be a catalyst, some sort of event to announce Aymn to the world. Mortius had no idea how to orchestrate such a thing.

Once they were on the road towards Beestreb, Aymn pulled his horse alongside Mortius'. They rode together at an easy pace, the sun's first rays piercing the sky behind them. One by one, they passed roads leading inland. To their left, the ocean stretched out to infinity; to their right, yellowed fields of tussock grass swayed in a gentle breeze. The road was empty, and Mortius felt an unfamiliar sense of peace.

'You still haven't told me why we're meeting those people.'

Mortius sighed. The day he'd have to tell Aymn the truth was coming—he could feel it, like the sense of malaise before an illness sets in—but he wasn't ready for it. Aymn hadn't spoken about Winter, about the connection he no doubt felt when they'd met.

'Larka is an old ... acquaintance,' Mortius said. 'Running into her was a stroke of good fortune. She's travelling with someone I was hoping to find, and I need to discuss something with both of them, something nobody needs to hear.'

'Then why am I here?'

'I don't expect any harm from Larka or her friends, but one should never go into an uncertain meeting alone.'

Aymn snorted. 'You've got some plan in the works, don't you?'

The corners of Mortius' mouth lifted. 'You're one for discernment.'

'I learned from the best.' Aymn looked over at Mortius. 'And I mean you, not Unner.'

'I wasn't aware you were paying so much attention growing up,' Mortius said. 'But I'm glad. You're right. I have a plan; I'm just trying to fit all the pieces together.'

'Would I be correct in assuming you'll let me in when you feel the time is right?' Aymn asked.

'Your assumption is correct.' Mortius paused, considering his options. 'Perhaps after this meeting.'

'What can I do to help?'

Mortius' smile widened. 'Get to know her daughter Winter. See what you can find out.'

The third road appeared and they turned down a dirt track. In the distance stood a copse of coarse-wood trees, exactly as Larka had described. Mortius led the way off the track, riding through the close-cropped grass towards the thicket. The trees were well spaced, and Mortius could see Larka and the others gathered in the copse's heart.

At the edge of the clearing, Mortius and Aymn dismounted and tied their horses off on a low-hanging but sturdy branch. For a few moments, they stood watching the other group. Hostility emanated from the two men, Rainer and someone Mortius wasn't familiar with. They were all dressed in the simple garb of lowkin farmers, though Rainer's iridescent eyes belied his true kin.

Only Winter showed nothing of the unfriendly emotions of her elders. Her grin spread from ear to ear as she looked at Aymn. The only thing holding her back was Larka's hands on her shoulders.

'Jesma has blessed us today,' Mortius said, nodding to each of them in turn.

'Indeed,' Larka said, her words clipped. 'This is Rainer moonkin.' She pointed at the man who'd once been a friend. 'And this is Hasting plantkin, our travelling companion.' She gestured at the unknown man.

Mortius inclined his head and laid his right hand over his heart. 'Mortius starkin, senior adviser to High King Reuben.' He drew Aymn forward with a hand on his shoulder. 'This is my nephew, Aymn starkin.'

Somehow, Winter's smile widened. With a subtle glance

back at Aymn, Mortius saw the expression mirrored on his face. Again, the cousins had eyes only for each other.

'Shall we step out?' Mortius asked.

Larka nodded and wove through the trees, Mortius in her wake, Rainer close behind. Mortius repressed a shudder. How easy it would be for his old friend to stick a blade through his back.

Once they were out in the field, Larka stopped.

'This will do.'

A small herd of cows crested a low rise some distance east. Each had a set of curved horns, their shape reminiscent of a first-quarter moon. Frieda's face swam before his eyes, the poison in her voice when she spoke of Reuben filled his ears. Mortius took a deep breath.

'So you've finally cast the mad king aside,' Rainer said, his gaze scathing.

'Not yet,' Mortius answered, wondering how far to trust the two rebels before him. 'But it is my intention to unseat him.'

Larka's eyebrows shot up. 'You've got some nerve.'

'Twenty-five years too late,' Rainer spat.

'Twenty-five years too late is better than never,' Mortius said. He didn't know how to placate Rainer. This fiery composure was something he'd never seen in him before. 'That's why I wanted to talk to you. I've already spoken with Beren.'

Rainer's face paled, but Larka scowled.

'Back then, we swore ourselves to Reuben,' Mortius said to Rainer. 'You relinquished that loyalty long ago.'

A quick step forward brought Rainer close to Mortius' face.

'You're admonishing me for deserting a madman?' Rainer snapped.

'Peace, Rainer.' Mortius held his hands up in front of his face. 'I'm not here to reprimand anyone.'

After a long moment of silence, Rainer took a step back.

'What do you want, Mortius?' Larka asked. There was a

weariness in her voice, a tiredness Mortius understood well. Reuben's decisions had affected their entire lives.

'He's far worse than he's ever been,' Mortius began. 'His paranoia is out of control. His mood swings are ... extreme. The Black Cloaks sit at our council meetings, gods help us all.'

Larka and Rainer shared a look that held some significance Mortius didn't understand. Behind them, the cows wandered slowly across the rise.

'Something is wrong with the land.'

Rainer snorted.

'No, I'm serious,' Mortius said. 'In Lashameg, they're birthing entire herds of stillborn calves. Now the sheep are starting to birth stillborns, and the llamas too. In Condor, the wood rots before it's cut. You were in Haba Sha, surely you heard about the fish?'

Larka shook her head.

'They're all dead before they're caught. Something is seriously wrong with Heredour, and it all started going wrong once we let Reuben get away with his deceits.'

'He may be mad,' Larka said, 'but how can Reuben being on the throne cause any of these problems?'

'I don't know.' Mortius shook his head. 'I was never one for the pursuit of philosophy, unlike my fellow starkin. But it gets worse. You know he's brought back the Law of Kaiāho?'

'Of course we know about the law,' Rainer said. 'We'd have to be living under a rock to miss that monstrosity.'

'There's also a star-caller loose,' Mortius said, charging ahead with what he wanted to say. Though Reuben had instructed them to keep that knowledge to themselves, Mortius found himself unable to obey. He had to make these people understand the depths of Heredour's problems.

Larka paled, but said nothing.

'Everything is going wrong, and I'm certain it's because of Reuben,' Mortius said. 'I think the raiders did something to him, put a curse on him, or some sort of spell. The way they used their powers was so different to us, they could have done anything.'

'You think the raiders did this?' Larka asked. 'And now we're stuck with a high king operating under some foreign curse?' She laughed, but there was little genuine mirth to the sound. 'Do you know how ridiculous you sound?'

'I sound like I'm the one who's been cursed,' Mortius said. 'You don't know me very well, Larka, but Rainer does.'

'Did.'

'When have I ever been one for hysteria or wrong-thinking?'

'Never,' Rainer said, though the admission seemed to cost him something. He grimaced.

'Exactly,' Mortius said. 'I've been by Reuben's side for most of the past twenty-five years. Something is very wrong, and even if it's nothing to do with the raiders, it starts with Reuben. He has to go.'

'Why are you out here?' Larka asked. 'Why not stay in the city?'

'I'm here under the guise of confirming how bad the regions are struggling. But really, I'm looking for three people. I just happened to find two of them in the same place.' Mortius wondered if Larka knew where Kali was.

'And why did you bring Aymn?' Larka glanced towards the copse where the others were hidden. 'Does he know?'

'Not yet,' Mortius said, shaking his head. 'I haven't found the right time to tell him.'

'But you mean to?' Rainer asked.

'I mean to see him seated on the Sun Throne.' There. He'd said it out loud. Though his gut roiled at the proclamation, it sounded better than he expected.

Larka's eyes widened. 'This is a joke?'

'No.'

'You would place the bastard son of a mad king on the Sun

Throne?' Rainer asked, incredulity filling his voice. 'A starkin boy? When you've got a perfectly good sunkin heir somewhere in the world?'

'Do you know where he is?' Mortius snapped. 'How long since you've seen Samson?'

The expressions on both of their faces told Mortius all he needed to know.

'Is she his?' Mortius waved a hand at the coarse-wood trees.

Larka glared at him for a long moment before nodding her head. 'That was the last time I saw him.'

Mortius tried to hide his surprise. There were always people claiming to have spotted Samson in Heredour, reports that made their way back to his ears. For over five years, he'd heard absolutely nothing, but to know that Larka hadn't seen him in eight or nine years ...

'Is he alive?' Mortius asked.

His face was stinging before he realised what had happened. Larka stepped back.

'How dare you?' she hissed.

Mortius placed a hand on his cheek. She'd slapped him. Nobody had ever slapped Mortius before. There were no lovers in his life, no jealous men or women to inflict their emotions on him. That was the way he wanted it, but the sting of Larka's slap stirred something deep within him.

'You're just as responsible for everything that's happened to him, to us,' Larka said, her lips lifted in a snarl. 'Unlike me, you have connections throughout the entire country, and probably beyond. Are you telling me you have no idea where my husband is?'

Lowering his hand, Mortius shook his head slowly. 'I've had no reports of him for over five years.'

Larka's snarl turned into a frown.

'Samson is alive,' Rainer growled. 'And regardless of where he is, he's next in line to the throne. Not your puppet boy.'

Aymn was so unlike a puppet that Mortius almost laughed. They knew nothing about him.

'What does Frieda think of your plan?' Larka asked, her eyes narrowing.

'Frieda has nothing to do with this.'

'Then she's the smartest one out of us all.' Larka pinched the bridge of her nose. 'If Frieda won't help you, what makes you think we will?'

'Because if there's one thing I know about both of you, it's that you love this country. Imagine. An end to the Law of Kaiāho. The removal of the Black Cloaks from the High Council. Hopefully, the resurgence of growth and vitality in the regions. You won't help me for the sake of it, you'll help me because Heredour needs you to.'

'I can't speak for Rainer,' Larka said, her eyes shifting sideways to the bulky-framed man, 'but there is only one way I will help you.'

'Which is?' Mortius could already tell he wasn't going to get what he wanted, but if she had some sort of compromise ... well, perhaps it was better than nothing.

'The problem is that Reuben's rule is built on a bed of lies. If there's anything the gods have taught us, it's that the truth must prevail, or we all suffer. The truth must come out, and when it does, Samson is the only logical person to take Reuben's place. Not Aymn.'

So. She wanted a part of his plan after all, just on her terms. Rainer nodded emphatically beside her.

'And how do you expect me to put an exiled person—who nobody has seen for at least five years—on the throne?' Mortius asked. The plan could work; it had always been his back-up plan anyway. The easier, more obvious route was Aymn, though.

'You have no faith in my abilities, Senior Adviser,' Larka said with a smirk. 'I will find him, and when I bring him to you, you will do what you must to ensure that the truth is uncovered and justice delivered.'

Without waiting for an answer, Larka turned and stalked back towards the trees. Rainer gave Mortius one last glare before following.

'Wait!' Mortius called.

Larka paused, but she didn't turn.

'If you want to find Samson, you must find Kali. I lost track of her many years ago, but she'll know where he is.'

After a few moments of silence, Larka turned, a disarming smile on her face. 'You really have no idea about us, do you?'

And then she was gone, disappearing into the tree line. Mortius sighed. None of that had gone to plan, but he shouldn't have expected it to. He glanced up at the rise where the cows had been. They'd moved on, making their way through the fields, but a single man stood on the hill, watching Mortius. A shepherd, from the look of his weathered clothes and tanned skin.

Cursing to himself, Mortius headed towards the tree line, just in time to see Aymn leaving the copse, leading both of their horses.

'Let's get out of here,' Mortius growled as he took the reins from Aymn, the bastard son of the high king.

43

JAMARI

FROM THE DEPTHS of a sluggish darkness, Jessandra opened her eyes. She blinked, her eyelids like coarse sandpaper. Was she drowning again? In the dim light, she could make out lumpy shapes surrounding her. People, she realised with a start, lots of people, all crammed together.

A stench hit her nostrils, a repulsive mix of urine and blood and sweat. She gagged, vomiting into her own lap. Nothing came out except water and bile, scratching her throat and bringing tears to her eyes.

Jessandra looked around as she wiped vomit from her face with the back of her hand, trying to remember what had happened. She was sitting on hard earth; the dirt packed flat and firm by many feet.

Her eyes began adjusting to the low light, and she studied the people all around her. Some were standing, others appeared comatose on the ground. Others were propped in a sitting position, just like her, resting against a wall. Pain ran down the length of her back as the rough wall pushed into her spine. Tears sprang to her eyes.

They were in some sort of outdoor cell. Three stone walls

and a single wall of thick steel bars opened to the sky. Low, dense clouds hovered just above the cell, pressing down with a strange weight that Jessandra felt in her chest. Some of the people stood pressed against the bars, the cold metal gripped between their dirty fingers as they called out in despondent voices.

Jessandra took a deep breath and pushed herself upright, using the wall to stabilise her shaky limbs. Sharp pain shot through her hands and her palms prickled with warm blood. Tears blurred her vision again, but bleeding meant she was alive. Swallowing her tears, Jessandra pushed herself off the wall, taking a few tentative steps.

'Where am I?' she muttered aloud.

A few people turned and stared at her. In the pitiful silence that swallowed the cell, her voice rang out loud and clear. A young man with emerald-green eyes walked over to her, his stride strong and purposeful.

'You're in a slave hold,' he murmured, keeping his voice low.

Jessandra baulked at his words, a lump rising in her throat. 'What?'

The man nodded.

'Where are we?' she asked.

'The only place slavers can trade in Heredour.' He looked at Jessandra expectantly.

'Jamari?' she whispered. 'How?'

'The same way everyone gets here. By ship.' The man shrugged and turned away from her, already disinterested in her plight.

'Wait!' Jessandra said. 'Why doesn't everyone just use their power to escape?'

Without turning, the man pointed up at the clouds. 'Black Cloak magic. None of us can feel any of our gods.'

And then he was gone, joining the others at the barred wall. A flood of memories surfaced to Jessandra's mind. She'd used

Setunil's power in that terrible fight with the miners. Her heart swelled at the thought, though she wasn't entirely sure how she'd done it. Closing her eyes, Jessandra sought a connection to the sky god. There was nothing to be found, though, reminiscent of how she'd spent the last few years—godless, powerless, fearful.

The man must have spoken truly. None of these people would simply lie here waiting for their fate if they could have escaped. She had no idea Black Cloaks were involved in the slave trade. A shudder ran through Jessandra's body and she doubled over, hands on her knees.

When the wave of nausea passed, Jessandra picked her way through the crowded cell. Her cloak was gone, along with the dress she'd borrowed in Sharvel. Pulling her arms around her body, Jessandra jostled for space until she was pressed against the cold iron bars.

A market spread uphill from where they were imprisoned. Grey, drab curtains protected stalls of all sizes, a reflection of the heavy sky above them. There were no trees or plants, no animals, no life she could see anywhere. The subtle hum of people talking drifted down from the market, though she couldn't see anyone.

Jessandra pressed her forehead against the cold bars and closed her eyes. Flashes of hazy, surreal memories came to her slowly. Waking in darkness, the ground beneath her swaying. Vomiting on a rough wooden floor. People, all around her. Stirring several times in darkness, the unstable ground making her shift violently against other bodies. The sounds of crying, soft whimpering—was it hers, or someone else's? A man, body silhouetted by light, staring at them. Half-awake, being carried down a ramp, the sky above grey and dismal. The ocean beneath her. Tumbling to the ground. An ugly ship, all grey wood and dark sails.

Opening her eyes, Jessandra was overcome with misery.

How had she become separated from Wave and Strath? They'd won the fight against the miners. They were escaping, making their way through the cursed, glittering town. But somehow, she'd ended up on one of those slave ships, and now she was stuck in a cell in Jamari.

A grim man strode down from the market. The wails of those around her rose to a higher pitch. Ignoring them, the man walked the length of the bars, staring at each prisoner one by one.

'You.' His voice was harsh, as if he didn't know quite how to pronounce the word.

Jessandra realised with a start that he was pointing at her. More terrifying than the realisation that she'd been chosen was the colour of his eyes. There was no hue to his irises, not even the strange iridescence of a moonkin. Blacker than the depths of night, his pupils seemed to extend out too far, contained only by the whiteness of his eyes.

'You,' the man spat, gesturing to an otherwise invisible gate in front of him. 'Now.'

Jessandra shook her head.

The slaver pulled a leather contraption from his pocket. When he shook out the crude harness, Jessandra almost vomited again. Leather circlets for binding wrists and ankles together, connected with rusting iron chains. At the top, a face harness held a thick, dirty bar at its heart. With a spike of disgust, Jessandra realised the bar was a mouthpiece.

'Now,' he growled.

She moved.

The other prisoners shuffled aside as she made her slow, pitiful way to the gate he'd already unlocked. The man reached into the cell and dragged her out.

Jessandra cried out in pain. She was already bruised everywhere, and his fingers were like a vice.

'Behave,' he said, the words sounding odd in his mouth. He jangled the harness in front of her face.

'Okay,' she pleaded. 'Okay.'

He tucked the vile thing into his belt and locked the gate behind her. The wailing in the cell subsided.

Keeping one hand tight around her arm, the man dug through his pocket and handed Jessandra a grimy cloth. She took it, staring at him uncertainly.

'Clean,' he spat.

'What?' she asked.

He gestured at her face with a thick, tattooed finger. 'Clean.'

As best she could, Jessandra wiped the grime and leftover vomit from her face. The material was rough and dry, though, and she scratched her skin more than cleaned it. She handed the cloth back to him, hoping she looked better than she felt.

'I think I'm in the wrong place,' she said, hoping to endear herself to the man. 'I'm a princess, heir to an important throne in Heredour.'

He looked at her with one white eyebrow raised.

'Please, sir. If my father finds out I'm here, he'll be very angry.'

'Shafit!' the man said. 'Ashna'agud.'

Jessandra squeezed her eyes closed. She'd already suspected he didn't speak the common tongue, but now she knew there was no point pleading her case.

The slaver forced Jessandra into a steady walk, steering her towards the market. She dragged her feet, pretending at weakness, studying the man as they walked. There was something about him, about his nightshade eyes, the tattoos swirling across his impossibly pale skin that she should have recognised. Memories of lessons she hadn't paid attention to tugged at her awareness, slipping from her mind like water in a cupped hand.

They scouted around behind the stalls and the stench from the cell began to dissipate. Canvas flaps lifted in a light breeze and Jessandra breathed in cool, fresh air that carried the tangy scent of salt.

The man led her between two stalls and into a large square full of well-dressed people milling about. These people had an air of impatience about them, a hint of self-serving importance Jessandra recognised well. Off to one side were more people, dirty and frail like herself, lined up in crude pens designed to hold livestock.

Jessandra began to sob. The slaver dragged her to a raised wooden platform in the centre of the square. She stumbled over the hard-packed earth, her whole body trembling. He caught her with rough hands. Taking her by the elbows, he manoeuvred her up three small steps to the platform. A wooden box at the centre served as a podium, and it was here the slaver forced Jessandra to stand.

From her vantage point, she could see most of the market. The square was lined with rough walls of straw and mud, but they opened to the sprawling market on one side. People moved about, looking as grey and dreary as everything else on this godsforsaken island. Jessandra shivered, despite the air around her being heavy with humidity. She forced her attention to the people in front of her. Those waiting in the square stood with all eyes on her, fixated by the young woman standing in nothing but a dirty slip. Unsurprised, Jessandra noticed there were no women in the crowd.

A new man, unlike the one who'd taken her from the cell, stood at one edge of the platform. He shouted in a variety of different tongues, most of which Jessandra didn't recognise, though he was clearly Heredourian. She wrapped her arms around her body, trying not to shiver. Every now and then, she caught words she could decipher thrown in among the other strange languages.

'Female, teenager,' he called to the crowd. 'Untouched.'

The word drew interested murmurs from the crowd.

'Pretty enough when scrubbed up.'

One of the men in the crowd shouted something in a foreign language, but the man ignored him.

'Worked as a serving girl for some highkin in Heredour. Good for all household duties, with the potential for more.'

The crowd began to mutter, creating a hum of noise in the square where before there had been relative silence. Jessandra felt her lips quivering but she held her tears back. Crying would be a sign of weakness she could ill afford.

'Starting bid at ten silvers,' the man shouted over the murmuring crowd.

The bidding began. The crowd showed a fair bit of interest in Jessandra; men shouted over the top of one another, calling out prices in the common tongue of Heredour. Jessandra pulled her arms tighter around herself, shivering despite the oppressive humidity. She looked at each of the men as they shouted their offers, swallowing her tears.

'Sold!' the slaver shouted.

Jessandra looked around in a panic. She hadn't been paying attention; she had no idea who'd won the auction for her body. A rough hand grabbed her elbow. The slaver lifted her off the platform and deposited her in front of a tall man who paid his dues in freshly minted gold coin. The money shimmered in stark contrast to the dreariness of Jamari. Jessandra lifted her eyes to face her new owner, a thousand beetles crawling beneath her skin.

The man who purchased her was tall and wiry, taut muscles quivering beneath his skin. His hair was a bright, shiny blond, and he conversed in the common tongue of Heredour. Even his rough moustache was blond, and the hair growing on his muscular arms was like spun gold. Underneath the hair, his skin was the golden brown of leaves in late autumn. Glancing up at his face, she saw the unmistakable amber eyes of the sunkin.

For a heartbeat, she forgot her troubles. Standing before him was like basking in the only ray of sun on a stormy day. Against the bleak market, the miserable sky, he seemed to glow. There was no doubt he was a sunkin, but why in all the gods was he in Jamari? More importantly, who was he? There were so few sunkin left in Heredour that Jessandra knew them all.

Her new owner grasped her by the elbow and marched her through the crowd of leering men. She shivered and stumbled over the ground, trying to escape their prying eyes. The sunkin's grip was firm and strong, reminding Jessandra that despite his highkin status, he'd just purchased her. Her life was no longer her own.

44

HEREDOUR'S DESERT

THE DESERT BORDERING the Lost Ocean and the Barancha Plains was an unforgiving place, but Wave didn't have the heart to care. Hot, dry winds blew red dust over the landscape. The sun beat down on the land with a particular ferocity, making it inhospitable for little more than a few scrubby plants and a host of reptiles.

The desert seemed to stretch on for as far as the eye could see, rolling sand dunes disappearing into the distance on all sides. Water was scarce; Wave felt its absence as a dryness in her bones, a hostility in her heart.

Coming into the desert had been Strath's idea. If there were more Black Cloaks, or even more of the unscrupulous miners, the first place they'd look would be the forested mountains around Kochee. Nobody without a death wish trekked into the desert, making it the perfect place for them to hide. They'd have to return to the town eventually, but Strath hoped to buy them some time.

Wave had gone along with his plan, following with slow, dragging steps, her insides numb. Now, she sat beneath the hasty shade cloth Strath had erected, staring into the desert.

Though she hadn't noticed at the time, their movements through the markets had been intentional on his part. He'd thieved all manner of things, from rope, to cloth, to string beans. None of it helped them much now, but at least they had a shady spot to rest during the midday heat.

For a little while, she'd had everything she ever wanted. The curse that had driven her away from Bindock was broken because there was no curse. She'd learned the truth about her father, her family, and her lineage, despite the pain it had caused at the time. And for the first time in her life, she'd had friends. Two people who cared for her as much as she cared for them, who would go out of their way to protect her, laugh with her, comfort her.

Her friendship with Jessandra had been so easy, forged from their shared position of not quite fitting into the world's expectations. And when they'd learned they were actually cousins, it had only solidified everything Wave already felt for the princess. A real connection with someone who understood her predicament, understood how her mind worked, understood her pain.

And now, she was gone. Snatched away by the Black Cloaks, no less. It had been Jessandra who warned them of the wizards' presence back in Sharvel, but they'd all been too busy with the miners to realise the Black Cloaks were also in Kochee.

Everything good that Wave had stumbled upon in the last few weeks was falling apart. Strath was sullen and brooding, the desert hot and unforgiving, and Jessandra was no longer with them. They had no passage to Veija-Mens, not that Wave wanted to go without her friend.

'You need to focus on magic,' Strath said from beside her. He was lying down, his hands resting on his abdomen. 'If you can harness it, control it ...'

'I don't care about that,' Wave said, her voice wooden. 'It won't make a difference.'

'You don't know that. What if you could find her?'

What if she could use the Black Cloaks' magic to find her friend? She'd do it, without hesitation. But she didn't know how she accessed their magic, and although she'd felt some semblance of control when she'd rescued Jessandra from the Kanrid, it was tenuous.

'If I could,' Wave said, 'you know I would.'

Too bad she had no idea who Hasting was, or where he lived in Condor. In his letter to X'olea, he'd offered to teach Wave what he knew. She pushed the unhelpful thought from her mind, the memory of X'olea's face adding a shard of pain to her heart.

Later, as the deep blues of dusk settled over the desert, Wave and Strath packed down their small camp. The sand beneath them radiated heat, but the air was already cooling. Stars winked at them, the moon a thick silver crescent. Shafts of burnt orange and violet marked the western sky.

Securing their cloaks, Wave and Strath trekked towards the fading light. A cold wind began to blow and they moved faster to keep the chill at bay.

'We must be getting close to the cliffs now,' Strath said as he peered across the endless dunes. It was only their second day in the desert, and they'd been travelling west since they stopped running. But the cliffs never appeared, and the desert continued into the distance.

'I can feel her,' Wave said.

'Jess?'

'The ocean.' Somewhere west of them, the deep push and pull of the sea called to her. 'It should be close.'

They walked on in silence. Among the never-ending visage of sand dunes, getting lost in her miserable spiral of thoughts was a fairly safe venture.

Wave bumped into something. She fell straight back, landing on her tailbone. A moment later, Strath was on the ground beside her, a loud grunt escaping him. They sat in stunned silence for a heartbeat. Strath leapt up and pulled a dagger from his belt, staring into the darkness around them. Wave imitated him, her useless fists raised. They stood back to back, circling around, but there was nothing visible that had attacked them. The desert stretched forever on all sides of them, lit in shadowed hues of silver and blue.

'What was that?' Wave asked when her heartbeat slowed.

Strath's brow was creased in a deep frown. 'I have no idea.'

Wave walked away from him, her hands thrust out in front of her body. Something hit her fingertips and she recoiled. Taking a deep breath, she reached her hands out again.

'What is it?' Strath asked.

Wave was silent, her fingertips scraping something she couldn't see. With both hands splayed, she pressed against the invisible shape, spreading her hands in different directions.

'It's ... it's a wall!' she cried in disbelief.

'What?' Strath ran up to her and Wave threw an arm out to stop him crashing into it.

'Put your hands out.'

Strath copied her and moved forward, feeling along the transparent barrier with his fingers. He turned to Wave, mouth open, eyes wide. With a shrug, Wave pushed against the structure. The desert stretched past the invisible barrier, the rolling dunes shifting beneath the starlight until they disappeared in the direction of the ocean. No matter how hard Wave pushed, the wall wouldn't give.

In silent agreement, Wave and Strath walked away from each other, keeping their hands pressed against the barrier. No matter how far they got from each other, the wall was still there, a distinct line cutting through the desert. Wave stretched her arms up as far as she could reach, but there was no end in that direction either.

Standing side by side once more, Wave and Strath stared at

each other in disbelief. After several long, speechless moments, Strath looked up and studied the stars.

'I don't know what this is,' he said, 'but I think it will lead us back to Kochee.'

Wave took a step back from the invisible barrier. Strath was right—the wall ran roughly north to south. Even though it stopped them from getting to the cliffs, they could follow the line it created as surely as the visual cue of the ocean.

'This is the work of the Black Cloaks,' Wave murmured.

Once she'd gotten over her initial surprise of running into an invisible object, she'd known immediately that magic was involved. The surface of the barrier sang beneath the touch of her skin, like a series of metal chimes caught in the wind.

'Probably,' Strath said. 'They have a castle, somewhere out here in the desert. The viper's nest.'

The tower from her vision and Jessandra's dream had been in the desert. The puppeteer, or spider-man, as Jess had called him, had been wearing a black cloak, though his hood was down. Skoa must have been showing her the seat of the Black Cloaks' power. Absentmindedly, she wondered if they all had such hideous faces beneath their hoods.

'Let's follow it,' Strath said, glancing up at the star systems above them. 'We're obviously not going to get past.'

They took to walking single file, keeping one hand on the wall so they didn't accidentally run into it again. An uncomfortable silence descended over them.

The barrier felt like cool water beneath Wave's hand, reminding her of a gentle, undisturbed forest pool. Dragging her hand along behind her was like running her hand over the skin of a body of water.

Pushing her fears aside, Wave let her mind drift. She wondered how she could explore this magic that she'd somehow accessed, this fusion of water and sun energy. Strath had been encouraging her to play, but she didn't know where to begin. Each time she'd used magic it had been in absolute desperation, times where her anger spiralled into an unfathomable rage. Surely the Black Cloaks didn't have to be in a violent fury in order to use magic?

Electricity, Strath had said on one of their many conversations during the hike through the North Claw. Wave tried to think of her father, the nonexistent sunkin, and the power he might have been able to harness. There were so few sunkin in the world, and certainly none where Wave had frequented, that she had no baseline for how Jesma's power might look or feel.

X'olea had always told her she spent too much time in her head; that sometimes, the answers lay in feeling, not knowing. Perhaps that was what Strath had been talking about when he was explaining Jessandra's intuition. Wave tried to let her thoughts go, focusing her attention back on the wall. There was a glow to its surface, a warm luminescence Wave could feel even though she couldn't see it. She let herself sink into the radiance, and in that moment, she understood the impossibility of electricity, of magic. The heat of the sun—its burning, fiery energy —combined with the mutable, viscous force of water generated a power unlike any of the other gods.

'I understand it,' Wave whispered.

Strath halted, turning to face her.

'What do you mean?'

'It's magic, like you said. I think I can get us through.'

'Why do you want to get through?' Strath raised an eyebrow.

'We don't know what's behind this barrier.'

'Desert.' Strath pointed at the rolling dunes stretching out before them.

'What if it's an illusion?' Wave asked. 'What if they're hiding something? What if the South Claw is still there?'

Strath shook his head at her. 'The South Claw is gone, Wave. Even the original story says so.'

'They must have built this for a reason, right?' Wave forged ahead with her idea, buoyed by the possibilities blossoming in her mind. 'The Black Cloaks don't do anything without a very good reason, even if those reasons are cruel.'

'What if they built it to protect us?'

'Protect us?' Wave laughed. 'Since when have you thought the Black Cloaks are our protectors?'

'Not since the day Ernad was taken,' he quipped. 'But you don't know if it's dangerous.'

'You wanted me to play with this,' Wave said. 'If I can learn to use magic ...'

Strath studied her, his gaze inscrutable.

'I have to try, Strath,' Wave pleaded.

He grimaced but gave her a curt nod. 'Do what you must.' He sat down on the ground, pulling his cloak tight around him.

Wave turned her attention back to the wall, spreading her hands across the surface. The sensation of water beneath her fingers, false as it was, centred her. Avoiding the anger she was so familiar with, Wave let herself fill up with Lerinial's power. Then she focused on the subtle glow she felt within the barrier, the pulsing seed of Jesma.

The glow grew, as did the heat she experienced in her entire body. Wave let her thoughts drift. She brought the glow and the essence of her water energy towards one another. When they met, sparks flew before her; lightning rippled through the darkness.

Wave closed her eyes. The key was there, at the edge of her awareness, tantalisingly close. A simple twisting, of her consciousness more than anything else, and she was thrown into a darkness more complete than a moonless night.

She blinked a few times. The desert was gone. Strath was gone. Wave was travelling at a great speed.

45

BEESTREB

ON THE WOODEN docks of the small coastal town of Beestreb, Larka and Hasting shouted at one another. Off to one side, Rainer and Winter stood hand in hand, watching the heated debate. The few sailors who still moved around the docks ignored the group. The sun was setting over the ocean, beams of umber, peach, and violet reflecting in the vast, shimmering water.

'Insane, absolutely insane,' Hasting said.

'You're only saying that because you're afraid to go home,' Larka said, taking a step closer to him. 'You're afraid to see the people you left behind, to face the life we used to have.'

'How dare you?' Hasting said. 'You know nothing of what I've been through. It was you who wanted to see Winter to safety in Veija-Mens, it was you who thought Sam might be there. And now you want to change the plan and travel to Sharvel?'

'I told you when we left Haba Sha!' Larka shouted, unable to contain her frustration. He wasn't listening to her, hadn't been listening since they'd fled Gardar Mae. 'Mortius is looking for Kali, but he has no idea where she is.' She stabbed at his chest with one finger. 'But we do. I would never tell him how to find her, but she deserves to know his plans, to know ours, don't you think?'

'And what about Winter? What about Sam?' Hasting threw his hands in the air. 'What about Siska and Wave?'

Larka squeezed her eyes closed. 'I was a fool to think I could help them. I have no idea where they are. It was folly, from the beginning.' She took a deep breath. 'Winter will be as safe in Sharvel as in Veija-Mens, if not safer. And even if Sam's not there, Kali or the others might know how to find him. Surely you can see that going home makes sense?'

Hasting glared at her for a long time, his lips a single, straight line. 'Fine.'

'Fine?'

'I'll find a ship to Kochee.' Hasting turned on his heel and strode towards the offices that sat in a row along the wharf, his hands clenched into fists at his sides.

Larka wanted to scream. Ever since Mortius had discovered them in Haba Sha, the actions she needed to take were becoming more obvious. But since that first conversation overlooking the ocean, Hasting had been set against everything she said, arguing with her, challenging her plans. She was on the precipice of telling him to go, that she didn't need him or Rainer anyway, when he'd agreed to travel to Sharvel.

The idea of going home felt strange to her too. Ever since Mortius had mentioned Kali, though, she knew there was nowhere else she could go. The path was clear. Kali was one of the few who knew the truth of Esra's death, of Samson's exile. If Kali couldn't help them, nobody could.

With Hasting gone, and Larka pacing the docks in frustration, Rainer and Winter moved towards her. Larka accepted the hug that Winter offered, her eyes large as she regarded her mother.

'Why are you angry, Mumma?'

Larka sighed. 'I'm not angry, sweet girl. I want to help your sisters, and I want to keep you safe. There's no easy way to achieve both, and Hasting and I disagree on the best way forward.'

'I can stay safe,' Winter said, nodding her head earnestly. 'I can.'

'I know you can, my love. But I have to think of the bigger picture, of things you don't yet understand.'

Winter nodded, though one side of her mouth drooped in uncertainty.

'Larka,' Rainer said, his voice thick with emotion.

'What is it?' Larka asked, acutely aware of the acid in her tone.

She had no doubt that he'd come to understand precisely who she was, but they'd never spoken of it openly. There just hadn't been a chance, and in truth, Larka didn't want to. She didn't want to hear empty placations for why he'd betrayed Samson, she didn't want to hear his reasoning for supporting Reuben all those years ago. She'd forgiven Kali with ease—but only because Kali had deserted the capital and the high king within the first year. Her conscience had gotten the better of her. Where had Rainer been all these years?

'I have done many terrible things in my life, Larka,' Rainer said. 'But participating in Reuben's ascension, playing my part in Samson's exile, for those things I could never forgive myself.'

Larka glanced around them, but the docks were empty now the sun had set. 'This is not the time, Rainer, or the place to have this conversation.'

'No,' Rainer insisted. 'I have bided my time; I have waited too long to speak these words to you.' He dropped to the ground, grovelling on his knees before her. 'I was there for all of it. All of the lies, the murder, the deception for a crown. And I cannot forgive myself, but I beg you, please forgive me on behalf of your husband.'

Larka rolled her eyes. If anyone saw them … but as she looked around, there was still no sign of another human. It was as if the gods had organised for the tiny wharf to be empty, just for this moment to unfold.

'You did nothing,' she hissed. 'Not when it counted.'

He looked up at her, his iridescent eyes crystalline with tears.

'You're right, Larka. When it was time for action, I did nothing. When it was time to speak up, I stayed silent. I can never forgive myself. But I have spent the rest of my life trying to atone for sins. Sins against myself, against Samson, against the crown, against the gods. I am unforgivable.'

He swallowed, his throat quivering. Beside him, Winter stood with eyes wide, staring at her mother in confusion.

'And when I tried to do the right thing,' Rainer continued, 'I lost everything I held dear, lost everyone I love.'

'You?' Larka spat. An uncontrollable rage filled her body, no doubt spurred on by the anger she'd felt at Hasting's rebuttals. Her hands trembled. 'You lost everyone? I've had to raise my daughters alone, isolated, in fear of our lives every single day. I go to bed each night and wake every morning alone not because my husband is dead, but because people like you made it impossible for him to be safe in even the most remote part of our country.'

She slapped him. The sound rang out like a hollow bell. Rainer clenched his teeth and bowed his head.

'No less than I deserve,' he muttered.

Larka's hand stung, ripples of pain radiating up her arm. Gods, she'd never inflicted violence on anyone in her entire life. First Mortius, now Rainer. What was wrong with her? The hurt in Winter's eyes drained Larka of all emotion, and she hung her head in her hands.

The silence lingered. Larka wasn't sure if it was only the

lonely hallways of her mind, or if the entire dock had fallen quiet around them.

When she lifted her head, the wharf was as empty as before, and Rainer looked up at her, his eyes full of sorrow. Since they'd met back in Gardar Mae, he'd given her his utmost loyalty, unwavering in his commitment to supporting her. In fact, he'd been more favourable towards her plans than Hasting had.

'I'm sorry, Rainer,' she said, sighing as if she wore the entire island of Heredour on her shoulders. Sometimes, it felt like she did. Raising three secret heirs to the throne was tiring, weighing her down in a way she'd never fully considered.

'You didn't deserve that,' Larka continued. 'I know you've suffered as I have. There is no comparison to suffering. Our pain is the same.'

Rainer offered her a tremulous smile. 'I see why Samson fell in love with you. You've a heart as big as the whole world, Larka.'

She wanted to laugh, but she felt hollow, like a wooden sounding board with no echo.

'Whatever you ask of me, I will do it.' Rainer looked at her in earnest, reaching for her hands tentatively. 'I pledge my life to you and yours.'

'Rainer, you can't,' Larka said. 'You have your own daughters to care for.'

'They don't want my help. I'm only a disappointment to their rebellious hearts. Hearts that I moulded. I meant what I said, Larka. I am yours.'

Larka sighed. She knew what it was like to have wilful daughters, set on their own missions, with no idea of what had come before. She thought of Siska, her well-meaning attempt to save Jessandra. A wiser girl would have let the princess suffer, but Larka couldn't lament her daughter's empathetic heart. It was only a reflection of what she'd once been like.

'Fine,' she said, placing one hand on Rainer's thick shoulder.

'I accept your pledge of allegiance, Rainer moonkin, though I make no promises to ensure your safety.'

Rainer took her hand and kissed it before standing once again. Somehow, he looked taller, prouder.

'Are you okay, Mumma?' Winter peered around Larka's arm. 'You look tired.'

'I am tired, my darling,' Larka said, pulling her into a tight hug. 'So very tired, but I am okay. I'm sorry you saw me hit Rainer.'

'Do we still like him?' Winter's face was all angles and creases.

'We do,' Larka said softly. 'Rainer will look after us, just like Hasting does.'

Winter smiled. 'Rainer always looks after us.'

Larka offered a small smile to the bulky man before her. If anything, she couldn't help but feel grateful for the strange bond that had formed between her daughter and the man who was once her husband's oppressor.

'Do you think Hasting will find us passage?' Larka asked.

'Of course he will,' Rainer said. 'Has Hasting ever let you down?'

Larka couldn't respond. There was only one person who'd never failed her, and it was Hasting. It should have been Samson, should have been the person she'd wed her heart and her life to, but it wasn't.

Hasting.

He was always there for her, even when she was unavailable for him. Their relationship was an unfair match of power, and for the first time, Larka saw the truth of it. Her heart sank in disappointment. How could someone as loyal and wholesome as Hasting still love her?

Half an hour later, Hasting returned, his face sour.

'I've found us a passage to Kochee,' he said, 'but it will cost us.'

'How much?' Larka asked. She had no money on her; once again, she was reliant on Hasting's good will.

'Our pride,' Hasting said. 'Rainer is an important highkin from Marbin. You and I, Larka, are his servants.'

She didn't blanch at the role; it wasn't the first time she'd played the subservient character.

'What of Winter?' she asked.

'Winter will play Rainer's child.'

Winter shuffled over to Rainer and tucked in beneath his arm.

'I can do it,' she said, her voice full of fervour. 'I can.'

Larka winced. Of course she could; their friendship had been set the moment Rainer walked into Hasting's house in Gardar Mae. Despite that, Larka felt somehow incompetent, as if she was no longer good enough alongside Rainer's presence. Wasn't that the essence of motherhood, though? To be needed, depended upon, until a child was old enough to cast you aside. Larka sighed.

'It's a price we're willing to pay,' Larka said.

Rainer nodded, confirming his agreement.

'Good,' Hasting said. 'We leave in two hours.'

Larka glanced at the last few shafts of orange. 'Two hours? They can't mean to leave during the night.'

'They do,' Hasting said. 'There's little danger in these waters, apparently. And if they leave tonight, they arrive in Kochee the day after tomorrow, in time for the morning markets.'

Larka shook her head. Travelling by ship wasn't her favourite, despite the numerous times she and Sam and Hasting had left the Swishdine Coast for Chaba-Canez. She had to trust that these sailors knew what they were doing.

'Do we need any other supplies?' Larka asked, resigning herself to another day and a bit on the ocean. The journey from Haba Sha had gone well, but it didn't make Larka feel any more at ease. While they were in Heredour, they were vulnerable.

Hasting shook his head. 'No, they'll feed us.'

'We might as well make our way down there now,' Larka said. 'No point hanging out here.'

Hasting nodded once and then turned, heading south down the dock. Larka and Rainer shared a final, significant look, before following him, Winter's hand clasped in Rainer's.

46

HABA SHA

'ONE WAY OR ANOTHER, Beren, this is happening.'

'Nobody has seen Samson for ten, maybe fifteen years!' Beren exclaimed, not caring if the others heard his words. He stood rod-straight, pulling a cold indifference around him like a royal cloak.

'There are options,' Mortius said. 'That's all that matters.'

Beren spat on the cobblestones. Rolling his eyes, Mortius tugged on the leather girth of his saddle, testing its tightness. With one foot in the stirrup, he mounted Sabré with the grace of a much younger man. The day blustered around them, the wind tossing humid, sticky air like a plaything. That familiar sickly tang of ocean water turning to slush as it joined the river hit Mortius' nose, and he crinkled his face in disgust. He couldn't wait to be out of Haba Sha. The whole place reeked of a misery that he couldn't and didn't want to fix.

'Will you stand by me, as was promised, Beren?' Mortius said, looking down at the man, a shadow of his former cunning self.

Beren's mouth was a tight, thin line. Rubbing his face with one hand, he huddled deeper into his coat.

'I'm good as my word, Mortius. You know that.'

The sallowness in his face and the blank desolation in his eyes told a different story, but there wasn't any more time to worry about Beren. There would come a time when he had to make a choice, and only then would Mortius know if he was true to his word, or a pathetic piece of slime. And if he was the latter, Mortius wouldn't hesitate to crush him.

The courtyard was full of Mortius' entourage, already saddled, waiting for the moment they would ride out. Dappled roans and silky chestnuts stomped impatiently, the sound of shod feet on cobblestones echoing around the enclosed yard. None of Beren's retainers or household were here to watch them leave. He stood alone, sullen.

'Let's go,' Mortius said.

Sparing one last withering glance for the Maire of Haba Sha, Mortius clattered away from the house, his crew in tow. They rode hard through the town, commoners crying out in surprise as they scrambled to get out of the way of the senior adviser.

At the banks of the Satin River, a wide, flat-bottomed barge waited for them, its gaudy streamers snapping and cracking in the wind. The captain greeted them with a deep bow from the prow of the flatboat.

Dismounting, Mortius took the reins of his horse firmly in hand.

'Remember, Sabré,' Mortius murmured as he rested his head against the stallion's nose. 'This is the calm, easy water.'

The horse snorted. After some initial resistance on the wide gangplank, Sabré gave in to his master. Step by deliberate step, the horse made his way onto the barge. Mortius led the stallion to a low shed in the middle of the boat, tying him to the hitching post. The building was designed to house cows and mules, creatures much shorter than horses, and Sabré stuck his head through the opening at the front, stretching his neck and snorting at Mortius.

'Keep the others calm, would you?' Mortius asked with a raised eyebrow. It'd be something to have at least one creature listen to him, to do as he asked. With a heavy sigh, Mortius watched as his men led their horses on board and stabled them.

At the rear of the crew, Aymn led his sometimes-wayward mare. Halfway up the gangplank, she stopped, tossing her head violently. Their position was precarious; even though the river wasn't deep or dangerous, a fall from this height was enough to break a horse's legs. Yll and the others rushed to the edge to offer assistance.

With a single hand, Aymn silenced them all.

'Back up, fellows,' Aymn said, his voice clear and authoritative.

The more time he spent close to the boy, the more Mortius became sure of his path. Samson was probably dead after all, and Aymn was a natural leader.

Speaking quiet words to his mare, Aymn stroked her nose, rubbed her neck. With slow, halting steps, the pair began to move towards the boat. Mortius was itching to get some time alone with Aymn. There hadn't been a chance for them to speak in private since their early morning adventure to the coarsewood copse. Since then, an unusual air had settled over Aymn. The difference was subtle; he was more quiet and reserved, and yet the other men jumped to answer his calls. A slight lift of his chin here and there, an almost imperceptible look of defiance when he watched Mortius.

The sense of standing on a ledge in the city, overlooking the destructive waterfalls, almost overwhelmed Mortius. A gaping chasm was opening wide in front of him, but he'd already made the decision to step off. As Aymn shepherded his mare into the shed, a shiver ran over Mortius' body and he rubbed his arms, trying to shake off the feeling of his own demise.

After a quick exchange of banalities with the captain, the barge was on its way north. There were several waterkin aboard, and alongside the captain, they crafted the current to push them upriver. Mortius guessed travelling by barge wasn't much faster than riding, but at least the horses would be well rested by the time they arrived in Triné's capital.

Haba Sha disappeared from view quickly. Mortius turned his face towards the vibrant, rolling plains of Triné. In the distance, groves of trees grew in clumps, offering shelter and shade for the cows that called this place home. The journey north would take at least two days. Though Mortius had impressed his desire for speed, the captain had reminded him that travelling this way took a lot of energy from the waterkin, and that they would need to rest for a night in Varachanas.

Bored, the crew had taken to playing dice at the front of the barge, enticing the captain to play with them. Sitting apart from them, removed but not disinterested, Aymn glanced between the game and Mortius. Gesturing to the back of the barge with a tilt of his head, Mortius padded down the worn planks.

A few open crates packed with tightly coiled ropes sat at the end of the boat. With one hand, Mortius held the ropes in place and flipped a crate over, perching on his seat in anticipation, his gut churning. Aymn stalked down the length of the boat, not meeting his guardian's eyes. Whether or not he'd seen Mortius do it, he mimicked his movements with another crate and sat, hands clasped in front of him.

For a long moment, the two men stared at each other. Mortius didn't want to reveal the truth of Aymn's birth now, out in the middle of the river, with all their men around them. Sharing family secrets felt like a private matter, something that should occur over wine in a secluded room. And yet, he knew he wouldn't lie to Aymn if he asked.

'You have something you wish to say?' Mortius said.

'Don't you have something you want to tell me?' Aymn retorted.

'I don't think this is the right time,' Mortius said. 'Or place.'

'You've been saying that this whole journey,' Aymn said. 'I've always trusted you Mortius, as was expected. But my trust is wearing thin.'

Mortius nodded. Aymn's words stung like a barb.

'Tell me the truth,' Aymn said.

'We're going to Marash Mountain after we visit the emperor.'

'Don't treat me like a child, Mortius,' Aymn said, balling his hands into fists. 'What have you been hiding from me?'

'There are many truths that have been hidden, Aymn,' Mortius said with a sigh. Why was he circling the very thing he wanted Aymn to know? 'Which truth do you want?'

'The truth about me, gods help us!' Aymn glared at Mortius. 'Who am I? Really?'

Mortius flicked his eyes towards the prow. Vir'n was watching them, but quickly turned his eyes back to the game. The others were laughing, engaged with the dice, the captain included. Taking a deep breath, Mortius spoke.

'You and I aren't related,' he said.

'I figured that much out already,' Aymn said, his voice stony. 'Who am I?' The last he ground out between clenched teeth.

Lowering his voice, Mortius leaned in towards Aymn. 'You're Reuben's son.'

There was no discernible change in Aymn's expression, but a muscle in his clenched jaw twitched, as if he'd known the answer all along.

'And my mother?' he growled.

'You've never met her.'

Aymn glared at Mortius, his gaze a column of fire. 'Who is she?'

Raising his hands in acquiescence, Mortius continued. 'Her name is Frieda. Once a noble moonkin.'

'And now?'

'A recluse in the city. A shadow of her former self.' Perhaps that wasn't true, but it was what everyone thought.

'Why?'

That one word, layered with so many meanings, held only dark answers.

'I don't think she could face what happened to her.'

'Is it a surprise that she was hurt because her child was torn away from her?' The words ripped themselves from Aymn's throat.

'It's worse than that. Frieda was in love with Samson. Not long before Samson's exile, Reuben—' Mortius paused, unable to voice one of the terrible secrets he'd held close to his chest for so long. He clamped his teeth together, biting his cheek until he tasted blood. If he was truly honest, he hated himself the most.

'Reuben ... what?' Aymn asked, the intensity of his gaze difficult to bear.

Swallowing his guilt, Mortius released his jaw.

'Reuben raped Frieda.'

Aymn clenched his fists together and dropped his head. They sat in silence for long moments, but Mortius could hear the heavy, rasping breath of his charge.

'And he blamed it on Samson, didn't he?' Aymn's voice was hollow, wooden. 'I've heard that part of the story.'

'Yes,' Mortius admitted. 'It was a way to secure the people's trust in him, to add to the reasons for Samson's exile.'

'Why did you raise me?' Aymn asked, lifting his head to meet Mortius' gaze. 'Why not her?'

Mortius glanced over at the fields of verdant grass. Cows dotted the plains, and soft, voluptuous clouds hugged the horizon.

'She couldn't,' Mortius said. He didn't want to hurt Aymn, but there wasn't any way to avoid it. 'She was so young, and incredibly traumatised.'

'She didn't want me,' Aymn said.

The resignation in his voice was a blow to Mortius. She hadn't wanted him, but nobody had blamed her. Who could love the child of a monster, the man who betrayed her trust, and everyone else's? Mortius had taken on the baby as a duty, but had discovered he cared for Aymn, in his own way.

'No,' Mortius said. 'She understood Reuben's true nature and wanted nothing to do with him. Unfortunately, that included you.'

Aymn nodded. 'But why you? Why not some wet nurse in the castle? Why not some orphanage in the lowkin district? Honestly, I'm surprised I'm still alive.'

'Nobody knew that Frieda was pregnant, including Reuben. She fled to her family's country estate before anyone found out.' Mortius sighed, overwhelmed by the memory. 'When she told me she couldn't bear to keep you, that you reminded her too much of the awful things he'd done, of the devastating loss of Samson, I knew I couldn't let you be raised by Reuben, or risk being cast out by him.'

'That wasn't your responsibility,' Aymn hissed.

'No?' Mortius asked, his eyes ablaze. 'I've sat by and watched every terrible thing Reuben has done. I couldn't let him raise another in his footsteps. I couldn't let him kill a baby. You're the child of two very powerful people. I had to save you from them both.'

'Save me?' Aymn shook his head. 'Why are we going to Marash Mountain?'

The subject change was so sudden that Mortius blinked, uncertain of his footing. Just like his father, Aymn's ability to control the conversation, to change its flow without warning was unnerving.

'You've never felt Everluof's touch, not truly,' Mortius whispered. 'I would know. I coached you into playing at being a starkin.'

'Because if I had responded to my true calling,' Aymn said, his voice little more than the buzzing of an angry wasp, 'I would have been named Kaiāho and sent off to Buduwai. You couldn't use me in your plans if I was trapped in that godsforsaken obelisk, could you?'

'I don't want to use you,' Mortius said. Didn't he, though? 'I want to see you delivered your birthright.'

'A birthright I didn't know I had until this very moment,' Aymn spat. 'And you think I'm going to wander into the sacred home of the highkin and declare that I actually feel the call of Wederlly or, gods forbid, Jesma? I'll still be named Kaiāho, still be sent to Buduwai. I won't do it.'

'Not if your true heritage is revealed. You can't be named Kaiāho then!'

Aymn rose to his feet, looking down on Mortius with a sneer. 'You're disgusting.'

'I know.' The words hurt more coming from someone else's mouth, though, someone who'd lived in his home, laughed at his terrible jokes.

'This isn't over, Mortius,' Aymn said. 'Not in the slightest.'

He turned and walked towards the prow. With a fervour that seemed natural, Aymn joined the game of dice, clapping the other men on the back as he sat beside them. With a final glare at Mortius, Aymn turned his back.

47

THE SOUTH CLAW

In a vortex of darkness, Wave's consciousness began to spin one way as her body twisted in the opposite direction. Nausea hovered at the edge of her awareness. She tried to let go of her thoughts, focusing on the concentric spirals unwinding before her and within her.

Her journey came to an abrupt halt. She stumbled and fell to her knees. Breathing hard, her stomach still churning, Wave looked up. She was in some sort of forest. Except it wasn't anything like the forests she was used to. Everything looked wrong. Trunks in shades of bright red shot up above her, ending in leaves of different neon hues.

Terror shuddered through her body. Wave pushed herself to her feet and ran. She broke through the tree line and found herself standing on the edge of a grassy plain. Her breath left her lungs in a strangled cry.

The image before her was familiar, yet entirely wrong. The plain swept away in all directions, but the grass swaying in the gentle breeze was a vivid purple, similar to X'olea's eyes. A bright sun sat high above her, but it was a brilliant, fluorescent blue that radiated silver rings outwards into a grey, metallic sky.

In the distance, Wave could see rolling hills covered in many-coloured trees, but none that were brown, or green, or even the fiery colours of an autumn tree. There was no sense of the ocean here, no sense of Lerinial at all.

Large black shapes spiralled in the strange sky. Wave swallowed, her heart beating fast in her chest. She'd been here before. The wrong, distorted colours were just as she'd seen in her dreams. That meant the shapes in the sky could only be one thing ... dragons.

As if summoned by the realisation, one of the shapes descended from the sky, landing before her with a thud. Tears fell from Wave's eyes as she stood paralysed in fear.

Black and skeletal, the dragon stood on its hind legs, rearing like a horse. Huge, bat-like wings spread to either side and a long, sinuous tail curled in the air behind its body. The head angling at the sky was reptilian, curling smoke blowing from two slitted nostrils.

Wave couldn't breathe. A dragon stood in front of her, one of the many beings who'd disappeared from Heredour so long ago that many doubted their existence. She should have run, but she couldn't move, couldn't think straight. Instead, her mind replayed the day she took her fellow students through Heredour's histories.

Dragons! Dragons! Dragons!

The dragon landed on its front legs, the ground reverberating with the force. Smoke streamed from its nostrils as it stared at Wave through large black eyes. Thin green slits for pupils regarded her with an almost human curiosity. Wave's mouth was as dry as the desert she'd just left behind, but sweat beaded along her brow. The dragon's gaze held hers, and there was a depth in its eyes, an intelligence she'd never encountered with any other animal, even Skoa.

One terrifying foot moved in front of the other as the dragon began walking towards her. The closer it drew, the warmer Wave became. When it was so close she could have touched it with an outstretched hand, the creature stopped. Too afraid to move, she stared into the dragon's eyes. Tears poured down her cheeks as it stared into her very soul, understanding her in the most deep, impossible way.

Welcome to the South Claw, Wave, daughter of he who was forsaken.

The voice reverberated through her mind, deep and ever-present, as if she'd always known its sound. Although the distorted world had shaken Wave's being, the voice of the dragon had a calming effect on her.

'I don't know how to talk to you,' she murmured out loud.

Use your speaking voice. One day you'll learn how to communicate like us.

'You said this is the South Claw?' Wave asked, gesturing around without breaking the dragon's gaze.

Sheared from the land, lost, forgotten. We are here, but where are we?

It sounded like a riddle, one she could never find the answer to.

But you came, blood of kings, breaker of nations, with no more thought than child's play.

'I didn't mean to end up here,' Wave said, reeling at the words echoing through her mind. 'I just followed the key, and the channel. The spiral opened up to me.'

An easy feat for you, but none else have come, not even the ones who left. Are we truly lost?

The words were drenched in pain and suffering. Fresh tears clouded Wave's vision.

'Your story has been hidden from us,' she said. *The Blood of the Ehta* had told her the truth of Setora and the stars, but nothing of the South Claw was recorded other than that the Black Cloaks had destroyed it.

The dragon lifted its head. A burst of fire shot from its

mouth, imbued with an anger Wave somehow felt in her body. The heat was brief but searing. Beads of sweat broke out on Wave's forehead. When the dragon lowered its head, a great sadness washed through Wave.

See our land, from our perspective. See what has become of our once great home.

The dragon lowered its body to the ground. When Wave didn't move, it nudged her with its head. Moving without any real thought, Wave climbed the dragon's legs, scaled its back, and tucked herself in behind its wing joints.

A few long strides and the dragon was in the air, long wings beating behind her. To her surprise, Wave felt secure, comforted by the resonant warmth from within the dragon's body.

High into the metallic sky they flew. The flying shapes revealed themselves to be other dragons, giant eagles, and strange, unknowable creatures. They flew over blue trees, orange shrubs, and purple grasses in unimaginable shades. In the distance, she could see the ocean, turquoise and crystalline, no different to her own world.

To the north, a great city stood, its whitewashed walls hugging the coastline in a series of blue-domed terraces. The dragon flew towards the city. Below them were manicured fields and pastures, and as the dragon flew lower, Wave realised there were people tending the plants. She covered her mouth with one hand. How? How could there possibly be people here?

Peering over the dragon's back, Wave saw that the city was full of people, humans just like herself. Some shielded their eyes to look up as the dragon passed low over the great city, others waved as if the dragon were a friend.

Then, they were out over the pristine ocean. Ahead should have been the North Claw, but all Wave could see was the vast, endless ocean. The dragon turned in a wide arc until they were facing land again.

Just like the ocean, the South Claw stretched into the

distance on all sides. Mountains pierced the sky to the south, but the eastern side looked as desolate as the desert from her own world. The dragon flew back to the field of violet grass, landing with a thud that sent Wave flying onto the grass. She rolled over her shoulder with ease, scrambling back onto her feet to face the dragon.

'Thank you,' she said, her voice breathy in her own ears. The words didn't carry the depth of her appreciation, but what else could she say?

Now you have seen our misery. Can you help us?

Wave stared at the dragon, its unblinking serpentine eyes regarding her solemnly.

'Help?'

We are tired of this place. It has been generations of dragons since we were separated. We want to go home.

'To Heredour?'

The dragon's chest sagged, as if the weight of its predicament had finally settled in.

Heredour. Our home.

'I don't know,' Wave answered. There was no way she could be anything but truthful to a creature this wise. And she didn't want to pretend she could do something she barely grasped.

I understand.

The dragon glanced up at the sky.

There is a way. You can learn how.

Wave didn't know what that was supposed to mean. 'I can try.'

The dragon's voice was silent in her mind.

'What name do you carry?' she asked.

The silence continued for so long that Wave became uncomfortable.

In the tongue you speak, I was once known as Tan'wyn.

'Tan'wyn,' Wave repeated aloud. 'Tan'wyn.'

It is time for you to return. You cannot help us from this place, and your absence won't go unnoticed by those who see all.

'I don't want to go,' Wave said, looking around in a panic, as if she could record everything before her in a few seconds.

You must. Your family needs you. Remember us, Wave star-caller.

'I could never forget,' she whispered.

Despite her desire to stay, there was a finality to the dragon's tone. Now that she knew how to get to the South Claw, there was no risk in leaving. And if Tan'wyn said she couldn't do anything while she was on this side of the barrier, she had to return to Heredour. She guessed that the Black Cloaks were the ones who see all, if her vision and Jessandra's dream was any indication of their true power. The last thing she wanted was to bring their attention to her, or what she'd discovered.

'Okay,' she said. 'I will learn.'

Your name reverberates through our history.

Tan'wyn's words were a mystery, so Wave closed her eyes, focusing on Lerinial, on Jesma. No matter how much she called to them, though, there was no response. No power of any kind came to her, not water or sun or magic. It was as if the gods had fled this world, this strange place the South Claw inhabited.

'I don't know how,' Wave whispered, her eyes still closed. She tried to ignore the panic thrumming in her chest at the absence of Lerinial's presence.

Hold the image of that which grounds you to Heredour in your mind.

Unbidden, Strath's face hovered in her mind's eyes. Strath, seated cross-legged in the silvery desert, waiting patiently for her. Strath, who'd guided her, held her, challenged her. Nothing else grounded Wave to Heredour in quite the same way, no one connected her to her world more strongly than he did.

Darkness surrounded her. Tan'wyn was gone. The purple plains and the ringed sun were gone. Wave's consciousness twisted again, spiralling in the opposite direction to the turning of her body. Her gut churned with the motion.

She burst back into the desert, landing on her hands and knees. The second journey took its toll on her body and she vomited onto the sand.

'Wave!' Strath's voice called. 'Wave!'

Wave wiped her mouth and pushed herself back into a squat. Night had wrapped its blanket over the desert. In the distance, a figure ran towards her.

'Strath?' she called. How had she ended up so far away from him?

By the time he reached her, she was on her feet. Strath wrapped her in a tight hug, the relief on his face palpable.

'I was so worried,' he whispered into her hair.

For a few moments, Wave let herself enjoy the feeling of being held in his strong grip.

'You won't believe what happened,' Wave said, pushing back from Strath so she could look up into his eyes. 'We have to go back to Kochee.'

Without waiting for an answer, Wave turned north and began walking. Strath jogged to catch up with her.

'What happened?' he asked. 'Where did you go?'

'The South Claw,' she answered. 'There's a way to save myself from being known as a star-caller, a way to save us all from the Black Cloaks' lies. I just have to figure out how. There's a way to bring the South Claw and its inhabitants home.'

48

JAMARI

JESSANDRA WOKE WITH A START. The room was dark, and a silhouetted man stood over her, hand outstretched. She cried out and flinched away from him, curling into the covers of the bed.

'Hush, child,' the man said, his voice gentle.

She tried to remember who the man standing over her was. Memories tumbled through her mind—flashes of pain and misery and loss—landing her on the slave platform, being delivered to the golden man, her owner.

On instinct, she scrambled away from him, but he was no longer standing above her. A lamp sputtered to life in the corner, illuminating the sunkin. Golden hair and beard glowed almost orange in the low light.

'We never got a chance to meet properly,' the man said. 'My name is Hela.'

He didn't move any closer to her, as if he respected her fear. It didn't make sense. If he was her owner, and she his slave, he could do anything he wanted to her.

'What happened?' Jessandra whispered. There were no

memories from when they left the market, and her mind felt sluggish.

'I, uh …' Hela cleared his throat. 'I had to sedate you. You got a little wild.'

Jessandra's eyes widened. 'Why?'

Even in the low light, Jessandra didn't fail to notice the colour that rose in Hela's cheeks.

'When I brought you here, you panicked,' he said, glancing down at the ground. 'I guess you thought I was going to have my way with you. You wouldn't listen to anything I said.'

Jessandra's heart pounded painfully in her chest and she peered under the covers. She was still in her light slip, as she had been when she woke in the cell.

'And you sedated me?' Jessandra choked the words out. Her mouth had gone dry, her tongue like a dead weight in her mouth. Had this creature taken her honour, made her a woman while she was unconscious? The thought was enough to bring bile to her throat.

'Only to protect you from yourself,' Hela said. 'And me.' He stretched his arms out into the light. The sleeves of his shirt were rolled up to his elbows, and the taut muscles of his forearms were raked in long gashes. Some were already inflamed, welts lifting ridges beneath his skin.

Jessandra covered her mouth with her hand. She had no memory of any of it.

'I understand why you're afraid of me,' Hela continued, lowering his arms. 'I purchased you, but I have no desire to own you.'

The dense feeling in Jessandra's mind grew heavier. Nothing was as it should be, and inside, she felt hollow, like a doll with no will of its own.

'Why?' Jessandra asked around her parched tongue.

'I was sent to free you.'

Jessandra closed her eyes, unable to comprehend the words he'd just spoken.

'Let's talk about it later,' Hela said. 'I've sent for hot water and a tub, and there's food and drink for you here.' He gestured at a covered platter on the small desk behind him.

A knock at the door announced two maids carrying a wide copper tub between them.

'I'll take my leave while you bathe,' Hela said. 'There are fresh clothes at the end of the bed.'

Without waiting for her to speak, he slipped from the room. Jessandra hid under the covers as the maids brought in buckets of steaming water and poured them into the big tub until the grimy window became fuzzy with condensation. One of the maids handed Jessandra a thick cake of soap, and the two women hurried out. Jessandra wrapped herself in the bedsheet so she could inspect the clothes Hela had laid out for her. A clean slip and stockings sat alongside a dark woollen dress and cardigan. Simple, but practical. Her boots, shiny with polish, sat on the floor beneath the bed. Jessandra smiled at them—those shoes had carried her through the North Claw, had seen her to safety time and again—then frowned. She didn't know what to feel.

Warmth seared through her body as she slid into the bath. She sat for a long time with her eyes closed, her head lost in the rising steam. When she felt warmed to the bone, Jessandra grabbed the soap cake and began scrubbing. Grime and sweat peeled off her in layers, and with it, much of the emotional pain of her ordeal.

Maybe Wave and Strath had sent Hela? Perhaps someone from Sharvel, someone like Kali? That wouldn't make sense, though. No matter who sent him, they had to have known she'd be in Jamari before she even arrived. The closest town by ship was Kochee—leaving from any other town would add several days onto the journey. Could Hela have been on the same ship as her? Gods, her mind was fuzzy. How was she supposed to get herself out of this mess if she couldn't even order her thoughts?

Hunger struck at Jessandra's belly like a sharp knife as she climbed out of the bath. She dried and dressed in a hurry, tearing off hunks of bread and scooping up the thick stew while she pressed her feet into her well-worn boots.

Just as she was pouring a fresh cup of tepid water, her stomach full of the heavy food, someone knocked on the door.

'Come,' she said, unable to mask the hesitancy in her voice.

The maids darted through the door, scooping up the towel and soap before carting the tub out onto the landing. Once they were gone, Hela sidled in, clicking the door closed behind him.

'Feeling a bit more human?' he asked, leaning against the doorframe.

Jessandra nodded, her hands clasped together in front of her. Never had she felt more uncertain, more unstable in her footing in the world.

'You said you were sent to free me?' Jessandra asked. Her mind had cleared a little with some food in her belly; perhaps whatever sedative he'd given her had finally worn off.

Hela nodded. 'May I sit?' he asked, gesturing to the chair next to her.

'Yes.' Jessandra scurried away, perching herself on the edge of the bed as Hela sat, leaning his elbows on his knees.

'I was tasked to rescue you,' Hela began. 'There are people, far away from here, and they want you to be free. They believe you're important.'

'My parents?' Jessandra asked. She didn't believe her father would go to this much trouble, but perhaps her mother couldn't bear the loss of two daughters.

'No,' Hela said. 'I can't tell you much about them, but you will get to meet them. We're leaving this awful place tonight.'

'You won't tell me anything about these people?' Jessandra asked. She'd always been overly trusting, but since leaving

Millen, she'd become a little more wary. The memory of Jai'til's reaction still rubbed raw.

'I can't, not yet.' Hela had the humility to look apologetic. 'It's not safe to talk about them here. But I can tell you that we're going to the Chaba-Canez Islands.'

Jessandra clenched her teeth together. The Islands had been the intended destination of her trio, but she had no way of knowing whether Wave and Strath would go there without her. She couldn't imagine Wave sailing happily off to Veija-Mens, knowing Jessandra was lost somewhere in the world. But then, what if Wave had been captured too?

'I can't go to Chaba-Canez,' Jessandra said, making up her mind. 'I have to go to Kochee. If you've come to free me, surely you can let me go where I need to?'

'Kochee?' Hela asked. 'What's in Kochee?'

'My friends,' Jessandra replied.

At least she hoped they were still there. She wouldn't let this stranger spirit her away from Heredour without first trying to look for Wave and Strath.

'We were looking for work so we could pay for our passage to Veija-Mens when the Black Cloaks took me.'

Hela sat up straight, pressing his hands into his knees. 'Black Cloaks brought you here?'

'I think they put me on a ship here from Kochee, though my memory is a bit blurry.'

'Why?'

Jessandra stared at him. 'What do you mean, why?'

'Most people don't earn the attention of the Black Cloaks, no matter their crime.'

Jessandra laughed, though the sound left a sour taste in her mouth. 'My friend and I are both being hunted by them.' She chewed her lower lip. 'I hope she's okay.'

Gods, let her be okay.

'Who are you, then?' Hela asked, studying her with his head tilted to one side.

'You don't know?'

'I have my suspicions,' he said.

'I don't know if it's wise to tell you,' Jessandra said. It wasn't hard to trust him—his easygoing nature and steady gaze made Jessandra feel at ease. Mere months ago, she'd felt the same way about Jai'til, though, and he'd betrayed her.

'There are few people who share your name,' Hela said. 'But I would rather you confirm your identity. If you are who I think you might be ...' He sighed. 'Well, it changes everything.'

There wasn't much point denying his suspicions. As he said, Jessandra was a name reserved for royal highkin. And if he had truly freed her ... maybe she owed him something after all.

'I am who you think,' she said after a long pause. 'Jessandra, daughter of King Mascerab, heir to the Marbin Province.'

'Heir?' Hela asked, as if that was the only part that was a surprise.

Jessandra nodded and explained Lenta's exile.

'I didn't know about your sister,' Hela said. 'I'm sorry.'

'Not as sorry as I,' Jessandra said. Talking with Hela was easy, and she tried not to let her guard down too much. 'I only wish I'd had the intelligence to realise she'd been named Kaiāho earlier.'

'So tell me,' Hela said. 'How did the only heir to one of the most important regions in the country end up trying to get a ship to Veija-Mens? I take it you weren't with your keepers?'

Jessandra snorted. She explained her story in minimal details, from her lack of calling, to Jai'til, to Siska helping her flee on Skoa.

At the mention of her handmaiden, Hela's face paled.

'What is it?' Jessandra asked.

He cleared his throat. 'Nothing.'

They sat in silence for a few moments.

'Who were you travelling with?' Hela asked, his voice as hesitant as Jessandra's had been not so long ago.

Closing her eyes, Jessandra's face softened into a smile.

'My friends,' she said. 'I met them by coincidence, or perhaps by the grace of the gods. We fought Black Cloaks together, stayed in a hidden town, learned all kind of things. But the Black Cloaks found us, and we fled. We made it all the way to Kochee. My friend, she's in more trouble as I am.'

'Who are they?' Hela's voice cracked as he spoke.

'Strath. He's from Sharvel. And Wave, who turned out to be my second cousin.' Jessandra opened her eyes. The memory of their faces made her feel better but didn't help her reality.

Hela's face was deathly pale. A line of sweat trickled from his temple, though the room wasn't warm by any means.

'Wave?' he croaked.

'Do you know her?'

'Yes.' He hung his head. 'Once.'

A conversation from long ago sprang to Jessandra's mind.

My father is Samson sunkin ... Kali said my father was nothing like that. That he was kind, and gentle.

'Gods,' Jessandra whispered. 'You're Samson.'

Hela nodded, his head still hanging low.

'You can't tell anyone,' he murmured.

'I'm not an idiot,' Jessandra said. How was it that her father's cousin—her best friend's missing father—had been the one to save her from a life as a slave? It was too impossible to be true, and yet ... was it any less possible than when she'd run into Wave and Strath on the street in Jindar? For a moment, Jessandra's breath caught in her chest. Were they all simply pawns in some cruel game of the gods, unable to make true choices, relegated to following the path set out before them, unbeknownst to them? The thought was crushing, weighing down on her like the low-hanging clouds that crowded over Jamari.

Jessandra took a deep breath, trying to settle her mind. Hela looked up at her.

'We're family,' he said with a half-hearted smile.

'I don't care,' Jessandra said. 'About me, or you. Wave is our family, and she is in trouble. We have to go to Kochee!'

'We're in luck,' Hela said, his smile fading. 'There's no direct passage from here to Chaba-Canez. All ships stop in Kochee first.'

49

BAY OF KOCHEE

Two DAYS on the blustering ocean was enough to remind Larka how little prowess she held in Lerinial's power. Hasting and Rainer both fared somewhat better, and Winter found her sea legs instantly. A favourite of the sailors, Winter had learned how to climb the rigging in her first hour and spent most of her time sitting up high in the crow's nest, her gaze on the distant, unmoving horizon.

Unlike the rest of the group, Larka spent the first night vomiting. She'd crossed the Lost Ocean many times as a young person, but it had been at least fifteen years since she'd travelled such a long distance by ship. She'd been too busy raising her daughters.

By the end of the first day, with her stomach empty and her limbs weak, Larka knew she'd finally grown accustomed to the swaying movements. Rainer secured her some simple food— bread and lentil stew—which she ate hesitantly, but soon enough, her strength returned and she was able to sleep.

The early morning sun cast the eastern sky in vivid shades of magenta as Larka joined the men at the prow. The ship was heading into the bay of Kochee; the white cliffs of Heredour's edge to their right, the jagged peaks of the North Claw to their left. Nestled between the mountains, desert, and cliffs, Kochee sparkled in the sunlight. The sight was impressive, and Larka smiled at the fond memories of her many journeys into the town. Returning to Kochee always meant she was on her way home, and the same was true now. The relief Larka felt in her body was unparalleled. How much tension had she been holding since she'd moved to the Plains?

Hasting wrapped an arm around her shoulders, offering her a small smile.

'We're going home,' Larka said, surprised by the well of emotion she felt.

'You were right,' Hasting said, his voice thick. 'It's been too long.'

At least he'd come around to the idea, despite his initial resistance. The closer they got to Sharvel, the more certain Larka was that she'd made the right decision. Tears clouded her vision for a moment, Kochee shimmering like a mirage in the distance. Larka blinked a few times, letting the emotion wash through her. Gods, she would have given anything to have Samson standing there with them.

'There's a storm brewing,' Rainer said, his gaze behind them.

Larka turned towards the stern. The western horizon was crowded with a growing mass of heavy, purple storm clouds. Sparks of lightning lit the darkness in different colours.

'We'll have to find an inn quickly,' Larka said, turning back towards Kochee. 'It's moving fast.'

'Shall we visit our old favourite?' Hasting asked, his smile lingering.

'The Zealous Rose,' Larka said, unable to hold back a grin. 'Definitely.'

'I've never been to Kochee,' Rainer said. 'I spent all my time in Lashameg and Condor. For a military man, my knowledge of Heredour is quite limited.'

'You're in for a rude surprise, then,' Hasting said. 'There is nothing quite like Kochee anywhere in Heredour, perhaps in the world.'

'Why does it glitter?' Rainer asked, his gaze encompassing both of them. 'My eyes can't make sense of what I'm seeing.'

As Hasting explained how the town was covered in gold leaf and gems, Rainer shook his head, his eyes wide in disbelief.

'The Kocheen hold little in the way of respect for the gods or the high king,' Larka said under her breath. 'They don't openly oppose anyone, though, because they're more interested in increasing their wealth.'

'So you could say,' Rainer said, eyeing Larka sideways, 'that they might be sympathetic to our cause?'

Larka screwed her nose up. 'I wouldn't go that far.'

Something barrelled into Larka from behind and she gripped the railing in surprise. A little body slithered between her and Rainer.

'You decided to join us?' Larka said, smiling down at her daughter.

'The barrelman said I had to,' Winter explained. 'He said we'll arrive soon.'

'Barrelman?' Larka asked.

Winter pointed to the crow's nest. The indistinct shape of a man, his gaze fixed on Kochee, waved at Winter.

'You already know more about ships than I do!' Larka said.

'And me,' Rainer muttered.

'I want to be a sailor when I grow up,' Winter said. Her grin split her face from ear to ear.

They laughed at her joy, even as Larka pushed her gnawing, nagging fear aside. Maybe Winter would be called by Lerinial and she could become a sailor. Unlike her sisters, though, it was getting harder and harder to avoid the impact the Law of Kaiãho would have on Winter.

'She'll be all right,' Hasting whispered, squeezing Larka's hand. 'We'll protect her.'

Larka nodded, turning her attention back to the now visible docks. The tall ship nosed its way through the deep water, slowly pulling up to a long pier. Other ships, sails edged in precious gems, rocked gently as they came to a stop. Sailors scrambled across the deck shouting at one another; Larka and her group stayed out of the way at the prow.

The other passengers disembarked as soon as the gangplank was secured. Once they were all gone, and the crew were organising the crates to be unloaded, Hasting led them down onto the pier. The wooden walkway was long; it would take some time to get to the town proper. Thunder grumbled through the air and flashes of lightning were reflected across the glittering mass of Kochee.

'Let's hurry,' Larka said, a sense of anticipation settling over her. No doubt this storm would bring with it some torrential rain.

They picked up their pace, weaving between stacked crates, coiled ropes, and milling people. Once they made it to the marina—the wooden platform that stretched the length of the shore—Larka paused. The anticipation in her had turned into a restless, fidgeting energy, almost as if she was being watched. She turned to look back at the storm. Half the sky was covered in clouds now, but the rain was still some time away.

'What is it?' Hasting asked, studying her face.

'I'm not sure,' Larka said, her stomach doing flips. 'The storm, I guess?'

Taking a deep breath, Larka turned away from the clouds.

'Shall we go find the Rose?' Hasting asked.

Larka shook her head. 'Not yet.'

There was something else, something she couldn't quite understand. It wasn't the storm—it was as if the gods were telling her to stay and watch. Was there danger ahead? Black

Cloaks? But the feeling that was growing inside her didn't feel like the dread of a bad thing coming.

Larka turned to study the slave ships at the far end of the port. Slavers had been stopping in at Kochee from Jamari for as long as she could remember. Seeing them left a bitter taste on her tongue, but even they weren't the cause of her hesitancy.

There were people everywhere. Sailors, merchants, passengers, and the Kocheen mingled side by side, glancing at the coming storm from time to time. Soon enough, the place would clear out. Maybe that's what Larka was waiting for?

'Gods,' Hasting whispered.

His hands covered his mouth, his eyes widening in shock. Larka followed the line of his vision, and her heart skipped a beat.

Striding through the crowd was a tall man with golden skin and hair, a teenage girl hurrying to keep up with him. Larka would have recognised him anywhere, and not for the stand-out amber eyes or the poise the man carried himself with. His face was the one she'd woken up to every day for ten years. He was the person who'd ensnared her heart and soul.

'Samson?' she whispered, as if what she saw was a mirage and not a real person.

Hasting rushed down the marina. Larka spared a glance for her daughter, but she was firmly planted on Rainer's hip. They both frowned at her.

'Come!' Larka called as she turned and followed Hasting.

Larka picked up her skirts and ran, weaving between the debris of unloading ships and the crowd of wandering people. Ahead of her, Samson and the girl were staring up at Kochee, completely ignorant to them.

Hasting reached them first, but only by a moment. Larka barrelled into her husband, wrapping her arms around his waist. Tears streamed down her cheeks and she sobbed, unable to speak.

'What in the—' Samson said.

He pushed Larka back, staring into her face, his eyes brimming with unshed tears.

'Larka,' he whispered, pulling her back into a tight embrace.

How long they stood like that, Larka had no idea. Perhaps it was an eternity, or only a second, but to Larka, it was everything. Their hearts beat in time, and the world seemed to move back into alignment.

Thunder clapped above them—a reminder that they were still in the world—and they let go of one another. Hasting and Samson pulled each other into a tight hug, their lost brotherhood rekindled.

Larka touched Samson's face, relishing in the feeling of closeness. Everything inside her ached, and her mind reeled in disbelief.

Surprise—and then concern—marked Samson's face as he noticed Rainer and Winter.

'Rainer's pledged himself to us,' Larka whispered. 'I have forgiven him.'

Samson nodded, but Rainer didn't move forward, his face a mask of uncertainty.

'It's okay,' Larka said, beckoning them forward. She lifted Winter from Rainer's hip and lowered her to the ground.

'Sam, this is Winter.' Larka placed a hand on her shoulder. 'Our daughter.'

Samson squatted down in front of Winter, his tears falling freely this time. Winter looked at him in confusion, then buried her face in her Larka's skirts.

'Winter,' Samson whispered.

'Give her time,' Larka said.

Samson rose to his feet with a slow nod. 'What are you doing here?'

'I won't say too much out in the open,' Larka said, her eyes

411

shifting over the people still milling around the docks. 'But the girls are in trouble.'

Samson glanced at his teenage companion. The girl wrapped her arms around herself, watching Larka with narrowed eyes.

'I know they are,' Samson said. 'This is—'

'Don't,' the girl said. She took a step towards Larka. 'You know who I am. Siska saved me.'

Larka gasped. 'How did—'

'Like you said, it's not safe to talk openly,' Jessandra said. 'Wave might still be here, and she needs me.' The princess looked around at the group. 'She needs us.'

Of course the princess had somehow ended up with Wave, and then Samson. Of course they'd all ended up in Kochee together. Were the gods mocking them, or helping them? Larka couldn't be sure anymore.

'I know what …' Larka began. Thinking about the suffering Wave must be going through was too hard to contemplate. 'I know what she is. How can we possibly help her when we can't go near her?'

'No,' Jessandra said, her tone clipped, one foot tapping the wooden dock. 'No, Setora's story was a lie. Wave isn't cursed. I've touched her, so has Strath, so have many of the people in Sharvel. She doesn't make others sick.' The princess balled her hands into fists. 'The Black Cloaks lied, and they rewrote our entire history. We have to help her.'

Wave had been to Sharvel. Swallowing, Larka wondered what she'd discovered there. What had Kali told her about their family, about their history? About Sam? There were too many threads weaving through the people around her, connecting to one another like a constellation of stars. What were the odds that the gods had let them come together accidentally? Larka didn't doubt Jessandra's words—the lies of the Black Cloaks were rampant throughout Heredour.

'Let's go to the inn,' Hasting said. 'There's a storm coming, and there's a lot we need to discuss.'

'I have to find her,' Jessandra said, her chin lifting as she spoke.

Larka was surprised to see the princess' defiance. All the stories Siska had shared were of a timid, uncertain girl, but the young woman who stood before her was full of ferocity. Her tone brooked no argument, and Larka could see the queen she would become, if the gods and her family let her.

'Do you have any idea where to look?' Larka asked.

'I don't,' Jessandra admitted. A hint of doubt crept into her features. 'But I can't just sit cosy in some inn while she's out here somewhere.' She lowered her voice. 'What if the Black Cloaks got her as well?'

'They're here?' Larka's voice came out as a squeak.

'We're going to the inn now,' Hasting said, stressing the last word. 'If they find all of you together ...' He threw his hands in the air.

'He's right,' Samson said. 'We're no good to Wave if we're caught.'

Jessandra grimaced. 'Fine.'

50

SHEBEDIE

THE SOUNDS of steel clanging and men shouting echoed through the training yard. Several storeys above them, Mortius leaned against the railing of a balcony, his cloak pulled tight against the crisp morning air. All of his retinue were down there, slashing at each other with curved scimitars as they learned the fighting style unique to Triné's army.

Aymn had taken well to the curved blade the empire's men wielded, not that it surprised Mortius. They'd started drills when he was old enough to bear the weight of the wooden training sword, and he'd become a formidable opponent as he grew into manhood.

When Unner had taken him as apprentice, Mortius had made sure that regular training was a part of their deal. Unner had a great appreciation for a trader who could wield a sword. Such a skill proved useful out in the world securing wares from wayward merchants.

Until today, Aymn had always been careful and precise in the way he fought, little different to his guardian. The man fighting in the yard below was someone altogether different—a beast full of undiluted rage, a man who'd just unlocked the pains of

414

his childhood. Mortius shook his head. This part of his plan was going all awry. Why had he expected anything different, though?

'Senior Adviser,' a man said from within the room.

Mortius turned away from the training yard. A servant bowed from the centre of the room, a delicate silver platter between his hands. The man was dressed in the unusual fashion of the Trinian who lived in the capital. From middle- and lowkin servants to the highkin who hung around the emperor's family like flies, all wore some version of a wrap-around tunic. The belt was a part of the material, tying around the back of the waist in bows of varying sizes based on the person's importance. Wide-legged trousers or long skirts covered the wearer's legs, and everyone wore a head wrap, though the styles differed from kin to kin. The servant before him was clothed entirely in grey, a small white turban wrapped tightly around his head. A large pin engraved with Emperor Kadesh's emblem held the headpiece together above the man's forehead.

'This arrived in the rookery earlier this morning,' the servant said.

A rolled parchment sat on the platter, its seal appearing unbroken. Mortius took the roll and examined the wax carefully. With a start, he recognised Juro's symbol—a setting sun and a rising moon sat opposite one another, pinpricks for stars between. The symbol of the united Heredourian army.

No longer caring who in Kadesh's retinue had read the scroll —and there was no doubt several already had—Mortius lifted the wax with his thumbnail and scanned the words scratched in Juro's rough hand. His eyes widened as he read, his knees buckling.

'Senior Adviser?' The servant's voice was a distant storm on the horizon. 'Sir?'

Mortius stumbled over to one of the few chairs in the room,

almost falling into its welcoming arms. In the background of his awareness, the servant hurried away.

Our worst fears have been realised.

King Vysidia has reported an army of raiders alighting all along the northern coastline. They are the same enemy as before. You must return to the city immediately.

Mortius tried to swallow, but his throat was dry. He coughed, choking on his own emotions. The servant was by his side in an instant, a copper cup of water in his hand. Mortius accepted the drink, swilling the cool liquid in his mouth.

Twenty-five years had passed since they last saw the raiders. Almost three decades of relative peace, if he excluded the persistent nightmares. Uncontrollable tingles ran up and down Mortius' spine and he felt bile rising in his throat. The familiar image of a terrifying painted face swam before him. Unknowable dark eyes, deep enough to swallow a man whole, still haunted Mortius to this day.

'More,' Mortius said.

The servant refilled the cup from a glass carafe and Mortius gulped the water down like a dying man. The timing of the raider's return filled Mortius with a sense of foreboding. He closed his eyes to try to alleviate the rising panic, but his mind flooded with memories.

Esra had been injured in the war, and as he recovered under the plantkin healers, Reuben had taken control of the fight. They were suffering, the High Army unable to turn the never-ending tide of the raiders. Reuben had summoned the armies of all the nations. Heredour had never fought as one until the day they all arrived—Marbin's infantry, Condor's archers, Triné's swordsmen, Lashameg's cavalry—and their combined forces drove the army of raiders back into the sea.

By then, it was too late. As the tide of war turned in their favour, Esra succumbed to a sickness the healers couldn't attribute to his injury. They guessed the foreign warriors must have imbued their weapons with some sort of slow-acting poison, though no other injured soldiers became sick like the high king.

On the eve of their success, Mortius stood in Esra's tent with Juro, Beren, and Rainer. There were other people in the room too—healers, officers, scribes—all of whom would be dead within ten years. Reuben and Samson sat on either side of the high king.

Uneven breath rattled from Esra's lungs. Samson, only eighteen, clasped one of his father's hands in his own, his head bowed towards the bed. Unlike his brother, Reuben sat apart from the high king, not touching him, barely looking at him.

Esra gasped, clutching his throat with his free hand. His eyes fluttered open, taking in the scene before him.

'You,' he croaked, raising a shaky hand towards Reuben. 'You did this.'

Despite the accusation, Reuben made no move, said nothing. Esra took a final, shaky breath. His hand fell to the covers, his eyes staring at the ceiling.

'Father?' Samson whispered. 'Father?'

——————

Mortius palmed his eyes, pushing the memory from his mind. He would never forget those final moments, nor the way Reuben had calmly turned to them and demanded their silence or their tongues. None of them had known then that he would blame Samson.

A shudder ran through Mortius' body. Why had the raiders

returned? They'd been defeated, their armies battered back into the sea. Had they spent the past three decades recouping their losses and planning to avenge their comrades?

'Can I get you anything else?' the servant asked, hovering by the door.

Mortius swallowed, his throat dry once again. He looked up at the grey-clothed man.

'What's your name?' Mortius asked.

'Rynar waterkin,' the servant answered. 'Of the emperor's personal retinue.'

'Rynar,' Mortius repeated. 'My men are in the training yard. Tell them to meet me in my rooms without delay.'

'Of course, Senior Adviser.' Rynar moved towards the door.

'Wait.'

The servant stopped. Mortius had to get word to the emperor and the grand prince, had to maintain some sort of diplomacy in what would be a rushed departure. They'd only arrived in Shebedie two days ago, and there hadn't been time for anything more than a formal greeting.

'Please pass a message to the emperor and grand prince,' Mortius said, choosing his words carefully. 'There has been a change of plans, and we must travel to the city immediately. I do not like to leave in this way, but I must do as the high king bids. The emperor should send one of his younger sons with us to confirm the urgency of our departure, if he wishes.'

Mortius took a deep breath. Rynar bowed, hinging from his hips, and hurried from the room. Wiping sweaty palms on his pants, Mortius pushed himself upright, feeling a little unsteady on his feet.

The others were already gathered in the sitting room of his quarters by the time Mortius arrived. They were covered in sweat and caked dust, all of them with the wide grins of men who'd exerted their energy well.

Except for Aymn. His face was neutral, his stance wary.

Mortius wished he could send him away, find somewhere to keep him safe.

'Thank you for joining me,' Mortius said, ignoring his emotions as best he could. 'Unfortunately, we have to cut our adventure short. Something urgent has come up in the capital, and it's imperative that I return immediately.'

The men did their best to hide their disappointment. Aymn narrowed his eyes.

'What is so urgent that we can't continue our journey into the regions?' Aymn asked. 'Senior Adviser.'

The title was tacked on as an afterthought, though the intention was deliberate, Mortius was sure.

'At this stage, I cannot say. I must confer with the high king first.'

'Then let us continue in your stead,' Aymn said. 'We can survey the regions as planned and learn the truth behind their maladies.'

Though they tried to hide it, the eyes of the other men lit up.

'Although I trust you would continue our mission with excellent results, I cannot keep good soldiers away from the capital,' Mortius snapped. His nerves were frazzled, and he didn't have the patience to deal with Aymn's contempt.

His words silenced the shuffling, fidgeting movements in the room. The men around him understood the message in his words, even if they didn't know the reason. The challenge in Aymn's eyes remained, but he nodded his head, acquiescing to his guardian.

'Good.' Mortius looked at his small crew. 'You understand that I can't speak openly of everything that occurs between myself and the high king, but let me say this. We ride hard, and we do not rest.'

Aymn swallowed. The others nodded in silent agreement.

'Go get yourselves cleaned up and pack your things. We leave in an hour.'

One by one, the group left Mortius' quarters until only Aymn stood before him.

'Is it because of me?' Aymn asked, his face composed despite the uncertainty in his question.

'No.' Mortius walked away from him, collecting stray belongings as he went. 'I would keep you far away from the capital if I could. But this is beyond our problems, Aymn. This is much, much bigger.'

A knock at the door stalled any response Aymn might have had.

'Come,' Mortius called.

Another servant, dressed almost identically to Rynar, stood at the entrance.

'Senior Adviser,' the man said. His eyes were paler than Rynar's had been; this servant was a skykin. 'I present to you Lord Lumer, seventh son of Emperor Kadesh, may he live long.'

Rich ebony skin set off Lumer's translucent, iridescent eyes. His head was wrapped in an elegant turquoise turban, its tail trailing over his right shoulder. Unlike the servants, there was no pin in his turban. The royal family needed nothing to distinguish them.

'All respect to the high king and senior adviser,' Lumer intoned, crossing his right hand over his heart and bowing slightly.

'All respect to the emperor and the grand prince,' Mortius said, offering a deeper bow. 'This is my nephew, Aymn starkin.'

Aymn bowed low but said nothing. Here, he was nobody.

'Please, Lord Lumer, step inside,' Mortius said.

Lumer crossed the threshold, smiling at Aymn and Mortius. He had a kind face, and Mortius realised that he was of a similar age to Aymn, perhaps a year or two younger.

'My brother said you have to return to the capital, and quite quickly.'

'This is correct,' Mortius said. 'It pains me that I wasn't able to spend more time with your father and brother.'

He wasn't pained at all. Time spent with the ancient emperor was entirely ceremonial and utterly boring, and time spent with his scheming eldest son was tiring. There were traditions to uphold, though, and as an emissary from Reuben, he should have spent several days meeting with the two men. Perhaps the only good thing to have come from Juro's message was being able to avoid them, though the price didn't seem worth it.

'We do what we must to serve the high king,' Lumer said, inclining his head. 'You offered for one of us to travel with you to the capital. It would be my pleasure to accompany you.'

'Indeed,' Mortius said. 'We'll likely have need of a royal ambassador from Triné.'

Ambassadors from each region were always present in the capital, sitting on council meetings and acting on behalf of their rulers. But they were puppets, highkin characters playing at being important. Having Lumer in Waterfall City, young as he was, would not only create a better connection with the southern empire, it would demonstrate what was needed from the other regions.

'I've yet to see much of Heredour,' Lumer said, unable to hide his excitement. 'Travelling with you would be a great honour.'

'The honour is ours, Lord Lumer,' Mortius said, noticing how Lumer glanced anxiously at Aymn. Perhaps the two young men would become friends on the road home. Maybe that was what Aymn needed now. Less time with older men, like Mortius and Unner, and more time with royal men his own age.

'We ride in the hour,' Mortius continued. 'And we ride fast. You'll need to bring few belongings.'

'Of course,' Lumer answered. 'I am an adept horseman. By your leave?'

Mortius nodded and the young lord left, his manservant trailing behind him.

'Triné has an ambassador,' Aymn said once the door was closed. 'Why do we need another?'

'We're going to need all the support we can get for what's to come,' Mortius murmured, immediately regretting opening his mouth. 'You should get ready.'

Aymn stepped closer to Mortius. His stubborn grey eyes were only a few inches below Mortius', full of the boy's anger. The flecks of gold were still there. Mortius pushed down the panic that fought for prominence in his body.

'If we're to go back to the capital,' Aymn said, 'then I want to see her.'

Mortius blinked. 'See who?'

'My mother,' he said, bristling. 'Frieda moonkin.'

Aymn turned and stalked away, banging the door to Mortius' quarters behind him. Mortius lowered himself to the edge of his bed. Of course Aymn wanted to see her. But what would happen if she agreed? And more importantly, what would happen once Aymn connected the dots between his father and the group of people they'd met in Haba Sha? What would Aymn do once he realised that Winter was his cousin?

51

KOCHEE

'WHAT DO you mean there's no library?' Wave hissed.

'I told you when we first got here,' Strath answered, his voice soft. 'They don't care for knowledge, or the gods. Only wealth.'

Wave mumbled a curse under her breath. How was she supposed to discover a way to bring the South Claw back if there were no libraries here? She didn't expect them to have the kind of texts Sharvel did, but to discover there were no books at all ...

They slid from shadow to shadow through the town. A storm had been building on the western horizon all morning, and the streets were growing quiet as the clouds drew closer. Wave hoped they'd be somewhere dry before it hit. In a dark alleyway between a cobbler's shop and a medium-sized stable, Wave paused and leaned against the wall.

'Then where do we find the elders, if not a library?' She lifted her eyes to the overcast sky. 'You said they still maintain that tradition here.' Thank the gods.

Strath cleared his throat, glancing at Wave before looking down the street the alley intersected.

'Well?' Wave asked.

'The elders stay in the merchants' guild.' He studiously avoided her gaze.

'The monstrosity of gold that's guarded by more infantry than I've seen in my life?'

'That one.'

Wave pressed her fingertips into her eyebrows and squeezed her eyes shut. When she'd landed back in the desert, her mission had seemed so simple. She could use magic to access the South Claw, and Tan'wyn had been so confident that she'd work out a way to bring them back to Heredour. But with each step away from the experience, Wave had become filled with a gnawing doubt. The children's stories and *The Blood of the Ehta* at least agreed on one thing—it had taken a bevy of Black Cloaks to shear the South Claw away from Heredour.

Against that feat of magic, what chance did she stand? Wave barely had any control over the magic she could access, and nobody to teach her any better. She certainly wasn't about to reveal what she could do to the Black Cloaks.

A library or an elder seemed like the next best option. Both had been Wave's best source of information since she'd left the Plains, especially if she counted X'olea as an unordained elder. Given how close Kochee had been to the South Claw, Wave hoped they held some sort of knowledge about what had really happened thousands of years ago.

'Please tell me you've got some clever scheme for getting in?' Wave asked as she opened her eyes.

'You're not going to like it.'

'Why am I not surprised?' Wave slid down the wall, squatting with her back pressed into the smooth surface. At least the Kocheen didn't bother to stud the walls of alleyways with gems.

Strath joined her, resting a hand on her knee. She opened her eyes, studying his face, the face that had become more familiar to her than her mother's. Despite the care she felt for him, her emotions were overlaid with a sheen of grief for the missing part of their trio. In the back of her mind, Wave knew the reason she was so set on bringing the South Claw home was because she had no idea how to bring Jessandra back.

'There's a bounty on your head,' Strath said. 'A large one.'

Similar posters to the ones they'd seen in Jindar had sprung up on all the shopfronts of Kochee since their last visit.

'I say we use that to our advantage.'

'Use me as bait?' Wave asked, disturbed by the apparent absence of fear in her gut. 'How will that help us find what we need?'

'Offer yourself to the guild, tell them they can take the reward.' Strath took a deep breath. The grimace on his face told Wave that he didn't like the plan either. 'And then we convince them of the truth of Setora's story and the South Claw.'

Wave snorted. 'An easy feat, especially when we have to convince them that everything they believe is a lie *before* they summon the Black Cloaks.'

'I don't like it either,' Strath said. 'But it's notoriously impossible to get an audience with the merchants' guild. If you have a better plan ...'

Glancing up at the sky, Wave sighed. Part of her no longer cared what happened to her. Let the Black Cloaks snatch her, she'd show them what she knew. But the sensible, terrified part of her reasoned that she had a job to do. Tan'wyn was relying on her, and somewhere in Heredour, Jessandra and her family needed her. The only way to help them all was to bring the South Claw home and reveal one of the Black Cloaks' many lies. She couldn't do anything while Heredour thought she was cursed.

'They don't know I'm a star-caller,' Wave said. 'The posters only say I'm a criminal. So maybe it won't be so bad.'

'What do you mean?' There was worry in Strath's hazel eyes.

'They'll be less fearful of me, and hopefully slower to run to the Black Cloaks.'

'I suppose.' Strath gripped her hand in a sudden movement. 'We don't have to do any of this, you know.'

'And what?' Wave shrugged her shoulders. 'Run away to Chaba-Canez to live out our quiet, peaceful lives? Do you really think the Black Cloaks will leave me be? They've never stopped hunting my father, just wait till they find out I'm his daughter.' Wave sighed. 'And anyway, I couldn't hide out on some distant island with what I know now. What about Jessandra? My family? Tell me you could sit on your hands for the next ten years?'

'Of course not,' Strath said, his voice husky. 'I just … I want to protect you, more than anything else I've wanted in my whole life. But I know neither of us could sit by and watch this madness continue.'

He lifted his eyes to hers. Wave's stomach flipped, but it had nothing to do with their impending visit to the guild. Her heart skittered in her chest, and her hand became sweaty beneath his. When she couldn't stand the intensity of his gaze any longer, she pulled her hand from his and did the first rash thing she'd consciously done in her life.

Wave reached for Strath's face and pulled it close to hers. She planted her lips firmly on his. After a moment's hesitation, he kissed her deeply, tangling his hands in her hair. His lips were soft, his breath as sweet as the wild apples they always snacked on. The world could have collapsed around them for all Wave cared.

After what felt like an eternity, they pulled apart. Wave rested her head on Strath's forehead, both breathing heavy.

'Let's do this,' she whispered.

He nodded, pulling her to her feet. They were only a few streets from the guild, but a light rain misted their faces as the golden walls came into view. An ornate, arched gate faced the street, gold leaf carved in unfamiliar inscriptions. A platoon of armed men lined either side; despite their matching uniforms, they looked little more civilised than the miners who'd attacked them days ago.

Standing at the centre of the gate was a man who was either the squad's captain or an overdressed herald. In one hand, he held a thick parchment scroll. His other hand rested casually on the hilt of a long, thin sword, and Wave realised with a start that his skin was so pale it was near translucent. He was the one they would have to convince.

From a nearby shopfront, Strath tore one of the wanted posters away with a grimace.

'Ready?' he asked.

Wave nodded, though she didn't think she'd ever be ready for this confrontation. How had she gone from the scared girl who was going to hide from the world to this moment, where she was about to turn herself in to the authorities in order to protect the people she loved?

She steeled herself, squaring her shoulders and lifting her chin while she tried to ignore the squirming in her stomach. When Strath grasped her hand, some of her resolve melted. Why couldn't they run away to Chaba-Canez, just like her parents had? Why didn't they deserve a simple, easy life? But Larka and Samson hadn't had an easy life, and neither would Wave. She took a deep breath as Strath led her towards the gates.

The man guarding the gate narrowed his eyes at them as they drew closer.

'Captain, I've come to present a gift to the elders,' Strath declared in a loud voice. 'I have the fugitive.' He thrust the wanted poster at the man and pulled Wave forward.

A badge was pinned to the man's chest—a diamond with five tiny stars hovering above—that was obvious now they were closer. Glancing at the other men, Wave saw their pins contained only the diamond. Strath had guessed correctly, then.

The captain peered at the image, glancing at Wave intermittently.

'This certainly appears to be her,' the man mumbled. 'Why present her to the elders? Why not claim the bounty for yourself?'

'The bounty is meaningless to me,' Strath said, keeping his voice loud so the whole platoon could hear him. 'I would exchange the criminal for something only the elders can provide. Something worth more than money.'

The man studied them closely. Wave lowered her head, attempting to look the part of the cowed prisoner.

'What would you ask of the elders?' he asked, his voice neutral.

'Knowledge,' Strath answered without hesitation.

The captain laughed, the sound loud and obnoxious. Wave winced. They hadn't considered what to do if they couldn't make it past this strange pale man. Some of the platoon sniggered. So much for a well-disciplined guard.

'Well, good luck with that,' the captain said, his laughter cutting short. 'Open the gates.'

Wave tried not to worry about what his words meant as two of the guards stepped forward and pressed a series of the inscriptions. Each symbol melted beneath their fingertips. When they stepped back, the arch was riddled with holes, but the golden gate swung inwards to a paved courtyard. On the other side, a smaller squad of armed men waited.

'In you go, then,' the captain said, taking a step to one side.

Above them, the sky opened. Rain fell in big droplets, drenching them within moments. With a cursory nod, Strath hurriedly pulled Wave towards the gate. They'd made it this far, and Wave tried to force her hammering heart to quiet. Perhaps their plan with the elders would go just as smoothly. They passed the line of men and were under the arch, peering at the disturbingly golden courtyard, when a shout came from behind.

'Hold the gate!'

Wave's heart flew to her throat. The voice was that of minced gravel, steel on ceramics, and a poorly played fiddle all at once. Only one race sounded like that.

'Keep walking,' Strath hissed.

Wave couldn't help herself. She peered over her shoulder, stumbling over the smoothest pavers ever made. Strath gripped her arms.

'No,' she whispered, twisting from his grip. 'No, no, no, no, no.'

The scene before her was one from her worst nightmare, one she'd never been creative enough to imagine. In the street before the gate, a large platoon of armed soldiers marched a bedraggled group of people forward, four Black Cloaks hovering at each corner.

Wave's knees went weak. Strath held her up, but said nothing. The group of people being herded by the Black Cloaks contained almost everyone Wave loved. Jessandra, Larka, her little sister, Winter. There were other people with them, grown men that Wave didn't know. She didn't care. Her eyes lingered on Winter's frightened face, on the firm but uncertain set of her mother's mouth. Beside them, Jessandra's eyes were alight with defiance, despite the hair plastered to her face.

There was a movement behind Wave, a shuffling of rich material, but she couldn't take her eyes off the group on the other side of the gate.

'We have to get out of here,' Strath said, his voice hitching.

'No.'

There was no way out, not for someone like her. The Black Cloaks had already closed the distance between them and the gate. Unless Wave learned to fly, or managed to summon a great eagle, there was no way to escape.

A dragon?

The thought hovered in her mind. She shoved it down. There was no time for useless ideas.

'This is quite the meeting, Dyafirah,' a curt voice said from behind Wave.

The captain bowed as the Black Cloaks shepherded the group through the gate. The eyes of Larka, Jessandra, and Winter all widened when they saw Wave and Strath. Terror crossed her mother's face, as if she'd seen a ghost. Behind them, a crowd of onlookers had gathered, peering through the gates with open curiosity from beneath umbrellas and jackets.

Strath had the sense to pull Wave backwards, away from the Black Cloaks, but they bumped into whoever was behind them. They scrambled off to one side.

'Stop,' the gravelly voice of the first Black Cloak said. 'Stop, girl.'

To their right, a group of opulently dressed merchants stood beneath a covered pavilion. They might have been the elders, or perhaps members of the guild.

'You,' the Black Cloak hissed.

'What is going on, Dyafirah?' one of the merchants asked as he fiddled with the tip of his dyed and pointed beard.

'This girl'—Dyafirah pointed at Wave—'is a dangerous criminal, a fugitive we've long sought.'

His hood shifted, and Wave thought she caught a glimpse of the tip of his nose, of a set of thin lips. She wasn't afraid of what was beneath the hood, even though she was terrified of the creature before her. The puppeteer in Skoa's vision had already shown her what they hid under their cloaks.

'Come,' Dyafirah spat. 'Nobody touch her.'

Wave squeezed Strath's hand and took a step forward.

'Wave, no,' he whispered.

'No.' Wave lifted her chin towards the Black Cloak they called Dyafirah. 'I will not come with you.'

'Fool child.' Dyafirah lifted his hand. 'I will make you.'

'You shouldn't touch me, Black Cloak,' Wave said. She shoved her hand into her pocket and pulled the star free, holding it between them.

The merchants gasped, shuffling back towards wherever they'd come from. Even the guards made an audible noise. None of the Black Cloaks reacted. Even the rain didn't seem to affect their cloaks; all four wizards stood dry and aloof.

'I'm no fool,' Dyafirah growled. 'I know what you are. But I don't need to touch you to overpower you.'

'So you believe your own lies, then?' Wave asked with a haughty laugh, even though she was trembling inside.

Everything about the Black Cloak stilled.

'You speak of things you know nothing about,' he hissed, the sound somewhere between the high-pitched wail of a newborn and the growl of a rabid dog.

'Don't I?' Wave said, baring her teeth at the shadowed hood. 'Don't I?' She raised her voice, so everyone in the court-yard and beyond could hear her. 'I've read *The Blood of Ehta*, wizard, I know the truth of Setora's story. There is no curse on me!' She reached behind her, grasping for Strath. He moved to stand beside her, holding her damp hand within his own.

Dyafirah laughed, if the terrible sound could be called laugh-ter. Wave winced. The merchants and her family covered their ears with their hands.

'It might be funny,' Wave said, raising her voice even further. 'If I hadn't verified the account myself.'

That silenced the Black Cloak. Everyone lowered their hands.

'That's right, Dyafirah,' Wave shouted, putting as much venom into his name as she could manage. 'I've been to the South Claw. I know what you've done, you and your kin.' She swept a hand towards the other wizards. 'You monsters have—'

Her words were cut short with a swift flick of Dyafirah's

wrist. Silenced by magic, she realised too late. She should have been more careful.

'Enough heresy from you, star-caller,' the Black Cloak said. 'It's time you fell into line.'

Wave realised her mistake. They were cornered. She might be able to use magic, but she still didn't actually know what she was doing. There were four Black Cloaks within metres of her, and her family was surrounded.

Dragons?

The thought pushed for space among the other terrified thoughts in her mind. She glanced at the group of people, finally paying attention to the men. Heart pounding, Wave realised she'd made another mistake. The man at the back, with his golden hair and amber eyes, was a sunkin.

He mouthed her name, his lips trembling.

Her father. Samson.

Dyafirah was saying something in an awful, guttural language. The words were imbued with magic, Wave could feel the electricity inherent in the words.

She was about to lose everything. Her freedom. The only friends she had. Her family. Samson—the father she didn't know.

There was only one thing she could do.

'Wait for me,' Wave called to her family.

Dyafirah hesitated.

Wave gripped Strath's hand and closed her eyes.

'Don't let go,' she whispered from the corner of her mouth.

She pulled water and sun energy together, the collision sparking the ground between her and Dyafirah. There was no need for anger now, only a deep desire to protect her loved ones.

Everything disappeared from view. They were travelling, Strath's hand held fast in her own.

52

KOCHEE

JESSANDRA WONDERED if she was dead. Even as the thought crossed her mind, though, images began to assemble in front of her. She blinked a few times, clearing her vision from the violent light that had consumed them.

They were in the courtyard of the merchants' guild, all gilded surfaces and ornate statues. The four Black Cloaks were still gathered around them, but the squad of soldiers were cowering on the ground, as were the merchants at the other end of the garden. Wave and Strath were nowhere to be seen.

'Wave!' Jessandra wailed. 'Wave!'

Her screams startled everyone into action. The platoon scrambled to their feet and the merchants helped one another up. The Black Cloaks made certain their magical hold over Jessandra and the others was secure. Jessandra screamed wordlessly in frustration. Any chance she had of touching the gods and their powers was gone, blocked by the Black Cloaks as it had been since they were captured.

'Jessandra,' Samson said, grasping her upper arms. 'It's okay.'

'It's not!' she sobbed. 'They made her disappear!'

'Hush,' he whispered into her hair. 'Let's not make it worse.'

His words sobered her, though they didn't stop her tears. The Black Cloak named Dyafirah turned towards them.

'I'm not strong enough, Larka,' the man called Hasting whispered, his words hardly registering in Jessandra's mind.

'Just Winter,' Larka breathed. 'Please.'

'What if they—'

'Silence,' Dyafirah croaked.

All eyes were on the Black Cloak, even the group of merchants.

'You.' He pointed at Jessandra. Her stomach felt as if it had fallen through her body.

'Me?' she whispered.

'You know the star-caller.'

Jessandra stared at the shadowed depths of the hood. How could she deny it? She looked around at the others, taking in the terrifyingly precarious situation they were all in. They hadn't even had a chance to get to the inn and devise a plan before the Black Cloaks had cornered them in the market.

Everyone around her was connected to Wave, but it seemed the Black Cloaks hadn't realised the depths of their entanglements. She exhaled a teary hiccup. If they took her, they might let the others go. She could keep Wave's little sister safe, and her mother, and Samson. Terror flooded her body. Her breath hovered in her chest as if it was stuck there. She could do it. She would do it.

'Yes,' Jessandra said, her voice trembling. 'Just me. These people have nothing to do with her.'

'No,' Samson said.

'I know the star-caller,' Jessandra said, raising her voice as Wave had done, ignoring the way it shook. 'But these people are only guilty by association with me. Let them go.'

Dyafirah growled. 'You take me for a fool, girl? I know who these people are.'

Jessandra swallowed. 'They have nothing to do with the star-caller!'

'Come here.' Dyafirah pointed to the ground in front of him. 'Disgraced heir of Marbin. You will be punished as your father never saw fit to.'

Larka squeezed her hand. More terrified than she'd ever been, Jessandra stepped forward to the Black Cloak. She peered up into his hood, noticing the edge of his long nose, the line of his lips.

'Where is she?' he spat.

'What?' Jessandra didn't understand. Hadn't he made her disappear, her and Strath both?

'I don't repeat myself,' Dyafirah said.

Jessandra blinked. 'I don't know.'

'Liar.'

A lightning bolt crackled above their heads. Jessandra swallowed the lump in her throat.

'I thought you made her disappear,' Jessandra offered.

Dyafirah turned away. The merchants shuffled back towards the main building. There was a crack, resounding through the air like a lightning strike. Dyafirah spun back to them, cursing in the tongue of the Black Cloaks. There was a commotion behind Jessandra, and she turned.

The group no longer looked the same, but it took her a moment to realise what had happened. Hasting and Winter were missing. Disappeared, just like Wave and Strath.

'What did you do?' Jessandra screamed, throwing herself at Dyafirah.

He waved a hand and Jessandra's movements halted. She was suspended in midair, one foot connected to the ground. When she tried to talk, her tongue wouldn't respond. Panic rolled through her. Even her eyes wouldn't move, though the rain continued to drip from her eyelashes. The only thing she could see was Dyafirah and the terrified merchants behind him. In the low light of the storm, the gold of the guild became a dull, almost bronze hue.

'Enough,' a voice called. Samson. His voice was like honey left to warm in the sun, so unlike the voices of the other two men who were travelling with Larka.

'I wondered when you would present yourself,' Dyafirah's voice grated, his attention directed away from Jessandra. 'You always were a coward, Samson.'

'Coming from the wizard threatening young people barely finished their training,' Samson said with a casual laugh, as if he was used to sparring with Black Cloaks.

Jessandra supposed he should have been. He'd probably been raised around them. It had been his father who wanted to integrate the Black Cloaks fully into Heredour's society, though it was Reuben who had taken the idea too far.

'A runaway heir and a star-caller deserve some special treatment,' Dyafirah said. 'Something I thought you would have understood.'

Lightning pierced the sky, blinding them all for a moment. The rain lashed at Jessandra's frozen body. She was already soaked, but now her immobile body was icy-cold.

'You've always been fond of tormenting the young,' Samson said, his words taking a vicious tone now. 'It was your idea to bring back the Law of Kaiāho, no?'

'Are you ready to come in?' Dyafirah asked, ignoring Samson's question. 'Are you ready to accept your fate for breaking your exile?'

Samson laughed again, long and loud. 'Oh, sweet little wizard. You have no idea just how royally I have destroyed my exile.'

There was a silence for a moment, as if Dyafirah was considering how to control Samson. The faces of Siska, Wave, and little Winter swam before Jessandra's eyes. What would Reuben do if he knew Samson had children? That by default, the throne would fall to them upon his death? Jessandra shuddered, though it was a sensation that happened internally. She wished she could move, anything to stave off the cold seeping into her bones.

'Let the princess go.' There was no lightness to Samson's tone now; he was every bit the commanding sunkin. 'She has no part in this.'

'Aside from being related to you, she ran away from her duties and she hasn't been called yet.' Dyafirah waved a hand in Jessandra's direction, and she fell to the ground in a heap. 'She's probably Kaiaho, just like her dirt-blood sister.'

'The only one with dirty blood is you, Dread.'

'We are the most pure!' Dyafirah screeched, his voice taking on a terrifying lilt.

It was the first time he'd become truly angry, Jessandra realised as she pushed herself up. In the background, Larka struggled against two of the armed men.

'The bastard children of two gods?' Samson said, his voice laced with casual laughter again. 'Too bad you never knew about Reuben's bastard son. You two would have had a lot in common.'

An unnatural silence fell over the courtyard. Jessandra shuffled over to Larka's waiting arms. There was little warmth to their embrace, wet as they both were, but it was a comfort Jessandra appreciated. Staring at the silent battle of wills occurring between her rescuer and her terroriser, Jessandra realised that Dyafirah wasn't affected by the rain in the same way they were. His cloak hung in neat folds, swirling around the ground at his feet. The hood hung loose around his head, as if it weighed nothing. Jessandra shuddered.

'Oh,' Samson said softly. 'You really didn't know.'

'Now they do,' Larka said, the words grinding out behind clenched teeth. 'Idiot man.'

Jessandra was surprised by the vehemence in her tone. She

was speaking of Samson, her husband, the man she hadn't seen in years. How could she hold such anger towards him?

Another clap of lightning lit the entire sky. The rain eased for a moment, and the golden walls of the guild glimmered.

'Your presence in the capital will no doubt provide a fruitful experience for everyone,' Dyafirah said, regaining some of his earlier composure. 'Before we see you to the headsman, that is. We've delayed long enough. Let's go.'

Panic spiked in Jessandra's body, but she was distracted by a large shape in the sky. She frowned, ignoring the Black Cloak that grabbed her upper arm. The others shouted and struggled against their captors, filling the courtyard with muffled grunts and cries, but Jessandra didn't fight back, her eyes locked on the sky. Another shape joined the first, then another, and another. They were too big to be birds, too big even for giant eagles.

Maybe Skoa had come to rescue them? But what help could a giant eagle be—or even a few of them—against the might of four Black Cloaks? One of the creatures descended towards them in a dizzying spiral. Jessandra's eyes widened as she recognised the shape.

Her mind must have been addled by all the magic, or the rain, or something else. Anything. There was no way the thing in her vision was a flesh and blood version of the drawing that hung in the schoolroom. It couldn't be possible.

The creature came even closer.

Someone screamed.

A jet of flames shot from the mouth of the winged beast, burning the gardens near the pavilion. The merchants screeched and ran. Jessandra couldn't move.

Dragons.

'Dragons!' Dyafirah's voice rang out across the courtyard. 'Cloaks, to me!'

53

KOCHEE

THE STORM CLEARED a little as Wave shot through the air on Tan'wyn's back. Through their mind bond, or whatever it was that connected their thoughts, she could feel his elation, his wonder at being home. Already, one of the other dragons had focused its attention on the merchants' guild.

'Tan'wyn,' Wave said gently, knowing now that he was listening to her thoughts. 'Please.'

Your family.

The ancient dragon dragged his head from the towering mountains of the North Claw and shot downwards in a dizzying spiral. Wave screamed and clutched at the scales of his neck. Just above Kochee's township, Tan'wyn pulled up sharply. Below her, Wave could see terrified people running in all directions throughout the town.

Warmth spread through Wave's legs, building in temperature. A jet of fire shot from Tan'wyn's mouth, melting one of the golden walls surrounding the merchants' guild. The heat in her body eased and she took a deep breath. Her family were down there. She could make out Jessandra, her mother and father. Nearby, the Black Cloaks rallied around one another.

Tan'wyn shot up into the air. The desert unfolded to Wave's right, rolling red sand dunes disappearing into the distance towards her childhood home. Tan'wyn turned back towards Kochee, and Wave studied the steep cliffs that marked the divide between Heredour and the invisible South Claw. She shook her head, focusing on the town as the dragon dove at another terrifying angle.

'Watch out!' Wave called as she saw the wizards raise their arms to the sky.

Tan'wyn spiralled sideways like a barrel tossed from a ship. Wave's eyes rolled back into her head in fear. A beam of some destructive magic shot into the air beside them, narrowly missing Tan'wyn's huge body. When they were right side up, Wave swallowed her fear. The Black Cloaks were trying to bring them down.

In the distance, Strath was tucked in behind the wing joints of Astar, another dragon. A jet of fire angled at the Black Cloaks from his mouth and the wizards scrambled out of the fire's way.

Her family were nowhere in sight now. Wave had to assume they'd followed the rest of the crowd to safety. Somewhere away from dragons and wizards and melting golden walls.

Tan'wyn and a third dragon hovered over the guild, sweeping their wings through the air slowly. The force of the false wind pushed the Black Cloaks to the ground. Wave smiled. What were four Black Cloaks against four dragons? Nothing.

'We've got them, Tan'wyn!' she said.

One of the Black Cloaks rolled onto his back. A bolt of electricity shot from the sky at a movement from his hand, striking the other dragon.

'No!' Wave screamed.

In her mind, Tan'wyn's anger echoed her own. The other dragon plummeted to the earth, crashing into buildings, rolling to a stop someplace distant. It didn't move.

'No!' Wave cried.

Without thinking, she pulled bolts of lightning towards her from the clouds. The rain had stopped, but the storm had left the sky riddled with electricity, just waiting for her call. Tan'wyn began to fly away, but one of the Black Cloaks, no longer buffeted by the other dragon, shot something at them. It pierced Tan'wyn's wing and he spiralled through the air, the pain lancing Wave's mind as if it were her own.

The bolts of lightning she'd summoned fizzled into nothing. The fourth dragon hurled fire at the Black Cloaks, as did Astar, but Tan'wyn was falling. Wave clung to his scales as he spiralled.

Hold on.

'Tan'wyn,' Wave mumbled, holding her arm as if it were his wing. The pain felt the same.

He beat at the air with his good wing to slow their fall, stumbling to a halt in one of the streets. Wave was thrown from his back. She tucked herself into a ball, rolling along the smooth pavers, the pain in her arm receding.

'Tan'wyn,' she said, her voice hoarse. 'Tan'wyn.'

Wave pushed herself to her feet and ran to the dragon. His body leaned against a building, his injured wing sprawled out beside him. It was torn like a rag, tattered and bloody.

'Gods,' Wave whispered. 'Gods, help him.' She placed her hands on his angular head.

Go, child of the stars. Your family needs you.

'I won't leave you.'

You don't need to.

He tucked his broken wing in close to his body and pushed himself upright. A visceral pain reverberated through Wave's body. Tan'wyn lifted his head to the sky and roared.

Wave hesitated a moment longer, then turned to face the town. Half of it was on fire; towering pillars of smoke surrounded her. Panic threatened to overwhelm her, but then she saw the two dragons spiralling around a central point not far away. Her legs moved without any conscious thought, taking her towards the heart of Kochee, towards the merchants' guild. The heavy pound of Tan'wyn's feet followed her.

The screams of people surrounded her as she ran. She couldn't spare a thought for the Kocheen, though, not when her family was at stake, not when she'd summoned ancient, impossible creatures from another dimension to save them.

Wave skidded to a halt before the gaping hole that had once been the gate of the guild. No walls were left, and the ground was a steaming, molten mass of gold. Three Black Cloaks stood together in one of the stone garden beds. The fourth wizard was a half-invisible mound among the gold. The others shot bolts of electricity at the two remaining dragons while they were buffeted by fire and wind. Strath was up there, in the sky, defending them.

Rage built inside of Wave, an anger unlike any she'd felt before. Henny drowning felt like a blip; Jessandra being pulled into the Kanrid was nothing compared to the rage that she summoned now.

I won't reach them.

'I will,' Wave said.

Sun and water came together for her, like she'd been using magic all her life. The elements coalesced into a vortex among the thin clouds above them. The sky lit up, as if Jesma himself was descending upon them. The dragons had enough sense to dart away from the guild, flying high out of the range of Wave's power. The light grew and grew until Wave was blinded. It didn't matter. She knew where the Black Cloaks were, the image of their fighting stance seared against her mind's eye like a silhouette.

Lightning sheared out of the sky, bolt after bolt after bolt piercing the ground within the guild. There was no end to the lightning, to Wave's rage. Her ears bled from the sound of each strike, but still, she pulled more electricity from the sky.

As fast as it began, the lightning was over. Wave fell to her knees. Tan'wyn's head was beside her, holding her up. Blinking a few times cleared the light from her eyes. The image of Kochee began to assemble around her. In the distance, three dark lumps were being consumed by the molten metal. Atop the garden bed, a lone Black Cloak nursed a limp arm. Smoke curled from beneath his cloak, and he howled in pain.

As if her attention had summoned him, the hood turned to where Wave wavered on her knees, her body slumping against Tan'wyn.

'This isn't over,' Dyafirah screeched. 'You're dead, star-caller!'

But he didn't come for her. Instead, he swirled his cloak around him, stumbling with the effort. Tan'wyn opened his mouth, a jet of fire spiralling towards the Black Cloak. It fizzled out before it reached the wizard.

Dyafirah tried again, and this time, the cloak swirled, wrapping him up into a spot of darkness that quickly disappeared. Then, he was gone. The other three wizards were dead, embalmed in gold.

Wave sent a faint prayer to Lerinial.

Please, let my family be all right.

Her eyes fluttered. She let go of Tan'wyn and fell forward. Time passed slowly as Wave tried to maintain her grip on reality, knowing she wasn't safe just yet. She focused on the feeling of the cracked pavers beneath her hands, the sensation of pain in her knees, the blood trickling down her cheeks.

A thud reverberated around her, but she couldn't lift her head.

'Wave?' Strath's voice, achingly familiar, called to her. He was distant, as if he stood on an island while she was swept away by the ocean. 'Wave, I'm here. We did it.' She felt his arms around her body, lifting her. 'I'm here, Wave, I've got you.'

'I know,' she whispered, letting her head loll against his shoulder. 'You've always got me.'

Everything passed in a blur of shapes and colours. The sounds of familiar voices around her—Jessandra, her mother, the warm-honey voice of her forgotten father—collided with the movement of Strath's gait.

Wave star-caller. You are not well.

Though she didn't have the energy to open her eyes or talk with her human voice, Wave found she could communicate in her mind with ease.

I'm okay, Tan'wyn. What can I do for your wing?

Once, the healers of Sharvel could fix our wings.

How will you get there?

The woman who birthed you has patched it. She has some skill. It will be a slow journey, but I will make it to Sharvel, if it still stands.

It does. I will go with you.

No. You need to go there now. Astar will take you.

I won't leave you.

I am home now, Wave. I am no longer alone.

Silent tears leaked from Wave's closed eyes. She didn't want to leave Tan'wyn, but she also knew that she had nothing left to give. Her mother had always been good with salves. Wave could only hope that after all Tan'wyn had done for her, he would be okay.

She felt Strath push her up onto a scaled creature. Unable to hold herself upright, she reached for the dragon with her mind.

Astar?

Wave. I will take you to safety.

My family.

We will take them.

Wave sighed. She felt a body slide into place behind her, a familiar arm wrap around her waist.

'Lean against me, Wave,' Strath said. 'We've got you.'

She leaned her head back against his chest, the waves of nausea subsiding now she'd stopped moving. Within moments, she felt the smooth step of thick legs beneath her, then the beating of wings through the air. They were up, safe in the sky. Wave smiled.

Astar?

Yes, star child?

Thank you. I owe you my life.

No. We owe you our lives. You have returned us to Heredour.

Wave felt the dragon's heart expand, the feeling washing through her body as if were her own.

You brought us home. We will lay our lives down for you. Always.

EPILOGUE

'Ready?'

Wave nodded, staring at the road leading back to Sharvel, but there was nobody there. This was the way she wanted it, but it didn't make it any less painful.

Beside her, Strath adjusted his heavy pack, settling it more evenly on his shoulders. Hasting squatted on the ground as he rifled through his own bag, his face a deep frown. A little apart from them, Samson leaned against a tree, his fingers intertwined in front of him.

'Are you sure you don't want to say goodbye?' Strath asked, his eyes searching Wave's. 'Not even to Winter?'

Wave shook her head. 'I won't be able to leave them if I say goodbye. It's hard enough as it is.'

Her family were well protected in Sharvel, as was Jessandra. Siska's face swam before her mind, and with a stab of regret, Wave pushed the image aside. They'd only been back in Sharvel for a few days—and Wave barely recovered from her wild feat of magic—when Larka had told her the Black Cloaks had her sister. The knowledge that there was nothing she could do to help Siska only pushed her to act on her plans as soon as she could walk.

'All right,' Hasting said, standing and looking between the two of them. 'It's time to go. Remember, keep your eyes closed or you'll be sick.'

'I'm going to keep mine open,' Wave said. 'I want to learn as much as I can.'

Hasting nodded and strode over to Samson. They held each other in a tight, brotherly embrace for a long time. Wave could hear them murmuring—she imagined they spoke of her mother, the person who bonded them. When they broke apart, Samson shook Strath's hand. The two men held each other's gaze for longer than normal, and Wave wondered what had passed between them. Was it about her?

When it was her turn, Wave let herself be wrapped up in the arms of the man who was her father. They'd spent some time together since their return to Sharvel, but there was still an awkwardness between them. Wave couldn't shake the sense of talking to a stranger who knew her too well.

'I want to say stay safe,' Samson said, looking down at her with his amber eyes. 'But I know that's not really possible for any of us.'

Wave closed her eyes and leaned her forehead against his chest. His face was still unfamiliar to her, but his voice ... the cadence of his words was a soothing balm to her soul.

'I'm so proud of you, Wave,' he whispered into her hair. 'Proud of everything you've become, despite the chaos of this life you've been given.'

She nodded, keeping her head buried as her eyes smarted.

'If anyone can bring the South Claw home,' Samson said, his voice thick with emotion, 'it's you.'

'I have to try,' Wave mumbled into his chest.

'I understand.'

'Look after everyone for me.' Wave pushed herself away from him. 'Especially Jessandra.'

Samson pursed his lips. 'I will.'

Wave took a deep breath. There was a definite chill to the air now it was almost winter, and the crispness offered her a sense of possibility. Maybe she could bring the South Claw back to Heredour. And if she did, she'd free herself from the illusion of the star-caller curse, but she'd also be exposing one of the Black Cloaks' many lies. She shivered at the memory of the raw power that had coursed through the air as Tan'wyn and the other dragons fought the Black Cloaks. The memory shifted into a feeling of dread, a deadweight in the pit of her stomach as she recalled the energy that flooded her body and allowed her to kill two Black Cloaks.

'Come on,' Hasting said.

Strath was already tucked in under one of his arms, gripping the back of his cloak with a white-knuckled fist. Swallowing her fear, Wave glanced at Samson once last time. He smiled at her, and for the first time in her life, his face was familiar.

A bird whistled in the forest and Wave glanced up at the sky. Silhouetted over the western mountains, a dragon winged its way towards Messenien. Tan'wyn's wing was still healing, but he'd explained to Wave that the other two surviving dragons— Astar and Syi'dor—were exploring the North Claw. They were communing with the descendants of the South Claw's giant eagles, reconnecting with the landscape of Heredour, and honing their intuitive knowledge of the world.

Wave nestled herself under Hasting's other arm, surprised at how safe she felt with him as her guide. He'd come to visit her while she was recovering, and the pair of them had been equally surprised that their true connection was through X'olea, not Larka. Just as he'd said in his letter, he promised to help her learn to control her magic, as much he was able to.

They were on their way to the desert. Wave hoped she could

teach Hasting how to jump to the South Claw, just as she had. It was clear that there were no answers on this side of Heredour, especially with the imminent danger of the Black Cloaks.

Too bad Dyafirah had escaped. Everyone would know of what had happened in Kochee. If she was honest, though, Wave didn't think she had it in her to murder him in cold blood. The others had died at the hands of her lightning, while she was blinded. She spent most of her nights awake, trying to convince herself that she hadn't become a monster like them.

'Don't let go,' Hasting said.

Strath pulled Wave into their trio so they were holding on to one another. The desire to rest her head on his shoulder was a powerful urge that she resisted. This might be her only opportunity to learn how to use magic to travel. She couldn't waste it on her heart's fanciful emotions, not when she'd had to be so strong just to get to this moment.

Muttered words fell from Hasting's lips, words Wave could only recognise as the language of the Black Cloaks by the awful, gravelly sounds they formed. Power emanated from him, a power Wave was starting to understand. Darkness began to consume the world around their group. Only a few steps away, Samson was already disappearing beneath a thick veil of darkness.

'Wait!' a voice cried. 'Wait!'

The sound broke Wave's heart, and she couldn't stop herself from looking up.

Jessandra stumbled into the clearing, desperation in her eyes. Twigs and leaves had caught in her hair and her dress was torn in places. Samson caught her as she threw herself at them.

'Wave!' Jessandra screamed. 'Don't leave me!'

Tears tracked down Wave's cheeks as she watched her friend disappear.

'I'm sorry,' she said, choking out her words through her sobs. 'I'm sorry.'

The forest faded along with the sounds of Jessandra's wails. Darkness surrounded them, consumed the world from sight. Wave buried her face into Strath's shoulder as sobs wracked her body. She would have given anything to bring Jessandra with them, but she knew she couldn't. Jessandra needed to go home. She was in the best position as a royal to prepare Heredour for what Wave was about to do. They all knew that the princess would never have agreed to be left behind, so they'd made the decision for her. None of it eased Wave's heartache, though.

Deep in Wave's cloak pocket, the star thrummed with energy, warming against her leg. With a frown, Wave glanced down without letting go of the two men on either side of her.

'Strath?' she whispered.

Despite Hasting's suggestion, Strath hadn't closed his eyes. He followed her line of sight and gasped.

'Gods,' he said. 'Is that ... the star?'

'Yes.'

All around them was a darkness so complete Wave thought she was drowning. The pocket that held the star was glowing, though, the light growing with each passing heartbeat. Wave and Strath looked at each other, mouths open in surprise. Somewhere between green and gold and white, the phosphorescent light expanded until it overtook the darkness, consuming them in its brilliance.

ACKNOWLEDGMENTS

When I first toyed with the idea for this book as a teenager, I never imagined it would take so long to see this story brought to life. A combination of imposter syndrome, general life distractions, and a fear of failure saw me falter and hesitate countless times.

Nearly 20 years on, this story and these characters wouldn't be in your hands without the support and encouragement from the following people, all of whom are so very dear to my heart:

Firstly, Mandi Kontos, my biggest cheerleader! Mandi showed me how to write my first draft to completion through sheer will power alone. How many nights did she sit beside me, writing into the wee hours of the morning as I pulled my hair out over a single sentence? How many times did she tell me to sit down, be quiet, and *just keep writing*? A bit of tough love was the kind of approach I needed to get the words down. I can say, without any doubt, that this book has only made it to publication due to her encouragement throughout that first draft, and every draft since. She's a writing performance coach, by the way, and the best of her kind! (www.dreamingfullyawake.com)

I can't go any further without thanking my mum. Everyone knows she is an absolute gem, a human so grounded and calm that you can't help but breathing easy around her. She's been my greatest support, backing my dreams of becoming a full-time author for as long as I can remember. In recent years, she took up reading fantasy (not her genre!) so that she could become my on-call beta reader. Her belief in both me and this story has often kept me afloat.

Speaking of people who keep me afloat, it would be remiss of me not to mention my husband, Tyler. Since the day we met, he's held space for me through the many ups and downs of this process. His undying belief in the power of creative practice always brings me home to the *why*—and without that sense of purpose, I would be lost. If not for his hand in mine as I walked through the shadowy depths of fear, this book would not exist.

Publishing a book takes a village of people to bring it to life. The gentle guidance and excellent eye for detail of my editor, Emily Marquart, allowed me to uncover the precious gem of this story. I'm quite sure that I didn't fully understand how to craft a story out of a bunch of scenes until Emily brought her wisdom into my life.

The creative genius of my cover designer, Jordan Lewerissa, is obvious to anyone who picks up this book. What's less obvious is his unending patience with me and my self-publishing journey, or his truly design-oriented mind when it comes to thinking more broadly than the cover alone. I couldn't have asked for a better partner in design.

My thanks to fellow indie author Abigail Hair for her wonderful map-making skills, and to Beth Attwood for her keen eye spotting my pet habit of dangling modifiers.

And lastly, to my original readers—those who reply to my newsletters, those who read my novella and are still here for the journey. In particular, Saskia Bebe, Gina Macauley, and Jenny Rogers: your excitement makes everything worthwhile.

ABOUT THE AUTHOR

Peta Hawker's love of books and storytelling led her to study a Bachelor of Writing and Publishing at the Northern Melbourne Institute of TAFE (now Melbourne Polytechnic). She currently works in a knowledge management team training authors and editing technical content.

Originally hailing from the southern parts of Australia, Peta now resides in rural Queensland with her family and three cats. A large part of her childhood was spent travelling the outback, and the diversity of the land generated a passion for living closer to nature. The incredible landscapes of Australia still inspire her work today. *Unwinding the Spiral* is her first novel.

www.petahawker.com